THE RIVER RUNNING BY

The River Running By

CHARLES GIDLEY

ANDRE DEUTSCH

FIRST PUBLISHED 1981 BY
ANDRÉ DEUTSCH LIMITED
105 GREAT RUSSELL STREET LONDON WC1

PHOTOSET BY ROBCROFT LTD, LONDON WC1

PRINTED AND BOUND IN GREAT BRITAIN BY
REDWOOD BURN LIMITED
TROWBRIDGE & ESHER

ISBN 0 233 97333 8

THE RIVER RUNNING BY

❧ *Part One* ❧

1

I

THE CURSE took the form of a frog left in the doorway of the stone hovel where Manoel lived with his young wife, Laurinda. The frog's mouth had been sewn up with coarse fishing twine, and its legs had been partially severed.

Laurinda was pregnant at the time, but the fishwives of Matosinhos suspected that Manoel was not the father. They knew that Laurinda had been meeting Carlos dos Santos, the engineer of the trawler *Novo Olho do Mar*; they had always said that Manoel was too old for Laurinda, and no one was surprised that Carlos was tired of his own wife Marta, a huge, domineering woman whose fat arms and legs had earned her the nickname 'Salsicha',—'Sausage'.

The curse worked. On Christmas Eve, 1920, Laurinda died while giving birth to a girl. The baby was named Natália.

Manoel treated the child as his own, and brought her up to believe it. But he must surely have known the truth: even the urchins in the street shouted it to his back when he went down to the harbour to board the *Novo Olho do Mar* – the 'New Eye of the Sea'.

His sister lived with him for some years after Natália was born, and she looked after the child while he went out fishing. But when Natália was five, the sister married a man from Aveiro, and moved away.

The old man and the girl lived on together in a closeness that would normally have been considered improper. Natália did not regard it as such however; she knew no better. And besides, in the winter nights when the rain and wind battered the little dwelling, it was good to share the warmth of his bed and to feel his protective arms about her.

7

Natália never discovered why it became necessary to move from the stone hovel that was their home. She was eight years old at the time, and when the old man told her to collect together her things, she did what she was told and wrapped them in a blanket.

They made their new home in a shack built out of driftwood from the beach, pieces of rusting corrugated iron and old packing cases. It stood in an area of waste ground in the valley behind the harbour, where the poor lived. Nearby were stinking piles of refuse where pie dogs scavenged and flies buzzed. The ground was littered with chicken bones, fish skeletons, spilt garbage. Little children with protruding bellies and dark, staring eyes mooched about at doorways of other make-shift huts.

Death in this community was commonplace. Many of the babies died in the first few weeks, and some mothers, too. When a baby died, it was laid out in a basket and surrounded by wild flowers picked from the pine-clad hills inland. Votive candles were lit, and for a night the child's body would have a place of honour in the shack where it had been so brief a visitor.

It was a matter of pride among the womenfolk to lay out their dead suitably.

The village of Leça da Palmeira and the sardine canning town of Matosinhos were separated by a river, which opened out into the harbour that is called Leixões. This river was more of a slow moving stream, often streaked with soap suds, for the clothes of the local people were washed in its water and spread out on the boulders and shrubs that lined its banks.

At low tide, smelly mud flats appeared at the river mouth, and these flats were spanned by four bridges. There was an ancient granite road bridge, a wooden foot bridge and two steel bridges for the tram and railways that linked Leça da Palmeira with Oporto.

When Natália was old enough to carry a basket of fish on her head, she began selling sardines in the streets of Matosinhos and Leça. Manoel went out in the trawler six nights a week, and between them they earned enough to eat adequately. They might have been able to afford a return to a proper stone house, but for reasons that Natália never discovered, Manoel was unwilling to do so.

Now that she was nearly fourteen, the young men who loitered outside the bars of Matosinhos would eye Natália appreciatively when she walked by. She went barefoot, and wore a cotton dress of pink and white checks: it had once belonged to an English girl, and had been given away to charity. But although she was becoming a woman in body, she was still a child in mind, and when men looked at her she avoided their glances and kept her eyes downward as she passed them.

She walked back from the town one late afternoon in October, picking her way barefoot along the track that led past the homes of other shack dwellers. She carried an empty fish basket on her head, and although she was grimy with dust and her dark hair was matted and ill-kempt, there was about her a certain individuality, a certain poise that caused people to look up and remark, 'There goes Manoel's girl.'

He was lying on the bed when she entered the shack: a powerfully built man, over sixty now, with watery eyes and skin smooth and papery like that of a well-baked potato. He was not asleep, and when the girl entered he rolled on to his back and lit a cigarette, greeting her briefly. He asked her if they were rich, and she showed him the few coppers she had earned from selling sardines.

She took a can and collected water from the pump in order to wash the dust from her face and arms and hair. While she washed, he smoked his cigarette and asked her what weather they would have that night. This was a game between them, for Natália had a reputation of being able to predict the weather and where the shoals of sardines would be found.

'You will have fog,' she told him.

'We shall have fog,' he replied. 'The *menina* is always right.'

'The sardines will be further out,' she said, drying her hair. 'A long way out.'

He finished his cigarette and collected his things for the night. He took with him a jersey and a *garafão* of wine and a tin box that contained some food and personal belongings.

Natália watched him. 'Don't you believe me?'

9

He put his hands on her shoulders and looked down at her tousled hair. Her predictions had begun to cause argument aboard the *Novo Olho*, and he was doubtful about repeating them. The last few catches had not been good ones, and there was a growing feeling that Natália's forecasts were bringing bad luck.

But Manoel was more concerned about another matter. Over the past months, he had asked Natália to share his bed more frequently. He had made love to her with great gentleness in the darkness of the shack. Neither had ever spoken of what went on; instead, a tension had developed between them: a tension compounded of love and guilt and fear. In the intimacy of the little hut where they lived, he could not but be aware of certain personal details. Natália never washed her hair or ate sardines during her monthly period: it was a widely accepted fact that to do so was inadvisable. Now, looking down at her, he recognised in her eyes his own misgivings. He was sure that she was overdue. It was as if she had washed her hair deliberately, to let him know. They both knew it, and both were afraid.

They embraced and kissed before he set out. She stood at the door of the shack, watching him stride away down the path toward the fishing harbour. The clock in the church of Our Lady of Sorrows struck six. It was kept ten minutes slow by Padre Preto, in order that the Devil might be confused.

Rui dos Santos and his brother Carlos were waiting with their nephews João and Pedro when Manoel arrived at the harbour beach. Most of the crew were interrelated. Manoel had become a member of the crew because Laurinda had been the cousin of José, the previous skipper. José had died some years before, of a tumour, and Rui dos Santos, a distant relation, had given up his small lobster boat to start fishing for sardines. He had brought with him his brother Carlos to be the engineer, and of course Carlos was the husband of the Salsicha.

The five men launched the dory now, and the brothers João and Pedro manned the oars and pulled the boat out towards the trawlers moored in the harbour.

These trawlers were called *traineiras*. They had graceful lines:

high bows and sweeping, counter sterns; two masts, and slim upright funnels. The weight of the nets stowed on one side caused them to heel over. Nearly all of them had guard dogs on board, and as the dory approached the *Novo Olho do Mar*, a brown mongrel raced up and down the trawler, barking and wagging its tail at the same time.

The men went aboard and the dory was hoisted on its davit. Steam was raised and the anchor chain heaved in on the capstan. Rui dos Santos and the dog went to the wheelhouse, and the trawler made its way out past the breakwater, the bow lifting to the long, smooth Atlantic swell.

Other boats of the sardine fishing fleet were putting to sea at the same time. The evening air was full of the shouts between boats, the barking of dogs, the thud-thump of engines. The *traineiras* headed out to sea, towards a huge setting sun. Looking at it, it seemed as if you could see the individual flames leaping from it—the effect of distant haze. Astern, the suns rays were for a moment brilliantly reflected in one of the windows of a house in Leça da Palmeira.

Once clear of the breakwater, the crew of the *Novo Olho* gathered on the foredeck to eat the evening meal. Pedro lit a charcoal grill and fanned it with a little raffia bat to make the coals glow red hot. Sardines were cooked and eaten whole except for the head, accompanied by chunks from a large crusty loaf and washed down with wine from the *garafão*. Each man wiped the flask's neck with the palm of his hand before and after drinking.

The sardine fleet was spread out now, some boats heading along the coast in the direction of the Boa Nova and Vila do Conde, and others south to the mouth of the Douro and Valadares. In each wheelhouse, the skipper scanned the horizon for signs of fish.

You could tell where the fish were because of the sea birds diving. By night, it was sometimes possible to see the shoal beneath the water.

João took a long drink from the *garafão* and replaced the cork. He glanced round at the others with a grin and then looked at Manoel. 'Well,' he challenged, 'And where does she say the fish will be tonight?'

11

The old man declined to answer. He shrugged, and shook his head.

'Doesn't she tell you any more?' João jeered. His face was reddened with wine. He had small eyes, a button nose, a white scar on his neck.

'It was never anything more than a game to her,' said Manoel.

'But you believed her,' João replied. He looked round at the others. 'You all believed her.'

In the wheelhouse, Rui dos Santos could see that the men were arguing, and he guessed what it was about. It was difficult for him, because what had started as a joke had now turned into a subject of argument every night. Some of the men wanted to ask Manoel what the girl had said, and to act on it, while others wished to have nothing to do with such superstition.

Now that the *Novo Olho* had had nearly a month of poor catches, Manoel was beginning to be regarded by João and one or two others as a Jonah. It had already been suggested that the old man was becoming a burden and should not be taken on any more trips. But Rui dos Santos had an uncle who was friendly with Manoel, and if Manoel were asked to leave the crew this would cause a difficulty with the uncle, in whose house Rui dos Santos, his woman and their five children lived.

Rui was not afraid of Manoel, but because he was nearly twenty years younger than the old man, he felt obliged to show him a certain respect.

The *traineira* headed north, about five miles out from the coast. It grew dark, and lights appeared here and there along the shore. The Boa Nova lighthouse began sending its fingers of light over the dark sea, and the *Novo Olho* chugged on and on through the night.

Some time after midnight, Carlos joined his brother in the wheelhouse. They were silent for a while. There was no need to comment on the fact that no fish had been found. But eventually Carlos asked the question that Rui had been expecting.

'Have you asked the old man yet?'

Rui shook his head, still staring forward at the dark horizon.

12

'Wouldn't do any harm to ask him,' Carlos observed.

Rui considered this for some while before opening the door of the wheelhouse and beckoning to Manoel, who sat on the bulwark nearby.

When the old man came to the door of the wheelhouse, Rui looked into the watery eyes and said, 'Where do you suggest we look tonight?'

Manoel shrugged. 'How should I know?'

'Didn't the girl say?'

'She said they would be a long way out.' He made a gesture of disbelief and glanced at the clear sky. 'She also said there would be fog.'

Rui nodded, pondering the possibilities. The child knew very well that if they did not find fish close to the coast then they would look further out. And if they did not find fish further out, it could be said that they did not go far enough out. As for fog, well – there was no hint of fog whatsoever.

The trawler rolled to starboard into the trough of the swell, and the light-dotted coastline seemed suddenly to rise up into the heavens behind Manoel's head. The old man maintained his balance easily, automatically. He glanced at Carlos, the engineer. Carlos had been the man Laurinda had loved. Carlos was the father of Natália. But instead of enmity between the two men there was an unstated sadness, a silent recognition of a bond between them. For each had loved Laurinda and now each, in different ways, loved Natália.

'I think it's better to ignore her advice,' Manoel said. 'Don't you think so?'

'We shall see,' Rui replied, and dismissed the old man.

After a further hour, because they had found no fish, Rui dos Santos put the wheel over and the *traineira* headed westward, further and further from the coast.

And in due course, they found the fish.

The shoal was like a pale silver cloud in the water. It was a big shoal, and the sight of it caused immediate action aboard the *Novo Olho do Mar*. Rui dos Santos rang down 'Slow' to the engineroom; Pedro and João moved quickly aft to launch the dory, and the remainder of the crew put away their bowls of cabbage soup and prepared to cast the nets. The mongrel dog

13

came out of the wheelhouse. It stretched, and then went for'd and lifted its leg against the capstan. It moved among the men, wagging, and avoiding being trodden on as they worked in their high rubber boots.

The dory was launched and the trawler manoeuvred so that the net went out in a long curve round the shoal. While they worked, the men spoke in soft voices, as if in awe of the size of the shoal. And quite suddenly, the moon rose, the air became cooler and damper, and the first signs of fog appeared.

It took nearly an hour to encircle the shoal with the net. When this had been done, the men gathered on the port side to pull it in by hand.

Manoel took up his customary position at the for'd end of the line of a dozen or so men. The net was cold and hard in their hands. Sardines clung to it here and there and were shaken back into the pool the net had formed alongside the boat.

As they worked, the men sang a wordless chant, a repetitive, rhythmical song that was started by one voice, taken up by others, repeated and varied by others yet. This tune was centuries old. No one knew its origin. Perhaps the Moorish fishermen used it. Perhaps even the men of Galilee once sang the same notes and the same harmonies. It is a tune that is nowhere written down, one that can be learnt only by going out with the sardine boats and witnessing the hauling of the nets.

Slowly, the net rose from the water. The circle it made grew smaller and smaller, until the sardines could be seen threshing about in their thousands.

It was a good catch. There was no doubt of that. The men pulled at the net with a will; their breath came out in clouds, and suddenly the fog closed right in, so that the fishing boat and the nets and the singing men and the dory toppling about on the water seemed to be a world unto themselves, a complete entity within a bowl of mist.

At length, the nets were hauled in sufficiently for the sardines to be loaded. The derrick was manned and a huge basket attached to the hook and tackle, to transfer the fish from the sea to the hold. With Manoel shouting the orders, the

14

basket was lowered into the mass of sardines, filled, and then winched up and tipped so that the fishes poured in a black and silver stream down into the bowels of the *Novo Olho*.

The fog was thick now. It settled on the eyebrows and clung to the nostrils. Lamps had been rigged for the men to work by, and their figures threw grotesque shadows on the fog bank. Over and over again, the basket rose from the water and the sardines streamed into the hold. After an hour of work the *garafão* was passed round for the men to take a drink. The work continued, and the hold filled up until the *Novo Olho* was low in the water and the men weary from hoisting the basket up and swinging the derrick back and forth.

When it was beginning to get light, and nearly all the fish were loaded, a noise was heard through the fog. It was an indistinct noise at first: the steady, distant beat of a ship's propeller.

The men continued their work, but having heard the noise they glanced at each other, in the knowledge that the *Novo Olho* was further out that night, and perhaps in the shipping lane.

The beat of the propellers grew slowly louder. The men looked up at Rui, who stood in the wheelhouse. He went to the back of the wheelhouse and took out a hand fog horn that was operated by pushing a piston down a wide cylinder. He took this contraption to the door of the wheelhouse, listened for a moment and then operated the horn. The noise of it filled the air, blotting out the squeak of the derrick, the splatter of fishes. It continued for several seconds, and when it stopped, the dog, sitting up in the bows, barked three times and then began to howl. It was a ghostly sound, strangely ominous, and the men stopped working.

Manoel, in charge near the derrick, hoisted himself up on the bulwark and shouted at the men to continue. But as he did so the noise of the propellers became much louder, and a ship's siren blared forth, far louder than the foghorn Rui had just operated.

At the same time, the little fog world of the fishing boat, the net, the dory and the yellow lanterns was invaded by the towering black bow of an ocean liner. The ship was upon them

15

immediately: there was no question of taking action to avoid it.

The bow wave lifted the trawler up and hurled it to one side. The loading derrick with the basket of fish went up in a high arc, and Manoel experienced a moment of flight through the air before falling into the sea.

He was underwater, and things were happening with a dreadful slowness. He knew that the ship was passing over him, was aware of its steel hull close to him.

The noise in his ears was like the pounding of some giant heart. He didn't know what it was until he felt himself sucked downward, under the ship's stern towards the huge propellers.

He was swirled downward into darker water, and accelerated through a vast mill. Dimly, he saw the curved blade of the propeller advance toward him and sweep through him, severing his legs from his trunk.

There was only a brief moment of consciousness after that, before the second blade struck, and his lifeless remains disappeared in the churning wake.

II

The foghorn on the Boa Nova lighthouse had been moaning for hours, and its long, mournful groan was the first thing that Natália heard when she awoke.

She lay on the bed amid a jumble of bedclothes and listened to the foghorn, the crowing of cocks, a lorry starting up in the village, dogs barking. She stretched her limbs, enjoying the last few moments before getting up and starting the day.

She could not lie in bed long. The *traineiras* would be returning to off-load their catches soon, and she would have to be there to meet the boat and collect the basket of fish to sell that day.

She stood up and stretched the last sleep out of her body. She sluiced water from the can over herself and put on her cotton dress and a much-darned jersey. She took a hunk of

16

bread and some goat cheese, and set off with her basket to the fishing port.

Some of the smaller boats were already in harbour and unloading their catches on the beach. The womenfolk were gathering on the quayside; lorries and ox carts were arriving: these would take some of the catch to Oporto, or to neighbouring towns. Part of the catch would be salted, part sold fresh and part put in ice to be canned in the local factory of Matosinhos.

Natália was known among the fish wives and was greeted by them as she made her way through the crowd to the quayside.

The first *traineiras* arrived: the *Maria de Luz*, the *Nossa Senhora de Fátima*, and others. Most had reasonable catches, but none of them good. Natália shouted down to one of the men aboard the *Maria de Luz*, 'Where's the *Novo Olho*?'

The man shrugged widely, raising his hands palm upwards. One of his mates shouted, 'You tell us, girl. You should know!' There was laughter: Natália's predictions were a standing joke.

Other boats came in. Most anchored in the harbour, but a few – the ones with better catches – came alongside the quay.

Natália continued to wait. There were only two boats still out: the *Novo Olho* and the *Santa Cruz*. The latter had a poor reputation. The skipper was inexperienced and would not enter the harbour in such fog. But it was unusual for the *Novo Olho* to be late in. Rui dos Santos was known as one of the better skippers.

As the morning wore on and the sun climbed higher, the fog thinned so that the breakwater became visible. Many of the lorries had been loaded now and were leaving for Oporto. Natália knew that if the boat were too late, a poor price would be paid for the fish.

And then, two *traineiras* appeared together out of the mist: the *Santa Cruz* towing the *Novo Olho*.

The sight of them caused much chatter and comment among the people on the quayside. Jokes were passed at the expense of Rui dos Santos and his brother Carlos. But when the people saw the catch that the *Novo Olho* had aboard, the laughter turned to amazement, for hardly a square inch of the *traineira's* decks was visible under the load of silver sardines.

The tow was cast off, and the *Novo Olho* drifted slowly alongside. Ropes were thrown up and secured. People shouted down to the crew, but the men made little reply. And on the harbour wall, Natália looked for the old man, but did not see him.

There was suddenly an awareness among the people that a tragedy had occurred. The women whispered asides to each other, and glanced across at the girl in the pink and white check dress, who stood by the bollard where the *Novo Olho*'s headrope was made fast.

Rui dos Santos climbed up the vertical ladder from the trawler to the quay. He was not a large man, but swarthy and straight-backed. He would have looked well as a Roman centurion. His face was heavily weatherbeaten and his arms hairy and muscular. He was a hardworking man, a loving father and, unlike his brother Carlos, a faithful husband. He liked his wine and his food and his coffee, and in ordinary life he was talkative and easy-going.

Now, as he approached Natália, he was tongue-tied. He stood before her, unable to choose words to explain what had happened, what he had done. How could he tell this child that they had discovered a part of the old man's body, but that it was considered better to do away with it there and then, to weight it and sink it? How could he explain that he and the crew had seen the accident as a stroke of fate, a punishment for their belief in her predictions?

He opened his mouth, hesitated, and then said simply, 'He is dead, little one. There was a collision. He was swept overboard and lost.'

Natália stared for several moments into his face, then turned and ran. She ran through the crowds of women and fishermen, between the piles of crates, and ox carts, past the circle of boys who were tormenting a bitch in whelp. She ran from them, through the streets of Matosinhos and along the path to the shack that was her home.

She entered and closed the door behind her. She stood clutching herself in the semi-darkness, horror and panic welling up inside her.

Within minutes, there were voices outside, and the door

opened. She found herself surrounded by women. They had come to comfort her. They wept over her and mourned on her behalf. Their tears were hot upon her shoulders, their bosoms damp with sweat and full of vicarious emotion. They enjoyed giving vent to their exaggerated sorrow, wailing and sobbing, patting her with their fat hands, clasping her to themselves until a feeling of total revulsion caused her to push them out of the hut and shut the door on them.

For a long time after they had gone, she stood motionless in the hut. The noises of the day went on outside, but she did not belong to them any more. Dimly, she began to wonder what had happened. A collision. What sort of collision? And if he had been swept overboard, where was he now?

She sat down on the bed and shivered. She didn't understand why she felt so cold. Her whole body shook; she clasped her arms round her shoulders, swaying back and forth silently.

Gradually the shivering subsided, and a succession of images passed through her mind. They were images of the past: memories of days of happiness with the man who had cared for her, the man she believed was her father. She recalled stories he had told her about her mother, who was young and the most beautiful woman in the village; who had died on the night she was born; stories, too, of his own childhood in the slums of Oporto in the days when Portugal had a king.

Time passed. She was unaware of how much time: a day and a night, certainly – perhaps two days and two nights. People came to the door of the hut and called her name, but she heard her own voice telling them to go away. She ate nothing. It seemed to her that she could never go out into the world again.

But in due course she was aware of an awakening within herself, and she emerged from the state of numbness and shock. She was able to recognise that he was dead and could never be alive again, and that it was necessary to leave the hut, to go out, and live.

When she emerged from the hut, it was a clear, still night. She walked down the path and crossed the river by the wooden footbridge, continuing down to the shore to the north of the village of Leça da Palmeira.

She descended on to the sand beach that had formed since

19

the building of the new mole and went to the water's edge. The Atlantic swell broke on the beach and the frothy water surged up, white, over her feet.

She walked northward along the wet sand, and the rotating beams of the Boa Nova lighthouse seemed to beckon her on.

She continued along the shore until she reached the little church built on the end of a slight promontory, not far from the lighthouse itself. It had not been her original intention to enter this church, but she wandered inside and found herself in the cool, stone darkness.

No candles were burning and no lamps were lit except for the tiny oil lamp that announced the presence of the sacrament. She went to the altar rail but did not kneel down. The sound of the Atlantic rollers was loud in the church, and moonlight spilled in through the open door.

She stared up at the figure of Christ in agony, the prim plaster features of St Joseph, the placid face of Our Lady, Star of the Sea. She felt she ought to pray, but no prayers came.

Another figure caught her eye. It was her own shadow on the whitewashed wall: a vast silhouette of a woman, not a girl. She looked at this shadow and was afraid. Who was this woman? It seemed to her that she was looking at the person she would be one day: a person who was as strange and remote as the shadow, and yet one that moved when she moved, was hers to control.

She raised her hand, and the shadow raised its hand in reply. She moved her head back, and the woman's hair fell away from her face to reveal a profile, a sloping brow, an open mouth, a neck, arched backwards. She turned, and the shadow followed her to the door of the church.

Outside, the first light of dawn was appearing. She left the beach and wandered among the sand dunes, her head light with hunger and fatigue. The sun came up and quickly dissipated the chill of the morning. It rose in the sky and the day gathered its heat until the sand burned and a haze formed inland.

But Natália was not aware of this, for she had fallen asleep among the dunes. When she eventually awoke, it was to the sound of people talking and laughing nearby.

20

❧ 2 ❧

I

BOBBY TEAPE peeled off his shirt, undid the old Rugby tie round his waist and lowered his trousers, revealing the full glory of his striped swimming costume.

'Last one in's a sissy,' he said, and punched Hugh Blunden in the stomach.

'First one in's a damn fool,' Blunden countered, whereupon Teape brought him down with a rugger tackle and the two friends wrestled in the sand.

It was Teape's thirtieth birthday: Fay Remington had organised a beach party as a celebration. It was usually somebody's birthday in the Oporto British colony, so there were quite a lot of beach parties.

The seven families and their friends had arrived soon after midday: they left their Austins and their bicycles on the track above the beach and carried the baskets of wine and food down to a suitable spot among the dunes. While the older ladies unpacked the lunch under the direction of Fay Remington, the young prepared for a swim.

Fay was in her fifties now. She was the wife of Dodger Remington, the co-director of Teape's Port. Their daughter Joy was engaged to Bobby Teape, and Fay was making a special effort to be the perfect future mother-in-law.

The younger members of the party were gathering round Bobby and Hugh. Sand flew everywhere, and a shower of it fell upon the green salad, making it a little too crisp. Teape was bigger and fitter than Blunden and succeeded in getting him by the ankle. To the delight of the younger children, he dragged him, roaring in protest, down to the water were they fought and splashed like overgrown schoolboys.

21

The sea was cold – it always was – and the undertow treacherous. The men chased the girls and the girls eventually allowed themselves to be caught and dunked. Joy Remington, who was fair with a piercing laugh and a fashionably flat chest, wanted to be dunked by Bobby, but they had argued that morning – again – and were not on speaking terms. She had to make do with Freddy Randall instead. Freddy was bronzed and athletic, but he was married to her sister, Madge.

The Remington picnics were always excellently organised. Fay was an American from Vermont, and unafraid of telling people what to do. For this picnic she had decreed that everyone wear stripes, so everyone did.

Lunch was the usual sort of thing. There were *bolinhos de bacalhau*, sardines, tuna, devilled eggs, fish mayonnaise and a variety of fresh salads. This was accompanied by chilled *vinho verde* and was followed by veal and ham pie, brown rice, cold chicken and a curry mould, with which was drunk an excellent Dão wine donated by Hugh Blunden. After that plates were changed for the dessert: grapes, melons, figs and nuts, most of which came from the Teape *quinta* in the *alto-Douro*.

After lunch there was coffee from vacuum flasks and Teape's tawny port.

The party split into groups. The ladies collected the plates together and packed them away; the younger children played in the sand; the older Remington offspring (James, Mark and Deirdre) went off with their friends Sally and Dee Millet, and the menfolk worked their way steadily through the remaining two bottles of port. Among them was Bobby Teape, large and athletic with short cropped hair and a booming laugh. He steadfastly ignored Joy's attempts to prise him away, and continued his conversation about American vines with Dodger Remington and Hugh Blunden.

When the ladies had packed away the lunch things, they began thinking about tea. By this time the men had consumed all the port they intended to consume and were ready to work off some of their excess energy. In the old days, when picnics were really picnics, they would have played Weak Horses or British Bulldog. But with only fourteen men and boys they had to settle for a game of *Púcaros*, which involved throwing terra

22

cotta mugs from hand to hand, some of which were filled with water.

It was all splendid fun until Joy – still trying to make it up with Bobby – deliberately threw a full beaker of water at him, whereupon he chased her, caught her and spanked her.

At first, this seemed to be just what Joy had wanted, but Bobby (who had done himself rather well on wine and Teape's Tawny) overdid the operation, and Joy lost her half-hunter in the sand.

'Why did you have to be so jolly rough?' she asked him.

Bobby shrugged. 'I didn't do it on purpose. It was an accident.'

'It was Granny Remington's. She gave it to me for my twenty-first.'

'I'm sorry.'

'You don't sound it.'

'I can't help what I sound.'

'Well you shouldn't have been so jolly rough.'

Freddy Randall organised a search. 'Come on everybody!' he shouted. 'No good having half a hunt for a half-hunter!' His four year old son caught this phrase and was to repeat it to the exasperation of several members of the colony for months to come.

The half-hunter wasn't found and anyway it was time to make a fire and boil water for the tea. Twigs and driftwood were collected and large quantities of China and Darjeeling tea were placed in a vast black teapot. Alice McNeil provided home-made scones and shortcake, and the party settled down to eat again.

'Ah,' said Madge Randall. 'I see we have company.'

Eyes turned to look where Madge indicated.

It was one of the girls from the village. She was very brown and thin, and wore a pink cotton dress.

Sally Millet said, 'I recognise that dress. It was mine. Mummy gave it away when I left the OBS. I was jolly cross.'

'Cast your bread upon the waters,' Freddy Randall said.

'Stare-bare, stare-bare, when you grow up you'll have no hair,' Joanna Millet chanted. She was eleven.

Her elder sister said, 'She probably thinks you look just as

23

odd as you think you aren't.'

'She doesn't look odd,' Joanna said. 'Just dirty.' She helped herself to two pieces of shortcake and gave one to her twin brother, Geoffrey.

'Can't we get rid of her?' Joy said. 'I hate feeling like an animal in the zoo.'

'Feeding time in the monkey house,' Bobby Teape said, and laughed heartily. He turned to the girl, who continued to stare at them, and motioned with his hand to get rid of her. '*Vai t'embora*!' he shouted.

The girl turned, swayed and fainted. 'Well I'm jiggered,' Bobby said, and went to help her up. She had fallen face down: there was sand sticking to her face and in her mouth. Her eyes opened and the eyeballs rolled upwards, showing the whites. 'She's right out,' he said, and picked her up in his arms.

He carried her down to the sea. He intended to sluice water over her face to revive her, but he was caught by a slightly larger wave and the girl was soaked. She regained consciousness and stared up at him.

She had thick brows and dark brown eyes. He helped her to her feet and steadied her. 'You fainted, *menina*,' he said. 'Are you all right?'

She nodded briefly and turned to walk away. He put his hand in his pocket and took out a note. Twenty *escudos*.

'Here!' he called after her. 'Take this. Get yourself something to eat.'

He put the note in her hand. She looked down at it as if she didn't know what it was for. Then the hint of a smile of gratitude came to her eyes. He knew then that he was excited by her, and was at the same time worried that the others might notice.

'Is she all right?' Joy called.

'Needs a good square meal, I'd say,' he shouted back. He returned to where the others were sitting.

'Did you give her money?' Joy asked.

'Yes.'

'How much?'

'Does that matter?'

'I was just interested. But if you're embarrassed about it, well – you needn't say.'

That was typical of Joy. She always managed somehow to make you feel in the wrong.

He said: 'I gave her twenty *escudos*.'

There was a general intake of breath. Madge Randall said, 'That's what I pay Etelvina for a month!'

'It was all I had,' Bobby said.

Joy brushed crumbs from her lap and folded her legs beneath her skirt. 'I expect she's laughing by now. I wonder how many times she's done that before. I expect she saw you'd be an easy touch, Rob. It's that big teddy bear look of yours.'

'I don't think she was a fake,' he said. Joy avoided looking at him. She made a pattern in the sand with her finger.

Fay Remington came to the rescue. 'I always give them food if they come begging at the door. At least that way you know your money won't be spent on drink.'

Joy stopped making her pattern and looked up at her fiancé. 'I think,' she said very deliberately, making quite sure everyone could hear, 'I think you rather liked the look of her.'

There was an awkward silence. Alice McNeil tried to control a giggle.

Teape said, 'I think that remark was in very poor taste, if you don't mind my saying so.'

'Oh heavens!' Joy laughed shrilly, 'The poor dear man took me seriously!'

She lay back on the sand and laughed up at him. He stood looking down at her, frowning. He said, 'Let's go for a walk, shall we?'

'Why?'

'I'd like to. Please.'

'Oh, all right then. Come on. If we must.' She stood up, shrugged to the others and accompanied him along the beach.

When they were well out of earshot, Teape said, 'I'm not prepared to go on like this, Joy.'

'I wasn't being serious, Rob. For heaven's sake!'

'It's not just that. It's not just what's happened this afternoon. You know very well what I'm talking about.'

'No I don't! I haven't a blessed idea!'

'You talk down to me the whole time. You belittle me.'

'Only in fun.'

'It's not fun for me. Anyway –' He stopped. 'I think we ought to break it off.'

'Oh.'

'What do you think?'

'I didn't think things were as bad as that.'

'Things aren't exactly bad. It's just that, well, I don't think they're good enough to make a happy marriage.'

She stared at him. 'You really are serious, aren't you?'

He nodded sadly. 'If you want to sue me and all that, I don't mind.'

'Don't be idiotic, Rob.' She gulped awkwardly, and burst into tears.

She had a good cry, and then turned it off abruptly. He remembered how she used to do exactly the same as a child. She hadn't changed. They walked on, and later he said, 'I would rather face up to it now than let things drift.'

She nodded and sniffed. 'Yes. Better this way. Before we hurt each other any more.' She looked up at him, but he was looking away, out to sea.

When they eventually rejoined the others, the remains of the picnic had been packed up and people were preparing to go.

Joy said in a loud voice, 'Well, you may as well all know. We've broken off our engagement.' Joy always delighted in the brutal truth.

Bobby was annoyed, and then almost immediately relieved at the thought that he would not have to suffer such remarks throughout a lifetime of marriage to her.

Fay Remington said, 'Darlings! My poor darlings!' She hugged Joy and squeezed Bobby's hand. 'What a brave, brave decision,' she added tactfully.

The picnic was over. They mounted their bicycles and pedalled home along the sandy track.

II

Although not one of the oldest of port firms, Teape's was

26

perhaps the most English and the most exclusive. The founder, Edward Teape, came out to Oporto in 1826. He brought with him his new wife and joined the firm of Quarles Harris & Co. where he stayed for three years until the death of an uncle made him the beneficiary of the family fortune. He then set up a port shipping business in his own name, being twenty-eight years old at the time.

Of his three sons, only one was to follow Edward into the family business. The eldest, George, lived as a painter and died in penury. Timothy was killed in India in 1850, and the youngest, Nicholas, stayed at home and worked for Hunt, Roope & Co. until he was in his late twenties, when he joined his father's firm.

Nicholas took after his mother. He was a dreamy fellow, softly spoken, and self-effacing. His father, a large and powerful man with an equally powerful personality, disapproved of this effete son who was to take over the firm. But he had no choice, for he died of a heart attack one afternoon at the Factory House, after a particularly good lunch.

Nicholas inherited a prospering firm. Teape & Co. shipped two hundred and twenty-three pipes of port to England in 1864, and in that same year Nicholas met and married Alice Hopkinson.

Alice is said to have 'invented' the beach picnic. She was a motherly person, whose generosity was fabled within the colony. She presented Nicholas with four girls and a boy, and the boy grew up like his grandfather: huge, ginger-haired and athletic. This was Charles Edward, and he was particularly popular in the colony.

Charles married Rosalinde Remington, the daughter of another port wine shipper, and she had three sons. The eldest, Nicholas (again) was killed four days after qualifying as a pilot of the Royal Flying Corps, in 1915. The second son (George) was killed at Brooklands motor racing track in 1928, and the third, Robert, was now finishing his dessert and washing his fingers in the brass finger bowl, under the eye of his elderly mother.

He and Joy had planned to go out for dinner that night, but after the picnic there had been some hurried rearrangements,

27

and they had ended up by dining at their respective homes.

Bobby was certainly from the family mould. Born in 1904 and educated at Rugby, he was considered a good sportsman and excellent company. Without his huge, benevolent presence, a party lacked something.

He had shared a house in the Oporto suburb of Nevogilde with Hugh Blunden for several years, shortly after joining the family firm, and the two bachelors had gained a reputation for living life to the hilt. But when old Charlie Teape eventually died, Bobby's mother asked him to come back and live with her at Vila Nova de Gaia. Bobby had agreed, but had insisted that they move permanently to their summer residence in Leça da Palmeira, eight miles to the north of Oporto.

Rosalinde Teape regretted the move. The house was appallingly damp, and the basic facilities were indeed very basic. But she was getting old, and Bobby was her one and only surviving son. She gave in to him, and made up for it by keeping him firmly under her thumb.

The news of the broken engagement had upset her. She wanted to see her son settled, and she had considered Joy a suitable match. She was a distant cousin, true, but Rosalinde was a Remington and had a strong sense of family.

'You'll have to find yourself a wife one of these days,' she said.

'All in good time, Mother.'

'There's been quite enough good time, to my mind. A little discipline and self-sacrifice would do you the world of good, my boy.'

'Yes, mother.'

'When I was a girl it was considered a duty among our class to have sizeable families, so that Britain should not be without capable people to govern her.'

'Yes, mother.'

'And don't "yes mother" me, either.'

'No, mother.'

Rosalinde Teape picked up a small lady in a large brass crinoline and shook it, tinkling a bell. The maid entered.

'*O vinho de port, Maria.*'

'*Sim Senhora.*'

Maria brought the decanter of port in its silver coaster and set it down before Bobby, who removed the glass bung and helped his mother and himself to a glass.

'This is the 1900, isn't it?' Mrs. Teape said.

Bobby shrugged. 'Somewhere around then, yes.'

Rosalinde Teape shook her head. 'I despair of you, dear, really I do. You should know!'

'Mother of course I know what it is! Just because I don't worship the stuff!'

'You can't hope to make a success of the firm unless you have some enthusiasm, Robert.'

'I do have enthusiasm. It's just that my generation isn't quite so earnest as yours. We like to underplay our hand a little.'

'Well if pretending not to care what vintage port you're drinking is "underplaying your hand", then I do not approve. Your father often said that a man had to believe in what he was doing in order to make a go of it.'

Teape bowed his head a little, acknowledging not for the first time the wisdom of his dead father. In the pause that followed, the grandmother clock chimed the hour.

'I have another birthday present for you,' his mother said.

'Oh really? Well I must say that's jolly decent –'

Mrs Teape held up a hand. 'This is not a present to be taken lightly. It is not a tangible present.'

She took up her glass of port, admiring the delicate colour of it. Nineteen hundred. That had been a good year, if her memory served her correctly. Not an important year, no. But a good one. Nicholas had started school with Mr Picken that year. And the Douro had flooded. Yes, she remembered that. She had gone down to the bridge to see all the shipwrecks it had caused. Charles was in his prime in those days: a handsome man, very upright, with a stronger face than his son. But Charlie Teape had slipped into alcoholism during the years after the Great War, and it had fallen to Rosalinde to keep the family firm together until one of the sons was able to take over.

It had been Rosalinde who had resisted the proposed merger with Randall, Brotherton & Co, she who had urged her husband first to make her a director of the firm and later to let go the reins altogether, when his illness turned him into a pathetic apology of a man, who had to be looked after night and day, like a baby.

His illness had lasted nearly two years. During that time, Rosalinde Teape established herself as the matriarch of Teape's Port. She began to run the firm on commonsense and thrift. She cut back on the lavish entertainment that went on every lunchtime at the wine lodge and used the money saved to pay off debts and purchase much-needed new stock. She insisted on new standards of cleanliness which at first horrified the Portuguese work force but later instilled in them a new feeling of pride. After the death of her husband, she bought out one of the directors with whom she disagreed, and made her second cousin James a partner. James, known in the colony as 'Dodger' – officially because of his prowess on the rugger field and unofficially because he never joined up – was one of the finest tasters in the trade. His partnership was of immense value to the firm: a wine is bought for its looks and its taste, and Remington's palate was to be one of the firm's most valuable assets.

More recently, Rosalinde had taken on Hugh Blunden. This decision had been against the advice of Dodger Remington but it had been a shrewd one, nevertheless. Blunden had money, charm, connections and excellent business sense. He was unmarried and happy to travel about the continent on the firm's behalf. Within a few years of his joining Teape & Co, sales to the continent and Great Britain were increasing for the first time in many years, and Dodger Remington had been forced to admit that Rosalinde had made a wise decision: her authority was finally established.

She looked up at Robert. He was very like his father in some ways. She hoped to goodness he didn't make the same mistakes. He smiled at her.

'Well? How much longer are you going to keep me in suspense?'

She placed her hand over his. Hers was an old lady's hand now. The skin was parched and brown and covered in freckles. The joints were swollen with rheumatism, made worse each winter by the frequent fogs that rolled in from the sea.

30

'I have decided to make you a director, dear.'

Bobby Teape beamed. 'And about time too, Mother, if I may say so.'

'If anything, I think I may be a little precipitous in this decision. Especially after what you have told me this evening.'

'You mean Joy.'

'I mean Joy, yes.'

'Oh.'

'Well. Aren't you going to thank me?'

He rose from his chair, leant across the table and kissed her on the cheek. 'Thank you, Mother. You're a sport.'

'Don't think this is something to be taken lightly, Bobby, will you?'

'Of course not. No. Absolutely not, in fact.'

'I'd like you to be happy, Robert. But happiness doesn't come easily. It has to be earned. By hard work. Integrity. And . . . and remember: you won't find it at the bottom of a bottle, either.'

'No, Mother.'

'I know you think I just say these things, but I really do believe them. It's so easy, so easy to just – '

'Just throw your life away. Yes.'

'Well. Mind you don't forget it.'

'I'll try not to.'

Rosalinde softened. She was very fond of Robert and could never get really angry with him. He was his mother's boy, of course, she knew that. But she hoped she hadn't spoilt him. No, she didn't think she had done that. 'And please do try to find yourself a nice wife, dear, won't you?'

'I'll do my best, Mother.'

'I would so like to see you settled. Settled and happy.' She raised her glass. 'Anyway. Happy birthday.'

'Do you want me to make a speech?'

'Not tonight, dear. I'll be going up to bed soon.'

He raised his glass. 'To the old firm, then.'

They drank the toast together, and when they put their glasses down, Rosalinde's eyes were a little dewy. She didn't stay for coffee. She said she was feeling a little tired, and went off to bed.

31

Bobby refilled his glass and took it out into the garden. The crickets and night insects were making a noise, and somewhere a long way off a dog was howling.

His mother's exhortations echoed in his mind. He chuckled and sipped his port. Joy – well, she was a nice girl. But not for him. Definitely not. No, the sort of wife he was after would not have a shrill voice for a start. Nor would she be for ever bossing him about.

Actually, he wasn't all that fussed about marriage. He was quite happy as he was. Quite comfortable really, what with his friends and his dogs, his shooting in the winter and tennis in the summer.

He relieved himself into the bushes, and as he did so he remembered the girl who had fainted on the beach that afternoon, and the shape of her young body under her wet cotton dress.

III

1934 was an eventful year in Oporto. Now that Salazar had declared his New State, a degree of stability in Portugal at last seemed a possibility. The Depression was drawing to a close, and a more optimistic mood prevailed in business.

In June, the President of the Republic opened the Colonial Exhibition, and in September the Prince of Wales made a surprise visit to the city, having travelled down by taxi from Corunna, where his host's yacht had put in on account of bad weather.

It was a good year for sport, too. The Portuguese Ladies' Tennis Championship was won by an Englishwoman, and the Espinho golf course was extended to eighteen holes. In the city, a sprucing-up operation was put into effect, and new tramways and pavements were laid.

Bobby Teape went up country for the partridge shooting at the end of October and his mother made one last visit to the office in Vila Nova de Gaia before starting her retirement.

Vila Nova de Gaia is a jumble of roofs and narrow cobbled

lanes. It is built on the steep hill on the south bank of the
Douro, looking straight across the muddy river to the city of
Oporto. The names of the port wine firms are displayed in
large white letters on the terra cotta roofs: SANDEMAN,
CROFT, TAYLOR, DELAFORCE, and all the rest.

Rosalinde approached the town sitting in the rear seat of her
black Rover saloon. The car crossed the river by the old
bridge, and threaded its way among ox carts, barefoot children
and women with baskets balanced on their heads.

The office of Teape, Sons & Company was approached by a
gate let into a stone wall. To enter these gates, the car had to
carry out a complicated manoeuvre in order to complete the
turn without damaging its polished wings. A bleep on the
horn, and the gates were swung open by a ten-year-old boy, the
son of Sr Pereira, the manager.

The car nosed its way along a short drive beneath a vine
trellis and drew to a halt outside the office entrance. Dodger
Remington was waiting to greet the old lady as she stepped out
of the car.

Dodger was a slight man, just over sixty now. He had shrunk
rather in the last ten years: his clothes were a little shabby, and
hung upon him loosely. He had been a first class scrum half in
his day, but that was a long time ago. His tufted eyebrows gave
him the look of a good-natured mongrel, and he had been
wearing the same straw hat for at least twenty years.

This hat he now took off to Rosalinde. They exchanged
their good mornings, and Remington followed the old lady
into the office.

Her visits followed an invariable routine. First, she went
through the account books, which she looked at in detail. She
examined the records of wine shipped in barrel, the prices and
wages paid at the recent vintage, the incidental expenses
claimed by Remington and Blunden and the three managers.
Conversation was limited while she did this, for Remington
knew exactly which books she wanted to see and what
questions she was likely to ask. She sat at the wide, teak desk
and he passed her the books and papers one by one, comment-
ing on an amount outstanding here, or a particularly large
order there. And as she went through these documents, she

added her initials to indicate that she had seen and approved them.

When she had finished, she looked up at Remington. 'Good. Shall we walk round?'

'Certainly, Aunt.' Rosalinde was not exactly an aunt to Dodger Remington, but a second cousin once removed. But she had been born a Remington, and the bond still held.

He led the way out of the office and into the *adega*, where row upon row of barrels of wine lay maturing and mellowing in the cool gloom, under worm-eaten rafters.

The old lady walked along between these stacked barrels, and greeted Joaquim, the old man who kept the records of temperatures and lot numbers. She paused to talk to him, asking in her execrable Portuguese how he and his family were, and comiserating with him over the foggy weather that brought on the rheumatism from which he, like the Senhora, suffered.

After visiting the *adega*, they proceeded to the bottling shop, where a small team of workers were filling bottles with Teape's Porto Seco, labelling them, corking and packing them.

They paused at the cooperage and from there went to the wine store itself, where the vintage ports lay in cobwebbed darkness. The bottles were stacked horizontally from floor to ceiling: thousands of them, though the exact number was a closely guarded secret, as it was an indication of the financial stability of the company.

The tour ended in the tasting room, where Remington discussed some of the new blends with Rosalinde. She was not a taster, and relied heavily on Remington. The room was not unlike a studio: it faced north, across the river Douro. Carefully labelled bottles of sample wines and brandies stood in rows on the shelves, and a large copper spitoon was available by the sink, for the taster never swallowed what he sampled.

Rosalinde Teape stood at the window and looked across the city of Oporto: the jumble of palaces, churches, solid Georgian houses and slums. On the river, four square-sailed Douro boats slipped gracefully along, each piled high with barrels. Remington was talking at some length about the comparative success of certain tawny ports, but she heard very little, aware

34

that she would not see this, her favourite view, many more times.

Remington had sensed that her walk round had been more thorough than usual, and so he was not completely surprised at lunch when she told him that this was to be her last business visit.

'I think it's time to hand over the reins to Robert.' she said. 'I want him to be a director in deed as well as in name. He is quite old enough.'

'We shall miss you,' he said.

'Will you? I'm not so sure about that. I expect you have all sorts of changes you'd like to make.'

'Things have worked very well, especially this year.'

'Yes. I don't see why they should not continue to do so, either. Mind you, I think you should keep a watchful eye on Robert. I would not like to feel that he was on probation, but on the other hand I should like to be kept informed as to how he is managing.'

She wiped her mouth with her napkin and sat back. The meal was over. 'Well. That's that. I won't keep you any longer.'

The car was summoned. Remington held the door open for her. She departed with grace and dignity, not for one moment allowing herself to display the feelings of nostalgia that she felt. They bade each other farewell, and Mrs Rosalinde Teape departed from the office of Teape, Sons & Company for the last time.

When she arrived home, she had a little siesta. She got up at four-thirty for tea, which Maria brought to her on the verandah. When she had finished and the trolley of tea things had been removed, she remained outside for the last of the sun, and read a magazine.

But she felt restless and had difficulty in attending to the printed page. For the first time in her life, she could not see the way ahead. She wondered if she had done the right thing. Was Robert really mature enough to take over the firm? He was such a careless boy. Careless? No. Carefree. She was afraid, too, that there was a weakness in his character, one which she could not identify but which she knew instinctively was present. Perhaps she had made life too easy for him, over the years. But there was little she could do about it now. If only he could get married to a really nice girl. A girl who would not only look after him, but support him morally. In a way, it was perhaps to the good that he and Joy had broken off their engagement. Joy was so waspish. Perhaps she would have mellowed as his wife. But again, too late now.

She looked out over the garden and allowed these and similar thoughts to come and go as they pleased. It had been like this when she had left school, she remembered. It was not the end of a paragraph or a chapter . . . more the end of an epoch in her life. If your life could be made up of epochs, of course.

But still. She was very lucky. Perhaps she might get down to some serious reading. Blackwoods was all very well, but it was rather light and racy in its style. She had always wanted to read the Russian novelists in translation. There was so much to do in life, and so little time to do it.

Her reverie was interrupted by the arrival of Amália the cook, a small stout woman with greying hair that was swept into a bun, so that her head looked like a cottage loaf.

'Ah, please, Senhora.'

'Yes, Amália?'

'Senhora we were going to have beans for dinner.'

'Yes.'

'Well I have asked the gardener to provide beans, but he refuses to do so.'

'Why is that?'

'He says they are not ready for picking.'

At that moment, the gardener appeared in the drive at the front of the house carrying a large quantity of spinach. He approached the verandah and doffed his battered trilby hat. 'Good afternoon, Senhora. I have brought the spinach for you to see.'

'The Lady did not ask for spinach,' said Amália. 'She asked especially for the beans.' She turned to Rosalinde. 'My Lady, the beans are young and tender, as you like them. If we leave them longer, they will quickly become too big and tough to eat.' She shot a withering look at the gardener. 'He is new, Senhora. He does not know how you like things done. I have told him and told him, but he takes no notice . . . '

Rosalinde held up her hand to stop the argument. 'I shall come and look at the beans myself,' she said. She pushed herself out of her chair, wincing at the pain in her joints. She wanted her stick, but it was inside.

The two servants exchanged a look of mutual animosity, and stepped aside as the old lady approached the steps.

Rosalinde was just a little dizzy. She saw the steps in front of her and stretched out a hand to steady herself on the sphere of stone that decorated the top of the balstrade, where the morning glory grew.

She put one foot forward, and again thought that she needed her stick. She was aware that she had stretched out her foot a little too far forward, and at the same time she stumbled, grasped for something to steady herself by, clutched air, and fell.

Amália screamed. Maria came running out of the house, and when she saw the Senhora lying at the bottom of the steps, she also screamed. They bent over their mistress and lifted her head. It sagged and lolled in their hands, and thick, dark blood oozed from the old lady's aquiline nose.

IV

At nine o'clock the following morning, Teape was scrambling up the mountain, high above the Douro valley, loaded double barrel twelve bore in hand, with his labradors Tagus and Minho leaping up over boulders beside him.

Spread out down the mountain were twenty or more other members of the shoot. The elderly and less agile remained on the lower slopes while the young and athletic, including Teape and Blunden, tried to keep some semblance of a line higher up.

Teape was dressed in an aertex shirt and flannel bags, supported by a Rugby tie. He had breakfasted on quantities of ham and eggs and bread and marmalade and coffee, and thus

37

fuelled, was in a fighting mood. Up and down the line, equally well-fed men were exchanging shouts, calling up their dogs, telling each other to hurry up or keep back as they advanced, beating the heather with sticks to drive the red-legged partridges out.

The first brace went up and António, some fifty yards to Teape's right shouted, '*La vai! La vai!*'

The birds came past like low level fighter-bombers. Bobby straightened, aimed and loosed off both barrels. Immediately after him, Freddy Randall fired, followed by Emidio Oliveira and all the rest, so that a great volley of shots echoed and re-echoed against the mountains on either side of the river.

Only one partridge fell. 'Mine!' shouted a voice, and there followed more shouts and laughter that ended when three more partridges went up.

There was game in abundance. That was what made shooting in the Douro country so different. You had to work hard for your sport, yes, but there was never any worry about limiting the number of fine birds you shot. Loose off as many rounds as you like, old boy. There's no such thing as a quota for the day.

So the dogs were kept busy. Their owners sent them off with the order 'Go fetch!' or, if they were Portuguese-speaking dogs, '*Vai buscar!*' and their black or golden tails wagged furiously in the heather and gorse as they sought out the dead and dying birds.

Down by the railway, uninvited guns stood by to look after any birds that managed to run the gauntlet of the fusilade unscathed. And if a partridge fell in the river, there were boats waiting to retrieve it.

The shoot continued until nearly two o'clock, when lunch was announced by a shout of '*Almoço!*' that was passed with boyish enthusiasm up the line. The guns, scratched by brambles, smeared with dust and cordite and sweating profusely, made their way down to the plateau of grass above the river, where a picnic meal was ready.

There was now much public school jollity. The behaviour of the men and dogs was in some ways strikingly similar. The dogs wagged, sniffed, panted, yapped, argued, got in the way and looked hopefully in the direction of the food. One of them knocked over a loaded shotgun, which went off harmlessly, but occasioned an outcry of protest followed by laughter.

The spoils of the forenoon's activities were gathered together and counted, and hung up in festoons, so that a photograph could be taken to preserve for ever a record of the victors and their victims. Teape and Blunden had a humorous argument about who was claiming how many, and half way through this argument one of the Portuguese dogs was caught eating a partridge. Its owner, Emidio Oliveira, a small, rotund and noisy man, kicked the dog sharply in the guts, and it went off yelping.

They sat down on the grass to eat.

Two hours later when the port was finished, the party broke up with many shouted farewells and arrangements to meet at the various *quintas* that evening.

Blunden and Teape took back eight brace of partridge to the Quinta das Rosas and when they arrived at the top of the steep and dusty path, the maids were ready to take the day's bag from them. Hot water had been boiled and baths prepared, and the gentlemen fell happily into their respective tubs to wash and change for dinner.

They sat on the verandah, an hour later, and watched the sun disappear over the mountain. They sipped their white port and listened to the wail of the steam engine as it made its way up the valley from Pinhão.

This steam train was known as the *Paciência*, or the 'Patience' train, because of its infuriatingly frequent stops and delays. The line followed the course of the Douro, and for many of the *quintas* in the upper Douro, was the only means of communication with the outside world. The Quinta das Rosas was no exception: there was no telephone and no road to it. Teape and Blunden therefore watched the arrival of the train at Rosas station, some five hundred feet below them, with a casual interest.

This interest increased when they saw the unmistakable figure of Dodger Remington alight.

'What the devil's he doing here?' Blunden said.

'Probably come to check up on us. See we're not misbehaving.'

They watched as the figure made its way up the path.

39

Blunden settled himself more comfortably in his cane chair. 'It's a long way to come for a drink.'

'Maybe he's run out of T.S.R.,' Bobby said, referring to Teape's Special Reserve.

They chuckled. Neither resented Remington's authority, but both were quite certain they could get on very well without him.

Teape went to the edge of the verandah, from where he could look directly down on Remington as he made his way up the path.

'Hullo there!'

Remington raised his hand in reply, and continued up the path. As he reached the verandah, Teape said, 'So you changed your mind. Very wise. We've had a splendid day.'

Remington shook his head. He had taken the hill a little too quickly, and was out of breath. Blunden said, 'You look as though you could do with a drink.'

Remington turned to Teape. 'Your mother's had an accident. She's in the British Hospital.'

'What sort of an accident?'

'She fell. Outside the house.'

'Is she bad?'

'She's an old lady, Robert.'

Teape frowned, and snorted with impatience. 'You've come to tell me I must go back to Oporto.'

'Yes. I think you should.'

'Damn!' Teape turned, took a few paces, and turned again. 'Damn! Trust the old lady to ruin my sport.'

Remington said quietly: 'I think I ought to tell you, she's in a coma.'

Teape walked to the end of the verandah. It was getting dark now, but a solitary eagle was soaring high above the mountains on the other side of the valley.

'I'll catch the morning train,' he said.

V

The organ in St James's church was in need of repair. The air supply system was faulty, so that the semi-breves were inclined to fade, and several of the notes were liable to burp and squeak in unpredictable ways.

The congregation was singing Ancient & Modern number 573 – All Things Bright and Beautiful. The church was full, because Rosalinde Teape had been well known and highly regarded in the British Colony.

Teape was in the front row, his face looking pink and oddly young, probably because he had had an extra short hair cut the day before. It seemed odd that they should be singing this hymn, but his mother had made a special request to the vicar, years before, that it should be sung at her funeral. As they sang it, he was reminded of his childhood before the war. They had lived in the big house at Vila Nova de Gaia in those days, and he remembered how his mother used to sing this hymn at the piano in the drawing room, and how she used to enunciate the words most carefully, as if to impress upon him exactly where responsibility for the creation lay.

The organ thundered and squeaked, boomed and faded, and the congregation sang words which have since been banned by the Church of England:

> *The rich man in his castle,*
> *The poor man at his gate,*
> *God made them high or lowly*
> *And ordered their estate.*

Human emotion is a fickle thing. It comes and goes at the most unexpected moments. It was during the verses of this hymn that Robert Teape found himself weeping.

Of course it was good that he should weep at his mother's funeral: he knew that, at heart. People would see, and later say to each other, 'Did you notice Bobby during the last hymn? He broke down completely.' But all the same, he would have liked to keep control. And why was he weeping? His mother had been seventy-three, and that wasn't a bad age. He had become

41

increasingly impatient with her authority over the past months.

She had lasted exactly seven days after the fall. She had remained in a coma for the whole of that time, and had not shown even a flicker of consciousness between the moment she fell and the time her pulse stopped in the early hours of the Saturday morning.

They were starting another verse.

> *The purple headed mountain,*
> *The river running by,*
> *The sunset and the morning*
> *That brightens up the sky . . .*

The author of that hymn might almost have been writing about the district of the Douro. Perhaps this was why Rosalinde Teape had been so fond of it, and perhaps, too, this was why these floods of sadness were welling up inside him. For it was as if he were not merely losing his mother but also a part of his life, a life that was rooted as deeply in the soil of Portugal as the vines upon which hang those small dark grapes that go to make the Englishman's wine.

When the hymn was over, and the wave of bereavement had broken over him, he felt better. He was able to walk along behind the coffin and stand by the open grave without showing further emotion, though he felt drained and unreal standing there in the blazing sunshine. The coffin was lowered into its slot, and he moved forward when the vicar gave him a nod, and scattered the traditional handful of earth upon it.

And that was that.

Afterwards, there was a reception at the Remingtons', and Fay came along and mothered him. 'You'll stay with us for a few days, Bobby, won't you?'

But Teape did not wish to be mothered. Nor did he want to be in Joy's company again, so soon after breaking off his engagement to her. 'Do you mind if I don't, Aunt Fay? I don't like to leave the house empty . . .'

'Shut it up! Send the servants off on a holiday!'

'No – really. I would rather not.'

'Well, my dear, if you change your mind you know there's

always a welcome for you here.'

So he went back to Leça, and when he arrived home, Amália and Maria both broke down and wailed their sorrow for the departed Senhora. Teape dined alone, and Maria served him watery soup and tepid *bacalhau* and a melon that wasn't ripe.

He sent for Amália and asked for an explanation.

'Oh *menino* Robert it will never be the same without her excellency the Senhora,' Amália sobbed, and hid her face in her apron, shaking her head. Maria joined in.

When this flood had subsided, Teape read them a lecture. For a start, he was no longer the *menino* Robert but the Senhor Robert. Secondly, though he also deeply regretted the departure of his mother, he did not regard this as any sort of reason for poor service or bad cooking. 'I expect my meals on time and properly cooked,' he said. 'Also, my clothes are to be washed and pressed and the gardens tended and the house cleaned in exactly the same way as before, is that understood?'

Amália nodded and sniffed. Maria curtsied as she had once been taught in a Portuguese household. 'The Senhor can be sure that I shall continue to do my best,' she said.

'Very well,' Teape said, and dismissed them.

But it was not 'very well' at all. During the days that followed, he found that he had neither the time nor the inclination to interest himself in household matters; nor did he have his mother's eye for detail that was so necessary to make sure work was done properly. Instead of correcting every shortcoming when it was noticed, as his mother had done, Teape was inclined to ignore some peccadiloes and explode with anger over others. This led to more tears and more tepid *bacalhau*.

He confided his problems to Hugh Blunden, at the office.

Blunden laughed. 'What you need is a housekeeper or a wife. Or a mistress, of course. Why don't you come back to Nevogilde? That house is far too big for you.'

'What do you expect me to do with the furniture? And the silver? And the linen, and the entire contents of the tool shed, and the trophy cupboard and my guns? And my dogs, for that matter.'

'Well – up to you, old boy. If you want to live in decadent

grandeur with a cook and a maid and a gardener, you can't really grumble if you find you have to tell them what to do now and again.'

So Teape stopped grumbling, and the furniture gathered dust and the bath grew a grey rim round it and Maria began to smell of Teape's Special Reserve.

The death of a parent – especially a parent with a strength of character such as Rosalinde's – can throw one off balance, and during the weeks after his mother's death, Teape felt unsettled. He went for long walks along the beach with his dogs and sat for hours in the evenings drinking, reading and putting off the moment when he would go up to bed.

Meanwhile, the November gales blew mist over the house, so that the walls sweated and the salt went into lumps and the sheets felt sticky and cold when he lay down between them.

VI

Natália walked along the wet streets of Matosinhos, a basket of fish upon her head, her back aching, her feet cold and wet in shoes she had found on a rubbish heap. In order to make herself heard, she had to shriek against the wind: '*Sardinias frescas! Sardinias frescas da costa!*'

On calmer days she would sing the words in a distinctive way: her voice had become known in the town, and by selling good quality fish and charging reasonable prices she was beginning to win regular cusomers.

She still lived in the shanty town by the Leça river. She rose early each morning and went down to the harbour to meet the returning *traineiras*; she took her basket of fish and went from door to door until all were sold. She fought against the tiredness that seemed to increase every day in order to clear a few *tostões*; and as there were ten *tostões* to the *escudo* and over eight *escudos* to the pound, her profits could not be described as large.

Natália knew, now, with complete certainty that she had

conceived and that a new life was growing inside her: she felt driven on by this knowledge to earn money so that she could eat and so that she and her unborn baby would live. Her life resolved about a single aim: survival.

She was successful – so successful that she began to take away the custom of other women who sold fish. At first, they tolerated it out of kindness and sympathy. But one afternoon in November when Natália felt ready to drop, the inevitable happened: she turned a corner and found herself face to face with the Salsicha.

The Salsicha was not one to mince words. She was a gross figure: her breasts sagged like great waterbags beneath her old green jersey. Her arms were red, and her nose bulbous and purple from the coarse wine she drank.

Her shouting gathered a crowd. 'If the *menina* thinks she can come here and take over my fish round, then the *menina* can start thinking again. The *menina* hasn't got a family to look after. I was selling sardines in this street when she was no more than a – a – '

'A pip in her father's tomatoes!' another woman shouted, and the bystanders laughed delightedly at the oblique reference to Natália's parenthood and the unfaithfulness of the Salsicha's husband. But while the joke was lost on Natália, in the Salsicha's case, it struck home. She lost her temper completely and hit out at whoever came near. She ran, shrieking, at Natália and fetched her a clip on the ear, then turned and went for the woman who had made the remark. People scattered, some laughing, some frightened.

Eventually, after a lot of talk and noise, she calmed down. The crowd dispersed and Natália made her way out of Matosinhos to sell her fish elsewhere.

She crossed the wooden bridge to Leça da Palmeira and entered the wealthier district, where a few large houses hid behind high stone walls.

A woman came to the back gate and beckoned to her. She crossed the road, and the woman, who wore a black apron, haggled a price for the few fish that Natália had to sell. The woman went inside to fetch small change, and Natália was left standing at the gate. She could see into the kitchen, and to her right, she could see into one of the front rooms. There were tall cupboards and shelves of silver and china.

A black labrador ambled out and wagged round her, and Natália thought she saw a movement in an upstairs window.

The woman came out of the kitchen with a plate for the fish and the required small change. She paid the girl, and the gate clanged shut behind her.

She continued to walk on down the road towards the sea. Her basket was empty now and light upon her head. The wind from the sea reached her as she came to the corner of a property wall and she shivered, increasing her pace a little.

It was then that she became aware of the car. It had come up behind her and had slowed right down so that it was keeping pace with her.

She looked back, and immediately recognised the face at the wheel.

VII

The car drew ahead a little, then stopped. He opened the passenger door and leaned across to speak to her.

'Come with me, *pequena*,' he said. 'I'll drive you home.'

She stopped, puzzled.

'Come on! Wouldn't you like a ride in the car?' He got out and stood with her at the roadside. The north wind blew sand and sea mist in their faces. He ushered her confidently to the passenger door. She hesitated. He laughed gently, reassuringly. 'You needn't be afraid. Wouldn't you like to sit down? You're tired, aren't you? Here – let me take your basket.'

She had never been treated in this way before. He was English, of course. She knew that. And the English were well thought of. It was the English who would stop their cars to allow you to cross the road, the English who paid their debts promptly, the English who built the big ships that were beginning to call at Leixões. And she was tired. She looked up at him.

He was still smiling. 'You don't have to,' he said. 'I'm not

46

'forcing you.' He spoke in a funny way. His Portuguese was easily understandable, but he drawled the words in the way the English always did.

She allowed him to take the basket from her, and he put it on the back seat. She got into the car and he closed the door for her before going round to the driver's side.

'Right. Off we go, then.'

He drove off. He had no plan in mind – was not even sure why he had left the house and gone after her. He had seen her from the window of his dressing room, and had remembered his feelings a month before when she had fainted on the beach. He remembered her dark eyes looking into his, the wet dress clinging to her body.

Now, he took it for granted that she would welcome an advance. Vaguely, in the back of his mind, he had the idea of making her into his secret girlfriend. There were others in the British colony who had made similar arrangements with local girls, so why shouldn't he?

He glanced at her quickly and smiled. She didn't smile back, but her eyes met his, and she didn't seem hostile. No reason why she should be, he reflected. Every reason to be damn grateful, in fact.

They reached the sea front. To the left, waves crashed against the Leixões breakwater, with its huge crane that dominated the harbour. The beach that ran northward was deserted, and the Boa Nova lighthouse almost hidden by a mist of blown spray. He realised suddenly that now she was in the car, he could take her wherever he liked. She was his.

'We'll make a little tour,' he said, and swung the car off the road and on to the track that ran along above the beach. He glanced at her again and she seemed to smile. He was encouraged and excited. Only a fish girl, after all. Probably had a brother somewhere, one of those grubby little urchins that pimped down by the harbour.

He hummed a snatch of tune. 'What weather!' he said. 'What weather!'

He glanced at her again. Her eyes were wide, and a little frightened. She said: 'I would like to go back now, sir.'

He laughed. 'No! You don't want to go back! We haven't

47

been anywhere!' He accelerated a little, and the Morris bumped over the potholes.

She clutched at her seat. They were a good distance from the road now. On one side the Atlantic rollers hissed and roared; on the other, pine shrubs clawed their roots into a stretch of wasteland.

He stopped the car and felt in the pocket of his Harris Tweed jacket. He had brought some chocolate for her.

'Here,' he said, offering the bar. 'For you.'

She stared at it, shook her head. He laughed and broke off a double row. 'Go on! Take it!'

Her mouth watered at the sight of it. She put it in her mouth, aware all the time of his blue eyes watching her. He looked so very English: his hair was neatly-trimmed and rather curly, and his red-cheeked complexion seemed to glow with health. It was as if she had suddenly been accosted by a god, a being from another planet.

She swallowed the chocolate too quickly and choked. She coughed and coughed, and he patted her back. When she stopped coughing, he allowed his hand to remain on her shoulders, and she felt his fingers stroking her neck.

He looked at her. She was very tense. She stared out of the car window, away from him, at the vast waves. They smashed down upon the beach, and the stones and sand rattled in the undertow.

His fingers ran up and down her neck, and he put his other hand over hers. She stiffened: his face was much closer to hers now. She could see the blond stubble on his cheeks, smell the wine and tobacco on his breath.

'I won't hurt you, *pequena*,' he said. 'I promise not to hurt you.'

His face came closer and closer. She didn't know what to do. She knew that he was looking at her, but she didn't want to look back. He kissed her cheek.

'There,' he said. 'That didn't hurt, did it?'

She sat very still. She didn't resist him, and he presumed that this was a sign that she wanted him to go on. He unbuttoned the top of her dress and revealed her right breast. He touched it gently: he pushed his fingers up, over the nipple and back down again.

48

She was shaking. 'Please – no,' she whispered. 'Please don't do this, your excellency.'

He was amused by her use of the formal address. He looked at her thick dark brows, her frightened eyes. He looked down at his own hand on her breast. 'It doesn't hurt, *menina*,' he whispered. 'It doesn't hurt at all.'

She began weeping silently. The tears went down her face. He didn't understand why. Perhaps it was because she was ashamed. He wanted to comfort her, soothe her. He pulled her towards him, and ran his fingers gently through her hair. 'Don't cry,' he whispered. 'You'll enjoy it.'

He had an idea. Perhaps she was attracted to him and yet frightened that he would not give her money. Perhaps she worked for some man as so many of these girls did. Perhaps she was desperate for cash. He took out his wallet and found a fifty *escudo* note.

'Look,' he said, showing it to her. 'Look what I'll give you.'

She seemed to freeze, and in that moment he believed that she had resolved to go through with it. She was just a bit panicky, that was all. Understandable, the first time. And he wanted her now. He wanted her badly. He wanted *it*. His heart was hammering and his fingers undoing more buttons. He was going to give her good money, and she was going to give him good value. He was going to do all the things that he had always wanted to do with Joy but which she had always so resolutely denied him. He was going to call the tune for once. He stuffed the note and the wallet back into his pocket.

'Now,' he said. 'Come on.'

She began to resist. She squirmed away from him and uttered a little cry of terror. He was suddenly angry. What right had she to oppose him? Fifty *escudos* was a lot. Far too much, in fact. You only paid these kids twenty at the most. Well, damn it, in that case –

He put his mouth down to her breast. It was something he had always wanted to do with a girl. She scrabbled at the door handle, but he grabbed her wrist and held it very tightly, tightening his grip further until she shouted with pain, and only relaxing it when she stopped struggling.

He was in control of her now. It was her own fault that he had to do it this way. She was to blame. If she had not resisted he would not have had to use force.

He opened his door and dragged her out by the wrist. She began struggling again, but he twisted her arm up behind her back as a warning. He felt that she had to learn and he had to teach. Maybe she was a virgin. Well in that case there had to be a first time. She would thank him for it, after.

It was damned awkward having to do everything with only one hand. He opened the boot and took out an old *liteiro*, a roughly woven mat that he had used to keep the back seat clean when the dogs were in the car. He put it on the wet sand in the lee of the Morris so that they could be sheltered from the wind. And because she resisted, because she was crying soundlessly, because her eyes were full of hatred, he became even more determined to do it, to do the whole thing. It was her fault, entirely her own fault. If she had behaved a bit more sensibly, he might not even have gone the whole way.

His hand went seeking downward through the side of her dress, under elastic. Her breath came in little sobs. She was like a frightened animal, a rabbit in a snare.

There. There it was. There. There.

He pulled her down. She was a mess of arms and legs. There were extraordinary silk bloomers under her long skirt: somebody's cast-offs, no doubt. They were difficult to remove: he pulled at them with his spare hand and they caught at her knees.

The wind shrieked and the sand blew. He pinned her down, and she turned her face right away from him so that all she could see was the underside of the car, the wheels, the black mudguards, and beyond them, the white Atlantic surf.

It was no good resisting him, but she still tried. She wanted to scratch him, bite him, kill him, but his hand was like an iron clamp round her wrist, and when he twisted it up behind her back, the pain was excruciating.

His breath came in great warm gusts against her face, and his Harris tweed jacket was prickly against her bare skin. She screamed and screamed, but the wind screamed louder. She felt his hand yanking at her, opening her, and she was suddenly afraid for a new reason: she knew that she was pregnant, and

50

she was now frightened more for her unborn baby than for herself. She stopped struggling. She lay there, shivering, trembling.

He said something in English she didn't understand. He was breathing through his mouth, and his hand was up, between her legs. She knew what he was doing, but her total experience of such things was with an old man, a man whom she believed to have been her father, a man who treated her with the utmost gentleness and love. This athletic Englishman in his tweed jacket and tweed trousers, his blond stubble on his reddened cheeks – he was doing something to her that was totally repugnant, something that made her feel physically sick.

For Robert Teape, the business was difficult, unsatisfactory and soon finished. Two or three thrusts, and the massive relief came. It was as quick as that. And once it was done, he wanted to finish with this sobbing child and get rid of her as quickly as possible; to return to the house before someone called and wondered where he had been.

He pulled himself out of her and she screamed and doubled up with pain. He stood up and hoisted his trousers, buttoned his flies. She got to her feet and pulled down her dress. She picked up the ridiculous silk bloomers that had given him so much trouble.

He took out his wallet and found the fifty *escudo* note. 'There you are,' he said. 'And count yourself lucky.'

She hesitated a moment, and he thought she was going to accept the money. He wanted her to take it. He wanted the business to become a transaction between them so that they were all square. But she spat directly in his face, and ran off, over the dunes and down to the shore. She ran with her arms crossed about her breasts, as if trying to retain something that was precious to her.

He drove home. He opened the gates himself instead of sounding the horn as he usually did to summon the gardener. He drove the car into the garage and got out. Then he found the fish basket. She had left it on the back seat. He swore under his breath and wondered what to do with it. There was a store next to the garage which was full of firewood, old sacks, garden tools. He put the basket in there. The gardener was new, and would not question it.

That done, he went into the house and poured himself a large whisky, which he drank at a gulp. He could not understand, now, what had possessed him to do it. He poured another whisky. I got away with it though, he thought. Yes, I got away with it. And she'll be all right. Didn't hurt her much. Just a little fish girl. Wasn't even a virgin. Happens every day.

The whisky was beginning to have its effect. He finished off the second glass and breathed out. My God! he thought. Can't go on like this. I must get away. Go to England. Anything. Find a wife. Anything. Anything.

❧ 3 ❧

I

THE EAST LONDON MEDICAL MISSION had its headquarters in the back streets of Islington, close to the Regent's Canal. The building was slightly larger than the grimy terraced houses that flanked it. Outside the door, a notice board displayed the hours of opening and the times of the Women's Meeting, the Sunday School and the Prayer Meeting.

Each weekday morning, the members of staff met for prayer before opening the doors to the public, and Doctor Warnes, a small Welshman with a lick of black hair scraped over his balding pate, would lead them in their supplications.

'Be pleased to grant thy blessing to our endeavours this day, O Lord,' he said, his eyes closed, but the lids fluttering as if they wished to open of their own accord, against his will. 'Let our work rise to thee as a sweet savour and an offering that is acceptable unto thee.'

Hurrying along the City Road, left into Shepherdess Walk, right into Dombey Street, Ruth Wilmot approached the mission. She was a tall, rather graceful girl of twenty-four, and had had her chestnut hair fashionably bobbed since coming down from Yorkshire the previous month. She wore the grey nurse's uniform of the Medical Mission, and her cap bore the initials ELMM. That morning, she had missed her train from Archway Station, and was late.

Children were playing in the street when she arrived at the Mission. There were always children about. Their mothers shut them out for the day, and they made a nuisance of themselves, running in and out of the Mission, stealing fruit from the barrow boys, playing football with stones, shouting, fighting, chalking on walls.

Doctor Warnes, when Ruth Wilmot complained that the children made work in the Mission almost impossible, had simply quoted, 'Suffer the children to come unto me.' And Ruth, who was inclined to be irreverent sometimes remarked to her good friend Suzy Laughton, 'We certainly suffer them. I only wish they'd go a bit more often unto him. Then he'd know what it was like.'

But Doctor Warnes had his own surgery, the holy of holies, and was rarely disturbed.

She nodded a good morning to the people queuing outside the Mission door and let herself in. She crossed the reception room and entered the Hall, where the small group of volunteer workers were completing their prayers.

'We ask that through our labours others may come to know of the peace of the Lord Jesus Christ. May they find spiritual as well as physical healing, O Lord, as we ask this for thine own name's sake, amen.'

Doctor Warnes opened his eyes and saw Ruth, who had slipped in beside Suzy Laughton.

'Ah. Miss Wilmot.'

'I'm sorry I'm late, Doctor Warnes – '

'Don't apologise. Better late than never, better never late.'

'Yes, doctor.'

He rubbed his hands together, a man among women, enjoying his role. 'Well ladies. To work.' And with that, he led the way out of the Hall.

The doors were opened and the queue of people shuffled into the reception area. There were expectant mothers, babes in arms, men and women allowed off from work to have minor ailments attended to. They brought their cuts and bruises and sprains, their infected eyes, oedemas, whitlows, boils, coughs, colds and fevers, and were briskly and efficiently attended to by Nurse Laughton, the only qualified nurse in the Mission. She was plump and capable. She always knew what to do. She passed on cases that she could not deal with herself to Doctor Warnes, but the vast majority were seen to entirely by her, assisted by Ruth. And while they worked, Suzy Laughton talked about what she was doing so that the patient would be reassured, and Ruth could learn.

54

They were pestered, as always, by children, who ran in and out, up the stairs and down again. They played catch with each other's caps, wrestled in the reception area and shouted obscenities in at the doorway of the Mission in order to shock the well-bred ladies who worked as volunteers.

'Is there nothing we can do?' Ruth said, but Suzy merely smiled and repeated, 'Suffer the children.'

But eventually, Ruth Wilmot's patience ran out. A group of ten-year-olds had rushed into the reception area and had nearly knocked over a woman who was on her way out after being treated for a scald. Ruth, seeing the woman wince, seized the nearest child by the collar and held him up so that she could look him in the eye.

'Now listen to me, you,' she said menacingly. 'I've had enough of this. There are people who are poorly here, and other people who are trying to work. This isn't a playground. You've no business to come running in here. Understand?'

The child looked up, grinning, slightly out of breath. Ruth noticed something about his hair. She turned to Suzy. 'Come and have a look at this. I think he's infested.'

Suzy came across and looked at the child's head. It was crawling with lice.

'Right,' she said to the child. 'What's your name?'

'Why?'

'Don't answer back. Tell me your name.'

'Billy Johns, Miss.'

'I see. Well we're going to wash your hair, Billy. Come along.'

The child protested. His friends watched in awe from the doorway. He began to struggle, but was held firmly by Suzy and Ruth, who frogmarched him to the large sink in the treatment room.

'Head down!' Suzy commanded, and exchanged a smile with Ruth. 'You've got bugs growing in your hair, Billy. So we're going to get rid of them for you.'

The child wailed, 'I don't want no hair washing!'

'Yes you do,' Ruth said, 'We can't have lice in here.'

The water splashed over his head and Suzy lathered his hair with disinfectant soap.

'It's gone in me eyes!' he shouted.

'Well jolly bad luck. You shouldn't have opened them.'

They washed, rinsed, washed again and rinsed again. 'Now,' Suzy said when they had finished and Ruth was drying the child's hair vigorously in a towel, 'Come back here in a week's time, understand, and we'll make quite sure you haven't got any more of those creepy crawlies, all right?'

Billy Johns nodded mutely. Ruth opened the door of the treatment room and he rushed out, into the road.

Immediately, there was a scream of brakes, and Ruth said, 'Oh my God!'

A car had come to a halt outside the Mission. Billy Johns, hair still wet, lay on the road. A man was getting out of the car: a man in his mid or late thirties, who wore a pin stripe suit. He looked at Ruth and said, 'There was nothing I could do. He ran straight out – '

Ruth and Suzy bent over the boy. He was conscious, whimpering. He sat up. Doctor Warnes was sent for, and examined him for broken bones. Billy was helped to his feet and assisted back inside the Mission building. Nurse Laughton accompanied the Doctor into the surgery. Ruth remained in the reception room. The man joined her, very overwrought.

'It was so sudden!' he said. 'He ran out without bothering to look. I feel terrible!'

She looked up at him, surprised and a little touched by his concern. So many people would have been angry. His face was rather long, and his hair thin. He had kind, grey-green eyes that looked out at her from beneath tufted eyebrows. 'I don't think he's badly hurt,' she said. 'Some grazes and bruises, that's all. Unless there's internal damage, he should be perfectly all right.'

He swallowed, and looked round at the people waiting for treatment. Sweat stood in beads on his upper lip. He swayed, closed his eyes, opened them and then collapsed completely.

'He's gorn and fainted, Miss!' one of the awaiting patients exclaimed helpfully. 'Fainted right out!'

Ruth knelt beside him. He was already coming to. 'Just keep your head down, that's the way,' she said.

He blinked up at her. 'I'm – so sorry – '

'Nothing to be sorry about.'

He sat up, shook his head. 'Be all right in a tick.'

'Shock, that's what done it,' a woman said. 'Isn't that right, Miss?'

'Probably, yes.' She helped him to a chair. 'I'll get you a cup of tea.'

He smiled weakly. 'I've never done this before. I can't imagine what happened.'

'It often affects people this way. An accident. You know.'

She went into the kitchen and made tea for him. 'There we are,' she said, adopting Suzy Laughton's brisk, efficient manner. 'This'll make you feel better.'

He accepted the cup and saucer gracefully and looked up into her eyes. 'I'm sure it will. Thank you so much.'

'I've put a little sugar in,' she said. 'It's good for shock.'

At the far end of the room, an old woman nudged the next in line and gave a large wink, nodding in the direction of Ruth.

The door to the surgery opened and Billy Johns was brought out by Suzy Laughton. He had a dressing on his forehead, where a large lump had risen. Doctor Warnes said, 'You're a lucky lad, Billy, aren't you?'

'Yes, sir. Can I go now?'

'Yes, but take it nice and gently, and if your Mum asks any questions, send her along to us and we'll explain what happened. Understand?'

The boy nodded, and limped out. Doctor Warnes turned to the driver of the car. 'I think you were lucky too, sir.'

'I was indeed.'

Doctor Warnes saw the cup of tea. 'What's this – preferential treatment?'

'He fainted,' Ruth explained.

'Ah. I see.' Doctor Warnes turned to Suzy Laughton. 'I think perhaps we had better have the gentleman's name, nurse. In case there are any further enquiries.'

'Of course,' the man said. He produced his card. 'Merriman's the name. Peter Merriman.'

Doctor Warnes went back into his surgery. Suzy said, 'Well I'm glad to see you're being well looked after, Mr Merriman.'

'Indeed I am. Thanks to – er – your assistant here.' He

smiled at Ruth, and sipped his tea. 'This really is excellent.'

'I expect you needed it,' she said.

'I did indeed.'

She looked down, embarrassed by the way he regarded her.

He finished his tea. 'Well,' he said. 'You really have been most kind, Miss – er – '

'Wilmot,' Ruth said, and Suzy looked at her in horror, amazed that she should volunteer her name so readily.

'Miss Wilmot,' he repeated.

She took his cup and he said he had better be getting along. When he had gone, Suzy Laughton said, 'I think he rather fell for you, Ruth.'

'Don't be so silly!'

'Not at all. His eyes went all misty every time he looked at you.'

'That was probably shock,' Ruth laughed. But she had the decency to blush, all the same.

A few days later, a letter addressed to Miss Wilmot was delivered to the Medical Mission by the afternoon post. Ruth read it out to Suzy Laughton.

Dear Miss Wilmot,

You will probably think it most improper of me to write to you thus, but since our chance meeting last week, I have repeatedly thought what a pity it is that having met once, we cannot meet again.

And having thought that, I asked myself, why shouldn't we meet again? So here I am writing to you to ask whether perhaps you might like to take tea with me one afternoon? I shall not propose a time or place at this stage, but simply ask you to write a short note if you would give me the pleasure of meeting again.

Believe me, I would much prefer to be properly introduced, so that all the forms of etiquette could be observed, but life in this modern world of ours is somewhat complicated, isn't it, and I am sure you will forgive this approach even if you choose to decline my invitation.

Yours very sincerely,
P.J. Merriman.

'Well!' Suzy said. 'What a nerve!'

'Do you think so? I think he sounds terribly restrained.'

'You won't reply, I hope?'

'Why not?'

'You have no idea who or what he is.'

'He seemed quite pleasant.'

'So do most confidence tricksters.'

'You're not suggesting he's up to no good?'

'I'm not suggesting anything, Ruth. All I'm saying is that I think you should be very careful. Really and honestly, I think it would be better to disregard that letter entirely.'

Ruth looked back at the letter. It was written with a thin nib, and the words ended with an upward flourish. 'I suppose it is a bit risky,' she agreed.

So she ignored the letter, and a fortnight later a second arrived.

Dear Miss Wilmot,

Please forgive me for writing to you again, but I keep wondering (a) whether my letter reached you and (b) if it did, whether you have written back and perhaps your letter has gone astray. Could you confirm you received my letter? It will put me out of my misery!

Sincerely yours,
P.J.M.

'Rather sweet really,' Ruth said after she had shown the letter to Suzy.

But Suzy urged the utmost caution. 'If you reply to him now, you'll give him an excuse to write again.'

'But it does seem rather rude of me.'

'He didn't have to write in the first place.'

'No. But it isn't as if he's a complete stranger.'

'But, my dear, you know nothing at all about him. He might be a complete rascal.'

'He didn't strike me as being a rascally sort of person.'

Suzy shrugged. 'Well, it's up to you, of course. But I would certainly not write back. I think it's asking for trouble.'

So Ruth ignored the letter, and three weeks later, another arrived.

59

Dear Miss Wilmot,

I cannot describe my feelings each morning when the postman fails to deliver a letter from you. I am sure you must have received my letters, and I can only presume that you are apprehensive of writing to a stranger like myself.

But consider: I could have called on you at the Mission where you work could I not? I could have pestered you, hung around in wait for you. I have not done this because I should hate to embarrass you. Could you not take this as an indication of my good intentions?

All I wish to say is that my invitation to tea still stands, and that if ever you care to write back, I shall be only too delighted to arrange a day. If I do not hear from you, I shall not trouble you further, but will understand that you prefer to be a ship that passed in the night – or rather, on a spring morning. But do please reply, even if the answer has to be 'no'.

Yours sincerely,
Peter Merriman.

Ruth received this letter without Suzy's knowledge, and she carried it about in her bag for some days, saying nothing of it and wondering what to do. Then one afternoon after work, when she was sitting in her digs, she read the letter again and decided that whatever Suzy Laughton thought, she, Ruth Wilmot, had a mind of her own. She took out her notepaper and fountain pen and wrote:

Dear Mr Merriman,

Thank you so much for your letters, and I apologise for delaying my reply. I would be happy to meet you for tea one day, and as I shall be in Harrods next Saturday, perhaps we might meet in the restaurant there at about four. But if you are not there, I shall quite understand.

Yours sincerely,
Ruth Wilmot.

When she had written this, she realised that her heart was beating faster and that her hands were trembling. It was a daring thing to do, and she felt guilty about saying nothing to Suzy about it.

She addressed the envelope and put a stamp on it. He lived in Sussex Gardens. She wasn't quite sure where that was, because she had only been living in London for two months, having come down from Yorkshire in the new year.

She went downstairs. Her digs were at the top of a four-storeyed house, owned by an impoverished solicitor and his wife. There was a smell of bacon and eggs in the hall, and the resident mongrel lay stretched out on the threadbare coconut matting.

She let herself out by the front door and went down the road to the post box. The GPO van drew up as she arrived and she gave the letter to the postman personally.

Back in her room, she stood at her window, looking down at the traffic going up Highgate Hill. She stood very still, thinking ahead to next Saturday, and wondering if she had done the right thing.

II

It all went very satisfactorily. He was waiting for her in the restaurant when she entered just after four. He was dressed in neatly-pressed grey flannels and blazer, and looked like an advertisement for gentlemen's soap.

They sipped their tea and ate hot buttered teacakes, while a string quartet played selections from Gilbert and Sullivan. He asked her about her work in Islington, and she explained how she had been teaching in a village school in Yorkshire until the previous December. She discovered that he lived with his mother in Sussex Gardens, and he that her parents had died when she was nine and that she had been brought up by an uncle and aunt.

Gently, the conversation proceeded. They discovered that both were church goers, that both approved of the disarmament negotiations Mr Ramsay McDonald had been conducting at Geneva; and both agreed that the recently elected German Chancellor was in fact no more than a puppet figure, who would soon be replaced.

They discussed the arts. He was a devotee of Bernard Shaw, and she was happy to listen while he explained why. He ordered another jug of hot water, and the quartet played 'Daisy, Daisy'.

She told Suzy Laughton all about it the following Monday. Suzy had been asked by Ruth's aunt to take her under her wing, and she felt responsible for Ruth's moral safety.

'I had a very unpleasant experience while I was training,' she said. 'London isn't Yorkshire. A girl on her own like you are, well, she's fair game to a certain type of man.'

'Peter isn't that sort.'

'Isn't he? Appearances can be very deceptive, Ruth.'

'There's really nothing to worry about. He's a perfect gentleman.'

'What did you talk about? Tell me all about him.'

'He's a sort of engineer. Something to do with hydro-electric schemes.'

'Isn't he much older than you?'

'Not all that much. About mid-thirties.'

'Ten years. It's quite a lot.'

'Well I liked him. He's mature. He served in the trenches for the last year of the war, and then he went to Cambridge.'

Suzy was still doubtful. 'I do hope you haven't started something – well, you know.'

'What on earth do you mean?'

'Well I hope he doesn't pester you.'

'Of course he won't. He's most awfully considerate.'

'Are you meeting him again?'

'Next Saturday. We're going for a walk on Hampstead Heath.'

'In that case I ought to come with you.'

'Oh Suzy!'

'I did promise your aunt –'

'I'm twenty-four!'

'Is he married?'

'Of course he isn't!'

'Have you asked him?'

'No, but –'

'Then you don't know.'

'My instinct tells me he isn't. I'm quite sure he would have said.'

Suzy Laughton sighed. 'You can't always rely on instinct. Believe me. I know.'

'Well, I shall ask him next Saturday.'

She put the question to him when they were walking by the Leg of Mutton pond. There had been showers and gales all day, and the pavements were still wet. Boys and their fathers were sailing boats on the pond, and nannies were pushing prams along, their uniforms blowing about in the wind.

'No,' he said. 'I'm not married. I very nearly married an actress a few years ago, but I wasn't exciting enough for her, and she went off with an Australian.' He looked at her quizzically. He had had his eyebrows trimmed since he first met her. 'Does that put your mind at rest?'

'Well I did wonder,' she said. 'It does happen, doesn't it?'

'All too frequently, yes.'

She was relieved, though she had not been aware of concern about it before she asked the question. It was pleasant walking with him over the Heath. She liked him because he was so mature. He had the confidence in his opinions to voice them and yet the humility not to be dogmatic about them. And he had a knack of making whatever they talked about interesting.

After that second afternoon together, he drove her back to Highgate and dropped her at her digs. The following morning a messenger delivered a dozen red roses with a card that read: 'Thank you for a splendid afternoon. P.J.M.'

She wrote back a letter:

Dear P.J.M.

You really are very naughty to send such beautiful flowers, but they are so beautiful that I forgive you this time. As soon as they arrived I bashed their stems (that is what you are supposed to do with roses) and put them in water, and they make a marvellous show in my otherwise rather humble abode.

But please, promise not to send me any more flowers. It is very sweet of you and I am very flattered, but I really do think you ought not.

Yours sincerely,
Ruth Wilmot.

He smiled when he read her letter. He liked the way she said she 'bashed' their stems. There was a streak of irreverence about her that he enjoyed. She made him feel young and twenty-four again. It was as if she had opened a door in his life, a door he had never before realised existed. He kept her two letters and read them when he came home from work in the evenings. He smiled to himself when he read them, and conjured up a picture of her in his mind's eye: large, cheerful, forthright, optimistic. Dear Miss Wilmot, he thought. My dear, dear Miss Wilmot.

The weeks went by and summer came. They met in parks, visited the Regent's Park zoo, went to Kew Gardens, picnicked in Hadley Woods. They wrote postcards and letters that began 'Dear P.M.' and 'Dear Miss W.' When they were together he was attentive, gentlemanly, kind, and quietly eager. He never embarrassed her, never took advantage, never tried to quicken the pace of their developing friendship.

They called each other 'Miss Wilmot' and 'Mr Merriman' for several weeks until one day she called him 'Peter' by mistake.

'Will you call me that from now on?'

'Do you think I ought?'

'Well, not if you feel you don't want to.'

'Perhaps it would be risky. What do you think? I mean you might call me Ruth.'

'I hadn't thought of that.'

And then she giggled, and her giggles gave way to laughter and he realised that she was teasing him.

'You're very cruel to me,' he said. 'You led me up the garden path.'

'Well – better that than the other way round.'

'I'll never do that, Ruth.'

In early June, she went to Sunday tea at his house in Sussex Gardens. He collected her in his car and the door was opened to them by the maid.

Mrs Merriman was short haired, rather masculine, and inclined to be abrupt. She looked Ruth up and down a little obviously. Tea came in on a trolley and the old lady talked about her husband the Brigadier. She dropped names, most of whom belonged to individuals she described as 'a very fine

64

man' or 'a most attractive woman'. All her acquaintances had a habit of possessing either extraordinary intellectual qualities or outstanding good looks or a title or all three.

After tea, Mrs Merriman showed Ruth the family photograph album: it contained row upon row of Edwardians and Victorians in brown and white suits and brown and white hats, sitting on brown and white verandahs where brown and white flowers grew in brown and white pots.

'Mater's a bit stuffy at first,' Peter said in the car on the way back, 'but she unbends once you get to know her. She's not a bad old stick at all really.'

'I was scared stiff,' Ruth admitted.

He laughed. 'So was she!'

They continued to meet throughout the summer. She went to tea at Sussex Gardens twice more, but found she could never really relax in Mrs Merriman's presence. She felt like a country cousin, and was constantly aware that the old lady would hardly describe her as 'a very fine woman' or 'an extraordinarily gifted person'. Every visit was like an interview for a much sought-after position in the family firm.

At the beginning of August, Peter told her that he had been given the opportunity to go out to Kuala Lumpur. The news came out of the blue.

'Will you go?' she asked.

'Probably. Yes. It's a splendid opportunity.'

They were lunching at Scotts. He had not taken her out to quite such a smart restaurant before and she had not even considered that he might have done so for a reason.

'What about your mother?'

'She's advertising in the *Lady* for a companion.'

'So you are going. Definitely.'

'Well – yes. Fairly definitely.'

'What will you be doing out there?'

'We have a project underway upcountry. I shall be advising on the sort of plant we need to install, and possibly scouting round for other likely areas that would be suitable for hydro-electric schemes. It's a big step up for me really.' He smiled, pleased to be able to tell her.

'And – if you go – when will you go?'

He looked at her steadily across the table. 'Mid-September.'

'You mean next month?'

'Yes. Another fellow had been earmarked to go, but he's gone down with stomach ulcers, poor chap. I was the next in line.'

'Oh.'

There was a long silence. He stared at her. She picked up her bag and looked for a handkerchief. She smiled with her mouth at him and gently blew her nose.

The waiter took away their plates. He paid the bill and they went out into the sunshine, down the Haymarket into Trafalgar Square and then on into St James's Park. He took her hand in his, and she held on to it tightly.

'Will they let you come back on furlough?'

'Not for two years anyway.'

She forced herself to be cheerful. 'I expect you'll have a marvellous time. A long sea voyage . . . where is Kuala Lumpur, anyway?'

'Malaya. The west coast.'

'I can just see you. Lounging about on a verandah having tiffin, or whatever they have out there. It'll be quite a change from Sussex Gardens, won't it?'

He frowned. 'Yes. I suppose it will.'

They drove back to her digs.

'Come up to my room,' she said.

'Are you sure we ought?'

'I don't care. Come on.'

He followed her up the three flights of worn stairs and into the little bedsitting room. He looked round at the shelf of books, the Bible on the bedside table, the vase of wild flowers they had picked only the week before.

'It's in a mess, like me,' she said. She looked at him hopelessly, trying desperately to smile. But the smile crumpled and she bit back tears.

He kissed her for the first time. The effect on both was devastating: four months of gradually increasing but carefully controlled mutual attraction was suddenly unleashed and allowed to flow freely between them.

'Marry me,' he said. 'Quickly. Before I leave. Come out to Malaya with me. Please.'

66

She wept, held his hands. 'If only it didn't have to be so sudden.'

'There's no doubt in my mind,' he said. 'I've been in love with you for months. But it wasn't until now that I had any idea of what you felt.

'Am I in love with you?'

'That's not for me to say.'

'I think I am.'

'I would rather you were sure.'

She smiled rather damply. 'Yes. So would I.'

'I don't want to push you into marriage. But on the other hand I know – certainly – that you are the only person in the world I have ever wanted to share my life with.'

'What about the actress?'

'It wasn't my *life* that I wanted to share with her, Ruth.'

'I'd like to have a day or two to think.'

'Of course.'

'I want to say "yes". But it is a big step.'

'I understand. It would be a mistake to rush into a decision.'

He kissed her again, and left her in the room. She went to the window, looked down at the car, waved to him as he drove off.

In the morning, she confided in Suzy Laughton.

'It is very sudden,' Suzy agreed. 'And you haven't know him all that long, have you?'

'Five months. But I am very fond of him.'

'Is that enough? Are you sure?'

'If only I could be sure of anything!'

'Surely you could wait two years. If you really love each other.'

They talked about it at great length, and gradually Ruth allowed herself to be persuaded into waiting. When she saw Peter, she echoed much of Suzy's line of argument.

'Although I do feel that I love you, Peter, I'm not completely sure that it isn't just a romantic sort of love that's got "Made in Hollywood" on the label. I mean – we've always been on our best behaviour really, haven't we? You've never seen me in a black mood, and I've never seen you when you're feeling tired or irritable. It would be so easy, wouldn't it, to arrange a quick marriage only to find a month later that it had been a ghastly mistake.'

67

He agreed, reluctantly. They decided that they would prove their love by putting it to the test of a two year separation. They seemed almost to vie with each other in making it difficult for themselves.

'We won't write to each other for six months at least,' she said. 'Much better to wait before writing: our emotions will have had time to settle down. We shall be able to view our relationship dispassionately.'

'I'm sure you're right,' he said. 'I'm sure we shall never regret it in later years.'

It was raining steadily on the day that Peter's ship sailed from Tilbury. He had sold the car, and Ruth accompanied him to the docks in a taxi. She went aboard the liner with him, saw his cabin, and later stood in the saloon with him.

'You'll write first,' he said.

'Yes. Next March.'

'But only if you feel quite sure, Ruth.'

'I shall do. I know I shall.'

He took her hands. 'It'll strengthen the bond, won't it? Strengthen it, or prove once and for all that it was never strong enough.'

The broadcast system announced that the gangways were about to be removed. They went out on deck, kissed for the last time. She went down the gangway to the quay.

The berthing ropes splashed into the dirty Thames water, and the tugs eased the liner from her berth. The ship sounded a long, mournful blast on her siren. Ruth waved and waved and allowed herself to cry at the same time without any attempt at disguising the fact, and on the deck, his figure in a raincoat and trilby waved back.

She went home by taxi. Alone in her room, she took a slip of paper from her bag with his address in Malaya on it. Box 72, Kuala Lumpar, Malaya.

She blinked back more tears, thinking of him having his first meal aboard the liner as it made its way out to the open sea.

They were right, of course they were right. She would prove how strong their love was, and their future life together would be the better for it.

III

She wrote to him promptly, six months to the day after his ship sailed. She was careful to avoid an outpouring or anything that might suggest a declaration of undying love. She told him all the news of the Medical Mission, her Christmas in Yorkshire with her relations and her hopes for starting a course in nursing at University College Hospital the following year.

... the daffodils and jonquils are out in the park now, and I realised that it is almost a year since you arrived with a scream of brakes outside the ELMM. My great friend Suzy Laughton is to be married this August, and has asked me to be a bridesmaid, which is very exciting. Her parents have a huge house in Essex: Suzy is marrying an up and coming psychiatrist who has already had two books published and has recently started his own practice in Wigmore Street. He came to the ELMM because he was doing research into child delinquency in slum areas, and of course Suzy has always been the person who has had most to do with the children in the area. They are buying a house in the Hampstead Garden Suburb, so I hope I shall be seeing a lot more of them both ...

She asked him about his life in Malaya and urged him to tell her all the details ('even the boring ones, because they won't bore me at all'). She wrote twelve pages and even then could have gone on.

I don't really want to stop this letter, because it's like talking to you again. But I shall post it off now and count the days until I hear from you. How long will that be, I wonder? I think the mail will take three weeks at least, so I suppose I shan't hear until the end of April at the earliest.

I needn't say how much I think of you, Peter. You are always in my prayers and thoughts and while I acknowledge that we were right to decide on this time of separation, I am quite sure that we have something so strong that a mere two years can do nothing to harm it. God bless you and keep you always,

With my love,
Ruth.

69

Having posted this letter, she waited in happy anticipation for his reply. It did not occur to her for one moment that he might not write back, and when May gave way to June and she received no word from him, she told herself that he was probably very busy, or that the mail had been delayed. She wrote again.

Weeks passed, and she decided that her first letter must definitely have gone astray. She wrote a third and fourth time, making excuses for him.

In August, a week or so after Suzy Laughton's wedding, she did something she had not really wanted to do. She rang up Mrs Merriman and enquired after her son. Mrs Merriman confirmed that he was well and that she had heard from him regularly.

The first seeds of doubt began to germinate in Ruth's mind. Had he cooled towards her? Worse, had he used his departure for the far east as a way of gently letting her down? Worse still, had he met someone else?

Suddenly she was seized by the vision of him in the company of a beautiful woman, sipping fresh lime juice as the sun went down. The thought of it made her feel sick with jealousy.

She wrote a fifth letter at the beginning of September.

Do you remember the third letter you ever wrote to me, Peter? You said that you would not write again for fear of being a nuisance, and asked me to reply if only to say 'no'. Now I am asking the same of you. If you don't want to hear from me again, do please say so and put *me* out of my misery. I have waited for some word from you since April now – nearly six months. I can't believe that you would 'drop' me like this. It just isn't in your character. I don't even ask a long letter of explanation or apology, but do please have the decency to write and *tell* me – however painful you may think it will be for me, it cannot be as painful as waiting for a reply and getting none . . .

She posted this letter with a heavy heart. September passed, and October. Suzy had left the Mission, and Ruth went through a time of intense depression, sitting in her room for hours on end, brooding on all the possible reasons why he did

70

not write. She began to lose weight, ceased to care about her personal appearance, and became thoroughly run down.

On a misty afternoon in November, she took a bus across London and rang the bell of Mrs Merriman's flat in Sussex Gardens. Miss Hughes answered the door: a neat and polished little woman with her hair done in plaited earphones.

'Miss Wilmot? Yes, I think Mrs Merriman has mentioned your name. Will you come in please?'

She was shown into the sitting room, where Mrs Merriman sat by the fire. On the piano was a large framed studio photograph of Peter. It was the first thing Ruth saw as she entered the room.

Mrs Merriman was as upright as ever. 'This is a surprise visit,' she said.

'I should have telephoned. I do apologise.'

'No need for that. We have few enough visitors as it is. Will you have a glass of sherry?'

'Thank you, but no.'

'I think we have a little gin if you would prefer it.'

'No – really.'

'Well in that case you had better sit down.'

Ruth sat. Miss Hughes stood at the door, round, rosy cheeked, expectant. She was clearly going to remain until invited to leave.

'I came to ask about Peter,' Ruth said.

'Oh? Why's that?'

'I wondered if you'd heard from him recently.'

'Is anything wrong with him?'

'Not as far as I know. It's just that I haven't heard from him. In the last few months, that is,' she added as an afterthought.

Mrs Merriman put on her spectacles and took a letter from the table by her chair. 'I heard last week. He seems very busy.' She opened the letter, scanned it.

'I've written – well, several times. But I haven't had any reply.'

'Well you can read this if you like. There's nothing private about it.'

'May I?'

The old lady handed the letter over. Ruth scanned the

71

address. It was unchanged. Box 72, Kuala Lumpur. She read the letter hastily, searching for even an oblique reference to herself. But she found none. It was his voice speaking, but not to her. Five sides of news from a son to his mother, and not the smallest hint about his private life out there.

She handed it back, and Mrs Merriman put it in its envelope. 'I suppose – has he ever mentioned me in his letters?'

'No. I can't say he has.'

Mrs Merriman took off her glasses and put them away in their box, which shut with a snap. Miss Hughes remained motionless by the door, drinking in every word and every implication.

Ruth felt tears coming. 'I can't understand why he doesn't write.'

'He's a grown man, my dear. He is old enough to know his own mind.'

She hated Mrs Merriman for that. She hated her, and she hated her henchwoman, Miss Hughes, with her rosy cheeks and the sleek black plaits of somebody else's hair over her ears that made her look like a radio operator at some secret listening post. She knew instinctively that Mrs Merriman was glad, glad that her son was abroad, glad that he was not corresponding with this tall, rather ungainly girl with a just noticeable Yorkshire accent who was definitely not-quite-one-of-us-dear. She wanted to say things, damaging things that would hurt the old lady in some way, to pay her back for her overweening satisfaction with her position, her late husband's rank, those rows and rows of brown and white predecessors who looked at you out of their brown and white past as if you came in with the cat.

But she kept all this back, forced a smile and said, 'Well. It was very kind of you to show me the letter. I was just passing, and I thought I might drop in. I'm glad Peter's having such an interesting time out there.'

'Are you sure you won't have a drink?'

'Quite sure, thank you.' She stood up. 'I'm sorry to trouble you like this.'

'That's quite all right.'

She held out her hand. 'Goodbye, Mrs Merriman.'

'Goodbye, my dear. And – don't blame Peter. Or yourself, will you?'

She was surprised by this remark. It caught her off guard, and the tears she had successfully held back surged out so that she choked on them, shaking her head, making for the door. Half blind, she went into the hall, collected her coat, allowed Miss Hughes to let her out. The black door shut behind her and she found herself in a thick London fog.

Deep, choking sobs overtook her. She set out along the pavement, hurrying away from that house and the photograph of Peter on the piano, the upright old lady, the cluttered sitting room.

The fog clung to her nostrils and eyelashes. It caught in her throat and made her cough. It was acrid, yellow fog, heavily laden with the tarry smoke of thousands of coal fires.

Motor cars crawled along, their headlights looming up from nowhere, the drivers leaning out of the windows to see ahead. She missed her way, tried to retrace her steps, and found herself in a complex of roads whose names she did not recognise.

Her journey home became a nightmare. She wandered through the backstreets of Paddington, found herself in dead ends, hailed taxis that were never for hire, waited at bus stops where no buses came. She asked directions from other pedestrians but found herself unable to follow them successfully. Finally, nearly two hours after leaving Sussex Gardens, a taxi stopped for her and crept back with her to her digs in Highgate.

She went up to her room and took off her wet coat. She felt damp all through and knew even then that she had caught a chill. She tried to have a hot bath, but the geyser wasn't working properly and the water was only warm.

Her temperature was rocketing already: she was shivering uncontrollably, and no amount of coats and dressing gowns piled on to the bed could make her feel warm. She curled in a ball, hugged herself, teeth chattering.

She barely slept at all that night. By dawn, she was almost delirious. The room was going in and out of focus; her whole body ached; her throat was so sore she could barely swallow.

73

She wondered if she might die, and worried about it because she knew that she had not tidied her drawers.

Mrs Bootherstone, the lumpy landlady with grey hair that escaped from the many clips and pins with which she tried to control it, came in to look at her.

'Oh dear, oh dear, oh dear,' she said. 'We've caught a chill, Miss Wilmot, haven't we?'

Ruth nodded, unable to speak. Mrs Bootherstone brought her some beef tea, but she was unable to finish it. The following morning when Mrs Bootherstone came in, Ruth asked if a doctor could come and see her. When he came, she understood dimly that she was to be taken to hospital.

Later that morning she was carried downstairs in the arms of two ambulance men who called her 'Luv' and made cheerful cockney remarks about having her as lively as a cricket in no time at all.

She was put in a private ward and given careful nursing. She seemed to be detached from what was happening to her, as if her mind had almost parted company from her body. At times she felt she could actually look down on herself as she lay in the hospital bed. She was aware of days and nights and the faces of people she knew: Suzy Laughton, Doctor Warnes, her aunt down from Yorkshire. Later, she went through a night of intense hallucinations: she talked with her mother, saw Peter again, flew easily over Highgate woods.

When she woke, she could see stars through the sash window. She lay there and watched the dawn creep into the sky. When the nurse took her temperature in the morning, she saw the look of relief on her face.

'Feeling better this morning I expect, Miss Wilmot?'

She nodded. 'Hungry, too.'

'You had us quite worried for a while.'

'What have I had?'

'Don't you know? Pneumonia of course.'

She felt rather pleased about that. I have had pneumonia and I'm alive, she thought to herself.

'Isn't it wonderful?' she said to Suzy Laughton when she visited. 'No one will ever see my untidy drawers.'

Suzy had brought grapes and books and flowers. She was as

74

brisk as ever. 'We're going to get you really well again,' she said. 'As soon as you leave here, you'll go and stay with my parents. Mother loves cossetting people, and you'll make up for the fact that she doesn't have me at home quite so often. You'll have lots of good food and she'll get a bit of weight on you. Understand?'

'Suzy you're an angel. What would I do without you?'

'Never mind about that. Just you make sure you get better nice and quickly.'

'I'll do my best.'

'And if I were you, I'd put that Merriman fellow right out of your mind. I was never entirely sure about him.'

When Suzy had gone, Ruth thought about Peter coherently for the first time since leaving Mrs Merriman's house. She decided that Suzy was right. What had happened had happened, and she must put it all behind her. This illness of hers would be like a door that she could close on the past.

The traffic droned by outside. She reached for a book, nibbled a grape. Peter has dropped me, she thought. Nothing I can do will change his mind. So be it. I shall go to convalesce at the Laughtons, and then I shall start afresh.

IV

The taxi drew up outside Laughton Hall on a wintry evening a few days before Christmas. Apart from a few lights on in downstairs rooms, the house was a bleak silhouette against a frosty sky.

The passenger of the taxi wore a heavy astrakhan coat with the collar turned up against the keen northeast wind. He directed the driver to place his two suitcases and a large cardboard box by the front door before paying him off. The taxi headlights came on, and the car moved off down the drive beneath the cedar trees.

The visitor launched into a rendering of 'Good King Wenceslas' in a powerful off-key baritone, slapping his gloved

75

hands together to keep warm as well as time.

Half way through the second verse, he knocked loudly at the door, and a few seconds later he was admitted by Winnifred Laughton.

He stopped singing. 'Aunt!' he exclaimed.

'Bobby! My dear boy!'

She enveloped him in a warm hug. She was a large lady: her bosom so generous that it seemed to weigh her down, and she bent forward permanently from the waist. Her voice was deep. It echoed around the large entrance hall that was hung with portraits of Laughton ancestors.

Teape brought his cases and the box of Teape's port inside, and while he was doing so, Theo Laughton emerged from the sitting room to welcome him.

'Robert my boy! How splendid to see you!' They shook hands. 'How long is it?'

'I was working it out in the train,' Teape said. 'Do you know it's very nearly eighteen years?'

'Is it as long as that?'

'I've put you in the room you always used to have,' Aunt Win said. 'Do you remember where it is?'

'Aunt!' he blustered. 'How could I forget!'

He went up the mahogany staircase and into the room he had used when on holiday from his prep school. He put his suitcase down, smiling to himself over half forgotten memories. He parted the curtains, looked out into the night.

Yes, he could just make out the walled garden and the little canal that ran along beside it, which served as an overflow for the fish pond. He remembered a summer holiday – it must have been in 1915 – when he stole a peach from the orchard and, finding it unripe, threw it into the canal. But it had floated, and Aunt Win had found it. She had asked him about it, and when he had denied all knowledge, she suggested a snake might have done it. In his innocence, he had seized upon this explanation, agreeing that this must have been the case.

He let the curtain fall back, ran water into the basin, washed his face and hands. He brushed his hair and looked at himself in the wardrobe mirror. Eighteen years! It was a long time. He could almost imagine his face as it had been when he was eleven or twelve. He could almost see it looking out at him from the mirror.

There was a log fire in the sitting room, and when he entered he was surprised and delighted to see his cousin, Suzy Laughton. He kissed her warmly and she introduced her husband.

'Darling this is Bobby, my favourite cousin. Bobby this is Maurice.'

'Your favourite husband!' Bobby laughed, and shook hands with Maurice Blakely. Blakely was a pale specimen with thinning hair. Teape classified him immediately as an intellectual. He could tell that straightaway by his suede shoes.

His other aunt was there, Grace, Win's sister. He kissed her on the cheek and she whispered a welcome. The large brown mole on her cheek was as prickly as he remembered it. She took his hand and squeezed it in a rather conspiratorial way. She had been a spinster all her life. She loved young men with long legs.

'And this is Ruth Wilmot, a friend of mine,' Suzy said.

Teape turned and saw Ruth for the first time. 'Ah!' he said, and stopped. She smiled, and they shook hands. There was a quiet gentleness about her that he liked. She could not be called beautiful, but on the other hand she seemed to radiate kindness: when she regarded him with her soft, intelligent eyes, he found himself hoping that she liked what she saw.

'Now, m'boy,' Theo said. 'What'll it be?' Theo was wiry and small. He had good capable hands that were hardened here and there from the frequent use of plane and chisel. He had been in banking all his life, and only in the last eight years, since his retirement, had he discovered a love for carpentry.

'Umm – a gin and It, if I may, Uncle.'

'A gin and It it is,' Theo said, and went to the cabinet to mix what he privately regarded as one of those confounded modern cocktails.

'Well then,' Aunt Win said when they were settled. 'Tell us all your news, Bobby. How is Portugal?'

'Had any good revolutions recently?' Suzy added.

'Not any more. We've got this new man Salazar in the driving seat now. He's the boy everyone's pinning their faith on.'

'There was a column in the *Times* the other day that made him out to be quite a financial genius,' Theo said.

'He's no fool, that's quite clear. He doesn't stand any nonsense. Just what the Pg.s need, to my mind.'

'Pg.s?' Ruth asked.

'Portugese,' Suzy explained.

'And the wine trade?' Aunt Win said. 'Have you had a good year?'

'Very early to say, Aunt.'

'Are you involved in the actual making of the wine, or are you merely the shipper?' Maurice Blakely asked.

Teape laughed, glanced at the others. 'I don't actually tread the grapes, you know. But I'm the johnny who does the blending.'

'I've told Maurice that we must come out and see a vintage one year, Bobby.' Suzy turned to her husband. 'One hasn't lived until one's seen the Douro country when they're harvesting the grapes.'

'I'm not so sure about that!' Bobby laughed. 'If you call doing without most of the normal creature comforts for three weeks "living" – '

'Don't believe a word he says,' Suzy said. 'These shippers – they live like kings.'

'And you're over here on business, Bobby, is that right?' Theo asked.

'Partly business, partly pleasure. And I hope to start sorting out mother's affairs, too.'

'Dear, yes,' Grace whispered. 'Of course.'

Teape sipped his drink, smiled awkwardly.

'Weren't you engaged?' Suzy said.

'Really dear!' her mother said. 'How tactless!'

Teape laughed. 'Oh – don't worry about that. Yes, I was. You remember Joy?'

'Only as a tiny baby,' Win said.

'Jolly nice girl. But we decided – well – we weren't exactly right. You know how it is.' He was aware that Ruth was looking at him. He glanced quickly across at her and their eyes met for a fleeting moment. He wondered what she was thinking. She had a certain serenity that he had never encountered before.

And there was something about her that made him just want to stare at her, in the same way he had once stared at Queen Alexandra when, as a boy, he saw her ride in a carriage with the old King for the Trooping of the Colour. Not that she looked a bit like Queen Alexandra. No, she was much softer, much more womanly than that. Motherly, almost. But alluring at the same time.

He looked away quickly, aware that he had been staring at her too obviously. Aunt Win excused herself to go and supervise in the kitchen. 'I'm afraid Cook may overdo the joint,' she explained.

Teape turned to Ruth. 'How do you come to know this splendid Laughton family?'

Suzy said, 'Ruth and I were working together in Islington.'

'Suzy taught me the ropes,' Ruth said. 'I don't know what I'd have done without her.'

'And are you still working there?'

'Well – not for the moment –'

'Ruth's been convalescing for the last few weeks.'

'Oh?'

'I went and caught pneumonia. Silly, really.'

'It doesn't sound at all silly to me.'

'It wasn't,' Suzy said.

'And will you go back to Islington to work?'

'No. I shall be starting nursing training in January.'

'Are you, though? That's very brave of you. Where will you do that?'

'U.C.H.'

'Ah. Now you've got me. What does that stand for?'

'University College Hospital,' Suzy said. 'It's in Gower Street.'

Ruth smiled, and he knew immediately that she was thinking, like him, that Suzy was rather keen on answering his questions for her.

Aunt Win came back and announced dinner. They moved into the dining room. The table was a large oval gate-leg, set with fiddle pattern silver and Edinburgh crystal. Teape sat between his two aunts, with Maurice and Suzy opposite and Ruth between Maurice and Theo.

The Laughtons prided themselves on being nearly self-sufficient. They kept hens and geese, pigs and a few cows. Their gardener, driver and handyman was a swarthy fellow known as 'Caesar' (a nickname he had earned for repeated use of the expression, 'See sir?' to Theo) and he provided fresh vegetables all the year round, while his wife made butter and cheese and bread, and set wide, shallow dishes of cream by the Aga cooker to make clotted cream.

Dinner was roast beef with crisp green Brussels sprouts, potatoes roasted in the juices of the meat, crusty Yorkshire pudding, carrots cooked in butter, gravy made lovingly from the roasting tin.

Teape ate heartily and enjoyed being the guest of honour. The conversation centred on Portugal for most of the time, as Aunt Win had been brought up in Portugal, and had not been back for many years.

'You see, I was a Remington before I married Theo,' she explained to Ruth, 'and my sister was Bobby's mother, Rosalinde.'

'The Oporto British colony is thick with Remingtons,' Suzy said.

'And Randalls and Millets,' Bobby added.

'They all intermarry, and breed like rabbits,'

'Suzy, really!'

'What about all that dreadful man who forged all those bank notes?' Theo said. 'That was a rum do if ever there was one.'

'You mean Alves Reis? They say he spends most of his time on his knees in his cell now. He's been converted.'

'Well I'm glad it's done some good, anyway,' Aunt Win remarked.

'Poor chap got a pretty raw deal if you ask me,' Maurice Blakely said.

'Oh? How so?'

'All he did was pursue the policy of the Portuguese government – albeit unofficially.'

'Maurice, darling!' Suzy said. 'Don't be ridiculous!'

'Not at all! The fellow simply had a few bank notes printed, that's all. The Portuguese government had been doing the same thing for months.'

Ruth appealed to Bobby: 'What exactly are we talking about?'

'A gentleman by the name of Alves Reis. He wrote a letter to Waterlows – the people who print money – on Bank of Portugal notepaper. Asked them for I don't know how many thousands of five hundred *escudo* notes. Persuaded a couple of dupes to take them into Portugal in suitcases.'

Ruth laughed. 'No! I can't believe that!'

Teape shrugged. 'It's the truth. Honest Injun. Promise.'

'But – you mean he got away with it?'

'For a year or two. He even wrote a second letter for replenishments. Had a special trunk made to bring them in.'

'Started a bank himself, didn't he?' Theo said. 'Bank of Angola or something.'

'Are you sure you're not all pulling my leg?' Ruth said.

'Not at all.'

'It's so utterly improbable!'

'Oh – it could only have happened in Portugal,' Teape said. 'Only the Pg.s could be so muddle headed. They didn't even have a system for checking the numbers of the notes.'

'Yes, but fair's fair,' Blakely said, 'That fellow Waterlow must have been a bit of a b.f. to agree to print the notes in the first place.'

'He probably wouldn't have for any other country. His only mistake was that he knew the Portuguese character too well.'

'I think you're being terribly unfair to the Portuguese,' Suzy remarked. 'I think they're a marvellous nation.' She turned to Ruth. 'It's a splendidly feudal country. The women beat out their washing on the river banks, and the children wave when you drive past.'

'Splendidly feudal habits, too,' Teape observed. 'You haven't travelled in the Oporto trams as often as I have.'

'What has that got to do with it?'

'Shall we say their personal habits aren't quite twentieth century?'

'You mean they spit? All latins spit. They're brought up to it.'

'What a charming conversation for the dinner table!' Aunt Win said. 'Really! What Ruth must think of us I can't imagine!'

The roast beef was followed by lemon meringue pie, and after that there was Stilton cheese and Teape's Special Reserve. The ladies withdrew and the men talked finance, golf and politics.

Half an hour later, when they joined the ladies, Teape took a seat on the sofa with his Aunt Grace. The conversation turned to child education. Blakely held forth for some while, enlarging on the importance of correct training in infancy and the Attitude of the Mother. During this conversation, Teape's mind wandered. He had nothing to say on this subject and found Blakely's earnest intellectual manner rather a bore. He didn't really like the fellow. He was a bit too clever by half.

And then, perhaps by accident, he caught Ruth's eye and they exchanged a private smile. Yes, she was bored too. Aunt Grace had once been a Sunday school teacher and was feeding Blakely with all the questions he enjoyed answering. Their eyes met a second time, and this time neither glanced away. He felt a thud of excitement: she is interested in me, he thought. She is attracted to me.

They started a little conversation of their own, but it was a conversation without words. It was a game of exchanged looks; not seductive or inviting looks so much as those which shared a growing awareness of each other. They were both on the re-bound; both needed to love and be loved. More important still, they needed to forget, and the source of their mutual attraction lay in the fact that Ruth was totally unlike Joy, and Bobby was completely different from Merriman.

They became mutually aware of this attraction; neither had ever engaged in such a silent conversation before, and each found it exciting beyond words. Aunt Win perhaps noticed something, for she said to Ruth, 'Are you too warm, dear? Would you like to sit further from the fire?' But Ruth shook her head and said she was happy where she was, and immediately after that brief exchange, another glance shot back and forth between them – a glance that made each tingle inwardly in wonderment that such a strong mutual attraction could exist so suddenly between two people.

Twenty-two sat down to Christmas dinner at Laughton Hall that year. Suzy's two brothers and their families came down from London and Canterbury, and Theo's niece and her husband and four children arrived from High Wycombe. For three days the house was full of people and children and dogs and noise.

Teape threw himself into the festivities with great enthusiasm. He went out with Casear to choose the tree, set it up in a brass bucket in the corner of the sitting room, organised the Laughton grandchildren into decorating it and finally lifted up one of the six-year-old grandaughters to place the fairy on the top.

In many ways he contributed to the great success of that particular Christmas. In the mornings his powerful baritone could be heard singing carols off key while he shaved with his Rolls razor. At breakfast, over a huge plate of steaming porridge and thick yellow cream, he regaled the children with ridiculous stories, shooting the occasional glance in Ruth's direction.

He presented a small envelope containing a brand new half crown piece to each child for Christmas, and a bottle of port to everyone else.

'Whatever am I going to do with this? Ruth asked when she unwrapped hers.

'Drink it!' he said.

'But I can't drink it all myself!'

'Then I shall have to come along and help you.'

'You shouldn't say things that you don't mean.'

'Ah, but how do you know I don't mean them?'

She laughed. He was great fun. The children loved him, as well. They pestered him to play with them, dragged him about, played practical jokes on him. And he would protest, but not too hard, so that from time to time he would suffer the ignomony of having flour poured on his head or cold water poured down his sleeve. Then he would roar in exaggerated protest and rampage about like a wild animal, scattering them round the house as he sought to revenge his loss of dignity.

But there were quieter times, too. One evening Ruth went upstairs to her room to change for dinner and heard Teape's voice reading a story from Winnie the Pooh. She stopped outside the door, watching without being seen. He was totally absorbed in the story about how Tigger came to the forest and discovered that the only thing he could really eat was Extract of Malt. And the children were equally absorbed: they sat around him on the bed, knees hunched under chins, pink from their baths.

Ruth saw this and loved him for it. She convinced herself that inside his bluff, jokey exterior lay the gentleness and love she needed.

But there was something else inside Robert Teape: something that never showed itself outwardly. For he was, in effect, on the run. He was trying to escape a memory that refused to let itself be forgotten. It was the memory of a thirteen-year-old girl's face, a look of hatred and revulsion. It was not with him always, but sometimes he woke at night and heard the wind outside, blowing over the fens, and he remembered the blowing sand and the white-crested waves crashing on the beach at Leça. He remembered the girl's face, her look of hatred. He could forget neither her shriek nor the shriek of the Atlantic gale.

He was afraid of these memories, and needed desperately to put them behind him. Ruth's serenity, her gentle contralto voice, her smile, her hair, the breathtaking curve of her breasts all awoke in him memories of better days, deep-rooted memories of his mother when he was a child. They were not so much conscious recollections as a dim awareness that Ruth presented what he needed to fill a void in his life. Teape was not a self-analysing sort of person, indeed he despised psychology in the same way as he despised modern art and Maurice Blakely's suede shoes, so he would have ridiculed the suggestion that he needed a mother figure, and that Ruth fitted the part.

VI

He stayed on for a week after Christmas at the invitation of his aunt. He and Ruth took to going for walks together in the afternoons. She wore a long coat with fur round the cuffs and collar. Her stay with the Laughtons had put colour back into her cheeks and a spring in her step.

'Do I walk too fast for you?'

'Not at all. I hate dawdling.'

'So do I,' he said. 'I like to get on with things.'

'What does that mean?'

'It doesn't mean anything really. I just like to get on. I don't like hanging about.'

She looked at him. 'You remind me of somebody, but I'm not sure who.'

'Henry the Eighth?'

'No, your ears are too big.'

'Lloyd George? Charlie Chaplin? Douglas Fairbanks?'

'No. I know. You remind me of Tigger. You're all bounce.'

'Thank you very much.'

'Please don't mention it.'

He chuckled. They walked on between frosty ploughed fields.

'And you know who you remind me of?'

'Who?'

'Promise not to say, "Don't be so silly"?'

'All right.'

'Norma Shearer.'

'Don't be so silly.'

'No. Honest Injun. You do look like her.'

'I'm much too big! I'm enormous! Bulky, even.'

'No you're not. You're not at all.'

'Oh no. I'm a mere will o' the wisp. Two laths and a rabbit skin. A fragile tiny thing.'

'Absolutely. Except the bit about the rabbit skin.'

'You're an ass.'

'No, I'm not. An ass is an Eyore, and I'm a Tigger. That makes you Roo.'

'Who's Kanga?'

'Aunt Win. And let me see, Suzy's Rabbit because she's so capable and sensible.'

'What about Maurice?'

'I think he'd better be Owl.'

'But do you think he can spell hot-buttered-toast?'

'Oh – sure of it. These trick cyclists can even spell TUESDAY.'

She giggled, and he caught her hand.

'Do you mind?'

'No. I don't mind.'

'It's sort of – comforting,' he said. 'Tiggers need to be comforted sometimes.'

'So do Roos.'

'Do they?'

'Everyone does. Everyone needs a bit of T.L.C., don't they?'

'What's T.L.C.? Something you gargle with?'

'Haven't you heard of Tender Loving Care?'

'Ah! You forget that I come from the backwoods of Lusitania. We aren't quite so well versed in the latest lingo over there.'

'Do you like it?'

'Portugal?'

'Yes.'

'I shall tell you a story. When God created the world, he made some places very hot and some places very cold, some places desert and others jungle. There were vast areas of rocks and mountains and equally large areas of grassy plains and deserts. But there was one place which had beautiful valleys, heather covered mountains, rivers, streams, long golden beaches, blue skies in the summer and rain in the winter to make all kinds of fruits and vegetables grow in abundance. Well, he called this place Portugal.'

'So you –'

'Wait a minute. I haven't finished. You see the Archangel Gabriel came along and said, "Look here, God, why have you made this part of the world more beautiful than all the others? It's got everything – rich soil, a wonderful climate, port wine, the seas full of sardines and the best rough shooting you'll find outside Scotland." But God said, "Hang on, hang on – " '

'I'm sure he never said that!'

'Oh yes he did. He said, "Hang on a moment. Just wait until you see the sort of *people* I'm going to put in this country."'

'That's cruel.'

'I know. It's a joke the Pg.s tell against themselves.'

'Which shows they've got a sense of humour.'

'Oh they've got that all right.'

'But you haven't answered my question.'

'You mean, do I like the place? Yes, I suppose I do. I can't imagine living anywhere else. The Teape family – well, it's part of the port wine tradition now.'

'I'd never realised there were so many British out there.'

'No one bothers to learn anything about Portugal. A lot of people I meet think it's part of Spain.'

'And your family's been out there how long?'

'Let's see. Somewhere around 1820. We're well rooted.'

'You're lucky.'

'To have roots? Am I? I hadn't thought of that.'

They were nearing the house, and could hear Caesar sawing logs. Teape let go of her hand and said, 'We don't want anyone getting the wrong idea, do we?'

'Are you sure you don't mean we don't want anyone getting the right idea?'

'The trouble with you, Roo, is that you have a nasty habit of hitting the nail on the head.'

She laughed and shook her hair back. They stamped the frost off their boots in the porch outside the scullery.

'Thank you for my nice walk,' she said.

'Please don't mention it,' he replied.

In the kitchen, Winnifred Laughton was making scones. 'What are you two laughing about?' she asked.

'No idea,' Teape said. 'Just giggling aimlessly.'

'There's a nice fire in the sitting room. Tea in half an hour.'

He kissed her on the cheek.

'I'm all floury, Bobby.'

'Aunt – floury or not – you're marvellous.' He turned to Ruth. 'Isn't she?'

Ruth nodded. 'He's right, Mrs Laughton. You really are.'

Teape ate a piece of raw pastry. 'Not a bad cook, either.'

87

She shooed them out of the kitchen, and they went into the sitting room, where Ruth allowed herself to be persuaded to play the piano.

Later that evening, when Win and Theo were preparing for bed, Win remarked to her husband, 'Do you know, I think Bobby and Ruth have fallen for one another.'

'What makes you think that?'

'When they came in from their walk this afternoon, there was something about them. A sort of glow of happiness.'

Theo folded his combinations and placed them over the back of a chair. 'Well that's very satisfactory, isn't it?'

'Yes,' she said. 'I think it is. I think they're a rather good match, don't you?'

VII

He began proposing to her in an underground tube train between Camden Town and Euston. They were sitting in the inward-facing seats, and could see their own reflections in the window opposite.

'I don't want to go back to Portugal,' he said suddenly.

'Why not?'

'At least – I don't want to go back without you.'

'We both have our lives to lead, Bobby.'

'Yes, I know. I know that.'

The train arrived at Euston. The doors hissed open, then closed. It continued on its way through the tunnel. He took out his handkerchief, blew his nose noisily, put the handkerchief away. 'Hell!'

'What on earth's the matter?'

'Matter? I'll tell you what the matter is. I've gone and fallen in love with you, that's the matter. I want you to marry me.'

She sought his hand, held it. The train arrived at Warren Street, then Goodge Street then Tottenham Court Road.

'You don't know very much about me,' she said.

'If you mean that fellow who jilted you – I know enough. Come to that, do you know enough about me?'

'Is there much to know?'

'Only that I need you. In an extra special way.'

They got out at Leicester Square. He talked to her as they walked to the escalator. 'You'd love Portugal. I know I run it down and make fun of it and the Pg.s, but there are compensations. It's a good life. We could put down roots. Make a home. Have children.'

They joined the crowd of people on the escalator. She stood on a step above him, so that she looked down on his head. He looked up at her and mouthed the words 'I love you'. Then he said aloud, 'Will you?'

They were reaching the top. She seemed to relax. 'Yes,' she said in a voice that made people nearby look round at them. 'Yes, I will.'

They stepped off the top of the escalator and he took her in his arms and kissed her. The crowd surged past them.

'What about my nursing?'

'We'll cancel it.'

'And the wedding?'

'As soon as you like.'

'In the spring?'

'In the spring.'

'Where?'

'Details. Mere details. In a church.'

He set off abruptly, taking her by the hand, running her through the station entrance to the street. He hailed a taxi.

'Bond Street,' he said to the cabby, and gave a large wink. 'I'm going to buy her a ring before she changes her mind.'

VIII

Teape went back to Portugal for three months and returned for the wedding in April. Ruth's aunt was unable to afford a wedding in Yorkshire, and so they were married in the parish church of Woodleigh Hall.

Hugh Blunden was the best man and Suzy the matron of

honour. There were four bridesmaids and one page. Theo Laughton brought the bride to the altar and the vicar, a new man who had played Rugby football for England, gave a sermon about the sanctity of marriage and the Great Adventure.

'These young people today are starting out on a life that will not always be easy,' he said. 'There will be times when they will need to remember the vows they have made. For while they will be bound as one person together they will, paradoxically, remain separate persons, with separate wills. There will be times when the self will have to give way: times when the will of one must be abdicated in favour of the will of the other . . . '

The organ thundered a toccata and the newly wedded pair emerged into an April gale that snatched Ruth's headress off at the moment the shutter of the official photographer's camera clicked.

At the reception, Hugh Blunden read out the telegrams of congratulation. Many of them were from friends and distant relations in Portugal. Two of them hoped that all their troubles would be little ones, and a third instructed them to go forth and multiply.

Everyone said what a handsome couple they made. Bobby wore a brown pin stripe suit to go away in which he liked very much but which Maurice Blakely later said made him look even more brash and colonial than he was. There was much clapping and laughing and throwing of confetti. Caesar arrived in the Humber wearing his blue suit and peaked cap. Boots and tin cans were tied to the rear fender, and some of Bobby's friends lifted up the back of the car, so that Caesar had great difficulty in driving off.

And then, just as they were moving away down the drive, amid cheers and waves and blown kisses, Hugh Blunden ran up alongside Bobby's window and thrust a last telegram into his hand.

'Just arrived!' he panted, and waved as the car pulled away.

Teape put the telegram in his pocket and turned to Ruth. 'Well Mrs Teape? What does it feel like?'

'It's like a dream!'

Caesar drove them to Croydon to catch the Imperial Airways flight to Le Bourget. Neither of them had flown

90

before, and it seemed a daring thing to do, to fly off together on honeymoon. They peered out of the aircraft window together as the plane climbed over the English countryside, and pointed out landmarks to each other excitedly.

When they crossed the coast Teape produced a bottle of Moet Chandon which Hugh Blunden had pressed him to take after the reception.

'We can't drink it now!' Ruth said.

'Why not? I can think of no better place.'

He began to undo the wire.

'Darling, you're the limit!'

'Here we go,' he said, working the cork with his thumbs. 'Here it comes.'

The cork sprang out unexpectedly and a jet of frothing champagne shot across the aircraft cabin. Teape shook with mirth. 'Came sooner than I expected!' he laughed, and winked broadly. 'We'll have to do better than that!'

She blushed from the tips of her ears to the cleavage of her breasts and looked away from him, out of the aircraft window.

'Ruth,' he said. 'It was only a joke.'

'In that case it was in very poor taste.'

He held the champagne bottle away from him so that the drips fell clear of his suit. 'You shouldn't take me so seriously,' he said. 'And anyway – we are married. Aren't we?'

She smiled a little and nodded. He filled the glasses and made a toast. 'To Tigger and Roo,' he said.

'To Tigger and Roo,' she replied, and they touched glasses and drank. When she looked at him, he looked away. He felt that she was seeing him in a new light. It was as if she were already divining the truth about him.

He took her hand. 'I love you, Ruth. I really do love you.' He took out a handkerchief and wiped his eyes.

She looked at him a little sadly. 'You're a sentimental old thing, aren't you?'

'Yes, I must admit I am.'

'I think I prefer you that way.'

'Just as well. I mean – bit late if you didn't. Jolly bad luck, in fact.'

That evening, over the *crèpes suzettes* in the hotel he said,

91

'Well – any minute now. Our big moment, eh?'

She smiled but said nothing.

'I suppose you'd like to go up first, would you? That's the way I believe it's done.'

'Bobby, I do believe you're embarrassed.'

'Me? Embarrassed? Not a bit of it. Well. Maybe. Not a dab hand at this sort of thing.'

'I should jolly well hope not.'

She left him sitting at the table sipping his coffee. After she had gone, he called the waiter and ordered a cognac. He told himself that it wasn't dutch courage, but then admitted to himself that perhaps it was. He finished his coffee, toyed with the balloon glass of brandy, sent for the bill.

When he took out his wallet, the telegram Hugh Blunden had given him that afternoon came out with it. He saw with surprise that it was addressed to Ruth at her Highgate address, and had been forwarded. He wondered if he should open it. After all, it might not be a simple congratulatory telegram. It might be bad news.

What if it were really bad news? The death of a loved one, perhaps. That would be an awful thing to give her on her wedding night. On the other hand, a telegram was urgent, and it was for her. Therefore she had a right to see it as soon as possible.

The waiter brought his change. He left a tip and walked out of the restaurant and into the lift.

Ruth was in bed, her brown hair loose on the pillow, the sheet up under her chin. His heart did a little somersault of affection when he saw her.

'I thought you'd got lost,' she said.

'Not me! You won't shake me off that easily!' He waved the telegram. 'We forgot to open this.'

'So we did. Who's it from?'

'I don't know. It's for you.'

He handed it to her. She opened it, frowning as she read it. 'Well?'

She was colouring. 'I – don't really understand it.'

She retained it a moment before giving it to him. He read:

DISREGARD LETTER. MERRIMAN.

'Merriman?' he said. 'Who's Merriman?'

'It's Peter.'

'You mean the fellow who – who –'

'Yes. Peter Merriman.'

'I don't understand. What letter?'

'Bobby, I don't understand either. I haven't had a letter.'

'Well are you expecting one?'

'No! Of course I'm not!'

'Seems deuced odd. I thought the fellow threw you over. You sure there isn't anything you ought to have told me, Ruth?'

Her eyes were very wide, and frightened. 'Quite, quite sure. And please don't look at me like that, Bobby.'

He shrugged. 'Well. Fine sort of telegram to get on your wedding night, I must say.' He looked down at it as though it had a nasty smell. 'I suppose he's written to you. Otherwise he wouldn't have sent this, would he? Well. No doubt we'll – you'll get it sooner or later. Then we'll know what it was all about.'

'Don't be angry with me.'

'I'm not angry.'

'Really not?'

He sat on the bed and took her hand. 'Well. Not really.'

'Wasn't my fault he sent it.'

'Better not be, Roo.'

'Have your bath then. Come to bed with me.'

He swallowed. 'All right then. Won't be a tick.'

He went into the bathroom and sang the Marseillaise as he ran the water. Ruth picked up the telegram from the bedside table. DISREGARD LETTER. Why had he suddenly decided to write after all this time? What had happened? Had he perhaps been through some terrible experience? Was he returning to England?

She found herself remembering him: his shy manner, his gentleness. She remembered the line of his jaw, the way he tilted his head slightly when he was thinking, the way he so often paused before answering a question.

The door from the bathroom opened unexpectedly and there was Bobby, resplendent in his striped Austin Reed pyjamas.

93

'Room for a small one?' he asked, and got into bed. The springs creaked. He was heavy, hot and hairy.

IX

After spending a week in Paris they took the Sud Express to Lisbon. For ten days they lived in luxury at the Hotel Miramar in Estoril. It was late April: the sun shone, but they were not quite in love. They saw the sights of Lisbon, shopped in Rossio, walked through the streets of the Bairro Alto, lunched in little restaurants on *sopa de Alentejana* and *bacalhau* and *pudim flan*. He took her one evening to a *fado* house (though personally he saw little in the mournful Portuguese way of singing) and the *fadista*, on being told that they were newly-weds, sang '*Coimbra*' for them.

They hired a car and drove out towards Sintra one day. They walked in fields where the spring flowers were like a yellow and white carpet, and later lunched on mussels cooked in wine.

In the train on the way north, Ruth said, 'I've never drunk so much wine before! My stomach doesn't know which way to turn!'

A car from the office met them at Oporto station. Their luggage was loaded into the boot and they set out along the steep cobbled roads of the old city and out towards Leça da Palmeira.

'Well,' Teape said as the car drew up outside a high, grey wall with iron gates. 'Here we are.'

On the other side of the wall, the top of a large square house was just visible among pine trees that all leant in a southerly direction.

'You mean – this is it?'

'Don't sound so disappointed.'

The driver sounded the horn. Dogs barked, and the gates swung open. The gardener, the cook and the maid awaited them. As the car moved up the slope through the gates, Ruth saw the house for the first time. The morning glory was out and the garden an untidy mixture of flowers and shrubs. The house itself had an air of wealth and decadence. The green paint on the shutters was peeling. The windows looked as if they had been shut for a very long time.

'What beautiful geraniums!' she said.

They were greeted, as they got out of the car, first by the dogs and then by the staff. Tagus and Minho, the two labradors, wagged and barked while Ruth was introduced to José the gardener, Amália the cook and Maria the maid. She insisted on shaking hands with each, and they bowed and curtsied to her. Amália made what Ruth guessed must have been a prepared speech, and Bobby translated: 'She says they want to welcome you to the house and she hopes that you will be very happy here.'

'Would you say that I am very happy to be here, and that I shall do my best to learn Portuguese quickly so that we can understand each other as soon as possible.'

They went inside. Everything seemed touched by the ghost of old Mrs Teape, of whom she had heard so much. In the dining room, there were shelves of china, silver and glass. The furniture was dark, solid and Victorian. The sitting room was cluttered with chairs and small tables, rugs, footstools, pictures, ornaments, antimacassars.

'Well?' Bobby said. 'Like it?'

'It's – very impressive.'

'But do you like it?'

She looked at him directly. 'Not as it is at the moment, Bobby. Did you expect that I would?'

He looked crestfallen. 'I hadn't really thought about it.'

She picked up a photograph in a silver frame. 'This is your father, isn't it?'

He nodded. She looked at the picture. It was of a man in his forties standing by a horse in the mountainous Douro country. He wore a battered straw hat tilted over his eyes against the sun. She put it back carefully, turned to Bobby. She took his hands.

'Funny old Tigger!'

'Dear Roo.'

'You'll let me do things to the house, won't you? You'll let me make my nest?'

95

'Anything you like. As far as I'm concerned, the house and the servants – they're all yours.'

'Come on then. I want to see upstairs.'

The bedroom was even worse than downstairs. When she saw the large bed, the mosquito netting tied in a knot, the bamboo furniture, she experienced a sudden shrinking feeling. And everything seemed very slightly damp. . . .

While she stood in the bedroom, he put his arm round her shoulders. 'It wasn't a bad honeymoon, was it?'

She smiled up at him, and he kissed her. It had been a good honeymoon in many ways, but there had been problems, the usual sort of problems.

'It was a lovely honeymoon,' she said.

Maria brought the luggage up. Ruth wanted to unpack it herself, but Bobby insisted that Maria should do it.

'But how shall I know where everything is?'

'You won't need to very much. She'll see to everything. All you have to do is tell her what you will be wearing and she'll make sure it's cleaned and pressed and put out for you.'

They went downstairs to the sitting room. He poured two glasses of white port. 'Here's to us,' he said, and as they raised their glasses, Maria came in with a sheaf of letters for them.

They were all for Teape except one, and that one was addressed to Ruth Wilmot and came from Malaya.

'Ah! The long-awaited letter!' Teape said. He handed it to her. 'Aren't you going to open it?'

'I'm not sure if I want to.'

'Why ever not?'

'The telegram – '

'Disregard letter. Yes. But that doesn't mean you can't read it.'

He sat down in an armchair by the empty fireplace, in front of which was a framed tapestry of angular roses. He started slitting open his own mail, snorting now and then at some piece of news that he read.

Ruth looked at him, observing without being observed. Marriage was an extraordinary arrangement. She had lived and slept with this man for nearly three weeks now. He was her husband, she his wife. They were married. They called each other pet names and were beginning to know instinctively what the other thought. And yet . . . in some strange way she felt further from him now than she had on that very first evening when their exchanged glances had felt like an electric circuit, they were so highly charged.

She looked at the envelope. Yes, it was definitely his writing. The man she had last seen standing on the deck of a P & O liner, his raincoat collar turned up against the rain.

Teape chuckled quietly as he finished a letter, and without glancing at her, reached for the next. Ruth opened the letter from Peter Merriman and began to read.

X

PO Box 12
Kuala Lumpur.
March 18th, 1935

My dear, my darling Ruth,

I arrived in Kuala Lumpur from up country this morning, and went to the post office as usual to collect the mail. I had virtually given up hoping to hear from you, and I wasn't surprised that there was no letter from you. But then, just as I was going, I overheard a remark from one of the Malay clerks behind the counter. He was asking what should be done with some letters that had been returned as incorrectly addressed. Something made me go back and enquire, and there were your letters, every single one addressed to Box 72 instead of Box 12.

What can I say? I had *longed* to hear from you, Ruth, and when no letters came, I spent hours deliberating whether or not to write. But I remembered our promise: I realised that you might have decided, after all, that you would rather allow our friendship to go no further.

How could I have been so stupid? Do you understand? Can you forgive me? And can you also forgive my mother, who has said no word whatsoever of your telephone call last summer? I have given much thought to this, and knowing her as I do, I can understand why she chose not to tell me. She has always been determined not to keep me tied to her apron strings, and I can well imagine that she thought she might be 'meddling' if she had told me of your call. I do hope you can forgive her: she is old, remember, and anxious to remain on good terms with me, no doubt.

I have read and re-read your letters, wept over them, wondered and wondered what to say and whether I can ever heal this terrible hurt you must have suffered. Is it too late? Will you believe me that not one single day has gone by without my thinking of you? That I have written a dozen letters to you, only to tear them up in order to hold to the promise we made?

But there is a gleam of hope in all this. If, as I believe, you can forgive me, or fate, or whatever it was that caused me to scribble my address so that a figure one looked like a figure seven – if you can forgive this, wait only a few more months, then we shall be together again and can start (– can we?) to pick up the threads of a friendship and – I believe – a love that can never be broken by anything or anybody. This trial of separation, uncertainty and unhappiness will be like the fire that gives tensile strength to steel: we shall have proved, finally, how strong is this bond between us – proved that nothing, nothing at all can ever cause us to lose our trust in each other –

Ruth got up from her chair quickly and went upstairs. She stood in the large bedroom whose windows looked west, through the pine trees, to the sea. She stood very still, holding the closely written sheets of Peter's letter at her side.

She looked round the room with a sort of horrified desperation, as if this were a trap that had been set for her, a trap in which she was caught fast and from which she could never escape. She looked at the mahogany tallboy, the massive wardrobe with thistles and leaves carved on the doors. She caught sight of her reflection in the long mirror by the dressing table.

She looked down at the letter again. She scanned its pages, the descriptions of life in the Malay jungle, of expeditions to the east coast, of tigers, turtles, mangrove swamps, unmapped mountains.

. . . Whatever happens, wherever I go and wherever you are, I know that I shall always love you. This is something that has happened to me, something that can never be changed by anything or anybody . . .

She closed her eyes, took a deep breath. Then, carefully, her hands shaking, she tore up the letter and threw it in the wastepaper basket that still contained a wisp of Rosalinde Teape's white hair.

'What was it all about?' Teape asked when she rejoined him in the sitting room.

'It was a mistake. He hadn't received some of my letters and he thought, well – he hadn't realised I was getting married.'

'So. All over bar the shouting, eh?'

She turned away. 'Not even any shouting,' she whispered.

'Good,' he said. 'Now. Couple of invitations here. Cocktails with the Randalls next Saturday. Dinner with the Millets on Wednesday. This is the beginning, Roo. You are about to be caught in the social whirl of the Oporto British colony.'

XI

Teape went to the office the following day, and Ruth was left to her own devices. She spent a morning looking round the house, discovering boxrooms, cellars, spare bedrooms, stores. She sat down in the dining room and started making a list of all the things she wanted to do to the house. She decided to have the whole place redecorated in order to do away with the dark woodwork and the depressing green distemper on the walls. She had ideas about reducing the amount of furniture in the sitting room, and enlarging the French windows. She wanted new carpets, too, and new lampshades to replace the faded tasselled affairs that reminded her, oddly, of Mrs Merriman's room in Sussex Gardens.

Towards the end of the morning, Fay Remington called. She wore a twinset and was very brisk.

.'What do you think of this perfectly ghastly mansion?' she asked. 'I thought I'd better come round on your first day, because I knew that if I were faced with making a home in this place I would just want to sit down and cry.'

They discussed Ruth's ideas.

'My dear I can see you are exactly what Bobby needs. You must shake him out of his rut. He's been bumbling along in this house since his mother died, and Amália and Maria have let things slip. So if he objects to the changes you want to make, don't pay any attention. Just insist.'

She told Ruth how to establish her authority with the household staff: how to insist on the highest standards from the start. 'They expect it of you, dear, believe me. The Portuguese need to be told what to do. If you show them you don't know your own mind, they will take advantage immediately and lead you a real dance. So many of the British wives out here grumble about their maids, and they really only have themselves to blame. Mind you,' she added, 'if I were you, I'd try and talk Bobby into moving house. Leça is all very well, but it's so damp. Gaia is so much nicer.'

They had lunch together, and later Fay took Ruth out in her car to call on Fay's daughter, Madge Randall, who lived in Foz. Alice McNeill was there, and the four ladies had tea together.

They returned to the house in Leça via the Matosinhos market.

'I don't usually go to the market myself,' Fay explained, 'Because everything comes to the door. But it's useful to wander round occasionally. The Pg.s always like to feel that the Senhora takes an interest, and of course if you come down here you can compare prices and make sure the woman who brings vegetables to the door isn't diddling you.'

It was nearly five when they arrived back at the house. Ruth invited Fay in, but the latter decided it was time to get back. 'My sewing woman's visiting in half an hour, so I'll say goodbye for now.'

Ruth went into the house. Maria and Amália were talking loudly in the kitchen. She listened, reflecting not for the first time on the ugliness of the Portuguese language.

She went upstairs to the bedroom. As she entered, there was a moment of terror. There was a man in her room. He was crouching on the other side of the double bed.

100

It was Bobby. He pushed himself up from his knees, looking flushed. Then she saw, on the floor at his feet, the pages of the letter she had torn up the previous day. He had been piecing them together like a jigsaw puzzle.

'I don't think you should have done that,' she said.

He was immediately defensive. 'Oh? Why is that?'

'I'm sure I don't have to explain, Bobby.'

There was a long silence between them. When at last he spoke, his voice sounded oddly forced. 'Do you still love him as much as he obviously loves you?'

She shook her head.

'You can't trust yourself to speak, can you? Why don't you have the courage to admit the truth? Do you think I didn't see the look on your face when you came downstairs yesterday? Do you think I am a complete fool?'

He picked up some pieces of the letter. His voice cracked: 'A love that can never be broken . . . this – something or other – between us. Us!'

'I can't help what he wrote, Bobby. And I did explain. He made a mistake. He didn't realise I was getting married.'

'Maybe, maybe. But you made nothing of it. You deceived me. You sneaked away so that I would not see the real effect it would have on you.'

'I did not deceive you. And I did not sneak away. And – and what sort of trust have you displayed by grovelling about on the floor putting those bits of paper together?'

'All right, then,' he almost shouted. 'All right! What about last night? What about last night in bed? Do you think I wasn't aware – aware –'

He turned away, let drop the pieces of letter. They fluttered down to the floor.

'What have you done, Ruth? My God! What have you done?'

He stood with his back to her and stared out of the window, westward to the sea. A gust of wind rattled the sash window suddenly, and Ruth looked about her, hardly able to believe that all this was actually happening to her, that she was married to him and that there was no going back.

❦ 4 ❦

I

THE WOMEN WERE STANDING among the piles of crates, the ox carts, the barrels of salt. They were gutting fish, throwing them into boxes and salting them, layer on layer. Their hands and faces were red. They wore large oilskin aprons, and thick socks over woollen stockings. Some wore shawls and others straw hats over scarves that were tied under the chin. Many were in black: once a widow went into mourning, she was unlikely to come out of it. Indeed, widowhood came as a relief as often as not. It brought an end to childbirth and seeing the money wasted on drink. Black cotton was the cheapest material you could get in the market.

In the harbour, dories were ferrying the crews ashore from the line of trawlers that had anchored a hundred yards or so from the quayside. These trawlers had, for the most part, unloaded their catches and the weight of their nets made each heel over so that their sweeping counter sterns and upright funnels were at drunken angles with the horizontal.

On the dock side, a derrick unloaded sand from a lighter. As each load was hoisted, the engine wheezed and clanked, giving off a cloud of steam that drifted about in the still air.

The drizzle made the people's faces glisten and the wide flat stones of the fish market shine. The men and women involved in the buying and selling of fish shouted and laughed, screamed, cursed, argued and spat. They stood in little groups and quarrelled about selling prices. They picked up individual fishes, feeling them for fatness and weight. They brought out leather purses, made bargains, agreed prices.

Through this crowd, Natália made her way towards a group of women who were gutting fish. One of these women was the

102

Salsicha, and when she saw the girl, she stopped working and put her fat, red hands on her ample hips.

'Ah,' she sneered. 'The Senhora has come to visit us. And what can we do for the Senhora today, may I ask?'

The Salsicha and the women who worked with her knew what Natália wanted, for it was an unspoken agreement among them that the widows and orphans of fishermen should be given a few fishes from each catch. In this way the dependants received a form of pension. Indeed, this was Natália's only way of earning a living: she sold the few sardines she was given, and with the proceeds was able to buy the bread and potatoes and olive oil that were her staple diet.

But the Salsicha resented Natália. She resented her lithe figure, her dark eyes, her hair. She resented her youth and her innocence, her natural dignity and the sound of her voice calling '*Sardinias frescas!*' when she went selling in the street.

The girl stood among the crates and baskets of fish. 'I've come for my sardines,' she said.

'So she has, has she?' the Salsicha said. 'She's come for her sardines. And what right has the Senhora to any sardines, may I ask?'

The other women continued to work, throwing the fish into boxes, salting them, sorting them. They shot sidelong glances at Natália, listening to every word that was said but showing no sign of their thoughts or reactions.

Some of these women were old. Their faces were not red like that of the Salsicha but brown like walnuts with black wrinkles. The Salsicha's mother was one of these: it seemed unbelievable that such a frail, gaunt frame had once given birth to what was now such an immense mound of flesh. But old Izaura had been well covered herself, once. Then the years of hunger and struggle had pared away the excess weight until she was nothing more than a skeleton covered in stretched, withered skin. She had no teeth now: her mouth was a small hole, and wrinkles ran outward from it like the spokes of a wheel. She stood on tottery legs upon which hung baggy stockings; her knobbled fingers wielded the sharply-pointed gutting knife with a frightening dexterity.

Natália looked at the Salsicha, said nothing, waited. The

103

women worked on, flinging the gutted fish expertly into the crates.

The Salsicha pointed across the harbour at a trawler that lay high and dry on the sand below the breakwater.

'What about the *Novo Olho*? Hasn't she seen? Beached. Cracked open. And all because someone listened to this one's advice. And she comes round here every day asking for "her" sardines. Shall I tell her something? It's she should be giving us the fish, that's what.' She jerked her knife at Natália. 'Go! And take your premonitions with you.'

Natália stood her ground. 'I never caused that,' she said, indicating the *Novo Olho*. 'The gales last month did that.'

'I can't hear her,' the Salsicha said, 'and I'll not waste my latin on her. Let her go and beg on the streets. It's all she's fit for.'

The girl ignored this remark and bent to pick up a handful of sardines. 'I don't want many. I'll take these.'

But the Salsicha lifted her hand and brought it down with all her strength on the side of the girl's face. The Salsicha was a big woman, and strong. Natália fell on the flag stones. A crowd gathered. The Salsicha let fly a stream of abuse. She called her a whore, a stinking bed louse. She told her to go away and shit herself.

Natália picked herself up, her eyes blazing. She faced this woman and repeated once more, 'I've come for my sardines.'

Just when the Salsicha was about to go for her again, a voice said, 'Give the child her fish and be done with it.'

People turned to see who had dared to contradict the Salsicha. It was old Izaura. She came forward, picked up some sardines and handed them to Natália.

'Here, *menina*. Take them. Go on.'

The girl accepted the fish, and pushed her way through the crowd, walking quickly away among the lorries and oxcarts.

There was talk, and laughter. The crowd dispersed. Some were disappointed: a fight between women was always worth watching, and this one had petered out too quickly.

After Natália had gone, the women continued to gut and salt the fish, and now they talked among themselves in order to justify the Salsicha's outburst. They agreed that there was a

104

curse on Natália. It had been said, for instance, that she had been the cause of the wreck of the *Orania*, the British ship that had been rammed in the harbour entrance the previous December. Natália had been observed at the end of the breakwater when the collision had occurred. Further, she had recently had a brief friendship with a boy who worked in Francisco's garage. But the boy had lost his thumb when an engine swung as it was lifted out of a lorry.

So they talked and gossiped, and the innuendoes and superstitious rumours about Natália were embellished and enlarged.

The day wore on. The steam derrick hoisted load after load of dripping sand from the lighter. At midday, charcoal stoves were lit, and the smoke from grilling sardines billowed in the drizzle.

In the afternoon, there was a small accident. An ox cart backed into a high pile of empty crates. The pile toppled and crashed down. Such things happened every day: they were not a cause for exclamation.

But on this day, when the pile of crates fell, they knocked down an old woman. She lay on her back on the wet stone. Her eyes were open and her face without expression. Her dried up lips opened to reveal a black, toothless hole. She sucked in air twice, three times, and then stopped breathing. Her eyes remained open, and her knotted hand still clutched the gutting knife, which was spattered with blood and scales and guts.

Later, it was recalled that the old woman who died that afternoon had been the one who had insisted that Natália should be given her sardines.

II

The people who lived in the shanty town above Leixões harbour contended with rain and wind, leaking roofs and sodden clothes. In winter, life was an unending battle against

105

cold and fatigue and hunger. The children begged at back doors; women scavenged the litter heaps. The men hung about street corners waiting for work to come to them. And each winter took its toll of deaths, whether from hunger or tuberculosis, cold or sheer exhaustion.

A few families fared better than the rest: those that used prostitution to provide drink for the man and meat for the family. The little boys of eight and nine would go out into the town and make knowing, inviting signs to the men who walked aimlessly and alone. And the mothers and sisters lifted their skirts behind walls and, bending forward, allowed the local men or the visiting sailors to achieve a quick and shortlived relief. There was no fixed price. Sometimes they gave themselves free of charge, in the knowledge that their generosity might be repaid in some small way at a later date.

But the prosperity such families earned for themselves was a mixed blessing, for girls lost their looks and grew listless; complexions that were once fresh and rosy became sallow and pinched. Sores appeared on the lips; the genitals itched and oozed; mothers and wives that had once been loved and fondled became hags, raddled with unmentionable disease.

In the spring, the excavation work began. The port of Leixões was being enlarged, and an inner harbour built. Lorries and bulldozers arrived, and gangs of men with heavy spades. The waste ground where the poor lived became a focal point, and the people who lived in the little tin-roofed shacks and hovels benefited from the cigarette ends dropped and loaves left unfinished. Wine was sometimes found in a discarded bottle, or meat on a chicken leg.

The gang of men who drove the bulldozers were a cheerful lot. They drew good pay and enjoyed their food and drink. They went down to the *tasca* near the church and sat over tumblers of red wine, and sometimes there would be an impromptu party; the women present would be bought drinks; the blind man who played the accordion would be brought in from the street to give a tune and the people would dance, banging their heels in a rapid rhythm on the stone flags, linking arms and whirling each other round.

In the day time, when the drivers of the heavy vehicles

106

stopped to eat a loaf of bread with garlic sausage, and swill wine from a *garafão*, they discussed the merits of the local girls and boasted of their conquests.

Joaquim Carvalho had his eye on Natália. They all eyed her, but Joaquim in particular. Whenever he saw her walking back from the river with a basket of washing on her head he would shout '*Olá, menina!*' and grin at his mates, his round, red face flushed with desire. 'That's the one for me, boy,' he would say. 'She's the one. Take a good look at her. I'll have her one of these fine days, just wait.'

His friends laughed at him. 'You're all talk, boy. All talk, no action.'

'All in good time. I'll get my boots off with her. She'll get a taste of my *pirri-pirri*, that's certain.'

The more he talked, the more convinced he was that what he promised himself would come about. He was a small man, and given to talking a great deal. He acted the role of clown among his friends and regarded the conquest of women as the one worthwhile occupation in life. But women rarely took him seriously, and most of the conquests he boasted of were imaginary.

Natália was the best looking girl he had seen outside a picture magazine. She walked in a certain way that gave him dreams at night: her bottom stuck out in a manner that seemed to him a definite invitation. As one of the shack dwellers, she was clearly fair game for any man.

He sat on the high seat of his bulldozer one afternoon and smoked a *Provisório* while he watched Natália coming down the path to the settlement of huts.

'Here she is,' he said. 'My little lovely. Good afternoon, sweetheart. How goes it? How about a bit of you know what?'

'He wouldn't say that if she could hear,' one of the other men remarked. This was Ricardo, a tall, dour man from Bragança. 'Why don't you go along now, if you're so keen on her?'

Joaquim grinned, sucked hard at his cigarette. 'Give me the wine,' he said, and when the *garafão* was passed up to him, he held it over his shoulder to drink from it. He smacked his lips, breathed out. He never took his eyes off the girl on the other side of the valley.

107

'So what are you waiting for?' Ricardo said.

Another man said, 'Take her a bit of your cheese. They'll do anything for food, this lot. I had it the other day for a pork roll.'

Joaquim took another drink of wine. 'I wouldn't mind,' he said, half to himself.

'All talk, no action!'

'Like a bet?'

'What?'

'Packet of fags?'

'Done.'

Joaquim grinned, happy to be the centre of attention. He glanced round at his mates.

'Well – why aren't you on your way?'

He climbed down from his seat, and the others exchanged winks and glances. One said, 'How'll we know?'

Joaquim said, 'You'll know, all right. You can come and listen outside if you want.'

There was obscene laughter. Joaquim revelled in it. He cleared his nose and spat. He flung his cigarette in the churned clay, and started out across the valley towards the hut which Natália was about to enter.

The other men watched. Joaquim was reaching the shack now, and the girl, unaware of what was happening, had gone inside. When he reached the hut, he paused outside and turned to make sure his mates were watching. He placed his hand on his biceps and bent his arm, fist clenched, in an unmistakable gesture, and the group of men by the lorries and bulldozers laughed and cheered. And then he entered the hut.

Natália turned quickly when she heard the door open. She was seldom visited, and no man had been inside the hut since old Manoel had left to go on his last trip the previous autumn. And although she was now nearly six months pregnant, she still managed to conceal the fact.

'What do you want?' she said.

Joaquim looked her up and down. At close quarters she was perhaps a little less alluring. She was barefoot, and her clothes were in tatters. Her manner was hostile, suspicious.

He smiled, and the very nature of his smile put her more on her guard. 'You look hungry, *menina*,' he said.

108

She made no reply.

He went on: 'Know what I've just eaten? *Bacalhau*, potatoes and beans. With plenty of oil and bread. It was good, I can tell you.' He rubbed his well-filled stomach. 'When did you last have a meal like that, now? Can you remember?'

Natália could remember. Six, eight months ago, when the catches had been good, they had eaten meals like that.

'But for a man, a meal isn't complete,' Joaquim was saying. 'It's not complete without something else. You know what that is?'

He took a step towards her and stretched out his hand. He nodded and smiled, showing a row of teeth that were yellow and decayed. He took hold of her jersey, that had once belonged to the housekeeper of Padre Preto. At the same time, Natália pulled herself away from him and picked up a blackened cooking pot. She swung it at him, and a quantity of cold soup made from cabbage and potatoes slopped over his shoulder.

There was a moment of confrontation between them then, before Natália threw the entire contents of the cooking pot at him. The mess of it hit him full in the face. It was slimy down his neck and thick in his hair. Half blinded, he cowered back from the girl, and now she hit him with the empty pot, raining blows on his head and shoulders. He protected his face with his hands and backing out, tripped and stumbled as he crossed the entrance.

A shout of laughter went up from the men who were watching. Joaquim paid no attention to them. Still covered in the mess of cold *caldo verde* soup, he walked back to his bulldozer and climbed up into the seat. He started the engine, revved, and jerked it into gear.

The noise of the engine drowned out the sound of his mates, shouting at him to stop. He was capable of steering the bulldozer across the valley and up towards the hut, but he was out of control in every other way. His only thought was to strike back, to regain the face that he had lost. He drove directly towards the hut, paying no attention when the girl came out and stood in his path, so that she was forced to jump out of the way at the last second.

109

He pulled the lever to lower the scoop. It hit the shack square in the entrance, smashing the boxwood construction and crumpling the rusty corrugated iron. The little dwelling collapsed immediately and without slowing the bulldozer. Joaquim swung the wheel and headed down the hill. He lifted the scoop, and planks and pieces of roofing, a tangle of bedclothes, pots, pans, cardboard boxes and washed clothes were all strewn over the ground and crushed deep into the clay by the big wheels.

The others watched him as he parked the bulldozer. He switched off the engine and took a packet of cigarettes from his pocket.

'No bitch throws soup over me and gets away with it,' he said. His hands trembled as he struck match after match in order to light his cigarette. When it was alight, he looked round at the other men, but they avoided his glance.

Ricardo said, 'You shouldn't have done that, boy. She's only a kid.'

On the other side of the valley, Natália surveyed the wreckage, and began to hunt about for the articles she could salvage.

While she was doing this, a woman came down from one of the other shacks. She was followed by her children: three serious-faced infants, barefoot, with sores on their legs, and faces ingrained with dirt and snot. The smallest was on the brink of starvation. Its belly was grotesquely swollen and the umbilicus stuck out like a thumb.

The woman watched Natália and said, 'There's no use building up your place again. The man came from the *câmara* today. We've all got to move. This is going to be part of the new harbour.' She considered a moment, then added: 'Anyway, you'll be all right. Only got yourself to feed. And if I were you, I'd keep it that way.'

Natália nodded dumbly, and continued her search.

The drawing room in the Remingtons' house at Foz was large, but cleverly furnished to give a feeling of homeliness as well as luxury. Fay Remington was a collector of Portuguese antiques, pottery and *objects d'art*, and the room was large enough to accommodate these and some of her favourite oil paintings, icons and beautiful oak furniture.

The ladies had withdrawn from the dining room, leaving the men at the table over the port.

'A car!' Madge was saying, 'How exciting! What sort of car?'

'One of those little sit-up-and-beg Austins,' Ruth said. 'Bobby's giving it to me for my birthday.'

'But can you drive?' Alice asked. Alice was small, curly-haired and chirpy. Ruth had taken to her on their first meeting, and they were now close friends.

'I'm going to start lessons next week. In Oporto. Mr Pereira from the office is going to chaperone me.'

'You are brave,' Madge said. 'It took me ages to pluck up courage to drive in this country.'

'But I thought you were brought up here?'

'I was, but I learnt to drive in England.'

Joy Remington had overheard part of the conversation, and joined in. 'You'll be all right provided you regard every other road user as a complete fool,' she advised Ruth. 'It's a case of the quick and the dead. And another thing: if you see an accident, don't stop and offer assistance.'

'Why on earth not?'

'Well the police here are convinced that anyone fool enough to hang around at the scene of an accident must have caused it, and they bring charges accordingly.'

'It happened to us,' Alice confirmed. 'On our way up to Viana a couple of years ago. We saw a man lying at the side of the road, stopped, and found he'd been knocked off his bicycle. So we took him to the nearest hospital, and a week later a policeman came round with a summons for Ian to appear in court. We ended up having to pay two *contos* in hospital fees.'

'That's awful!'

111

'That's Portugal,' Joy corrected.

'So I suppose you'll be popping about all over the place now,' Madge said.

'I hope so. But I'd like to use the car to some good. All this terrible poverty one sees . . . I'm sure there must be ways in which one can help.'

'It's not easy,' said Madge.

'Surely it can't be that difficult! What about these children that beg in the streets?'

Joy said, 'Didn't you know? They're professionals. They don't keep the money you give them. They hand it over to some grey-faced man who stands in a doorway.'

'It's quite true,' Alice said. 'I've seen it happen.'

'Well what about making clothes for some of these poor little scraps you see wandering about half naked in Matosinhos?'

'Fine, provided you can guarantee their fathers won't sell the clothes to buy *bagaceira*.

Alice saw Ruth's questioning look. 'It's the spirit they make from the grape skins after the grapes have been trodden. Real firewater.'

'Aren't you all being rather defeatist?' Ruth said. 'I can't imagine it's as bad as you make out.'

Madge shook her head. 'My dear, there is nothing you can do. Really nothing. You just have to accept that this is the way things are.'

'Well what about a clinic? Surely we've got the skill to give basic medical assistance – '

But Joy was shaking her head. 'It's not as simple as that. You see – anyone who wants to practise medicine in this country has to pass the Portuguese medical exams. It means that the doctors and nurses have a sort of monopoly. And if anyone so much as catches a common cold within a year of your treating them, you'll get the blame.'

'And the bill,' Madge added.

'All right then. What about a soup kitchen?'

The others looked at each other. Alice said, 'I don't see why we shouldn't try that.'

'Would Bobby let you?' Madge asked.

'He'd jolly well better had!'

112

'You're a breath of fresh air!' Alice laughed. 'And if you decide to go ahead with your soup kitchen, you can count on me to come and help. I think it's a wonderful idea.'

The men were coming back from the dining room. They were full of Teape's Special Reserve, and Freddy Randall had been having an argument with Ian McNeil about Wellington's strategy during the peninsular wars.

'We've been hearing all about your new car,' Madge said to Teape.

'You have, have you?' Teape went to Ruth and put his arm round her. 'I hope you haven't been airing the state secrets, Roo?'

'My word, no! Perish the thought!'

'Look at them!' Freddy said. 'The bride and groom. What a damnably lucky fellow you are, Teape.'

Joy needed to change the subject. 'I've got a bone to pick with you, Freddy.'

'Oh?'

'You're on the committee at Espinho, aren't you?'

'For my golfing sins, yes.'

'Well. I was playing a twosome with Maisie Lowndes the other day and a gentlemen's foursome shouted "fore" at us and insisted on playing through. They were really very unpleasant about it.'

'How very unfortunate.'

'It was more than that. They said they had a right to play through. We told them that was utter rubbish, but they insisted. They said it was in the rules.'

'Ah. Of course they were right there. Who were they?'

'No names, no pack drill. But whoever heard of a twosome having to give way to a foursome?'

'But you were a ladies' twosome,' Teape said. 'That's why they had precedence. Isn't that so, Freddy?'

'Absolutely. Ladies play at Espinho as a privilege, not a right.'

'But that's ridiculous!' Ruth said.

'Not at all,' Freddy said. 'It's a gentleman's club. Simple as that.'

'So jolly bad luck and never mind, what?' Teape added.

'I think that's most unfair,' Ruth said. 'And ungentlemanly.'

'Oh – you just have to get used to it dear,' Fay Remington said from the other side of the room, 'The men are a law unto themselves. Just wait until the summer ball at the Factory House. The ladies aren't even allowed to use the main staircase! We have to go up the back way.'

'Well I'm not going up any back way,' Ruth said, and flushed.

Freddy Randall turned to Teape. 'I can see you're going to have to have a serious *tête-à-tête* with your good lady,' he said lightheartedly.

'That's right,' Teape said, and looked at Ruth. 'I shall have to teach you to walk to heel, dear.'

'You can go and jump in the fish pond first,' Ruth said.

'Women of Oporto – rally to the flag!' Madge laughed.

'Another blow for the emancipation of British womanhood!' Alice added.

'What a load of tommy rot!' Freddy said.

'Absolutely right!' Teape agreed, and they both laughed.

The maid came round with the coffee, and the evening continued. It was just another dinner party at which the same faces appeared, year after year. Ruth had lost count of the number of dinner parties, tea parties, tennis parties and beach picnics she had attended. She had made friends with several members of the Colony now, and knew that as the wife of a port wine shipper, she was being accepted as one of them. But she could not help feeling a little apart from them still. She was reluctant to identify herself with all the problems that took up so much of their conversations: the eternal comparisons of the quality of the maids and how much they should be paid, the almost obligatory admiration of newly acquired clothes and possessions, the whispered gossip about illicit affairs that were going on between shippers and the wives of other shippers; and, as a continual theme tune with an infinite number of variations, the steady flow of abuse and condescension that was poured upon the Portuguese behind their backs.

In the garden, the men relieved themselves into the shrubbery, clamping cigars between their teeth while buttoning their flies. Freddy Randall, Dodger Remington, Christopher

Millet, Hugh Blunden, Bobby Teape: they knew each other well, worked or competed with each other, had attended the Oporto British School together or at different times. Most of them were inter-related, for cousins had married cousins and brothers and sisters had married sisters and brothers. There were few families that could claim no link with the Remingtons or the Millets or the Randalls, for these three families had been breeding sons for the battlefields of Europe and Asia and Africa since the eighteenth century. They perpetuated among themselves a certain code of behaviour, a fixed set of desirable qualities. Was a fellow a useful cricketer? Did he play tennis? Was he a good shot? Could he ride a horse? Did he know how to behave? Could he take his drink? And what was he like as a taster? By such criteria was a man judged; these were the ingredients that were required to make a gentleman in the Oporto British colony.

The guests departed at eleven o'clock. Many went on foot or by tram, but this evening the Teapes travelled home in the new Austin 7 that had recently arrived from England.

'Bit of a tight squeeze!' Teape said as he fitted himself in behind the driving wheel.

The engine started on the first pull of the starter knob, and the gear shift made a reassuring clunk as he put the engine into first. There were shouted goodnights, and the Austin ground its way up the drive, its headlights illuminating the pine trees by the gate.

When they reached the Boa Vista, Teape manoeuvred the car off the cobbles and on to the tram lines, and the ride became considerably smoother. He switched off the engine, and they coasted all the way down the wide avenue to the round-about at Castelo de Queijo, the 'Cheese Castle', built as part of the coastal defences in the eighteenth century. Leaving the tramlines, the tyres rattled and bumped over the cobbles as they drove north to Leça da Palmeira.

'Let's stop by the sea!' Ruth said over the noise of the engine and the road.

'Not tonight! I'm for bed!'

They arrived at the gates and drove in. Ruth felt a twinge of disappointment. It was such a beautiful night: she had hardly

115

spoken to Bobby that day, and it would have been pleasant to share a few moments with him under the stars. She wished that he could just occasionally be a little more romantic.

When he came into the bedroom after his bath, she was brushing her hair at her dressing table.

'I was talking to Madge and Alice about trying to do something worthwhile in the village,' she said.

'Oh yes?'

'We thought we might start a soup kitchen.'

He was taking off his silk dressing gown and hanging it behind the door. He turned. 'A soup kitchen? What the dickens is a soup kitchen?'

'Just a little place where we can give the needy soup and bread. I don't think we could do it more than three times a week, but it would be something.'

'You mean a sort of charity thing.'

'Not a charity thing, no.' She smiled at him in the mirror. 'Just a common or garden soup kitchen.'

'With Alice McNeil. I suppose this was her bright idea, was it?'

'No. I thought of it. But I think she would be keen to help if I started it. I wondered if you could ask Pereira at the office if he could find a place for us.

'It's out of the question.'

She put her hairbrush down and turned to face him. 'Why?'

'I'm not having you dishing out soup in some grubby little charity joint in the backstreets of Matosinhos, Ruth.'

'I can hardly believe you mean that, Bobby.'

'Well I do, so you'd better get used to the fact.'

'You mean – you're forbidding me to do it?'

He smiled, but without humour. 'Put it like that – yes. I'm forbidding you.'

'But what am I to say to Alice McNeil? We discussed it. I never thought for one moment – '

'Perhaps you should have thought. You must remember that you are a member of the colony now. There are certain basic standards expected of you, unlike Alice McNeil.'

'But she's a member of the colony!'

'No she's not. Ian isn't a shipper. He has nothing to do with

116

the port wine trade. He sells insurance.'

'I – I really don't know what to say. You astound me.'

He laughed, relaxing. 'No need to say anything. No need to be astounded. Come to bed. Be a good Roo.'

She finished brushing her hair. The silence seemed to build and harden between them. Her mind was full of the injustice, the sheer pig-headedness of his attitude. But in spite of the lighthearted conversation that had taken place earlier that evening, she was by no means a supporter of the latest craze for women's emancipation. She believed that having promised to love, honour and obey her husband, she should do just that. So she swallowed her anger, got into bed with him, lay down beside him and reached out to him: she welcomed his masculine hardness against the softness of her breasts and would have been happy to give herself to him had he made an advance.

But he didn't, and after a while he turned over on his side to go to sleep.

There was a dog howling in the distance, and his mind was still full of the little duel he had had with Ruth. There was no doubt that he had taken the right line: no doubt of that whatsoever. And what he had said that evening at the Remingtons' had not been entirely a joke. Ruth did need bringing to heel. She was inclined to be wilful and had had things too much her own way. They'd patched up that business over the letter, of course. That had been a bad start, and he had resented her anger at what he considered to be thoroughly justified suspicion. And then there had been the tussle over the redecoration of the house. Perhaps he had given in to her too much over that. It had been she who had insisted on having the walls plain white, when he would have preferred blue. She had made the final choice of carpets in the sitting room, and that choice had been against his advice. Everybody said how well everything looked, of course, and he had to admit the colours she had chosen did go well together, and she may even have been right about having the walls white. But all the same, it was a question of attitude. He was the master of the household and she should damn well know it. Not a question of not loving her, no, not a question of that. Quite the reverse, in fact, for if he did not care for her he would not be so inclined to insist that

117

she recognise his authority. And she had gone too far over this soup kitchen business. She should not have presumed that he would approve. She should have asked him before discussing it with the McNeil woman. And he didn't like her seeing so much of the McNeils, either. Ian McNeil was a nice enough chap, but he wasn't colony, and nothing could change that.

He was becoming sleepy, but sleep would not come. He turned over, heard one o'clock strike downstairs. He turned over again.

Ruth said softly, 'Are you awake?'

He grunted.

'I can't sleep either.'

He grunted again.

She put the bedside light on and started untucking the mosquito net.

'What are you doing?'

'Feel like a little something,' she said.

He blinked in the electric light as she left the room and went downstairs. She came up again a few minutes later with a couple of home-made biscuits and an opened bottle of mineral water.

She offered him a biscuit. 'Like a nibble?'

'No thanks. That is – yes please.'

She perched on the side of the bed and took a drink of the mineral water straight from the bottle. 'No crumbs in the bed, mind,' she said, and handed him the bottle. 'Have a glog.'

'Thank you.'

'I'm – sorry about the soup kitchen,' she said.

'That's all right.'

'It's just that – well – I do so want to do something useful.'

'You are being useful. You're being my wife.'

'Yes. I know that, and it does come first. But it upsets me to see so much poverty and to do so little about it.'

He reached out and took her hand. He turned her engagement and wedding rings round and round. They were quiet for a while, but it was not an angry silence. When she had finished the mineral water, she went to the window. It was a hot June night. She could see the loom of the Boa Vista lighthouse flashing in the distance, and the only sound was the ringing note of a *grilo* in the garden. She turned.

'Shall I tell you something?'

'Please do.'

'Well, it's a little early to say definitely, but I think – in fact I'm nearly certain – that I'm going to have a baby.'

He reached out to her and she went back into bed. He held her in his arms and called her his darling beautiful Roo.

'Make love to me,' she whispered.

'Isn't it dangerous?'

'Of course not!'

He was getting a little better at it now, and managing to make it last longer. When they had finished, she lay in his arms, and for the first time they fell asleep like that, her head nestling against his shoulder.

When the cocks started crowing at four-thirty, Bobby Teape awoke and remembered, with pride, that he was to be a father. He lay on his back and watched the light creep into the sky and his imagination raced years ahead, planning games and hobbies and schools for his son. It had to be a son. He smiled to himself in the half light. He'll follow me into the wine trade, he thought. And one day I'll hand over the reins and he'll be head of the firm.

IV

It was summer again, and the beach at Leça was crowded every weekend. You could tell the English boys, because they were the ones who wore baggy trousers held up with school ties. The Portuguese youths wore swimsuits made by Jantzen. They flexed their bronzed bodies before the elder sisters of the English boys and made sure that when the elder sisters took a dip, they did also. They shouted to each other and played football ostentatiously, heading and kicking the ball expertly to each other for the benefit and wonderment of the young ladies, who pretended not to notice.

There were lines of beach tents along the shore, and each line belonged to a different bathing woman who hired out tents for a few *escudos* a day.

119

Some of the English had their own tents, and you could tell these, because they were the only ones facing the harbour mole rather than the sea. At a glance, it looked as though these tents were owned by people who wanted nothing to do with anyone else on the beach, but the real reason lay in the fact that their owners – the Millets, the Randalls and the Remingtons – preferred not to have sand perpetually blown into their eyes and into their food by the prevailing north wind.

Not all the English placed their tents thus, but on the other hand, the English certainly stuck together. Their line of tents was strictly British Territory; the games of beach tennis or cricket were played to British rules, and the sandcastles were of British design.

There were others who bathed, and these were the peasant families who came from inland. They had heard tell of the British custom of dipping themselves in the sea, and came for the beneficial effects this was believed to have on the constitution. The women, dressed in voluminous black skirts and chaste black bodices, would be led into the sea by their menfolk and – regardless of their bloodcurling screams – dipped backwards in the breakers. That done, the mothers would collect their infants and subject them to the same treatment.

Overseeing all these activities was the beach guard. He wore a grey uniform and carried a whistle. It was his duty to see that no one indulged in any form of impropriety or immodesty. Strict regulations as to the type of bathing costume to be worn were enforced: ladies were required to wear skirted costumes, and the public display of the male nipple was forbidden.

To the north of the lines of beach huts, there were others yet that spent their days on the beach and in the sea. But they were not on holiday, for these were the women and children who were employed in gathering seaweed. They used heavy wooden rakes, and carried the weed up the beach, placing it in piles above the high water mark, and it dried in the sun and was sold as a fertiliser.

Among these people was Natália. She had moved away from the Leça valley now, and had made herself a home in a little stone ruin she had found among the dunes, a hundred yards or so inland from the sea. She had joined the gang of women who gathered weed, because they did not know of her reputation. She worked every day, spending hours in the water, starting at dawn and finishing at dusk. In this way she managed to earn enough money to buy food to keep herself alive.

She was always hungry, however. She had never known such hunger before: as soon as the man who employed her gave her the few coppers she had slaved for that day, she would go into the village of Leça, buy the cheapest bread and gnaw her way through it ravenously.

But however hard she worked, it seemed that she never had enough of anything: never enough money, never enough food, never enough sleep, never enough warmth at night. It was as if she were on a treadmill that was going too fast for her: gradually she was slipping lower on the wheel. It was only a matter of time before she slipped off it altogether.

And then one afternoon in mid June, she collapsed under the weight of a load of weed. Her legs gave way beneath her. She sank to her knees in the burning sand, unable to go on. She wanted to be sick, retched, brought up a dribble of bile. Her head sang; the sky burst into fireworks when she opened her eyes.

People helped her up, relieved her of the hated wooden rake, the stinking weed. They told her to go home, get some rest. They asked her if she was all right now and she said yes, yes, she was all right.

She wandered off, dazed, among the stunted pines.

The people returned to their work. It was not entirely unknown for a person to collapse from exhaustion, and although Natália was no longer able to conceal the fact that she was pregnant, no one suspected that the birth was imminent. She would be all right, they told each other. And if she wasn't, who cared? There were plenty more who were only too willing to take her place.

V

The stars wheeled silently, imperceptibly. She lay in the little stone ruin which she had made her home, shivering at times, sweating at others, dreading always the moment when the next pain would come: a searing, splitting pain that made her mouth open in a silent scream to the heavens.

She was not ignorant at what to expect: she had often heard the women discussing their many experiences of childbirth, and had seen them fussing about, filling water pots, washing out rags when a delivery was due. She had even seen a new born baby wet from its mother's womb, the umbilical cord sticking out like a finger from the navel, tied off with a clean piece of cloth. Yes, she knew what to expect.

But she was afraid, nevertheless. She had asked no one for help, had told no one that her baby was due; now, she was frightened by the horrifying inevitability of what was happening to her.

Why had she not asked for help? Partly because there was no one at all whom she knew well enough or trusted sufficiently. But shame was at the heart of it: though she had never been instructed in the ethics of such matters, she knew that fathers should not beget children in their daughters' wombs, and as far as she knew, the old man who had shared her bed and had caused her to conceive had been her own father. Perhaps it was shame, too, that prevented her screaming aloud.

Another pain. Were they coming more frequently now? She could not be sure, but she thought so. To the north, she could see the pale fingers of light cast by the Boa Vista lighthouse as they circled silently in the darkness, and these, together with the slow movement of the stars she could see through the broken roof, gave her a primitive sense of time.

She had made her preparations. During the previous week, she had managed to gather together a little store of food and water to sustain her after the birth of the child. She had filled an earthenware pot with water, washed out a collection of rags, and sharpened her gutting knife on a boulder until the blade shone.

Yes, these pains were becoming more frequent. She tried,

after this latest one eased, to breathe more deeply and slowly. She lay and listened to her own breath, and the breath of the wind among the pines, whose roots clung to the sand like old fingers. She slipped in and out of a trance-like condition, half hypnotised by the circling bands of light, the sound of the sea and the murmur of a distant crane, unloading a ship in the harbour of Leixões.

But there was another sound, and she was suddenly alert, all her senses straining to identify what it was. At first, it sounded like a twig being rapidly scraped up and down against the wall: it was a rapid, almost breathless sound. And suddenly she recognised it for what it was: a dog, sniffing and panting.

Carefully, she reached for a large stone, picking it up soundlessly from the rubble of the wall which gave her shelter. She tensed, searching the darkness, trying to find a direction.

The dog panted, sniffed and panted again. She turned her head this way and that, unable to see it, but aware that it was close.

Again the sound of panting, and now it gave way to a brief whine, and the sound of a movement, somewhere over to her left. She threw the stone with all her strength, and there was an immediate scuffle and the dog – or whatever it was – ran off. She lay back, and was almost immediately engulfed in another pain.

How long would this go on? The slow movement of the night shadows and the gradual sliding away of the stars brought a feeling of indescribable timelessness. It was a sensation that was hers and hers alone: unshared, unspoken. Strange thoughts and memories drifted in and out of her consciousness: the single cry of a night bird became suddenly, in her mind, the shrieking of gulls in the harbour on that foggy morning when the *Novo Olho* had returned without old Manoel; the dark shapes of bushes and broken stone walls took on the form of a host of people, who seemed to be watching her silently.

Here was another pain. She arched her neck, gasped, whimpered, panted. And with this pain, she felt the waters break. This was something she had heard about, but which surprised her all the same. What had gone wrong? Was it

123

blood? She didn't know. All that she knew was that she was alone and that now, now that it was too late, she did not want to be alone. She wanted a voice to coax and comfort her, a hand to hold, someone to urge her on and encourage her in the way she had heard of when babies were born in the shanty town. She wanted – suddenly she saw in her mind's eye what she wanted: it was her own mother, the woman who had died giving birth to her, the woman whom Natália saw, in her mind's eye, as the kindest, gentlest and most wonderful woman who had ever lived.

She began to wonder if she would die, as her mother had died, and the thought of it made her even more afraid. What if the baby survived, but she did not? What if she died here, among these broken walls and hideous pines? What if that animal returned, that dog . . .

But here was a new pain, and now she recognised that what must happen would happen, and that each successive pain brought some sort of conclusion, whether it was a new life or a new death, a little closer.

Time passed. Surely it must be soon, now? She watched the moon's lip clear the broken wall, aware of the beginnings of a massive movement within her. It was a movement which she was half afraid to permit, but which she knew must be allowed to run its course: one that she could choose to accelerate but one that, if she delayed too long, would choose for her.

The pains became suddenly worse, and almost continuous: they came upon her like waves crashing upon a shore. They swept over her, great white-capped rollers of agony that took her with them, swept her on, until she knew that she could fight them no longer and that the time had come to go with them: to give her whole being up to what must take place, whatever that surrender might mean.

She screamed, for she no longer had control, nor did there seem any necessity for control. Her screams went unheard, but they served their purpose nevertheless. She screamed, panted, pushed, screamed and panted again.

The world – the universe – moved. It was happening, it was happening: he was coming out: the dome of his head was there, there in her hands: wet and smooth and moving on, on, outward.

124

And then, when this was happening, she saw the eyes in the darkness, eyes that glinted orange-red, that blinked independently. She struck out at them with her hand and felt saliva and warm fur. Her teeth bared in the darkness: she scrabbled for another stone, found one, lashed out. There was a sudden yelp, and the eyes were gone and something was plunging and rustling from her, through the brambles and the pines.

It was as if the baby had waited for her to deal with the threat before continuing its outward movement into the world, for now she was aware of the last massive contraction and this whole new life slithered out of her.

She was shaking uncontrollably now: bewildered, frightened, shocked. She lay back exhausted, panting, recovering her strength for the next stage. When it came, the relief of it was immense: she heard herself give a little laugh of hysteria and triumph. It was nearly over. All that had to be done now was to cut the cord.

Trembling, she felt for the knife which she had placed on a boulder near where she lay, along with the store of food. It was not there. She searched with her hand in the darkness, panic rising within her. She must find the knife: she must find it in order to cut the cord.

It must be there. She must have dislodged it when she threw the stone. Carefully, she felt with her hand in a series of widening circles, until she was rewarded by the feel of the cold blade. She took it in her hand: she was shaking with fatigue, and unsure now whether to cut the cord or to wait – and unsure also if she waited, what she should wait for.

She felt for the baby, discovered the thick lifestring. She could delay no longer: she put it between thumb and blade, and severed it.

Immediately, as the blood gushed out, she knew what she had done wrong. Sobbing and screaming with terror lest the baby die, she grasped the cord in her hand, squeezing it tight to stem the flow, throwing the knife away with her free hand and scrabbling for the rags that she had put by. She ripped cloth with her teeth, made strips, bound the cord tightly round and round, uttering little cries and prayers as she did so.

The bleeding stopped. At the same time, she heard what she

thought was the whining of the dog, but as she reached for another stone, she saw the dim outline of her baby, she saw his fists clenching and unclenching, and knew that he was alive. His eyes were tightly shut, but his mouth was open, and now he let out another cry.

For a moment, she didn't know what to do with him, but then, half sobbing, half laughing, realising that she was all that he needed, Natália took him as he was, wet and slippery in her arms, and wrapped him, and held him to her breast.

✧ 5 ✧

I

THE VINTAGE was over for another year and now, in the early part of November, there were a few days of clear blue skies without wind. This was known as the Summer of St Martino: a time when the city of Oporto seemed to pause for breath before facing the winter; when the swifts and house martins prepared to fly south. The first sweet chestnut vendors appeared on the streets now, and blue smoke from their ash-whitened ovens billowed about in the squares where the plane trees shed yellow leaves.

James Remington crossed the Douro from Vila Nova de Gaia by the lower bridge and made his way past the jumble of vegetable and fish stalls on the Cais de Ribeira. He wore a dark suit and carried a silver-topped walking stick. Leaving the riverside, he walked up the hill between yellow-walled slums where washing hung out of windows and the sewers ran in open gutters. He turned right when he reached the Rua dos Ingleses, and made his way unhurriedly towards the Factory House of the British Association.

Far from being any sort of factory, the Factory House in Oporto is the formal headquarters and meeting place for the members of the British port wine firms. Constructed largely of granite, and presenting a facade of arches and balconies, it is unmistakably British in its air of entire confidence in the permanence and stability of the port wine trade.

Remington entered the large and chilly vestibule and went up the massive stone staircase to the members' writing room, whose walls are lined with bound copies of *Punch*, *The Times* and other gentlemen's papers. Here, the members of the Factory were now assembling for the customary Wednesday lunch.

127

Hugh Blunden was there, and Freddy Randall, Johnny Millet, Bobby Teape – nearly all of the shippers in fact, for, with the vintage and the first weeks of the shooting season over, most had returned to Oporto to catch up on work in their various offices.

The air was thick – not with cigarette smoke, for smoking was banned until after two o'clock – but with conversations about the prices and quality of grapes, the latest jokes, anecdotes, rumours. The atmosphere was one of restrained bonhomie: they sipped their glasses of white port, rolled it round their tongues, mentally comparing it with their own products. They taunted and ribbed each other with well known standing jokes: they called each other 'my dear fellow', 'old chap' and 'old boy', each vying with the next man to appear more relaxed, more urbane, more knowledgeable, more British.

Lunch was laid out on a sideboard in the dining room, and the shippers helped themselves, uninterrupted by the attentions of waiters: a custom which allowed them to talk freely, and one which served to enhance the exclusive reputation of the Wednesday lunch.

Bobby Teape was with Hugh Blunden and Freddy Randall, and the other director of Brotherton's, Johnny Millet, had joined them. Remington sat near them, but was not part of their conversation. He was not of their generation, and had long since stopped trying to keep up with their particular form of public school banter. He listened to their conversation, enjoying it and yet not taking part.

'The fellow's a showman, that's all,' Randall was saying. Randall was always the one who was in the know. He had a knack of reading the right newspapers, retaining the pertinent facts. 'He knows what the people want to be told, and he says it.'

'Shouts it at the top of his voice, more like,' Teape said.

'Maybe so,' Randall replied. 'But he's certainly putting the country on its feet.'

Blunden turned his lethargic blue eyes on Randall. 'But, my dear boy, at what cost? The fellow's a braggart and a bully if you ask me.'

'All I'm saying is, if Salazar can learn a few wrinkles from him on how to run a country, then it'll be no bad thing.'

'The quest – the question is,' Johnny Millet stammered, 'Does the fellow drink – drink port?'

Randall smiled. 'An ex-corporal? I doubt it.'

'Probably swills that revolting beer of theirs,' Blunden added.

'That's beer is it?' Teape put in, mock serious. 'I always thought it was Brotherton's Tawny.'

Freddy Randall turned to Millet. 'I have always had my doubts about young Teape, you know, Johnny. I mean if the fellow can't tell tawny port from German Pilsner – '

'Abso – absolutely!'

They chuckled and took their plates to the sideboard to replenish them with veal in wine sauce, oily rice and fresh salad.

After the meal, the port was passed. The large, cut glass decanters proceeded slowly in a clockwise direction (providing you were not viewing them from under the table) and the members were invited by the honorary treasurer to name the shipper and the year of the vintage.

Dodger Remington, sitting opposite Teape, sniffed deeply from his glass and recognised it without having to taste. But he had named the vintage correctly too often at the Wednesday *almoço* to be anxious to do so again. Rather, he was interested to see what the younger generation made of it.

Freddy Randall said, 'I think it may be one of ours.'

'Nineteen-oh-eight?' someone else suggested.

Blunden said, 'It hasn't the body of an oh-eight.'

Teape breathed in the aroma of the port. It was a good one: the rather cautious manner of the older shippers gave evidence to that. He took a sip, recognised it immediately and set the glass down on the polished table with a strange feeling of exaltation. Years before, as a child, he had found it difficult to believe that it could be possible to recognise a year or a blend and put a name to it. But it was possible, and when recognition came it was positive and unmistakable. This wine was, without doubt, the wine he had drunk on the evening of his thirtieth birthday, just over a year before, the day he had broken off his

129

engagement to Joy Remington.

'Teape's nineteen hundred,' he said.

'Absolutely right,' the honorary treasurer confirmed.

Remington smiled. 'Well done, Bobby.'

Teape laughed, pleased with himself. 'Takes a Teape to know a Teape!' he said. He turned to Freddy. 'What was that you were saying about German beer? Eh? What?' And he laughed again, triumphant.

Dodger Remington saw, and was pleased. Teape had never managed to guess the vintage at a Wednesday lunch before. This little success was good for his self-esteem and, what was more important, good for the reputation of the firm. For it was a curious thing that a wine shipper who was well thought of by the members of the Factory was unlikely to fail – rather in the same way that a prime minister needed to command the respect of the House of Commons before he could command respect in the country. Now that Teape had achieved this little breakthrough, he would be a better taster: he would have more confidence, would be more willing to experiment, less hesitant. It would have been easy to forestall him, and claim the accolade for himself. But Remington had remembered the advice of his cousin Rosalinde, and was quietly carrying it out.

Later that afternoon, Teape sat in the corner seat of a tram as it jerked and trundled its way along the coast towards Leça, his wide brimmed trilby hat tipped over his eyes, enjoying the semi-stupor that his lunch and wine had induced.

He was still pleased with himself for guessing the year of the vintage. Remington should have known it of course. Remington was regarded by some as the best taster in the port wine trade and he had succeeded in chipping that reputation.

The afternoon sun sparkled on the surface of the sea and slanted across the wooden tram seats. Teape felt unusually content with life, and when the tram eventually jerked to a halt at the Leça terminus, he alighted and walked off towards the Rua Ferreira whistling tunelessly to himself and wondering what was for tea.

The sound of the baby crying reached him before he opened the gate. He went up the steps to the front door, threw his hat at the hat stand, missed, picked it up and shouted, 'Hallo! I'm back!'

There was no answer. The sound of the baby crying came from the cellars. He frowned, went to the steps leading down, and as he did so met Ruth coming up. She was wearing her Medical Mission apron, and her hair was tied in a scarf. She was a little flushed and carried a basin.

'What the devil's going on?' he asked.

She kissed him. 'Sorry about this, darling. Tea's in the sitting room. I'll just go and tidy up, then I'll explain all about everything.'

She went on upstairs. He entered the sitting room and helped himself to tea from the trolley. While he was doing so, he saw a registered letter on the desk for him. It was from the family solicitor in England, and when he opened it he found that his mother's probate was at last settled. He was still looking at the list of securities that had been made over to his name when Ruth joined him.

He looked up. 'Have we started a nursery or something?'

'Not exactly. But I think I've found a new maid.'

'I thought we were going to take on Amália's niece?'

'Yes, we were, but this one – ' She stopped. 'Promise not to get angry with me?'

He stirred his tea. 'That depends, doesn't it?'

'You remember the girl I told you about? The one who was coming to the door for food a few weeks ago?'

'You haven't gone and taken her in, have you?'

'Don't get cross, Bobby. I haven't had a chance to explain yet. She came to the back door this morning with her baby.'

'So you have! Oh my God!'

Ruth was suddenly angry. 'Will you please let me explain!'

'Tell me the worst, then.'

'She came with her baby and asked me to look at him. She was frightened – he had a fever of some sort. Well – you would not believe the state that child was in. I took him up to the bathroom and undressed him. It was quite horrible. Stank of urine. Covered in sores. Dirt – dirt ingrained in every crease of skin – round his elbows, his armpits, his neck, his bottom, behind his knees – ' She broke off, shook her head. 'It made me weep. And I discovered the cause of the fever. Ticks. I found eight of them on him. Eight. I've spent most of the afternoon cleaning him up.'

'And you've invited the girl to stay on as the new maid, is that it?'

'No, I haven't said anything to her about being a maid.'

'Yet.'

'Not yet. But I don't see why I shouldn't train her. I'm sure she'd be only too willing – '

'Of that I have no doubt.'

'I can help to bring the child up – '

'Which is probably exactly what she hopes.'

'Well why shouldn't she hope, Bobby? Why shouldn't she? And why shouldn't we make the effort, just for once, and offer her a little Christian charity?'

'There's a difference between Christian charity and downright stupidity.' He snorted and shook his head impatiently. 'You're so innocent. You can't see the risks involved, can you?'

'Wouldn't it be worth a small risk, don't you think? Wouldn't the fact that we – you and I – were doing something to help these people rather than take a quick profit from them – wouldn't that outweigh the risks? Why is it – why do we have to treat them like – like an inferior breed?'

He laughed. 'Because they are, that's why.' He took two scones from the trolley and ate them at the same time.

She pushed a strand of hair back, watching him as if he were a total stranger. Then she continued, quieter and more controlled now: 'Don't you understand that I need to do something like this, Bobby? Can't you see that if I have to spend my whole life making small talk at lunch parties, playing golf at Espinho without doing something . . . something worthwhile, something to help, I shall become, well – not only dull and frustrated but unhappy. Bitter. Do you want that?'

He swallowed a gulp of tea. 'There are ways and ways, Ruth. Ways and ways.'

132

'That doesn't mean anything. What is it – I suppose you think this child is too poor, do you? Or perhaps a little too close to death. You're afraid it might die on you, is that it?'

He turned back to face her, searching out a piece of scone from a back tooth with his tongue. 'If you want to have a foster child, there are orphanages. Genuine cases of need. This child, well, for all we know she may be a confidence trickster.'

The words hit her: she remembered Suzy's prejudice against Peter Merriman, and her almost identical words of caution.

'If you remember,' she said, 'On the very first day that I arrived in this house, you told me that as far as you were concerned, the running of the household and the staff was my affair. This girl – she may well prove ideal. She's young, not unintelligent, willing. You said yourself that it would be a good idea if I trained up a new maid before I had the baby.'

'Maybe, maybe. But not if it means I'm taken to court for abducting a minor.'

'I'm not abducting her.'

'Her parents could accuse you of doing so.'

'She doesn't have parents. Or relations for that matter.'

'Or so she says.'

'Why must you be so distrustful of her?'

'My dear Ruth, you haven't lived in this country very long. It's a sad truth that you simply have to regard everyone as a scoundrel until he or she proves otherwise. And you forget that I, ultimately, have to be responsible for the decisions you take. I carry the can if things go wrong.'

'I understand that. But do credit me with a little common-sense. I got Maria to talk to this girl and find out about her. Apparently she used to come selling fish at the door not so long ago. She's not unknown round here.'

He stared at her. 'She's a fish girl?'

'Yes. What difference – '

'Where is she?'

'I've put them down in the servant's room in the basement. There's a tap and a basin down there, and she'll have a little privacy.'

He was already moving towards the door, putting his teacup and saucer down. 'I want to see her. Now.'

'Darling, I've just settled them. Can't you wait until tomorrow?'

He ignored her, going out into the hall. She went after him, put her hand on his arm. 'Let me go first. I don't want to frighten her. Or wake the baby.'

She lit a lantern, and he followed her down the stone staircase to the cellars. She opened the door to the servant's room, and the yellow light spilled into the bare, whitewashed cell.

The girl was lying on the bed, her knees drawn right up to her chin. The baby was asleep in a cradle that had been made out of a fish basket placed on an orange box.

'I found the basket in the shed,' Ruth whispered. 'Isn't he sweet?'

But Bobby Teape was staring at the girl. She was not asleep: her eyelids were moving, as if she were deliberately keeping them shut. Then, for a brief moment, she opened them, and it seemed that she looked directly into his soul.

III

He turned abruptly, pushed past Ruth, his footsteps ringing on the stone steps as he went up to the hall. He continued upstairs to his dressing room.

When she entered, his back was to the door and he was staring out of the window.

He didn't turn. 'She can stay until the baby's better,' he said, 'and then she must go.'

'Why?'

'I've already told you why.'

After a long silence, she asked: 'When I told you she was the fish girl, why did you immediately want to see her?'

He looked round. His mouth went into a strange shape, and he eyed her as if wondering how much she could be trusted.

'I didn't want to tell you this,' he said, 'but I feel I must.' He took a deep breath. 'She's a child prostitute.'

134

'How do you know?'

He laughed awkwardly. 'You forget I've been living here for some years. Walking about in Leça and Matosinhos. You get to know faces. I've seen her soliciting. Now she's landed herself in trouble and she comes along to the first kind face to ask for a home. And of course she's found one in you.'

'I'm not ashamed of that.'

'Not a question of being ashamed, Ruth. Simple case of making a mistake, that's all.'

'But I don't feel I have made a mistake. You didn't see her face when I gave her a glass of milk. The look of gratitude. The relief. And what if she is a child prostitute which, by the way, I doubt. What of it? Is that her fault? Is that a bar to her receiving help from us?'

He turned away. 'I am not having her in this house. That is final.'

She stood so quietly behind him that he became unsure whether she were still there. But eventually he heard a stifled sob, and when he looked round he saw that her face was covered in tears.

'Why do you have to be like this?' she wept. 'Why can't I be allowed to have her? Why? I thought you loved children, Bobby. I thought we were the same over this sort of thing. I remember watching you read to the children at the Laughtons – only last Christmas. I think that was when I began to love you. And now, when we have our first opportunity to do something positive, in the way I thought you would like – you just say "no". I don't understand. I thought you would be only too pleased. I even expected that it would be a happy surprise for you, that you would be as enthusiastic about the idea as I was. Am. And you – you just trample the whole thing into the ground. I feel suddenly that I don't really know you after all.'

He shook his head and grunted.

'Are you the same person I married? Are you?'

'Of course I am.'

'Well, why in pity's sake can't we take this girl in? Can you give me one good reason, Bobby? One single good –'

His fist crashed down on the chest of drawers. 'I have said no! Can you not understand? No! Now get out before I really lose my patience.'

135

Her eyes widened. She caught her breath, stood her ground. 'All right,' she said quietly. 'I'll get out. But understand this, Bobby. Your attitude has shocked me more than I can explain to you. And at this moment, I don't want to be in the same room as you. So I'll leave. Not because you tell me to go, but because I wish to go.'

He remained standing in the room for some time after she had gone and later, when he had bathed and changed, he went down to dinner, which they ate in total silence.

IV

The silence continued throughout the evening until they were about to put the light out, when Ruth said, 'Can we try to make it up before we go to sleep?'

This was one of her foibles. She had once quoted to him, after one of their lesser squabbles, 'Let not the sun go down upon thy wrath', and had insisted that they should always try to forgive each other before going to sleep.

He snorted. 'Nothing to make up as far as I'm concerned.'

'Then will you at least think about the possibility of keeping her?'

'I have already given my decision, Ruth. So I'd be grateful if you'd stop trying to get round me under the guise of making it up. Goodnight.'

He switched out the bedside light and turned on his side, away from her. Later, he felt the bed shaking gently as she sobbed to herself.

They didn't speak at breakfast, and when he came home after work, he went straight out with the dogs. It was dark when he returned, and he went up for his bath, deliberately spending a long time over it in order to avoid her company over their customary evening drink.

When they sat down to dinner and Maria had served the soup, Ruth said, 'This is ridiculous. We can't go on not talking like this.'

136

He shrugged.

She persevered. 'The baby's made an enormous improvement. Even in one day. I tried to find out a bit more about the girl. She's called Natália.'

'How extraordinarily interesting,' he said, not looking up from his plate.

'She's a strange child. She stares at me all the time, almost like a dog. She'll eat anything I put before her. Quite pathetic. I tried to find out how old the baby was, but she wouldn't say. Maybe she didn't understand my Portuguese.'

Maria removed the soup plates and withdrew into the kitchen.

'I went out and bought some clothes for her and the baby. I thought if we're going to put them out on the street again, at least I could make sure they would be reasonably warm.'

He said nothing.

'Do you object?'

'You don't give me much choice, do you?'

'I'll pay for the clothes and medicines out of my own savings,' she said. 'So that your capital won't be eroded.'

'Ah! So we're moving into the realms of sarcasm, are we?'

'At least it got a reaction out of you.'

He snorted with contempt. Maria served the main course, her dark eyes darting from Ruth to Teape, trying to divine the cause of the conflict.

After dinner, Teape sat in his arm chair and read a detective novel. Ruth settled down to embroider a baby's smock. It was to be for her own baby: as she worked at the cross-stitch, she glanced from time to time at Bobby.

'Why do you have to keep looking at me like that?' he asked eventually.

'Am I not even allowed to look at you, then?'

'Not in that holier-than-thou way.'

'I'm not being holier-than-thou. I just hate this petty argument, that's all.'

'I'm not arguing.'

'Aren't you?'

'No. I'm reading a book.'

'Well can I ask just one favour of you?'

'What?'

'I've been trying to find out from Natália who the father of her baby is.'

His eyes narrowed. 'Do we need to know that?'

'Darling of course we do! We might be able to get some sort of maintenance out of him.'

'We're not in England, you know. She probably doesn't even know herself.'

'Oh she does. I'm sure of it. But she won't say. At least, she won't tell me. I wondered if you could ask her. You know what my Portuguese is like. You'd be able to explain why we wanted to know.'

'I've no desire to quiz her, thank you.' He returned to his book.

Ruth watched him for a while. There were times when he could be unbelievably pigheaded, and this was one of them. There was no point in opposing him. The only thing to do was to accept it with as good a grace as possible. But she could not withold a small sigh of resignation.

'Never mind,' she said. 'Doctor Rebelo's coming to see me tomorrow. I'll get him to have a word with her.'

Teape continued to look at the open book on his lap for some minutes, but he read not a word. He closed the book, stood up, went to the french window.

'How old would you say the baby was?'

She looked up. 'I tried to find out, but she seems very vague about even that. I wouldn't say much more than three or four months.'

He parted the curtains and saw only the reflection of himself in the dark window. Three months . . . that would mean to say that the baby would have been born in August. And nine months back from August was November. He remembered the look of hatred upon her face, that late afternoon a year before. Had she come back deliberately? Had she planted those ticks on the baby to give it tick fever, so that she would have an excuse to appeal to Ruth's better nature? What would she say to Doctor Rebelo tomorrow?

He turned. Ruth was still sewing. He watched her for several seconds. She was wearing a brown dress that she had had before they were married. She was careful with her clothes, careful with the housekeeping money. She tried hard to be good to him, to apologise if ever she felt she was in the wrong.

'Look,' he said, 'Don't bother Doctor Rebelo with it. I don't mind seeing the girl. I'll have a word with her.'

She looked up, immediately ready to forgive. 'Darling, will you?'

'Perhaps I've been a bit – well – hasty over this business.'

She reached out her hand to him, and he went over to her chair and took it.

'You're a funny old Tigger,' she said. 'You love changing your mind, don't you?'

'Do I?'

'Of course you do. You're always saying "no, thank you" and then turning it into "yes, please".'

'I haven't said she can stay.'

'But you will think about it.'

He frowned. 'We'll see.'

'And will you ask her about everything tomorrow?'

He cleared his throat, looked away. 'Rather do it now. Get it over with.'

'Shall I come down with you?'

'No. No, I'd rather see her here. Alone. She's more likely to open up to one person than two.'

'Yes, you're probably right. It'll be less embarrassing for her.' She began to put her sewing things away. 'I'll go and fetch her.'

She stood up, but before going to the door she went to him and took his hands. 'Thank you, darling,' she said. 'I appreciate this.'

When she was out of the room, he poured himself another glass of tawny and sat down again in his armchair. He twirled the glass absently, holding it up to the light of the standard lamp. It was very difficult to know what was the right thing to do: what would cause him the least pain in the future. He had acted foolishly and wrongly a year ago, he admitted that to himself. Perhaps he was being offered, in some strange way, a means of making amends.

His thoughts were interrupted when they came to the door

and Ruth said, 'Here's Natália, Bobby.'

He turned, and Ruth gave him a private smile before she withdrew and closed the door.

The girl stood with her hands at her sides, but defensively, as if at any moment he might lunge at her. She wore a long skirt that nearly reached the floor, and a knitted jersey whose sleeves came down below her wrists. She was thin: dangerously thin, and there was a wary, gaunt look in her eyes that held a mixture of fear and distrust.

He beckoned. '*Venha*,' he said. 'Come.'

She took a couple of steps closer. They faced each other. He put the glass of tawny port down on the table by his chair.

'How – how is the baby?' he said at last.

She stared back at him, wordless, challenging. Could he see a meaning in that stare? It was almost as if she was the interviewer and he the interviewed.

'The lady of the house has told me that she would like to employ you here. Would you like that?'

She nodded, and whispered a barely audible assent.

He tapped his knee with his fingers, shot a glance at her, looked away again. If only he could know – positively – what sort of game she was playing: whether she had come to the house by accident or by design.

'Do you have a home?'

She shook her head.

'Father? Mother? Relations?'

Again, she shook her head.

'Your name is Natália, is that right?'

'*Sim*, Senhor.'

He stood up. He was very much taller and heavier than she. He did not want to frighten her, but on the other hand he was determined to instil respect. He looked down at her and she looked back, her eyes steady but still wide with fear. He walked away, stood at the window, parted the curtain. For the second time that evening, he came face to face with his own reflection.

He turned. 'Very well. Listen carefully, Natália. I will give my permission for you to be employed in this house – '

Her eyes widened further.

140

'– on one condition,' he went on. 'You must swear never – never –' He broke off, wiped the beads of sweat from his upper lip with the knuckle of his forefinger. 'You must swear never to tell what happened. Do you understand?'

'I understand.'

'Swear, then.'

'I swear.'

'Make the sign of the cross.'

She hesitated, then crossed herself, her dark eyes never for one moment wavering from his.

He relaxed a little, nodding more to himself than to her. 'Good. Now then, Natália, who – who is the father of your child?'

Her eyes darted sideways. This was the question she had always dreaded, the question she had known all along that she would one day have to answer. The Englishman looked down at her, his eyes very blue and his face fiery and red.

'I don't know his name,' she replied. 'I think he was a trawlerman.'

He felt a surge of relief. She knew which side her bread was buttered, this girl. She was going to co-operate.

'Has the birth been registered?'

'No, Senhor.'

'There'll be a fine to pay. He's more than a month old, isn't he?'

She nodded.

'Well then. We shall pay that for you. And when they ask you who the father is, you just tell them what you've told me, right? They'll register the father as *inconhecido*, that's the normal way of it.'

She glanced about the room, marvelling at the luxury, the oil paintings in gold frames, the polished writing desk, the Globe Vernica book case full of leather bound volumes, the crystal decanters in their silver coasters on the sideboard.

'Very well,' he was saying, 'I shall tell the lady of the house that you may be employed here. But if ever you say one single word about – about what you know – I'll turn you out on the street in disgrace. Understand?'

'I understand well, Senhor.'

'Good. So. Go to your room. Go.'

She went to the door and tried to open it, but was unused to doing such a thing. She pushed at the knob instead of turning it, and he had to do it for her. For a moment, they were side by side again, and he was conscious of her as a girl: her eyes looked up at him, eyes that held a strange quality of wariness, suspicion and perhaps – though he could not tell – hatred. He opened the door and she went out into the hall, collecting the lamp to go back to the cellars.

After she had gone, he stood in the middle of the room and wondered if he had done the right thing. Perhaps he should have stuck to his guns and refused to have her in the house. But what if she had told the truth to Doctor Rebelo? What if Ruth had found out? Was his marriage – his whole life – worth such a risk? There had been no alternative, no alternative at all. And perhaps, as he had thought earlier, this might be a way of making amends.

He joined Ruth in the bedroom. She was already in her dressing gown.

'Well?' she asked. 'Did you find anything out?'

'Not very much. She thinks it was a fisherman, but she doesn't know his name.'

'How terrible!'

'Can't say I'm surprised.'

'I should have her examined, I suppose.'

'Examined?'

'Medically. She may well have venereal disease.'

That shook him. 'I – hadn't thought of that.'

'We can't be too careful. If she is what you say she is –'

'I see what you mean. Yes.'

'I'll get Doctor Rebelo to do it tomorrow.'

He nodded, and started pulling off his tie.

'Did you say anything to her about staying on?'

'Yes,' he said gruffly. 'I told her I'd have a word with you.'

She came to him and put her arms round his waist. 'Darling! Thank you!'

'That's all right. Don't mention it.'

She kissed him. 'Funny old thing.' She put her hands up his back, inside his jacket. 'Come on. Bath and bed.'

142

Later, as he was dropping off to sleep, she said suddenly, 'By the way, I never asked you what that registered letter was you had from England.'

'It was mother's probate.'

'It's come through?'

'At long last.'

'Oh. Good.'

'Don't you want to know how much she left us?'

'Not unless you want to tell me.'

'Guess. No, don't guess, I'll tell you. Just over seven thousand.'

'Pounds?'

'Good Lord no! *Contos*. Multiply by twelve if you want it in pounds.'

After a silence, she said rather quietly, 'I'm not sure I want us to be as wealthy as that.'

He smiled in the darkness. 'You'll get used to it. We'll have herds of children and spend it on their education.'

'I'll concentrate on having Small first.'

He stroked her arm. 'How have you been? The last few days?'

'A bit queasy in the mornings. Not too bad.'

'I thought of a name for Small, by the way. If it's a boy.'

'Oh?'

'Edward. After the founder of the firm.'

'That's a coincidence.'

'Why?'

'Well when I went down to fetch Natália this evening, I asked her what she was going to call her baby. She told me. His name's Eduardo.'

V

The cellar room had no window, and there was no furniture except the trestle bed, the makeshift cradle and an old table. The baby awoke in the early hours of the morning. The noise of his crying echoed in the bare, yellow room. Natália tried to

143

feed him, but she had no milk, and this made him cry all the more.

She sat on the bed in the candlelight, looking down at the baby in her arms. The more he cried, the more she felt trapped and imprisoned in this bare room. She longed to be outside, under the stars again, but the thought of the cold and hunger of her previous existence prevented her from taking the child and leaving.

The door opened and the lady of the house entered, wearing a long pale blue dressing gown. She took the baby from Natália, comforting him in English, holding him over her shoulder, patting his back. She beckoned to Natália to follow her, and they went up to the kitchen, where Ruth warmed milk and put it in a bottle. She made the girl sit down in a cushioned wicker chair by the stove, and gave her the baby so that she could feed him from the bottle. She could not speak Portuguese well, and she communicated with sign language and single words. The baby stopped crying and sucked at the bottle, his eyes closed. Natália looked down at him and then up at Ruth.

She could not understand at first whether the lady was happy or upset. She was smiling, and yet there were tears in her eyes, tears that welled up and flowed down her face. She pointed to herself.

'I also,' she said in her strange Portuguese. 'I also will have a baby.'

Natália understood that, and they smiled to each other, aware suddenly of the bond between them.

The first grey light of morning filtered in through the window; they sat there, in the large, warm kitchen, and the baby sucked noisily at the bottle. When he had finished, Ruth demonstrated how to bring up his wind, and they exchanged a smile of triumph when Eduardo succeeded in producing a full-bodied burp. They went back to the cellar, and Ruth watched while the girl put the baby back in the cradle. He snuffled, found his thumb, sucked contentedly. The fever had gone from him already.

Ruth pointed to herself again. 'I am going to teach you,' she said. 'You will be a servant, but also a friend. I want only one thing of you, and that is the truth. You must always tell me the truth. You understand?'

144

Natália nodded.

'Whatever happens,' the lady repeated, 'you must always tell me the truth.'

The lady of the house left the room, and Natália continued to sit on the bed in the candlelight.

It was strange, she reflected, that the man had made her promise to withold the truth, and that the woman had insisted on the opposite. Both in their different ways had treated her as if she belonged to them. But she knew inwardly that this was not so, that she belonged only to herself, and that she would tell the truth or withhold it according to her own judgement rather than that of any other person.

VI

There was a great deal to learn. It was bewildering and amazing to Natália that the lady should take so much interest in her. She was shown how to bath and change the baby, how to warm the milk and test its temperature by allowing a little of it to drip on the wrist. She was taught how to make her bed every morning and to air the blankets.

She stood in her room while the sewing woman took measurements for her maid's outfit, and a week later it was delivered: a gingham dress in blue and white check, with a white apron. She looked at herself in the large oval mirror by the front door, amazed at her own image. When selling fish she had seen girls dressed similarly: they had come to the back doors to buy sardines from her, had handed money to her.

Amália set her to work in the kitchen. She scrubbed tables and floors, polished silver, peeled potatoes, gutted fish. And in this last at least she was already an expert: she knew how to take the bone out of a sole while leaving the fish virtually whole, and her skill in this respect won praise from Ruth.

After a few weeks, she was allowed to serve supper at the table for the first time. She had been taught how to serve the dishes from the left and to remove them from the right; to

145

whisper '*com licensa*' as she did so and to move quietly and calmly, speaking only if spoken to.

Nevertheless, she was extremely nervous on that first occasion, and her hands' shook as she put the plate of soup down before Teape. She never ceased to be impressed by the sheer size and redness of his face and the sound of his breath whistling among the hairs that grew in his nose. She no longer hated him, but instead treated him with caution. She had noticed that unlike the lady of the house, he never looked at her directly, and sometimes she wondered if he would ever again demand from her what he had demanded on that windswept beach. She knew that if he did so, she would break her promise to him and tell the lady what he had done to her. But Natália did not want that to happen; she was becoming increasingly devoted to Ruth, and regarded her more and more as the mother she had never known, the mother who had died giving birth to her.

The Teape household now ran smoothly. Maria overcame her initial jealousy of the new maid; Ruth's Portuguese improved rapidly as she spent more and more time teaching Natália, and Bobby Teape, seeing the happiness that the presence of Natália and her son brought to Ruth, decided that his decision to allow the girl to stay had been a right one.

In the country, too, things were apparently going smoothly. The streets were clean; the monopolies were beginning to show good profits; the churches were full, and the people of Portugal seemed to be accepting that the discipline Salazar was imposing was good and just, and that Portugal was once more on the road to the greatness she had once enjoyed.

But in exactly the same way that the Teape household contained within itself the seeds of disaster, so too were the seeds of revolution already being sewn in the New State. For Salazar – that introverted, sallow, political spider who sat in his study weaving intrigue – was a believer in the theory that democracy was the enemy of the state, the breeding ground of Communism. And to stamp out this evil, he reorganised his secret police force and invited experts from Nazi Germany to come to Portugal and advise on training techniques. Few people knew, in those early years, that the bull lash and

146

electric handcuff were being used to soften up the political detainees in the special cells of Caxias, Peniche and Aljube prisons. No one bothered to question why certain individuals 'fell out of the windows' of the police headquarters in Lisbon. Instead, there was a growing feeling of national pride: Portugal was at last beginning to prosper, and Salazar was being hailed as the saviour of his country.

The attitude to Portuguese politics among the members of the British colony was more or less uniform, and Bobby Teape provided a typical example of it. As far as he was concerned, Salazar could pass any damn law he liked, so long as it didn't interfere with the making of port wine and the shipping of it, at large profit, to various parts of the world.

The autumn rains started in late October that year, and apart from a few days' respite in early November, continued day after day, for several weeks. This was Ruth's first winter in Portugal, and she found herself longing for a crisp frosty morning to break the endless succession of days that started with the sound of water splashing down off the gutterless roofs.

Teape went down to Lisbon on business towards the end of November, and Ruth went into Oporto on the same day to do her Christmas shopping. She parked in the centre of the city and spent a long, wet day in search of presents which would have taken her a matter of half an hour or so to buy in a London store.

On the way home, she had a very minor accident with a taxi, which stopped abruptly in front of her. She skidded on the wet tram lines and dented one wing of the Austin. It was not a serious bump, but the taxi driver, seeing that she was a woman, decided to make a profit out of it. She stood in the rain and listened to the torrent of Portuguese which he poured out: a torrent which she eventually stopped by taking out her purse and asking him simply, 'How much do you want?' He accepted a figure which represented about three times the cost of the repair, and Ruth drove on to Leça.

When she arrived home, she discovered that she was bleeding. It was still raining, and she felt like screaming at it to stop. She was in pain, and she wanted to be in England. The

147

very sound of the maids talking in the kitchen set her on edge. She wanted to see the Yorkshire dales again, hear a thrush sing, feel the bite of an autumn morning on her cheek.

Instead, she went to bed and looked out of the window at the monkey puzzle and palm trees and listened to the rain.

When Teape arrived home two days later, he was met by Doctor Rebelo, a small, sympathetic man who wore horn-rimmed spectacles and highly polished shoes.

'I'm afraid your wife has suffered a miscarriage,' he said. 'There is no danger of haemorrhage as far as I can see, but she does need plenty of rest.'

The doctor left, and Teape went upstairs. He found Ruth sitting up in bed, looking pale and drawn.

'I met Rebelo on his way out,' he said. 'He told me.'

Her face crumpled, and she wept.

'I'm sorry darling,' she sobbed. 'So sorry.'

He shrugged. 'Can't be helped, can it? One of those things.' He sat on the bed and took her hand. 'Not the end of the world, you know.'

'I so wanted him, Bobby. For you. For both of us.'

He looked away from her, out of the window. It was still raining.

'I feel so useless,' she whispered. 'I feel I've failed you.'

He couldn't think of anything suitable to say to that, so he patted her hand and tried to cheer her up. 'Poor Roo,' he said. 'Never mind.'

She controlled her tears. He sat on the bed and held her hand. The rain eased for a few seconds and then came down again with renewed force.

'We'll try again,' she said. 'Won't we?'

'Of course we shall. Of course we shall.'

But nevertheless, he felt cheated. He thought of all the plans he had made. The unborn baby had become a person in his mind: he had imagined him as the eldest of several children, the renewal of the Teape family, his successor in the firm, his firstborn, his heir, his *son*.

Ruth was crying again. She was sobbing almost silently, her body shaking, her hand moist and cool in his. He wished she would stop: she only made matters worse by crying like this.

'Poor Roo,' he muttered. 'Poor Roo.'

He stood up eventually and excused himself to go and change.

'Bobby,' she said, when he was at the door.

'What?'

'Please don't blame me. It wasn't my fault.'

'Why should I blame you?' he asked. 'What a ridiculous thing to say!'

On the landing, he met Natália who was coming upstairs with a pile of freshly ironed laundry. She stepped aside for him and their eyes met. And it seemed to him, in that briefly exchanged glance that she was enjoying a small triumph at his expense: I have succeeded and your wife has failed, her look seemed to say.

He went quickly into his dressing room and covered his face with his hands, overcome suddenly and unexpectedly by emotions which he did not really understand.

❧ 6 ❧

I

THERE WAS A LAW that said you had to wear shoes. The poor people hated this law. Shoes were a luxury they could not afford. But they bought shoes – the cheapest – and only wore them when they had to. Sometimes they walked along barefoot, carrying their shoes. In the towns, they would occasionally wear only one shoe, carrying the other so that they could slip it on if they met a policeman.

It was not unusual therefore that Marta, as she walked inland from Matosinhos one morning, wore one clog and carried the other. But the sense of purpose with which she waddled along that day was unusual.

She had always been fat. When she was a girl, her father had called her his Pudding. Later, she was known to her friends as Bola, which was short for *bola de Berlim*, which meant doughnut.

But in those days when she was the Pudding or the Doughnut, she was a cheerful giggly lump who made up for her size by a certain willingness to grant favours to the boys. A young fisherman had made her pregnant in due course however, and her father had insisted that the boy – Carlos dos Santos –marry his daughter, the Pudding.

For a few years, the marriage was a success. Carlos withstood the jibes and winks of his friends, because Marta possessed two of the most essential qualities for the ideal wife: not only was she able to please him in bed, but also at the dinner table.

He called her his Salsicha, his Sausage.

When Carlos tired of her and started going with other women, the Salsicha became a changed person. She knew that her husband was having affairs, and she was powerless to stop him. She looked at the slender girls who caught his eye, and

150

became eaten up with jealousy: a jealousy for which she compensated by eating more and more. And when she heard the rumour that Laurinda, the wife of Manoel, was pregnant by Carlos, the Salsicha had felt compelled to take action.

That was sixteen years ago. Now, she was returning to the marshland for a different reason. For she had seen the girl Natália in the market the previous day, dressed as a maid and in the company of an English lady.

Marta did not enjoy the sensation of jealousy, but was driven by it. It was like an animal inside her, a force that acted independently, using her as a vehicle. She would have liked to be a friendly, lovable girl again. Part of her was that girl, even now. But another part acted because of this alien motivation that dwelt within her, of which she could not rid herself.

It took her nearly the whole morning to reach the swamp. When she arrived, she tucked her skirt up into the elastic of her knickers, revealing the immense thighs which had earned her the name her husband had given her.

She waded into the mud, and it oozed up between her toes. Bubbles rose round her as she went deeper; she searched the water among the reeds, bending and pouncing from time to time.

Eventually, she managed to catch a green frog as it swam desperately to escape her reddened hands. She held its legs fast and looked at it closely. The creature's bulbous eyes flitted left and right, and its heart pumped rapidly. She placed it in a square of cloth and tied up the corners so that it could not escape. She waded out of the reeds, untucked her skirt, picked up her clogs and set out on her return journey immediately.

When she arrived at the little stone bungalow close to the fishing harbour where she lived, she heated up some macaroni and potatoes for herself and ate a large plateful, with plenty of olive oil and some slices of blood sausage.

Then she got down to work. She took out a thick needle and some fishing twine. She threaded the needle, and making sure that the frog did not escape, carefully undid the cloth.

The reptile lay tense in her grasp. She took the needle and, ignoring its vain strugglings, inserted it through the lower lip. Its wide mouth distorted grotesquely as she did so, and she had

151

to tighten her hold on it in order to prevent it escaping. While the mouth was open, she put the needle through the top lip and drew the twine taut so that the mouth was pulled closed.

Once the first stitch was in, the rest was easy. She sewed up the mouth with six coarse stitches, knotting the twine to ensure that they would not come undone.

It was by now late afternoon. She pondered whether or not to break the legs, but decided not to. After all, she only wished this curse to bring poverty, unhappiness, bad luck. Death was not required, this time.

She put the frog back in the piece of cloth and set out once more, crossing the foot bridge into Leça and making her way up the Rua Ferreira.

When she reached the back gate of Number 154, she tossed the frog over, rang the bell, and hurried away down the road, her dress becoming caught between her fat thighs, which rubbed together as she waddled along.

II

Natália was ironing in the kitchen, using two flat irons which she heated on the stove, changing them round as the one in use cooled. Outside, on the back steps, Eduardo was playing by himself, making a careful pile of little stones that he gathered from the driveway.

Natália sang quietly to herself as she worked, folding shirts and handkerchiefs and pillow cases neatly, and piling them in the basket beside her. When the bell at the back gate rang, she stopped singing and listened. It was unusual for the bell to ring without warning, for the gate was normally used by tradespeople, and they announced their arrival with the customary street cry that served as their trademark and advertisement.

She put the iron down and went out of the kitchen. The dogs had started to bark when they heard the bell, and the black labrador called Minho was now making little charges at something on the ground, just inside the gate.

152

When Natália saw what it was, she turned back and ran inside, gathering up Eduardo in her arms. She went quickly into the sitting room where the Senhora was sitting at her desk, writing a letter.

Ruth looked up. Now that she had lived in Portugal three years, her Portuguese was becoming fluent. 'Whatever's the matter, Natália?'

The girl trembled, white-faced. The dogs barked and barked. '*Ai, minha Senhora!* She's just put a curse on me.'

'I've put a curse on you?' Ruth asked, understanding the use of the third person to mean herself, as was normally the case when a servant addressed her.

'No, not the Senhora. It's – somebody else – '

'I don't understand. Who?'

'Please come. Quickly.'

Ruth followed her through the hall and the kitchen, and descended the steps to the back gate. She silenced the dogs, then saw the frog.

'It's a frog, that's all,' she started, then caught her breath and drew back as she saw the stitches that had been put in its mouth.

Natália hung back, trembling and sobbing with fear.

'Don't touch it! It's a curse! It means death!'

'Don't talk nonsense. Bring me a pair of scissors. There's a pair on my dressing table. Off you go!'

Still holding Eduardo, as if to protect him from the evil, Natália hurried into the house and returned a minute later with the pair of nail scissors. She watched as her mistress carefully cut the stitches and removed the fishing twine.

'There we are,' Ruth said in English. 'The place for you is the pond, Mister Jeremy Fisher. You'll feel a lot happier there.' She carried the frog round the house and placed it on the stone surround of the goldfish pond. It sat for a moment, the pulse in its neck throbbing visibly, then leapt into the water and swam downwards, disappearing among the water lilies.

Natália looked at Ruth as if she had performed a miracle. She poured out her thanks, explaining that as Ruth had removed the stitches, the curse would no longer work and that the person who had done this thing to the frog would be the one to suffer.

153

'But whoever would want to place a curse on you?' Ruth asked.

'I know who it is,' Natália explained. 'There is a woman who hates me, a woman who would like to see me dead.'

'But why?'

Natália shook her head. 'I don't know why. She has always hated me. For as long as I can remember.' She smiled, and lowered Eduardo to the ground. 'But now this curse she has made will work against her, because you have undone it and the frog will be able to eat and live and take his revenge.'

Ruth was shocked. 'You mustn't think like that, Natália!'

'Why not?'

'You must never think of revenge. It doesn't work. It never works.'

Natália shrugged. The Senhora clearly knew little of such things, and it was pointless to argue with her.

'We shall see, Senhora. *Vamos a ver.*'

III

The *Paciência* left for the upper Douro from São Bento station, Oporto. The engine had a brass bell-topped funnel and the words 'MINHO E DOURO' were displayed in brass letters on either side of the boiler. It puffed its way through tunnels, over precarious bridges and under sheer faces of overhanging rock.

The line rarely left the course of the Douro: a river that now, in early October, was no more than a swiftly running stream but which, when the winter floods came, could be turned into a vicious brown sinew of water that carried all before it, including – in the worst years – the ships at anchor in the estuary.

The arrival of this train at each of the sleepy stations on its route towards the Spanish border was something of a social occasion, for in many cases the train was the only link villages had with the outside world. When the locals heard the wailing siren approaching along the valley, they would go to the

154

station in order to hear the latest news from down the line.

The crates of chickens and bags of seed were loaded and off-loaded; women in black came along with baskets upon their heads, and passengers boarded and alighted while the station master passed the time of day with the engine driver.

And while the train stood at each station, the heat of the sun that was trapped and reflected between the mountains shimmered over the soot-blackened roof and turned the passenger compartments into ovens, so that the sweat evaporated even as it formed.

After much talking and shouting and laughing between the people on the platform and those in the carriages, the station master blew on a shepherd's horn and the train pulled slowly away, the clouds of steam vanishing almost immediately in the bone-dry air.

As there were no ticket barriers at the stations, anyone could board the train without any official check as to whether he had paid for his journey. This made the presence of a ticket inspector essential on the *Paciência*. But because the train had no corridor, the inspector was required to be a nimble and athletic fellow, for instead of proceeding in a dignified and rather severe way along the train as is the way of most inspectors, he had to swing his way from door to door along the outside of the train, taking refuge in the carriages when it passed through tunnels or over bridges.

Suzy and Maurice Blakely were startled, as the train rattled along under a sheer piece of mountain, to see a sunburnt face at the window and, a moment later, to be asked for their tickets. Maurice produced them and, having punched them, the ticket inspector vanished as miraculously as he had appeared.

'You don't say *"gratias"*,' Suzy said. 'You say *"obrigado"*.'

'*Obligado*, then.'

'*Ob-ree-gaa-doo*. You have to roll the *r*s.'

'As we're only going to be in the country for another five days, I can't work up very much enthusiasm for a detailed knowledge of the language. They all sound as though they've got their mouths full of hot chestnuts when they talk, in any case.'

'That's a very poor attitude, Maurice. If you want to say thank you to them, you may as well learn to say it properly.'

'Yes, darling. Three bags full, darling.' Maurice looked at his watch. 'Would you say there was a remote chance of our actually arriving at our destination within the next – what shall we say – three or four hours?'

The train ambled its way inland. Towards evening, one and a half hours late, it at last pulled into Saborinho station, and the Blakelys alighted, stiff from their journey and dazed by the strangeness of this rugged mountain country.

They were met by Bobby, Ruth, three dogs and the maid. Suzy and Ruth had not seen each other since Ruth's wedding. They kissed warmly, and kissed again.

'Three and a half years!' Suzy said. 'Where has all that time gone?'

'You haven't changed a scrap!' Ruth laughed. 'You've no idea how good it is to see you!'

Suzy smiled, but inwardly wished that she could say the same, for Ruth had indeed changed: she had lost weight and looked tired. Suzy remembered that she had looked rather similar four years before, in the autumn before she went down with pneumonia.

Maurice and Bobby shook hands. Bobby was much the same, perhaps a little heavier, a little coarser. 'Don't carry those,' he said to Maurice. 'Let her do it. That's what she's for.' He indicated the maid, a girl of seventeen or so, barefoot, who wore a simple blue and white check dress. She smiled to Maurice and took the two cases from him, putting one on her head and carrying the other in her hand.

They followed her up the steep and dusty path, and the train continued on its journey, its siren echoing and re-echoing among the mountains. The path led past low whitewashed farm buildings to a large chalet, built on a spur of rock, which dominated the whole valley. Flying from two flag poles were the Portuguese and Union flags.

'Natália will show you your room,' Ruth said as they reached the top of the steps to a wide verandah. 'There's a jug of hot water for you, and make sure you close the windows before you light the lamps because otherwise you'll have a room full of mosquitoes.'

156

'And if you want a bath, help yourself to the Douro!' Bobby added.

When they had washed away the grime of their journey, the Blakelys came out on to the verandah, and the four sat beneath the vine trellis and watched the light of day fade behind the mountains. The silence was such that it was not necessary to speak as loudly as normal: indeed, the voices of women talking somewhere on the other side of the valley could be clearly heard.

They sipped their glasses of white port and ate roasted nuts and the soft, oily seeds of pine cones. A candle guttered on a low table, and a toddler ran out of the house and stood looking uncertainly up at Maurice, who sat in a wicker chair.

'Hullo!' he said. 'What's your name?'

'That's the maid's brat,' Bobby said.

'Eduardo,' Ruth explained. 'Natália's little boy.'

'Of course!' Suzy said. 'I remember your writing about him.'

Ruth beckoned to the child. '*Olá! Venha cá, menino!*'

Eduardo gave a seraphic smile and ran towards her. But he tripped on the hard stone flags and fell headlong. He lay on his front and yelled at the top of his voice. Natália came hurrying out of the house and scooped him up, full of apologies.

They went inside for dinner. They sat at a long table with a white cloth, and their shadows wavered in the lamp light. Natália waited upon them impeccably.

'How old is she?' Suzy asked when she was out of the room.

'We've never been able to find out,' Ruth replied. 'But she couldn't have been more than fourteen when she came to us.'

'I must say you've trained her remarkably well,' Maurice remarked.

'Hardly surprising,' Bobby said. He turned to Ruth. 'You've done little else, have you?'

'I'm sure that's not true!' Suzy put in quickly.

There was an awkward little pause.

Maurice said, 'You haven't started harvesting the grapes, then?'

Bobby shook his head. He was inclined to be abrupt when questioned about the making of port. 'Too early,' he said. 'We had a cool spell last month, and they're late.'

'So we might not see the *vindima* after all,' Suzy said.

'Depends how long you stay. I'd give it another five days at least.'

'How sickening. That's all we've got.'

'You can't hurry grapes.'

'No. Of course not.'

'How do you decide when to tread them?' Maurice asked.

'We wait till they're ripe,' Bobby said.

'Bobby!' Ruth exclaimed. 'It's not quite as simple as that! I mean – you have to agree a date with the farmers, don't you, and they always want to pick earlier than you do.'

Bobby turned to the other two. 'If there's anything you want to know about the vintage, just ask Ruth. She's quite the expert these days.'

'Well you're jolly lucky to have a wife who takes an interest,' Suzy said.

Ruth changed the subject. 'You must tell me all about your new house,' she said, and Suzy, taking the hint, talked about their recent move to the Hampstead Garden Suburb, and their eldest son's new school, Byron House, where a poet called John Betjeman had once been a pupil.

It was not an easy meal. The ladies stayed at the table for the port, and Teape had an argument with Maurice over the likelihood of war. Listening to her cousin, Suzy realised that something had gone seriously wrong between him and Ruth: he rarely missed an opportunity to make an obliquely wounding remark, and the buoyant good humour he once possessed now seemed to have turned into a slightly forced bonhomie. She wondered what could have happened. Ruth had never hinted at anything in her letters, but now there was a look in her eyes that almost pleaded for help, and Suzy decided, before she went to sleep that first night, to broach the subject at the first opportunity.

They were shown round the *quinta* the following morning. They walked down the hill to the long shed which contained the granite *lagares* where the grapes would be trodden and, on a lower level, the *armazém*, where the new wine was stored in barrels and where the raw must would be piped into a huge wooden cask, and mixed with brandy.

They emerged, blinking in the sunshine. Suzy looked up at the terraced mountains and said, 'There's a sort of feeling of anticipation, isn't there? Don't you feel it? It's so quiet!'

'It'll be noisy enough in a week's time,' Teape said.

'I suppose it will. Such a shame we'll miss it.'

Teape slapped his thigh. 'Well. Work to do.'

Ruth asked: 'You're going over to see Espírito Santo?'

'And a few others.'

'Wait a minute,' Maurice said. 'Espírito Santo. Isn't that the Holy Ghost?'

'It's a common name out here. Ayres Espírito Santo is one of the farmers who supplies me with grapes.'

'I thought you grew your own,' Maurice said, indicating the vine terraces with a sweep of the hand.

'We do, but we also buy in grapes from other farms.'

'So Teape's port isn't necessarily made from Teape's grapes?'

'Shhhh!' Ruth laughed. 'Trade secrets!'

'And you go and visit other farms, do you?' Maurice asked.

'That's right.'

'On foot?'

'Mule.'

'May I come with you?'

'You'll find it damned uncomfortable.'

'I don't mind that.'

'Well we shan't expect you back much before dinner,' Ruth said. She turned to Suzy. 'We could take a picnic down by the river, if you like.'

The men went off to the stables, and Ruth took Suzy back to the chalet to collect their lunch and swimming things. They walked down to the Douro together, and found a beach of pebbles and some smooth boulders which offered a little shade. Ruth spread out a *liteiro*, and they dabbled their toes in the brown water. She was much more relaxed than she had been the previous evening, and Suzy wondered if perhaps she and Bobby had simply had an off day or a petty argument. But then Ruth made a remark about the drawbacks of life in the Oporto British colony, and Suzy noticed the same look of pleading in her expression that she had seen the day before.

'Do you enjoy living out here?' she asked.

159

Ruth looked at the water rushing along at her feet. 'I like Portugal,' she said carefully, 'and I've nothing against the Portuguese, even if they are infuriatingly inefficient sometimes.'

'But are you happy?'

'Does it matter very much if I'm not?'

'It matters to me.'

'I think happiness is important, yes. But not essential. I think if you have something worthwhile to do, then it is more important to do that than to be happy. The question is, am I doing anything worthwhile?'

'And are you?'

'I'm not sure.'

They sat in silence for a while. A fish jumped. Suzy said: 'I know I'm Bobby's cousin and all that, but I'm also your friend. And I wouldn't be much of a friend if I couldn't see that something was wrong between the two of you.'

Ruth picked up a tiny pebble and threw it into the river. She wanted to talk, but it was difficult to start.

'There is something wrong, isn't there?'

'Yes. I suppose there is.'

'Would children have helped?'

Ruth nodded. 'It's strange how important it becomes. When both of you want a baby, and no baby comes. And especially – ' She stopped, frowning.

'Go on. Tell me.'

Ruth smiled. 'Are you sure you want to hear it all?'

'Of course I do.'

Far away down the valley, there was a distant explosion. A road was being blasted. The report echoed.

'He was wonderful, the first time. Very loving, very gentle. Forgiving. But looking back, it was his very forgiveness that was misplaced. As if it had been my fault that I had had a miscarriage. Then, when I lost the second one, I even felt guilty because a few days before I had been throwing a stick for the dogs, and that became the reason, and I was to blame again. Since we lost the third one – no, since *I* lost the third one – well, I feel I've failed him. He seems to have given up as far as I'm concerned. I'm a dead loss. I organise the house and help him entertain. Outwardly, we're an ideal couple. You know what Bobby's like with a couple of drinks inside him. The life and soul of the party. But when the guests have gone, it's a different story. We're like strangers.'

'But don't you try to discuss it?'

'I used to. But it's very difficult with Bobby, you know. I can never get him to come to grips with the fact that – well, we aren't as happy as we might be. He gets emotional very easily, and I think he's almost afraid of facing reality because he knows that it will hurt. So the result is, he pretends that things are better than they are. I want to help him – help both of us – but he keeps me at arm's length the whole time. And the absurd thing is, he can also be very jealous. He always has to know exactly where I'm going or where I've been as if I'm a sort of . . . child. And if I sit and talk to a man at a party, he's unable to believe that I'm not on the brink of an affair.'

'Would it help if I talked to him?'

'Don't you dare! He'd think I'd asked you to. Better to leave well alone.'

'But – these miscarriages. Have you seen a specialist?'

'Here in Portugal, yes. But they haven't been able to give a definite diagnosis.' Ruth laughed. 'Natália says I should eat more sardines.'

'Maurice says that it's sometimes possible for a woman to miscarry for psychological reasons.'

'I don't know about that. Though I could list a lot of little – factors. None of them very important, but they all add up.' She looked up the mountains. 'I think that's Maurice and Bobby,' she said, and pointed to two men on mules making their way slowly along the skyline.

They watched the two men for a few moments.

'Tell me about – what did you call them – the other factors.'

'I suppose it's the house, mainly. I've never felt at home in it. It's damp, and whatever I do, I always feel that his mother's looking over my shoulder to see that I'm doing it as she would have wished. And I know you'll think this is silly, but I've heard noises. Always when I'm alone. As if the bedroom furniture were being rearranged. I've told Bobby about it and he says he'll believe it when he sees the ghost holding its head under one arm. Typical Bobby, you know. But it doesn't help. I long to get out of that house, but he's completely set on staying. He likes his beach walks and hates change of any sort. If tea is ten minutes late he thinks the household organisation is on the verge of collapse. It's not even as if the house were a family seat or anything. It's only rented. We could up sticks and go any day we liked. But he says the rent is a bargain and we'd be lucky to get anything better. I'd like to build somewhere – or possibly renovate an old *quinta*. But no. So we stick at 154, Rua Ferreira and I expect we shall stay there for the rest of our lives.' Ruth smiled sadly. 'I hate criticising him like this. He's a dear in many ways, and I'm still sure we could be really happy together – even without children. But there has to be some give and take, doesn't there?' She relaxed a little. 'It's wonderful to be able to talk like this. I suppose I've been bottling it all up.'

'What about your friends out here? Don't you have anyone you can talk to?'

'There's Alice McNeil, who I told you about. I get on very well with her. But Bobby is convinced that her husband – Ian – has a soft spot for me, so I have to be very careful there. And the trouble with a small community like ours is that everyone gossips about everyone else, so unless you're prepared to join in, you can't make any sort of friendships. I go and play golf at Espinho with Alice McNeil and Madge Randall, and I sometimes play bridge at the Remingtons. But I don't really do so by choice. I don't think I'm a bridge and golf sort of person. But there's so little else to do. I hate the colony gossip, and I refuse to join in, so sometimes I feel a bit like a spy in their midst.'

'We have the same circuit in the Hampstead Garden Suburb. But at least in London there's a wider selection of people to choose from.'

'Sometimes I sit having tea with the Remingtons or the Randalls or the Millets and listen to the same old chit-chat about Mrs X's husband who's having an affair with a girl half his age and I want to scream! I suppose it was naïve of me not to realise that it would be like that in a small community. Do you know I discovered that a rumour went round that Bobby and I had to get married? Would you believe it?'

'You did marry rather quickly, Ruth.'

'Yes, we did. I suppose we were both in a hurry. Bobby had lost his mother and I – well, you know all about that.'

'Did you ever hear from Peter again?'

'No. No – never.' Ruth felt herself flush. She had never told anyone about the telegram and the letter from Peter, and this was the first time she had told a direct lie about it. She watched a line of bubbles tumbling about in the fast moving water. Perhaps Peter was at the bottom of it all. Perhaps that single factor had soured her whole marriage, had made Bobby continually jealous, always on guard, always possessive of her.

In the silence of the afternoon, sitting in the sunshine, the picnic basket tucked under a rock to keep cool, she found herself thinking about Peter all over again. Quite recently, she had had a dream about him: she had been sitting at her desk, reading that very last letter of his when she had suddenly become aware of him standing at the door. She wanted to turn and look at him, but had found herself unable to do so, as if she were held by some invisible vice. Now, she thought of him again, remembering their walk together through St James's park on the day he told her he was going to Malaya. She remembered him in her room in Highgate, his lips against hers.

She stared down at the river, and her eyes filled with tears.

'Are you very unhappy?' Suzy asked.

She took a breath. 'If only he could give me just a little of the tenderness, a little of the love, that I need. If only he could be the way he was before we were married.' She turned to Suzy and tried to smile. 'But it's no use saying "if only", is it? We have to make the best of what we've got.'

They collected the picnic things together and began walking back along the river path, eventually turning up the hill, over the railway and on up to the Quinta das Rosas. The path led between rows of vines from which hung heavy clusters of small, black grapes.

The men were already back when they arrived at the chalet. They were sitting in wicker chairs on the verandah, still hot and dusty from their mule ride.

'What's this?' Bobby roared goodnaturedly as the ladies

reached the top of the steps. 'Late for tea! Not good enough by
Jingo by Jimminy! Not good enough at all!'

IV

As the sun rose over the mountain, the skyline brightened
until the topmost crags and olive trees became for a moment
sharply outlined by slivers of brilliant light. This light bathed
the valley: it made every colour more brilliant; every vine and
wall and smooth river pebble was picked out by it, given its
own surreal shadow. And as the disc of the sun cleared the
mountain top, its heat could be felt immediately. The very
rocks seemed to brace themselves against it.

Teape, in grey flannels and aertex shirt, came thudding
down the path to the river. He peeled off his clothes, stood
massive and naked for a moment, then dived into one of the
deeper pools.

It was cold but not icy. He felt the stones of the river bed
brush his chest, then surfaced, striking out powerfully against
the stream. He swam with all his strength, just managing to
prevent himself being swept down, his head turning to one
side every fourth stroke in order to take a gulp of air.

He swam for a minute then left the water and towelled
himself dry: huge, naked, a little freckled and very hairy. He
gasped and grunted, pulled the shirt over his head and knotted
his old school tie round his waist to keep up his trousers.

When he had dressed, he chose a clear space on the bank and
did twenty press-ups in quick time. That done, he collected his
towel and returned up the path to the *quinta*.

It was the first day of the vintage, and the Blakelys were
returning to Oporto by train that day, on their way back to
England. He was glad they were going: the vintage was no
holiday, and he had never liked guests when there was so much
work to be done. On some *quintas*, ladies were not allowed at
all: this had been the case at the Quinta das Rosas until
Rosalinde Teape took over the reins and insisted on overseeing the vintage herself. Teape had a good mind to put the

164

clock back and reinstate that rule. Women asked damn stupid questions about the quality of the grapes and whether it would be a good year and at what stage you added the brandy. They seemed to regard it as a duty to ask as many questions as possible, as if they were on some sort of school outing and would be required to write a composition about it afterwards.

Perhaps it was the very simplicity of the process that made him reluctant to explain it. You hired a gang of women to pick the grapes, a gang of men to bring them down in baskets and an accordion player to keep the peasants happy. You threw the grapes into a stone tank and paid men and boys to walk up and down and play the fool all night, crushing them with their feet. Then you drained all the juice into a big barrel, put a bit of grape brandy with it, and hoped for the best.

You usually got it. Of course you could make the process sound as complicated as you liked by talking about sugar content and acidity and specific gravity. But port was basically what it had always been: the juice of Douro grapes whose fermentation has been stopped by the addition of grape brandy.

It was after the making of the wine that strange things began to happen to it. For a port, as he had so often explained to visitors to the wine lodge down at Vila Nova de Gaia, is in many ways like a human being. It likes to be handled gently, especially in its old age. Some wines – the vintage ports – are like geniuses: they need no blending, for they are excellent by nature. But some need to be mixed and educated by the taste of others. All of them will, at some stage of their lives, reach a peak, their high point of quality. Some reach it early, others late. In some, it will last but a year or two, and in others it will be maintained for decades. Some ports die young; others seem to last for ever. There are cheap ports that are like cheap people: they are bawdy and brash; their colour is not subtle and their taste is blatantly sweet. There are everyday ports, the professionals, who give good service, good value for money. And then there are ports which are great: ports for drinking only on special occasions, whose colour and aroma and taste defy any attempt at description because of their excellence.

Teape's thoughts ran along this analogy as he made his way

past the farm buildings, acknowledging the cries of 'good morning' from Bernadino the farm manager, and Ayres the old toothless muleteer.

He stopped on a spur of rock just below the verandah of the chalet, and looked out over the thousands of vines which stood like motionless battalions to his left and right.

My property, he thought. My *quinta*. My grapes. My wine.

He wondered about himself. Had he reached his own peak? A feeling of vague unrest and dissatisfaction had been troubling him for some time. He had wondered, on occasion, if making port wine was a good way to spend your life. For however much you praised a wine, however much you discussed it, revered it or paid for it, it remained, after all, only a drink. It was flushed through your system in exactly the same way as the cheapest beer. He remembered how his mother had once said that he would never succeed unless he had enthusiasm. Sometimes he had misgivings that perhaps he lacked sufficient enthusiasm for making port.

He sat down on a low wall, savouring the stillness of the morning. A donkey brayed on the other side of the valley, and the sound of it hung about between the mountains for some time. Voices in the far distance made him look round. A dozen or so women were making their way down the mountain towards the *quinta*, laughing and talking among themselves. They were the first of the pickers to arrive from neighbouring villages. The happy anticipation at the beginning of the vintage could be heard in their voices even at this distance.

He smiled to himself. This is why I make port, he thought. Not because all this belongs to me, but because I belong to all this. I am a part of it. I need these vines, these people, these old buildings more than they need me.

He was about to climb the steps to the chalet when he overheard Ruth's voice, above him.

'It's been wonderful,' she was saying, 'Just to be able to talk about it all. You've no idea how much better I feel for it.'

'I only wish I could do more,' he heard Suzy's voice reply. 'But do remember – if ever you need to get away, we'll be delighted to have you. Jump on a boat or a train and come over.'

166

Ruth laughed. 'I can just imagine what Bobby would have to say to that! He wouldn't hear of it!'

Suzy lowered her voice a little, but Teape could still hear the gist of what she said. 'You mustn't let him trample on you. Don't be a doormat. Dig your toes in now and again. You'd be surprised how effective it is.'

He remained stock still, hidden by the orange trees and shrubs that grew below the verandah. When he heard them go back into the chalet, he waited another minute and then, humming determinedly to announce his presence, made his way up the steps and into the breakfast room.

V

'It was not a happy fortnight,' Ruth wrote to Suzy after returning from the vintage. 'Bobby was not in the best of moods: the grapes were not good this year, and I think we are all becoming concerned about the situation in the world. But all the same, I do wish he could be just a little more sympathetic. There have been times recently when I have felt that he would be quite happy to see the back of me –'

She stopped writing, read what she had put, and tore up the page. She was about to put the pieces in the waste paper basket, but changed her mind. She was almost sure that Bobby looked at torn up letters, and she did not want to make matters worse between them by letting him decipher what she had just written and rejected. So she made a little pile of the torn up pieces on the flap of the desk.

She tried again, but found herself stuck for words. Her mind drifted: she sat listening to the rain and wind that buffeted the sash windows, looked out at the pine trees in the garden, bending before the gale that had been blowing for the past two days.

Life was becoming an unending fight against depression: a fight in which she felt completely alone. She had begun to wonder if she was suffering from some sort of neurosis: if

167

perhaps the sounds she had heard in the house, her feeling of unhappiness, her inability to elicit Bobby's affection – if all these were symptoms of something wrong in her emotional make-up. She had been troubled, too, by increasingly frequent memories of Peter Merriman. Often, before going to sleep, she would find herself thinking of him, wondering what had happened to him, where he was, what he was doing. Such thoughts troubled her and she tried to resist them: she was frightened that they constituted a form of infidelity and might themselves be cause for further unhappiness.

While she sat and wondered what to write in her letter to Suzy, the cook came to the door of the sitting room and knocked discreetly.

'Yes, Amália?'

Amália smiled as if she brought good news. 'Senhora – José has brought something he would like to show you. He is at the back door.'

Ruth followed the cook out of the sitting room, thinking to herself that here was something she could tell Suzy, for José had gouged a piece out of his forehead while chopping wood the previous week, and she had taken him to the hospital to have him patched up.

He was waiting at the kitchen door. He took off his cap to her, sweeping it low in a gesture of genuine respect, the three clumsy stitches revealed on his forehead.

He held up a small sack. 'A present for the Senhora,' he said.

'They are very good,' Amália added. 'I shall cook them in butter.'

'What are they?'

José gave her the sack, and as she accepted it she realised with horror that whatever it contained was alive.

The gardener and cook, expecting her pleasure and gratitude, were surprised by her reaction as she opened the sack.

It was full of birds. When she saw them, she looked away involuntarily, and gave a little sob of horror.

José looked puzzled. '*A Senhora não gosta?*'

She shook her head. 'No. It's very kind of you, José, but – no.'

'But Senhora,' Amália said, 'They are excellent to eat.

168

Senhor Teape likes them very much. His mother used to order them for special occasions. I cook them in white wine and butter and garlic, with a few mushrooms – '

But Ruth was already taking the sack into the drive, her hair being blown about by the wind, a flurry of drops falling from the trees. She upturned the sack and emptied it on to the wet gravel. The birds fluttered and flopped at her feet, some dead, some able to hop and beat their wings. She closed her eyes, turned away, ran into the house.

She stood in the sitting room holding on to the back of a chair so tightly that her knuckles were white. When she heard the tinkle of the tea trolley, she did not look round. She was not aware how long she stood there: time seemed to have no value.

Bobby arrived home. She heard him rev the car before switching off, march into the hall, up the stairs. When he came down, having changed into his comfortable clothes, she was standing by the french window, still gripping the back of a chair.

He helped himself from the trolley. He ate scones two at a time and washed them down with gulps of tea.

'What's up this time?' he asked eventually.

She gazed out of the window. 'I never knew you liked eating sparrows.'

He laughed. 'Ah! They arrived, did they? José told me he was going off trapping. They catch them on the rooftops in the city, you know.'

'It must be very dangerous work.'

He spread blackberry jam on a scone, bit into it and poured more tea. 'Sarcasm's not your strong point, Ruth. I'd steer clear if I were you.' He drank the tea in three gulps. 'Not having any tea?'

'No thank you.'

Even the sound of him eating, swallowing, was offensive to her. She willed him to hurry up, finish his tea, take the dogs out.

'So that's what it is this time, eh?' he said. 'You're upset because José has gone out of his way to get one of the local delicacies for you.'

169

How could she ever make him understand that it was more than simply the sight of those helpless, seething sparrows?

'Nobody cares, do they?' she said, turning to face him. 'They let children starve and the sick go uncared for. They kick dogs, beat horses and cook little sparrows in butter and white wine. Amália doesn't care. José doesn't care. You don't care. Do you?'

He shifted uncomfortably.

'Do you?' she repeated.

'For God's sake, Ruth! Stop making a mountain out of a molehill!'

She turned away from him again. The sash window rattled in a gust of wind.

'Look,' he said, 'Why don't you tell me what the trouble is, eh? Why don't we sort this out once and for all?'

When she spoke, it was as if from a great distance. 'I have told you over and over and over again what the trouble is. I have told you that I hate living in this house. I've tried and tried and tried to get just a little love, a little tenderness, a little affection out of you. I've tried to welcome you when you come home, talk to you, be friends with you. But I get nothing back. Nothing. Every afternoon you arrive home and stuff yourself with food and you look through me as if I don't even exist. Well I do exist. I'm Ruth. Remember? Ruth Wilmot.'

He made little grunting noises, shrugging with impatience. 'I can't for the life of me see why you're making such a fuss.'

'No,' she said, as much to herself as to him. 'I didn't think for a moment that you would.'

He slapped a fist into his palm. 'Well. Think I'll brave the elements. Take the dogs out. Perhaps you'll feel better by the time I get back.'

She heard him collect his mac and boots from the cellar steps and whistle the dogs out. When he had gone, she went to the desk and collected the pieces of her letter. At least he had not noticed them. She smiled sadly at the fear of him they represented. That she should actually be afraid of him! She remembered frosty walks in Essex before they were married; holding hands with him in Paris and Lisbon on their honeymoon; the fun they had had in those early months of their

170

marriage: the shared jokes, the walks, the picnics. She remembered these things and asked herself over and over again, What's gone wrong? What's gone wrong?

And in the wind and bluster of a north-westerly gale, Bobby Teape strode along the beach toward the lighthouse on the Boa Nova, his hands thrust deep into his mackintosh pockets, the dogs racing on ahead, the spray and sand blowing up over the beach and the stunted, deformed pines that grew inland.

What the hell, what the hell, he thought to himself. She'll get over it. Give her a couple of days and we'll be having the big apology, the big reconciliation. Dinner at Mario's, lobster and champagne. Making love when we get back and special efforts all round. And maybe she'll get pregnant again. Yes, and then have another miscarriage.

It seemed that his marriage – his life – was becoming nothing more than a series of patched up crises. He laughed bitterly to himself. He was beginning to recognise the pattern.

VI

She was reading her Bible when he came into the bedroom after his bath. He had no objection to her reading the Bible, but he couldn't help wishing that she wouldn't do it quite so often and for quite as long.

He got into bed and took a detective novel from the bedside table.

I'm damned if I'm going to speak to her if she doesn't want to speak to me, he thought to himself, and finding his place, started to read.

She put her bedside light out and settled down to sleep. He continued to read for a further half hour before doing likewise.

Damn stupid woman, he thought.

He listened to the wind and rain. He had had a long discussion that day with Hugh Blunden about planting vines below the railway line. Brothertons had done so some years

171

before, and the vines showed every indication of being very good.

'I want to increase the output of white port,' he had told Hugh. 'That's where the market can really expand. A good white port – well, it beats sherry into a cocked hat any day of the week.'

Blunden had said they would never get anywhere without an advertising campaign. 'Look what Sandemans are doing,' he had said. 'No wonder they're leading the field. If you say "port" to the average Englishman, the only name he can think of is Sandeman.'

'Maybe, but Teape's port has never been for the average Englishman, Hugh. Don't forget that, there's a good chap.'

He smiled to himself in the darkness, remembering the conversation, pleased at the point he had scored. Yes. White grapes below the line, that was the thing.

The bed shook.

She was crying again, sobbing to herself. He had given up trying to do anything about it. She often cried at night, but when he tried to help, she only told him that he couldn't understand. She said he didn't know how to love, that he was incapable of real affection. Well. Perhaps he might feel a bit more affectionate if she could manage to be a little more cheerful. But all she ever did was moan.

Her sobs died down. He felt himself beginning to fall asleep. His thoughts drifted into a muddle of theories about advertising, white port, the height of the Douro the last time it flooded, the years of the various ports he had been using to blend the next batch of Teape's Special Reserve.

And then he woke up with a start. Ruth was out of bed, getting dressed.

'What the devil are you up to?' he asked.

But she was already leaving the room, closing the door gently behind her, going downstairs.

He listened intently, heard the front door open and close, and later the squeak of the front gate. He lay on his back, undecided whether or not to go after her. Hell! he thought. What the devil's she playing at?

He threw back the bed clothes and swung his feet on to the

172

floor. He went into his dressing room and put on trousers and a jersey over his pyjamas.

Outside, the wind hit him with surprising force. He was aware, suddenly, that he was worried about her. He ran down the road, wondering where she might have gone.

Sometimes she walked out to the end of the harbour mole, and he wondered if that was where she was now. When he reached the coast road, he turned left down the slight hill to the harbour and past the huge crane that had been placed there during the mole-building operations.

The waves were crashing against the cement blocks on the seaward side of the mole, and sending explosions of white spray upward into the darkness. He ran along the mole in the slight shelter of a wall, but became quickly soaked by falling spray. When the bigger waves broke, there was a heavy thudding sensation underfoot, like the burst of a bomb nearby.

He found Ruth right at the end of the mole, by the flashing red light that marked the harbour entrance. He stopped some yards away from her, afraid that when she saw him she might do something – might even jump off the mole into the dark water.

She stood with her back to him, wearing only a skirt and blouse. When the light flashed, he could see the side of her face. She stared into the darkness, unperturbed when a huge wave broke against the mole and the spray whipped over her.

Seeing her like that made him wonder, what sort of person is she? She was so difficult to understand: in some ways she needed his affection, needed to be told that he loved her; and yet in other ways she seemed to possess a certain inner strength, an inner self which she kept locked away from him at all times. Looking at her from the darkness of the wall was like seeing this inner self revealed, and he marvelled at it.

She turned and saw him. He went to her immediately: they stood a yard apart, like people in a dream.

'What happened?' he asked, but his words were snatched by the wind and she didn't hear. He held out his hands to her and she took them. He pulled her towards him, held her closely, stroked her bedraggled hair.

He wanted to say things, wanted to make new promises, wanted to tell her all that he would do for her. But the words were for some reason blocked inside him. He held her very tightly, and began to shiver.

When they reached the road and were clear of the spray, he walked along with his arm round her shoulder.

'We'll move house,' he said. 'Start looking for a place this weekend. All right?'

She looked into his eyes and her expression told him that she was back inside herself again, safely locked away from him.

She nodded. 'All right,' she said.

❦ 7 ❧

I

THE QUINTA DO MOINHO VELHO, or 'Old Mill Farm' stood at the head of a valley that ran down to the sea, close to Valadares and about six miles south of Oporto.

To get to the *quinta*, you left the main road and bumped over a dusty track that led along one side of a eucalyptus wood and ended, inevitably, before a wall and a pair of high gates.

Inside these gates was a sunny courtyard formed by the wall, the stables and the house, whose main rooms faced south and west, so that the windows overlooked the five acres of vegetable gardens, orchards, flower beds and woodland. A little way from the house was a metal windmill for raising water from the well, and a large granite tank. A magnolia tree shed creamy petals nearby, and figs and walnuts ripened in the sun.

The Teapes bought Moinho Velho in the spring, but did not move in until late July. In the intervening weeks, Ruth spent hours with the building contractors, explaining exactly how she wanted the windows enlarged, the fireplaces restored, the cupboards fitted. She motored about the countryside picking up antiques and shopping in the market towns for the soft coloured furnishings, the hand-woven carpets and the solid oaken furniture for which she had longed so often in the house at Leça.

In the last weeks before the move, Amália, José and Maria decided that they would remain at Leça rather than move across the river to Valadares. But Natália, with no other prospect of a place to live or work, accepted Ruth's invitation to continue in service at the new house.

From the moment they arrived on that blisteringly hot day at the end of July, Ruth sensed that she would be happier in this house. She set about organising the unpacking and putting away with an enthusiasm she had not felt since her days in the East London Medical Mission, six years before.

Teape was aware of the change in her. And now that the pieces of oak furniture had been placed in the positions she had planned for them; now that the shelves of Portuguese pottery were up, and the pictures hung on the freshly white-washed walls; now that he saw, for the first time, the sunlight slanting down upon the black and white tiles she had chosen for the hall, he knew with certainty that the decision to move had been the right one.

Eduardo also liked the new house. On the first day, he made friends with the gardener and the cook, Joaquim and Fernanda, who lived together in a two room cottage on the property, a little way down the hill. Joaquim worked all day in the vegetable garden: he had three grown up children and was happy to make friends with this chunky little four-year-old, whose deepset eyes looked out from beneath a mop of chestnut hair. Eduardo followed him about, watched as he pulled the lever to put the vane of the windmill in the position to turn the sails into wind so that a jerky stream of water was pumped into the water tank. He stood by solemnly as Joaquim guided the flow of water from the tank along the ditches and aquaducts that led between the neat patches of tomatoes, beans, beetroot and spinach, so that Fernanda, using a bowl as a scoop, could fling the water over the vegetables, her wide bottom straining in her skirt, varicose veins like blue snakes in her legs.

To the north of the vegetable garden were windbreaks of bamboo, and beyond them a hill that was studded with pines and boulders. Here, Eduardo sometimes went exploring. Lizards rustled and dashed at his approach, and when he sat down on a smooth stone to see how far he had climbed, he could look down upon the *quinta* and see his mother beating the dirt out of the clothes on a cement slab behind the kitchen. He enjoyed that, for she often sang as she worked, and heard at a distance, her voice was oddly pleasing to him.

They slept right at the top of the house, he in a tiny box room next to hers. Sometimes in the late evenings, when her

176

work was over for the day, she would take him on her lap and sing quietly to him: he would put his arms round her neck and she would hold him closely, so that her breasts were like soft cushions against his face.

The lady of the house was kind to him, too. She spoke to him in her funny way and asked him all sorts of questions, encouraging him to talk, teaching him already about numbers and letters. He liked to watch her in the afternoons when she sat outside in the shade, reading one of her books. She sat so still, the book in one hand, her other hand resting lightly round the ears of the black dog they called Minho. Eduardo would stand a little way from her, amazed that anyone could sit so still and so peacefully. Sometimes she would see him standing there and look up and smile the good smile of hers, beckoning to him and talking to him.

He would stand by her chair, shy, not understanding all that she said but happy nevertheless simply to be in her presence, to fill his nostrils with her fragrance, to see her beautiful hands and gently rounded fingernails, so different from his mother's work-hardened hands and the pungent smell of her natural odours.

Teape, he regarded more as a god than a human being, whose will dominated the whole household. He went to work each morning at nine o'clock and returned at half past five. He gave orders: orders to Joaquim, to Fernanda, to Natália – even to his woman, the Senhora. Once, Eduardo had placed his feet inside the Senhor's heavy leather brogues that had been put outside his dressing room door for polishing. He marvelled at the sheer size of them, but when his mother saw what he was doing she scolded him, telling him that he must never, ever touch anything that belonged to the Senhor again.

Eduardo's awe and fear of Teape was also mixed with a certain fascination, and the slow, soft stare of the little boy eventually irritated and angered Teape until one day he turned to Ruth and said, 'Why the hell does he have to hang around all the time?'

'It's only natural, darling,' she replied. 'He has to look up to some man or other. You're his father figure.'

Teape looked away, down the valley to the short stretch of

horizon visible beyond the pines. 'I don't like the maid's brat hanging around,' he said.

She reached out a hand to him. 'He looks up to you. Can't you give him just a little in return? I do wish you could like them both more. Natália's so sweet to me. There are all sorts of little things that she does without my ever asking.'

He grunted. 'I would steer clear of allowing her into any sort of friendship, Ruth. It can lead to all sorts of difficulties.'

'It surely can't do any harm to treat them as human beings.'

'I'm perfectly civil to her. It's just that I don't like her snotty-nosed infant gazing at me all the time as if I were some sort of animal in the zoo.'

'Well you do look rather ferocious, darling. And it's not often you see a Tigger in his natural habitat. Perhaps he thinks you should be put behind bars.'

'Any more of that and I'll put you over my knee and give you what for,' he said, and his lips pursed in the beginnings of a smile.

She held his hand and looked at the auburn hairs and freckles on his arms. 'Things are better, aren't they?'

'Things?'

'Us.'

'Oh. Yes. I suppose they are.'

'You don't regret moving?'

'I miss my walks on the Boa Nova.'

'But do you regret moving?'

He looked at her. 'Early days, yet.'

'Go on. Be a devil. Admit it. You love this place.'

'It's not bad,' he said, and she knew that this was as much as she would get out of him.

'I thought we might have the party on Saturday week,' she said. 'I'm going to get Joaquim to make a nice long trestle table, and we'll all sit down to lunch under the trees. And if we top up the water tank, the children can swim.'

He nodded. The children. Not their children of course, but the children of the Millets, the McNeils, the Pratts: all the other young marrieds who were making a life for themselves under the Portuguese sun. He glanced at Ruth, and shared with her that all too familiar pang of disappointment that they had had no children of their own. She was twenty-nine now, and he would be thirty-five in October. Next spring would see their fifth wedding anniversary. Everything was so uncertain: events in Europe seemed to be running downhill, out of control. The world leaders were making pacts, alliances and agreements: they seemed hypnotised by the delusion that a signature on a piece of paper was something upon which they could rely. They scurried from capital to capital, waving their pieces of paper as if to dry the ink, proclaiming victories for good sense, peace in our time. But at the same time, men were being called up for military service in Great Britain, and the Navy had been mobilised. Every night, when the Teapes listened in to the BBC News service, the rift between Britain and Germany seemed to have deepened. Now, in mid August, war seemed inevitable.

Perhaps he should not have bought this house. Perhaps he was a damn fool. Randall said that the Portuguese might well throw in their lot with Hitler, and although Franco did not seem too enamoured of the Nazi leader, he might consider it in Spain's interests to change his mind. Rumours were going about that the German war machine could snuff out France and the low countries within a few weeks. And if that happened, it wouldn't be long before Nazi staff cars were going up and down the Boa Vista, and Gestapo Blackshirts were sitting behind desks in the Factory House.

'Well?' Ruth said. 'What do you think?'

'Think?'

'About the party.'

He patted her knee. 'Yes, darling. Whatever you think best.'

II

It was the biggest lunch party that the colony had seen for some time, and it took place in a strangely unreal atmosphere of anticipation. The day before, news had come through that Germany was invading Poland, and that women and children

179

were already being moved away from the cities in Great Britain.

When the guests arrived, they stood about in groups in the shade of the walnut and fig trees, sipping their drinks and talking about the crisis.

There were forty-four places laid at the long trestle table under the magnolia tree. Jugs of wine had been placed along the centre of the table, which was set with a white damask cloth, little bowls of flowers and silver that gleamed in the dappled sunlight. Nearby, a smaller table had been laid for the children, with coloured table napkins and jugs of home-made squash. Natália and the new maid, Ana, hurried back and forth bringing out bowls of salad and rice, cold meats, fish and pastries.

'We can't just stand around talking about war,' Ruth said quietly to Bobby, and he nodded and went into the house. A few minutes later, he emerged wearing a very old fashioned full length swimming costume that had once belonged to his father and was made of wool, with wide, horizontal black and white stripes. The guests separated as he ran towards them: they cheered and laughed as he plunged, with a massive splash, into the water tank.

This was the signal for the children to join in, and a water fight developed, principally between Bobby and the Millet children on one side and Christopher and Sally McNeil on the other.

Ruth joined Alice McNeil on the low stone wall above the rose beds.

'He's marvellous with children, isn't he?' Alice said. 'Ian could never let himself go like that.'

They watched as Sally and Christopher dragged Bobby along the side of the water tank and threw him in. They were cheerful, mischievous children, with curly fair hair like their mother and bright, intelligent eyes. They had run round to the other side of the tank now, and were preventing him from getting out. He lunged about, roaring underwater and making a noise like a sea lion.

'He's only an overgrown little boy himself,' Ruth said.

'Well at least he knows how to relax, which is more than can be said for Ian.'

180

They looked across at Ian McNeil, who was talking with Dodger Remington and Johnny Millet. Ian, a tall, narrowly built man in hornrimmed glasses, was rolling a pebble about under his shoe, talking very seriously while the other two listened, nodding gravely.

'He's so pessimistic,' Alice said. 'He says that he feels as if the whole world is about to plunge into an era of wars and lawlessness. He thinks we're about to enter a period similar to mediaeval Britain.'

There was an extra loud roar, a shriek and then a splash. Bobby had jumped in with Sally and Christopher on his back. 'What a wonderful place this is,' Alice said. 'Weren't you lucky to find it?'

A more mature shriek came from behind them, and Hugh Blunden appeared from the house in swimming trunks carrying Joy, who kicked and squealed.

'Isn't it about time those two got married?' Ruth asked when Joy had been thrown in.

Alice laughed quietly. 'Oh – my dear, I don't think Hugh wants to get married, does he?'

'Why not? I thought he was just about the most eligible male in the colony.'

'It depends what you mean by eligible.'

'Whatever does that imply?'

'Don't you know about Hugh?'

'No?'

Alice smiled a little secretively. 'Perhaps I shouldn't tell you.'

'Well now you've thoroughly whetted my curiosity, I think you'd better.'

'He's one of those,' Alice said quickly.

'One of those what?'

'Oh Ruth! You really are incredibly innocent sometimes! Can't you see it? I mean he's – pansy. Effeminate.'

Ruth's face fell. 'Oh,' she said. 'Oh. I must say the thought had not even crossed my mind.'

'The trouble with you is, you're too nice.'

Ruth smiled faintly. 'I almost wish you hadn't told me.'

'Well you did ask.'

'Yes. Yes, I did, didn't I?'

Hidden among the pines and bamboos, a little way up the hill behind the water tank, Eduardo crouched, watching. He saw the English pushing each other into the water and was amazed that the children should treat the Senhor with so little respect. He saw the Senhora sitting on a low wall, talking to her friend who often came to the house for lunch. He also saw his mother going to and fro, fetching and carrying, her arms brown against the white tablecloths and her dark hair tied back with a ribbon, specially for the occasion. He watched the confusion among the guests as the decision was taken to sit down to lunch and the Senhor, his voice booming, told everyone exactly where to sit. He saw the large quantities of food that were eaten and the replenishments of salad, rice, meat, fish and wine that were brought to the table by his mother and Ana. He heard the gusts of laughter, the exclamations, the smash of broken glass.

Later, after the party, he stood with his fingers in his mouth and watched his mother and Ana working their way through the piles of washing up, while the sun sank towards the horizon and the guests, who had stayed for tea and evening drinks, decided it was time to go.

It was hot in the kitchen and the women smelled of sweat. His mother's hands were red and damp, and she was wet under her arms. She worked on and on, wiping plates, glasses, cutlery, pots and pans, while Ana stood grunting at the big stone sink. Ana had grey hair and stubble on her chin like a man. She was often short of breath. That was why she grunted.

When the work was done, he was taken down to the cottage where Fernanda lived with Joaquim. There were other people there, people that Eduardo had not seen before. Dogs went in and out and the people sat at a wooden table and ate grilled sardines and boiled potatoes. There was bread and wine on the table, and everyone talked at once.

Very late, when the wine was nearly all gone and Eduardo was nearly asleep, they persuaded Natália to sing.

He was transferred to the lap of Fernanda, but he preferred to stand. He slipped down on to the stone floor, and the old woman put her hands on his shoulders.

The plates of sardine skeletons were still on the table, and so were the nearly finished glasses of wine, the crusts of bread. Cigarette smoke twisted upwards. Natália stood by the table in the light of the oil lamp. She sang in a husky contralto which had surprising power. Her head was thrown back and her eyes closed. Her brown, muscular arms stretched downwards at her sides as if to force the notes out more completely. The men looked at her approvingly, and started clapping as she reached the climax of each song.

Her voice rose and fell in the quietness of the evening and Eduardo, wide awake now, gazed up at her in happiness and pride.

From where he stood, it seemed as if the oil lamp that hung from the ceiling was a crown of light which she wore upon her head.

III

There were eleven hens and one cock. Fernanda fed them in the early mornings, and when she came to their enclosure they all ran towards her. Often, he helped her collect the eggs. Some of them had straw sticking to them and some were warm and soft from the inside of the hen. The cock had dark red pieces of skin that hung underneath his chin, and when he crowed he went on tiptoe. Sometimes he chased after a hen and held on to it with his legs, and that was how he made chickens because Fernanda said so.

There were rabbits in a hutch by the henhouse, and these rabbits had fur like one of the Senhora's coats and blue eyes like the eyes of the Senhor. One of the rabbits escaped once and the dog, Minho, killed it. The rabbit sat still and waited for the dog, and only began to run away when it was too late. The dog held it in his mouth and shook it, and the rabbit screamed and when Joaquim made the dog drop it, the rabbit made little squeaking noises and its feet twitched as if it had now decided to run away. Then it lay still, so that it could be dead.

When the wind blew strongly, the windmill went round and

round very quickly, so that you could not see the separate blades of it, and the green tips of the blades became a blur against the sky. At other times when there was hardly any wind, the blades went very slowly round and round, and he could imagine himself sitting on one, going round and round and round and round. When the wind changed, the vane that stuck out at the back caught the new direction and turned the windmill to face the new breeze and when it turned it made a mournful squeak that he sometimes heard at night.

Yesterday there had been a party, and in the evening his mother had sung those songs. They clapped, and she had worn a crown of light. She sang again and they clapped again and her crown flared and hissed, and the skeletons on the plates watched, eyeless.

Today there was no wind, so the blades were still and the water in the tank black and smooth. If he moved his head he could see the sky and the windmill, upside down, in the water. And if he moved it again he could see a boy looking at him, a boy that was himself but not himself.

You could float in the water if you wanted to. Or you could jump in, go to the bottom and come up like the English *meninos*. You could splash about if you wanted or swim like the dog, Minho, using your arms and feet.

If you took your trousers off you could see yourself and you could also see it in the water, only it was the underneath, the part you couldn't usually see, and if you turned round and looked sideways over your shoulder you could see the other side, too. Also, if you put your head between your legs and then looked into the water the boy that looked back at you looked very strange indeed, his hair falling, but falling upwards, like –

It was very cold and it filled his mouth when he took a breath and made him swallow and swallow and swallow – swallow much more than he had ever swallowed, and when he took another breath more water came in and although he wanted to shout he couldn't because something was inside him so that he could not breathe and anyway he was underneath again and it was black, a sort of green blackness, and when he came up the sky was not blue any more but red, red, and he put up his hands

184

to hold on to the air and pull himself up, but instead found himself swallowing, trying to cough, but being unable and quite quickly the light faded and went out and he was suddenly travelling very fast, faster than the wind, up and up and up and up, so that he was flying, and there was a roaring in his ears, a roaring blackness that stopped abruptly with every other sensation.

He was coughing and being sick. Hands were pressing down on his back, and water was flowing from his mouth. The ground was hard; someone's fingers were in his mouth, pulling at his tongue. Somebody – a woman – was wailing, sobbing, praying. The hands stopped pressing on his back and lifted him gently up, and when he opened his eyes properly, he saw that the Senhora was carrying him, and he looked straight into her face all the way back to the house, along the hall, up the stairs and into a bedroom that was not his.

She towelled him dry and put him between crisp, sweet-smelling sheets and the Senhor appeard carrying the cut glass brandy decanter and a crystal glass, and his clothes were dripping wet. When the Senhora saw him standing like that in the doorway she laughed and said something to him. He looked down at himself and at the same time the bell rang at the front gate and somebody sounded the horn of a car.

IV

Teape opened the window and looked out. Ana was opening the gate and the car bumped over the ledge and into the courtyard.

Teape said, 'Hullo, there!' He looked straight down on the car, a Standard coupé with the hood down. Christopher and Sally were sitting in the back, and Alice in the front passenger seat. Ian McNeil looked up.

'We were on our way past, so we thought we'd drop in to make sure you'd heard.'

'Heard? Heard what?'

In the bedroom, Ruth straightened, listening. Teape's bulk filled the window. A pool of tank water was collecting on the floor where he stood.

'We're at war,' McNeil said. 'Britain and Germany. As from five p.m. today.'

V

She came to him in the evening, after Ruth had gone up for her bath. She found him standing outside the sitting room. It was a windless night and he was gazing up at the stars. His cigarette gleamed momentarily in the darkness. She made a little noise to announce her presence.

He turned. 'Yes, Natália?'

She joined her hands across her apron, facing him in the darkness.

'I wish to thank you,' she said.

'It was nothing.'

'The Senhora also. I wish to thank her.'

'We only did what had to be done.'

She looked up into his face. He was a big man, yes, but he was lost for words and his lips moved awkwardly so that she knew he was troubled.

'I simply wish to thank you,' she repeated.

He gave a stiff little bow, trying to remain the master, trying to keep her in her place as a servant. But she knew – they both knew – that for that moment they were not master and servant but man and woman, rankless and equal.

When she had gone, he turned back and stared upward at Orion and the Plough and the great mass of stars that crowded the heavens. He remembered the sight of Eduardo's naked body, half submerged in the water tank. He saw again the little feet, the buttocks, the wet, dark hair and the blue lips as Ruth gave him artificial respiration. He remembered how he had prayed fiercely, silently, that the boy might live.

He smoked the last of his cigarette and went into the house. When he entered the bedroom, Ruth looked quickly back into his eyes.

186

'Natália came and thanked me,' he said.

'I thought I heard you talking.'

He took her hands. 'Ruth,' he whispered. 'Ruth.'

'I know, darling. I know.'

They stood together, and there were no more words to say, for much had already been said and now, at the outset of war, it remained only to enjoy while they could the peace and happiness which they had so recently found.

VI

There was excitement at first, with the news of the bombing of German ships at Kiel, the sinking of the *Athenia*, and the arrival of British soldiers on French soil for the second time within twenty years. In Oporto, the Consul called a meeting at the Factory House to pass on the advice of His Majesty's Government that British nationals in neutral countries should remain where they were. At that meeting, one of the shippers put everyone on their guard against spies, and for months afterwards Teape made a joke of it by looking under his soup plate before lunch.

But after the first weeks of war, the news from Poland and Finland seemed to have little bearing on the lives of the British in Oporto. Life jogged along – albeit a little uncertainly – much as it had in the past.

Ruth became pregnant that autumn, and Teape insisted that this time she should take special care. For the first four months, she had breakfast in bed every morning and a rest every afternoon. An extra woman was employed to come in daily and clean the house so that Natália could be released to work as Ruth's personal maid, and this brought them into even closer contact than before.

The baby was born on 20 June 1940, the night Paris fell. Ruth had entered the British Hospital in Oporto two days before, and had undergone a difficult delivery that was nearly three weeks premature.

Teape was the proudest of fathers. 'Look at that, look at that,' he said when he saw the baby for the first time. 'Isn't she beautiful? Isn't she marvellous?' And when the nurse pointed out that Ruth had done very well, too, he added: 'Yes, yes, of course you have, haven't you, sweetheart?' and sat down on the bed, taking her hand, his eyes watering and his mouth puckering in an emotional smile. 'Easy as shelling peas, wasn't it?'

They had long discussions about names. They considered Nicola, Joanna, Patricia, Anne, Elspeth and even Edwina. But the baby was finally named Stella Rosalinde Teape and christened in her great-grandfather's baptismal shawl at the church of St James's, Oporto.

It was quite clear from the outset that Stella Rosalinde was to be the light of Bobby Teape's life. While he was naturally reluctant to hold her or have anything to do with her if she was wet or dirty, it was his greatest pleasure to take her in his arms when she had been bathed and feel the warmth and incredible softness of her head against his cheek, and to allow her tiny hand to grip his thumb.

Many of the younger shippers were joining up now. Freddy Randall and Johnny Millet were already in uniform, and Hugh Blunden had surprised everyone by volunteering for service in the Royal Air Force, along with several others. Teape, seeing them go, was torn between his duty to his country and his natural inclination to protect his wife and child.

After September 1940, rumours started that Hitler, having failed to conquer Britain, might now thrust westward into the Iberian peninsular. A joke went round that all he had to do in order to conquer Portugal was pick up the telephone and tell Salazar he was on his way, to which the reply went that Portugal was therefore quite safe from attack, because the appalling telephone system would provide adequate defence.

Towards the end of the year, however, the rumours became more ominous. The Remingtons owned land up at Vimiosa where wolfram was mined, and Dodger Remington had contracts to supply both British and German customers. He had heard that Portugal was next on Germany's list, as it would provide invaluable bases from which to attack allied shipping and supply routes.

As if in confirmation of this rumour, Churchill let it be known that British families in Portugal should be evacuated. The Consul called another meeting at the Factory, and everyone was warned to be ready to move at a moment's notice. Nobody knew how or when the order to move would come, but everybody had to be ready. Suitcases were kept packed and petrol tanks filled. And the jokes about spies ceased to be jokes when a British ship that left Leixões one afternoon was promptly sunk by German aircraft the following day.

Teape found himself in a difficult position. He had put a lot of his inherited capital in buying up land for the firm, and a further sum in acquiring the Quinta do Moinho Velho. He now believed that it was his duty to fight, but was loathe to leave until Ruth and Stella had been safely evacuated. He had some money in England, but could not touch it, and he was therefore faced with the prospect of selling up the house in order to raise enough money for Ruth to set up a home elsewhere.

He delayed through the winter of 1940 and into the spring of '41. By May, the first families were already departing: some to South Africa, some to Britain, others to Canada. Nearly all the men had joined up. James Remington was in command of a motor torpedo boat at the age of twenty-six; Geoffrey Millet was at Sandhurst, and Joy Remington was driving an ambulance in London.

In June, Teape decided that he too must now go and fight.

'But only when you're safely out of Portugal,' he said to Ruth one Sunday afternoon when he had told her of his decision.

'What about the house?'

'We'll have to sell up. You'll need capital.'

'Not if I go and stay with the Laughtons.'

Teape shook his head. He now took a pessimistic view of the war, and believed that England might well be over-run. 'No. I'm not having you in Britain. It would be a case of out of the frying pan into the fire. Canada's the best place.'

'Darling, I know no one in Canada! I've no desire to go there!'

His temper flared. 'I've no desire to go and fight in the trenches,' he said, still pathetically ignorant of modern warfare.

'I'm sorry.'

'It's all right.' He smiled sadly. 'Don't mention it, Roo.'

'Do I have to go?'

'I think so.'

She looked towards the water tank where the pram had been placed in the shadow of the magnolia. Stella was awake, and the pram shook as she kicked and gurgled to herself.

'It seems so secure here,' Ruth said. 'Such madness to leave it.'

'They probably thought that in Poland. And Czechoslovakia. And France, and Holland.'

'Alice has decided to go on the next available ship.'

'I know.'

They sat in silence for a long time, and eventually she said, 'If I have to go, I'd like to go with her.'

He nodded. 'I'll wait until you've gone, so that I can sort things out and then, well . . . it'll be my turn.'

'Yes,' she echoed. 'Then it'll be your turn.'

VII

Natália was in tears.

'Senhora – I shall have nowhere to live.'

'I know that, Natália. I know. But what am I to do? I don't want to leave this house, nor do I want to leave Portugal or you or Eduardo. But Senhor Teape is going to join the army and he does not wish me to stay here on my own. Don't you understand that?'

'I am afraid that you will never arrive where you are going and never return here in Portugal.'

'Nonsense!'

'I am afraid for you, Senhora, for you and for *menina* Stella –'

'Now don't start that all over again. We shall be perfectly all right, and when the war's over –'

'My lady, I have nowhere to go!'

'Listen. I shall give you some money, not very much, but enough to help you in the first weeks. Surely you have friends or relatives somewhere? Didn't you once say that your aunt lived in Aveiro?'

'She would not even know me. She has not seen me since I was a *menina*.'

'What about the people in Matosinhos? The people your father knew? Couldn't they help?'

'Senhora, I have told you many times, my father had no friends. I am hated there.'

'I wish – I really wish I could do more, Natália. But I can't. You will be able to stay on here until the house is sold but after that – you will simply have to do the best you can. And if – when – the war is over, we shall come back to Portugal. You must ask for us, try to find us again. We may even live here again. But wherever we are, we shall want you to be with us.'

Natália now put her head in her hands and wept without any attempt at control.

'Natália . . . please don't . . . don't . . .'

'Ai, Senhora!'

'Here you are. One thousand *escudos*. Keep it for when you really need it, understand? Now go upstairs and fetch the luggage. The car will be here any minute.'

'I beg of you, my lady, believe me, there is bad luck –'

'Natália – I said go and fetch the luggage. Now go. Go!'

'Yes, my lady. Certainly, my lady.'

VIII

The SS *Oriole* was a stately vessel with a tall funnel and counter stern. The red ensign clattered and flapped in the fresh *nortada* that was blowing, and the decks were busy with men loading cargo and preparing for sea.

Cars and taxis were drawing up on the jetty, and the first families were already embarking. There had been only eight hours notice of departure, and Ruth was dazed by the suddeness of it all. Bobby, lifting the luggage from the boot, was frighteningly quiet and aloof: his mouth was set in a hard line, and his voice had an odd, defiant ring about it. The McNeils arrived a few minutes after the Teapes; Christopher and Sally were wearing their Oporto British School uniforms and looked unusually clean and well behaved. Christopher McNeil had been told by his father that he was to look after his mother, and was taking this instruction as seriously as only an eleven-year-old son can. He stood very uprightly in his grey shorts and blazer, and looked round the almost empty harbour.

'I thought we'd be going in a convoy,' he said.

'Shhh!' his mother said. 'We're not supposed to talk about it.'

They went up the sloping brow to the ship with Stella in a carry cot. The sun was setting now, and some of the harbour lights glimmered and were reflected in the wind-ruffled water. One of the crew took them down two decks to a small cabin; Alice and Ruth were to sleep on the bunks, the children on camp beds and Stella in the carrycot. The men brought the heavier luggage down, and as Stella was by some miracle asleep, she and the luggage were left in the cabin while the Teapes and McNeils returned to the deck.

'Cable me immediately you arrive in harbour,' Bobby said. 'Wherever you are. Send me a telegram. I must know where you are.'

She nodded, looking across the harbour to the jumble of roofs and trees in Leça, hardly able to believe that only two years before she had lived under one of those roofs herself.

'And when you write to me, always – say –' He stopped, swallowing and blinking. 'Always say you love me,' he whispered. He took a deep breath and let it out in three sobs. Over the loudspeaker system the voice of the Chief Officer announced: 'Attention please. All ashore that's going ashore. The gangway will be removed shortly.'

She stared up into his face. 'Don't wait,' she said. 'Kiss me and go. Now. Please.'

Then they were in each other's arms, both sobbing, and suddenly he had let her go and was going away from her, down the brow and on to the quay.

When he reached the bottom of the gangway, he stopped, turned, and raised his hand. As she raised her own hand to wave back, she felt suddenly cold, in the way she had so often felt in the house at Leça, and she remembered Natália's repeated warnings about all the premonitions she had had. A shiver ran up and down her spine: she was terrified, and convinced that she would never see Bobby again.

He had opened the car door but could not bring himself to get in and drive away. He looked up at her hopelessly. There was now a large crowd on the quayside; their upturned faces stared up at the ship, which now let out a tentative hoot on its siren.

A few feet away from Ruth, some members of the crew were standing by to cast off the berthing wires. They argued among themselves, and Ruth heard what they said without having to make an effort to listen.

'Look,' one was saying, 'It stands to reason. If bloody Gerry's started taking a swipe at Uncle Joe, 'e's not going to have as many bullets spare to use on us, is 'e?'

'Who says anything about taking a swipe at Uncle Joe?'

'I told you. Ruddy Sparks got it on the radio 'alf a hour ago. They've walked into Russia.'

'So what?'

'If you was to clean your bleedin' lug 'oles out, you'd know. That's what I was just saying, see. If Adolf's pointing 'is pop guns at the Ruskies, 'e won't have many spare to point at us.'

'What if 'e takes over Russia like 'e done in France?'

'Never 'appen, Mate. Joe Stalin won't never let 'im.'

'Want a bet?'

''Alf a dollar.'

'Five bob.'

'You're on. Five bob, each way, on Joe Stalin.'

'Who said anything about each way? You put money on a 'orse each way, means 'e can come in second.'

'Well I don't know that, do I? Not a gambling man, see –'

'Excuse me –'

The men turned to see a woman in her thirties, one of the passengers, in pearls and pullover, tweed skirt, stockings and lace-up shoes.

193

'Yes, Ma'am?'

'I couldn't help overhearing – did you say that the Germans had invaded Russia?'

'That's right, Ma'am. Been a special bulletin. Massive attack, they called it.'

'Are you sure?'

'I'm blood – I'm positive, Ma'am. Was in the wireless office when it come through, see. No error.'

The woman looked down at the jetty, then back at the man, a tall, narrowly built individual with thinning black hair and huge, yellow teeth. 'You really are positive?'

He shrugged. 'Well. That's what they said. Don't usually get things wrong, do they? BBC, I mean.'

The woman turned this way and that. On the quay, a mobile crane was moving into position to lift off the gangway. She went quickly along the deck and spoke to an officer who was to supervise the operation.

'Excuse me, officer. I've decided not to go.'

The officer looked unperturbed. It wasn't the first time evacuees had changed their minds at the last moment, and it wouldn't be the last. 'You'll have to hurry,' he said. 'This brow's coming off in a couple of minutes.'

She looked quickly back at the crane. The jib was already being lowered so that the strops could be made fast to the gangway. She was suddenly gripped with a new fear: that she might not be able to get off the ship in time. She ran down ladders, along corridors, lost her way, doubling back and eventually finding the cabin.

Stella was awake now. Ruth scooped her up in one arm and collected her overnight case with her spare hand. The rest of the luggage, she decided, would just have to go with the ship. She struggled back up the ladders and met Alice and the children on her way along the deck to the gangway.

'What are you doing?'

'I'm not going.'

'But Ruth!'

'It's no good. I can't. I know I can't.'

Alice gripped her by the arm. 'You're staying on board,' she said quietly. 'Don't make a scene. It's for the best. You know it's for the best.'

194

'I can't. I can't!'

'For goodness sake take a hold on yourself,' Alice whispered, her Scottish accent suddenly more pronounced. 'This sort of thing does nobody any good.'

But Ruth, seeing that the strops were already made fast to the gangway and the order already being given to hoist away, snatched herself free and shouted, 'Wait!'

'Too late, Madam,' the officer replied.

But it was not too late. She pushed past him, Stella in one arm and her case in the other hand. She ducked under the frayed wire strops as she went down the gangway and was met on the quay by Bobby.

'What – why – ' he started.

'I'm not going,' she told him, and there was triumph, defiance and happiness in her voice. 'They've invaded Russia. The Germans, I mean. They'll never come here now.'

The crane groaned and the brow rose in the air behind them. 'I'm staying in Portugal,' Ruth shouted above the noise. 'I don't care what anyone says. This is where I belong.'

Orders were passed and lines cast off. In the gathering darkness, with a cluster of passengers waving from the deck, the *SS Oriole* slipped quietly out of Leixões harbour, bound for a secret *rendez-vous*.

IX

The only member of the family who wasn't sea-sick was Christopher. He slept on a camp bed in the corridor outside the cabin, and was up early each morning for breakfast. While other passengers groaned and retched, he tucked into a large plate of porridge and tinned milk, toast, margarine and bright orange tea. The *SS Oriole* wallowed her way out into the Atlantic, and Christopher made friends with the officers and crew. When lifeboat stations were exercised, it was Christopher who was used as a model for the new lifejackets that had been issued, the ones with lights and whistles attached. On the second day out, he was invited to the bridge to watch the gun's crew at practice, and the Chief Officer, who had taken a liking to this rather serious, intelligent child, showed him how to sight the sun with a sextant and bring its image sailing down to the horizon. When porpoises appeared round the bows, he explained to Christopher that they were a sign of good luck.

The weather improved on the third day, and Alice and Sally appeared on the deck for the first time. That evening, the ship joined a convoy, tagging along at the end of a column of ships. The wind had lightened and was now from astern: the smoke from each ship's funnel rose vertically and gathered in a hazy cloud above the convoy. While Sally and Christopher were trying to decide whether there were twenty-six ships or twenty-seven, a naval corvette came close alongside and an officer carried out a shouted conversation with the master of the *Oriole* by megaphone. As the corvette increased speed and headed away, into the swell, its bows dipped and the spray flew right over the bridge.

That evening, the McNeils knelt down together in the cabin and Alice prayed aloud for the safety of the ship, her husband and all her loved ones. She asked that those in authority might make wise and courageous decisions and that the war might be quickly ended.

The torpedoes struck in the early hours of the following morning. There were two heavy explosions and the ship seemed to stop dead in her tracks. The lights went out between decks: there was smoke, shouting and chaos.

'Everything will be all right provided you keep calm and do as I say,' Alice told her children. She made them put on their lifejackets and follow her up the ladders by the light of her pocket torch.

On deck, the night was pitch black. Men were shouting orders, marshalling passengers, preparing to lower lifeboats. A woman was screaming hysterically, and a steam safety valve was making a deafening noise. The ship had already tipped over to one side. From the bridge, three Very lights soared into the air and the figures of the officers were momentarily silhouetted in their glare.

Sally shouted, 'Are we going to jump in?' She was wearing only pyjamas, and clutched a much-loved doll called Elizabeth.

196

'Just stay with me, darlings,' Alice shouted over the noise of escaping steam. 'Just stay with me. If we have to jump, we'll all stay together.'

The men were having difficulty releasing the lifeboat. It seemed to have jammed against the davit. An officer took charge of the group of passengers that included Alice and the children. 'We'll have to use the rafts. This way. Quickly now.'

They followed him along the deck and watched as he used a knife to release the rafts. They splashed into the sea. He turned to them, his face white and haggard. The ship was heeling over alarmingly now. 'Right. Jump! Jump and swim clear!'

Sally began to cry. Alice reassured her. 'We'll be all right, darling.'

Christopher shouted, 'Let's all jump together. Like at the Teapes!'

Other passengers were already jumping, their nightclothes billowing up as they descended out of sight into the water. Alice took Christopher and Sally in either hand and they climbed over the guard rail.

'One – two – three – '

The waves were massive. Alice found herself struggling in the black water with no idea where her children were. She heard Christopher nearby. 'Over here, Mummy!'

Hands reached down and pulled them into the Carley float.

'Where's Sally?' she shouted as soon as she had joined Christopher in the raft, but he stared back and shook his head.

'Paddle!' a man in pyjamas told her. 'Paddle!'

'I've lost my daughter!'

'Can't be helped. We've got to get clear of the ship!'

They paddled with their hands, looking back as the ship tipped further and further over and finally capsized. A man leaned across to her and said, 'Don't worry, love. She'll have been picked up by another raft.' He said something else, but his words were swept away as a wave lifted them and broke over them.

The very first light of dawn was in the sky now, and they could make out the shape of a ship approaching, and the occasional glimpse of other rafts and lifeboats. 'Shan't be long now!' one of the men said. 'They'll have us out of this lot in no time.'

The ship – a modern freighter – came slowly up to them. Scrambling nets and ladders had been lowered over the side. The swell lifted the raft rapidly upward, almost to deck level, and then the ship's side seemed almost to rise up out of the water, they descended so quickly. After waiting their turn in the queue of rafts, Alice and Christopher chose their moment and leapt onto the scrambling net, climbing upward to the deck, where they were met and ushered below to one of the messdecks, and wrapped in blankets.

Other passengers who had already been picked up sat on benches, staring at each other, numb with shock. A man came round with a large kettle of cocoa.

'My daughter,' Alice said. 'She's only eight. My daughter.'

The man handed her a mug. 'Come on, love. Get a bit of this inside you.'

She held the mug while he poured the cocoa. At the same moment the whole ship jerked, and a stream of the nearly boiling liquid went over her wrist. Seconds later, there were two more explosions as the cargo ignited. The lights flickered and went out.

There was panic then. People stampeded to the ladder and the weak were trodden underfoot. A torrent of water came down on their heads through the hatch, and tables and benches slid together into a heap.

Alice wrapped her arms tightly round her son.

'It's all right, Mummy,' he shouted. 'I'm all right.'

In the darkness, a man's voice, cracked and high pitched, shrieked, 'Jesus God! Jesus God! You bloody bastard!'

Later that day, the escorting corvette picked up eleven survivors and reported, among many others, the names of Alice McNeil and her two children as missing, presumed drowned.

X

The cellar was cool and quiet. He came down the stone steps and put on the electric light, whose bare bulb gathered cobwebs about itself.

The bottles were stacked in the archways, their ends outward so that they resembled the cordite in a ship's magazine. Each separate year had been carefully labelled so that any vintage could be selected without difficulty.

Here were the 1900s. Only a couple of dozen left of these. He remembered going down to the cellar in the old house at Vila Nova de Gaia and seeing hundreds of them when he was a boy. Those were the days, just before the Great War, when he was at school and Canon d'Albertanson was headmaster. His father had been the best tennis player, the best cricketer and the best company in the British colony then, and he, Bobby, had reason to be proud of the title 'Charlie Teape's boy'. He had been proud, too, of his elder brothers: he remembered the day Nicholas departed by train to join the family regiment, the 5th Irish Lancers, and how disappointed he had been a year later to learn that he had decided to leave the cavalry and join the Royal Flying Corps. Secretly, he believed that Nicholas had thrown his life away unnecessarily. He should have stayed in the family tradition and fought on horseback as so many of his ancestors had done. Teape had even regarded his death (caused by an inadvertent spin during a training flight) as something of a divine punishment on the family. Nicholas had put glory before duty, so Nicholas had died. That was the way Bobby had viewed the matter at the age of eleven, and he promised himself that if he went to war, he would not make the same mistake himself.

He moved along to the next archway, carefully removing a bottle to inspect the label. These were the 1904s, his birth year vintage, and he read the words he had read so often before: 'Specially bottled on the occasion of the birth of Robert Edward Teape, 7 October 1904'. He replaced the bottle. Not quite so fine a vintage as the 1900, but they would last a few years yet.

Here were the 1908s, the ones he had bought for Ruth as

part of his wedding present to her; a really beautiful wine, and he wished that he had more than the five dozen he had laid down. It was sad that Ruth had never really appreciated good port. She was happy to drink it, but was unable to detect the nuances of taste or to admire a really fine colour or bouquet such as this wine possessed.

He passed on, along later vintages: 1912s, 1920s, 1922s, 1924s. All of them good, some excellent. These were his dog days, the vintages of his public school and university years; years that he associated with dorm raids, cricket matches, learning to shave, afternoons on the Isis. They were also years when he began to see the gradual change in his father: the transition from an energetic man in the peak of health to a pitiable creature whose breath came in gasps, who repeated himself endlessly, who forgot where he had left his keys, which day of the week it was and whether he was going out to dinner or not that evening.

While Bobby looked back on those years with sadness, he recognised their worth all the same, for he had learnt from his father's weakness and was continually on guard against the creeping alcoholism that had ruined so many port shippers' lives. And what, after all, was a father for if his son could not learn from his mistakes?

He reached his large stock of '27s. Almost as good as the 1912s, these, but still young, still only in their teens. 1927 had been the year his brother George had started motor racing in earnest, in spite of his mother's protestations. His had been a brief, spectacular career; heavily built, fair haired and strikingly handsome, George Teape had captivated the hearts and imagination of the motor racing enthusiasts and sports writers. He had lived the life of a hero for nearly a year, adored by a string of young women in cloche hats and clinging dresses, wined and dined in the most expensive clubs and restaurants, paraded shoulder high after each successive racing triumph. It had ended abruptly on the Mountain Turn at Brooklands, when his Leyland Thomas rolled and burst into flames. The national newspapers carried the picture of the accident on their front pages.

1931 held memories of a vintage when Joy Remington had

come up to Quinta das Rosas, and they had danced to the music of an accordion while the treaders sang and clapped in the *lagares*. That was the autumn he had realised for the first time that there was perhaps more to life than eating and drinking, playing tennis and shooting partridge. He had not exactly courted Joy, but had acknowledged her presence more often and taken to accepting more of the invitations of Cousin Fay, who was anxious to see her eldest daughter up the aisle.

1934. He paused to stare at the bottles, still comparatively new and shiny. Not one of the great vintages by any means, and the year was not one to be proud of. That was the year he broke up with Joy, the year his mother died, and above all, the year of his first encounter with Natália.

He shuddered a little, remembering.

When Ruth had agreed to leave Portugal, he had thought to himself that her departure and the sale of the house would at last be the means of getting rid of Natália. But now, with Ruth determined to remain in Portugal come what may, the Portuguese maid seemed to be even more closely involved with the family than before. She adored Ruth and would do anything for her; she doted on Stella and regarded looking after her more as a privilege than a chore. She was becoming part of the family, making herself indispensable, so that it was becoming unthinkable that she should ever leave.

At least I am making amends, he thought. She and Eduardo are clothed and fed; they are happy and in good health. Perhaps what has happened is for the best; perhaps this is the way it had to be.

He glanced round at the crates of non-vintage ports: Teape's Double Dry, Teape's Special Reserve, Teape's Bandmaster – the ports they drank every day. He wondered, a little wryly, whether his palate would be affected by the coming forced abstention.

He looked at his watch. The Lisbon train left at ten-thirty, and it was now nearly nine. He took one last look round, wondering when or whether he would see all this again and then, switching off the electric light, returned up the steps from the cellar.

He found Stella in her playpen. He crouched beside her and

201

looked into her dark blue eyes. She gripped the vertical wooden bars and her jaw jutted out in that strangely determined way of hers. He lifted her up and held her cheek against his face, to feel again that incredible softness. He whispered and talked to her, walking about the room with her. He held her at arm's length, gazing into her eyes, and realised at that moment that she, Stella, would be the final and ultimate reason for fighting and surviving; for going and for coming back.

These thoughts were too much for Bobby. He bit his lip and his eyes filled with tears.

'I think it's time we went,' Ruth said behind him. He turned. She stood at the door, and he wondered how long she had been watching him.

He nodded, not trusting himself to speak, and lowered Stella back into the playpen. He kissed the top of her head, told her to be a good girl and marched quickly out into the hall.

The car was already loaded with his baggage, and Joaquim and Fernanda were waiting to open the gates. Minho wagged round his legs and the older dog, Tagus, stood by the front door, grey-muzzled, wagging from a distance.

He felt large and clumsy. The sun beat down fiercely.

'Off we go, then,' he mumbled. 'Off we go.'

Ana came out and curtsied to him. He accepted the good wishes of Joaquim and Fernanda.

'Have you said goodbye to Natália?' Ruth asked him as he was about to get into the car.

'Not really.'

'She went into the village to buy *pãosinhos*. I thought she would be back by now.'

'We can't afford to wait.'

They slammed the doors and he started the engine. Joaquim and Fernanda opened the gates and held the dog. The big black Jowett bumped over the sill and out onto the dust track.

On their way towards the main road they met Natália coming the other way. She stood aside on the verge, holding Eduardo back to keep him clear of the car. Bobby raised a hand in acknowledgement and farewell.

As the car swept past, its wheels raised a cloud of dust that hung about for a long time in the hot, still sunshine.

❊ 8 ❊

I

WHEN HE CAME HOME she was playing at the back with Eduardo, and Natália was scrubbing clothes on the slab. She was five. It was 1946. He had a moustache, and when he picked her up he smelt of tobacco and his bristles pricked her cheek. He was huge and he had a boomy voice and there were hairs on the back of his fingers. He was very jolly-jolly and what-have-we-got-here and he gave her a doll. She clutched the doll and hated it even more than she had hated every other doll, and only thanked him when her mother reminded her. Then he called her Miss Funny Face and she said that's not my name and he said what is your name? and she said Stella Rosalinde Teape and he looked at her mother and they both laughed and kissed each other. That was when she first noticed that her mother had changed: she had had her hair permed in Oporto and it looked too wavy and false, like a wig. She was wearing a suit which she didn't often wear and that looked wrong, too. She was different in other ways, sort of fussy and anxious and telling her off when she wouldn't have usually told her off. They talked all the time, to each other, not to her. They talked about things she didn't know about, 'all the news' was what they called it and suddenly it seemed as if neither had time for her, that she had been given her doll and that she should go away and play with it, there's a good girl. So she went upstairs and banged the doll's head, gently at first, gently, experiment-ally, on the brass rail at the bottom of her bed. A bit harder later, just a little harder, until the back of its head was cracked open so that she had to hide it in case he found out, and in the morning, after she had knocked on their door and had been told to go away and come back later and knocked again and

203

eventually been allowed in, in the morning, after they had told her that no, she could not come into bed – after that, he asked her where her doll was and what her name was to be, and her mother said yes, what's happened to it? and she had been obliged to bring it along, and he had found out about the bashed-in head, and his lips went a horrible shape which meant, she later learnt, that he was specially angry, and his face had gone sort of dark and she was afraid of him. But he quickly became cheerful and never-mind-never-mind and later what-have-we-got-here all over again, and produced a fluffy rabbit which was to have been for her birthday but he said why-not, why-not and so she was given that as well. But Fluffy Rabbit could never take the place of Ferocious Animal, the one with a zip up the middle for keeping your pyjamas in. Ferocious Animal slept with her and had the sort of arms you could put half round your neck, which was a comfort when the dog in the village, the one they kept tied up all the time, howled in the night.

II

Things changed. Before he came back, every morning, she had gone into her mother's bed and snuggled close, and if ever she had had a bad dream her mother always took her into her room and sometimes she slept the whole of the rest of the night, waking up in the morning and having a surprise because her mother was there, soft, close, comforting. And far back, so far back she had only a dim memory of it, there was a big green room at the top of a building, which in fact was the billiards room in the Factory House, and she went there with her mother and lots of other ladies who made bandages and sent parcels to England. When they got home they had tea and in the evenings after her bath they sometimes sang clap hands till daddy comes home. Before he came back they were always having exciting conversations about what it would be like when he returned, how wonderful it would be to have Daddy home, and sometimes her mother got out the photograph albums and showed her all those pictures, the pictures of the wedding in England and that one of them walking along a road in Paris and all the others of people doing silly things on beaches and that's Uncle Theo, poor Uncle Theo, who died and this is dear old Tagus who had to be put down and this is you at your christening, weren't you sweet? and that's old Joaquim who used to live in the cottage where Natália lives, and this is Quinta das Rosas and when Daddy gets back we shall be going there I expect, and when Daddy gets back we shall be doing this and that and when Daddy gets back the other. Always when Daddy gets back. But when Daddy got back, things changed. Everything changed.

III

She didn't understand what went wrong. It should have worked out the way they had expected it to, but it didn't. In ways it did, of course, in fact on the surface it seemed to work out exactly the way it was supposed to, for all sorts of new things began to happen. They went up the Douro for holidays and on expeditions to Viana or Aveiro at the weekends. People started coming for drinks and for dinner. Things were done to the house and garden. Rationing stopped and she was given a bicycle for Christmas and a watch for her birthday. Yes, in a way it did work out, because he was often in good moods and teased her and tickled her and read to her and gave her piggy backs and swam in the water tank with her and on her birthdays and at Christmas organised games and took charge of everybody, laughing a great deal and saying by-jingo-by-jimminy. But on other days, awful other days, there were arguments and scenes and battles, the reasons for which she could never remember, he with his head bent over his plate (it was always worst at meal times) and she troubled, unhappy, and after he had left the room she had gone to her and said, 'Never mind, Mummy,' that time she had cried and it had been horrible, frightening. That was the beginning of those long

205

years of being difficult. She knew, in a roundabout way, that she was being difficult, but she didn't know why. She didn't enjoy the tears and shouts of hatred, the slamming doors, the hot tears into her pillow; she didn't enjoy them, but they just had to happen, to let go the pressure that had built up not only inside her but also within the whole house, as if she were the weak part of the balloon, the part where it had to burst. And she was told repeatedly that she must try, try very very hard to control herself, and was asked, what would happen if Daddy and Mummy behaved like that? and then she realised something she had never realised before: grownups were stupid and most of the things they said were stupid. The same people came for the same drinks and said the same things. They talked about Atlee and Churchill and the stupid atom bomb. They admired each other's houses and each other's children and they asked her how she was getting on at school, to which she answered, abruptly, 'All right,' and stared them out so that they had to look away, nervous of her. School was stupid too, at least it was very nearly stupid. Most of the things they gave you to do were too easy and they made you spend ages and ages on the same things so you got bored, bored, bored with it and started copying down everything Miss Maybury said so you could read it out loud in her voice during break and that made them laugh, but they were all stupid as well, because they laughed for the wrong reasons. But – but – although so many things and people were stupid there was, underneath, a frightening sort of feeling that she was not the same and yet would like to be. Not the same, obviously, for she was taller than everyone else her age. She looked down on them, was unable to be one of them, was left off their birthday party lists, left out of their stupid games, the games she would like to think were not stupid so that she could enjoy them. She would have given up being top of the class, winning at sports, getting reports that said, 'Excellent work'. She would have been happy to give up all that, in order to be like them and to be interested like them in all those stupid conversations and secrets and things that made them giggle. But she was difficult. It shouldn't have worked out that way, but it did. And she could never understand what had made her difficult, what had gone wrong.

Her head was too big and her bottom stuck out. Her hair flopped and her hands were silly. She hated her name and hated her face and her eyes looked out at you, the you in the mirror, sort of darkly, as if that you was really another person, and perhaps it was.

V

When 1950 came, it was like turning a corner, because that was the year she was going to be ten, and it was as if the whole world had started again and they were suddenly living in the future. That was the year her parents went away for a holiday in the spring, a second honeymoon, because they had been married fifteen years. They went to France somewhere and for a fortnight she was looked after by Aunty Suzy who wasn't really an aunt but a cousin. Aunty Suzy always knew the answer to everything and told you stories about how she knew Daddy when she was a little girl and he was a little boy. Aunty Suzy had four children and they were all at day school in London and enjoying it very much, and Uncle Maurice was her husband and he was a sort of doctor, whom she hadn't met. Almost every afternoon Aunty Suzy went upstairs and had a snooze, and while she did so the house was so quiet and still that the only thing to do was to mooch about in the garden and wait for Eduardo. Eduardo was nearly fifteen. His voice was cracky and his chin sort of furry. He worked on the *quinta* in the very early mornings before he went to work at the lodge, where he was learning to be a cooper. A cooper was somebody who made barrels and it was very difficult because you had to get it just right so that everything fitted, and sometimes they made a fire in the courtyard outside the cooperage in order to heat the iron hoops, and that was in order to make them grow so that they would fit over the newly-made barrels and shrink tight when they got cool. Eduardo had thick dark hair with gingery strands in it and his eyes looked at you when you

207

weren't expecting it and when he started to make friends he didn't seem to mind if you tried to stare him out but just grinned back, and one of his front teeth had grown crooked and that made him look crooked, but in a friendly way. He didn't have many hairs on his arms and he didn't say a great deal, but he often smiled and she liked that because you didn't have to say anything back, just stand there and look at him, watching him, especially in the early mornings, wielding the heavy hoe above his head, bringing it down into the April earth, turning it up, making it ready for the rows of lettuce and beans and tomatoes that would grow in those squares with ditches round them. When he didn't know she was there he sometimes sang in his strange, cracky voice, and because he was working at the same time, the sound of it came jerkily, jerking each time the hoe bit into the red earth. Also, when he wasn't looking, she saw him doing it into the bamboos and he made it arch, glistening in the early sunlight, and splatter against the long green leaves and the pale stalks and the next time she saw him he looked up from his work and smiled his crooked tooth smile, and it seemed to mean more, and only a few days after that in the evening when she was watching him, he put the hoe down and came over to her and sat down and lit a cigarette and invited her to sit down also, talking to her in a way that made her forget about trying to stare him out. He was very grown up, smoking his cigarette, and she was nearly ten. He held her hand and patted it with his own, and she saw that the fingernails were broken and caked with earth because he had been pulling out weeds; he patted her hand with his, and she liked it and when he asked her if she would come and see him again she nodded, yes, and agreed to keep it a secret.

VI

When they came back from their holiday, their second honeymoon, they seemed much happier, and there was a very big party in the evening that summer, the summer she was ten, and people danced and she was allowed to stay up late, and even when she was in bed the music went on and in the morning her mother said she hadn't had an evening like that since before the war. It was on that day, when Natália was still clearing up, that a lorry arrived at the gates and the men delivered a stone statue of a boy with no clothes on, a statue that her father had bought in France, and there was much discussion about where it was to go. Eventually they decided that he would go in the square between the four rose beds, and the regular gardener, Pedro, and Eduardo were told to move one of the big millstones that had always leant up against the side of the house in order that it could be used as a base, because it was round and her mother thought it would be a good idea. When they moved the millstone, they uncovered the ants' nest and Natália bought a kettle of boiling water to pour on them and the ants panicked, racing backwards and forwards carrying eggs that were much too big for them, and Natália poured the boiling water over them and they died in their thousands. Her mother said, poor ants, and in the evening asked her if she knew what a millstone was for and how it was used, and that was an easy question because she had visited a windmill with Aunty Suzy one day when they went to Aveiro, and she had seen the sails hurtling round. They had gone up the winding staircase and seen the two millstones, the top one going round and round, and the steady stream of grains falling between them and coming out like white sawdust that rose in little clouds and made people's faces smudged with white, like clowns. So they put the statue of the bare boy on top of the millstone and she could see it out of her window in the mornings when she looked out to see if she could see Eduardo. And some weeks later her mother told her the story about Jesus and the children, and made her find the place in St Matthew and read it aloud: whoso shall offend one of these little ones which believe in me, it were better for him that a millstone were hanged about his neck and that he were drowned in the depth of the sea. That was why her mother had thought of the idea of the little naked boy standing on the millstone and when her father overheard her mother explaining about it, he started an argument with her, an argument

209

that went on and on, the first real argument they had had since coming back from their second honeymoon and he said he wished he'd never bought the bloody thing in the first place and she wailed, nothing I do is ever right. She heard that bit quite clearly, when she was listening on the stairs.

VII

There was a Christmas when they went to the Remingtons and Uncle Dodger was in a wheel chair, so deaf that you had to shout in his ear, and they made her go and talk to him and he gave her a present, a tiny gold charm that was a rabbit to put on her bracelet, the one she never wore, and when you went close to him you could see into his nostrils and he had yellow skin and pale brown freckles on the backs of his hands, freckles that were so big that they joined up, and lots of other Remingtons were there, James and Phillipa and their family and Joy, who had never married, and Deirdre and her husband Arie who was a Dutchman and was always laughing and slapping his thigh, but they couldn't have children and were going to adopt; and she overheard her mother say to her father that Uncle Dodger was incontinent, so she looked it up in the dictionary on Boxing Day, the *Little Oxford Dictionary* that Aunty Suzy had sent from England, and it said, 'lacking self restraint, unchaste,' so she looked up 'unchaste' and it didn't have it so she looked up 'chaste' and it said, 'pure, virtuous, modest; pure in taste or style, unadorned,' and it all made her wonder what Uncle Dodger had done because he looked a nice old man really and she would have liked to have him for a grandfather because he wasn't stupid and had kind eyes and tiny little eyebrows that grew out in spiky tufts. But he died only a few weeks after Christmas, and that was the first time she saw a real coffin, because she went to the funeral and there it was.

210

VIII

When people came to dinner her father was different. He was all jolly-jolly and by-jingo and what'll-you-have and he liked talking about port. Often he had arguments with Hugh Blunden about how to sell port and what sort of port was easiest to sell. Hugh Blunden wore polished black shoes and a blue suit. He had wet lips and a big stomach and when he smoked a cigar the end of it went damp and soggy, and he was always telling stories. He stayed very late usually and her mother once called him 'that awful man'. In the evenings before dinner if there were guests who were also customers, her father would offer them a drink, saying, a glass of Red Portugal? and then he would tell them how port started and how the red wine was called 'Red Portugal' and he would quote that same rhyme that he always quoted: Be sometimes to your country true, Have once the public good in view, Bravely despise champagne at court and choose to dine at home with port. Then they laughed and that always made him pleased because he liked people to laugh at what he said. When there was no one in for dinner, especially in the summer evenings, he often walked up and down outside breathing through his mouth and muttering to himself, his hands behind his back, sometimes looking at the ground and sometimes looking at the sky, and when he did that he was thinking about blends, which years to mix with which years and how to make it taste right with the nutty flavour he was always talking about. Once or twice a year she went with her mother to the lodge in Vila Nova de Gaia and they would find her father either in his office or upstairs in the tasting room with the window that faced north, like an artist's studio, her mother said, where you could look out over the Douro. Boats with square sails still brought some of the wine down the river in barrels that were laid in rows on the quayside, to be collected in oxcarts later and taken up the hill to the lodges to mature. In the tasting room was the huge copper thing like the end of a trumpet or one of those old gramophones which they spat into, a great stream of golden red spit that dribbled downwards. There were rows of bottles and test-tubes and everything was labelled and she was expected to ask questions. They always did the same tour when they visited the lodge, walking through the place where all the barrels were kept and looking at the extra big barrel, the tonel, with the family coat of arms on it and saying good morning to old Tomaz Leitão do Espírito Santo, which meant Thomas Sucking Pig of the Holy Ghost, and every time they went into the bottling plant her father explained that it was only since the war that they had started bottling vintage port in Portugal. Further down the hill was the cooperage where Eduardo worked. Usually he was busy doing something, sawing or using the adze or sweeping or bending the iron hoops, and he always seemed engrossed in what he was doing. Her mother would ask her father, quietly, how he was getting on, and her father would say he was a very promising lad, and she would make a point of watching him working. Then, just as they were leaving he would look up at her for the first time and although he didn't smile she knew that he was thinking a smile and she thought a smile back. She was eleven and he was sixteen. No one else knew anything about it.

IX

That Easter, the Easter before she was going to be twelve, they went to England to see the school. Craybourne House, it was called and it was a Country Seat. There was a driveway of gravel that went up the hill past rhododendron bushes and when you came round the corner there was the school, with tall square chimneys and latticed windows and wisteria growing up the walls. It had oak doors and a leather-bound book for visitors to sign their names. Inside, there was a particular smell of polish and at the end of a long wide corridor there were huge mirrors so that as you walked towards them you could see your father in his new tweed suit that your mother had helped him choose at Austin Reed, and your mother in her jacket and skirt and smokey blue pullover and single row of pearls and yourself between them in your dress from Dickins and Jones and your

212

Oporto British School blazer over it. There was a visitors' room where you had to wait while your parents talked to the headmistress in private, and later you were called in and said how-do-you-do to Miss Robson the headmistress, who asked you if you liked living in Portugal and you said it was all right, and tried to stare her out, but she stared back with her baggy eyes very steadily and asked, what does all right mean and you said it means there's not very much wrong with it and your mother caught her breath and said really Stella I'm sure you can do better than that and Miss Robson nodded and said yes I'm quire sure you can and then ignored you and talked to your parents about how you would travel back and forth. They said you would be staying with relations in Hampstead or Essex, and when they eventually stopped talking about you in front of you which you hated more than anything else, Miss Robson shook hands with your father and with your mother and then with you and said she was looking forward to seeing you in September, and you said nothing at all because the whole conversation was stupid: nobody had meant anything they had said. In the car on the way back to Hampstead they argued about it and he said boarding school's just the thing for you my girl by jingo by jimminy and the sooner you go there the better for all concerned.

X

They stayed at the Blakelys in Hampstead and in the mornings they had cornflakes and toasted Wonderloaf and tea out of pottery mugs. She had four Blakely cousins, Julian, Paul, Tristram and Jennifer. They were all doing very well and looked like Uncle Maurice once looked, with soft downy skins and dark eyebrows and long eyelashes and soft woollen pullovers. Julian played the piano and Paul was good at art and Tristram wore glasses and was Gifted and Jennifer was a Darling. They had a spaniel called Willy and Uncle Maurice was always looking things up in books and encouraging them by asking difficult questions and helping them to find out the

213

answers for themselves. When he wasn't doing that, Uncle Maurice sat in his study and worked at his typewriter, and her father called him a trick cyclist which made her mother say 'sshhhh' because she was afraid he would hear. They played Monopoly because of the rain and at mealtimes her father teased her and was much nicer to her than he ever was at home, even making her laugh sometimes which was good up to a point but not when it made her too much the centre of conversation and interest because then she could feel them all looking at her and seeing how big she was for her age and that made her do and say things which she didn't want to. That happened on the last day but one, the day after she dropped her marbles in the Tate Gallery, when there were two other guests for lunch, and they all sat down to table together, Uncle Maurice at one end and Aunty Suzy at the other and everybody else including the children and some extra guests all in between and they had filthy soup like jellified sick, which she left, and roast beef and Yorkshire pudding and the grown-ups had wine and her father started talking about port all over again and the guests, who came from Kent, asked all the right questions and her father gave all the usual answers about port having to be well-educated and how different ports were like different people. And she said that's right, some ports are boring like you, and that started an argument between them which at first was meant to be funny, but which went wrong because she said you're always talking about your stupid port, and Teape's port is no better than any other, it's just a question of advertising and he said you don't know what you're talking about and she replied oh yes I do because I heard Hugh Blunden saying it and he said Mister Blunden to you if you please and she copied him, if you please and the argument got worse and suddenly she realised that something was wrong, something her mother had once said would one day happen and she didn't know what to do about it because they were all looking at her and the longer she stayed at the table the worse it felt and eventually the only thing to do was to get up and run out of the room and he shouted at her, come back here, but her mother said 'Bobby' in a specially urgent way and when she got up to the bathroom it was all over her skirt and she knew

214

they must have seen because they had watched her go from the table and the skirt was stained with blood and now they would also be able to hear her crying and she felt she would never be able to face any of them, ever, ever again.

XI

On Sundays they went to St James's Church. She had to go because her mother insisted. Once she had tried to refuse, but her mother said think, he gave up so much for you, can't you give just one hour every week for him? Her mother was a person who never lost her temper. She wore glasses for reading and parted her hair in the middle and enjoyed A.J. Cronin. She helped at the women's functions, made sandwiches, visited people when they were ill, consoled, advised, listened. Her mother kept a rockery garden in which she planted shrubs and plants: wild orchids she found on walks, rock roses, tigers' eyes, brilliant flowers in miniature which she dug gently from the earth with a tiny trowel. Her mother had made the tapestry covers for the kneelers in the church and it was she, now that Mrs Remington was getting on and doing less, who organised people and talked them into taking part in the fêtes and jumble sales and outings that the Busy Bees organised in aid of the various charities and orphanages which the church patronised. Her mother was always busy, but never too busy to listen. After the holiday at the Blakelys she felt much closer to her mother because they were both women. Being a woman was frightening in one respect. There was nothing you could do about it and it became more and more obvious as time passed. It was like leaving No Man's Land and moving finally into the female camp, when you would have preferred to stay just you. But in addition to being frightening it was also exciting because you knew that men were looking at you, looking at *them* and you were glad because you had something that they could not have and yet wanted and envied you for having. So in the evenings you looked at them in the tilting

215

mirror on the dressing table and saw yourself, white where the swimming costume went, and also the glass animals, the elephant and the rhinoceros and the giraffe which you kept on the dressing table, the ones which a distant aunt had given you for successive Christmases. You looked at them and were secretly proud of them, and they were like a secret source of power which were yours to use in any way you liked.

XII

On that last day, Eduardo throttled a hen. He went down to the hen house with Natália to choose one and when he held it up for her she blew on its chest to separate the feathers so that she could make sure the skin was yellow and the chicken therefore good for eating. Eduardo grinned and showed his broken teeth. He put the hen under his arm and took its head in his hand and warned her to look away, but she said she wanted to see. Just before he did it, the chicken seemed to know, know what was going to happen as if Death is like an important visitor who sends a servant on ahead to announce his arrival. Eduardo twisted the head and tugged it at the same time. There was a sort of barking noise from the chicken and it was dead and Natália plucked it that morning on the step outside the kitchen. It was her last day, and that was why they killed the chicken. Laurinda, the new cook, made stuffing with bread-crumbs and onions and herbs. The kitchen was busy with the comings and goings of Laurinda and Natália and Etelvina, who was the new maid and was being trained and was unbelievably stupid although she was nineteen. Natália prepared the vege-tables and sang songs about food and departed lovers, and Eduardo, who was working in the garden with Pedro, joined in, his voice distant but clear, and she wanted to go and talk to him but somehow it was impossible because in the last months she had felt shy of him and they had not spoken, only looked, for she was twelve and turning into a woman and he was seventeen and becoming a man. In the evening the Randalls came to dinner and she was allowed to stay up. The glasses shone in the candlelight and Natália served delicately-carved white chicken meat from a silver dish. Her father held a glass of tawny to the light and invited them all to admire the soft rose-golden colour, and they drank her health before she went up to bed. The taps in the bathroom were of polished brass with ceramic tops and had C for hot and F for cold and the hot water came in sudden steamy spurts, coughing its way out because it was so difficult to heat it without overheating it and anyway all the plumbing was wrong and her father cursed it daily when he shaved in the mornings. The uniform hung in her wardrobe: a blazer with pink and green stripes and a straw boater with a pink and green band. A white blouse and a dark green gym slip. A pink and white dress for Sundays and brand new shoes. She opened her window and looked out into the darkness. Pinpoints of light flashed on and off under the trees – fireflies, they were – and many other insects chirruped and sang. Down by the cottage, a match flared. It was Eduardo. She saw the cigarette glow each time he sucked it. The light was on in the bedroom and although she could not see him she knew that he must be able to see her, and was watching her. She raised her hand and waved, and the point of light that was his cigarette moved in an arc as he waved back. And then, because she wanted to say goodbye in a special way, she took off her dressing gown without bothering to draw the curtains, not allowing him to see everything but knowing that he would see enough, not hurrying to put on her nightdress and blowing him a very quick kiss before she drew the curtains, which had a pattern of peacocks sitting in trees. When her mother came in to say goodnight she was already in bed with Ferocious Animal and her mother sat on the bed and said well darling, you're coming to another milestone aren't you? and talked about how she felt when she was a little girl and had to be away from home for the first time and how she thought it was important, as you grew up, to take some of your childhood with you and never leave it all behind, and when she kissed you goodnight there were tears in her eyes because she was not really as happy as she should be, not as happy as they had been in those long-ago days before he came back.

217

XIII

The music mistress was Miss Cumming and she was like a soft vole, with downy skin and hooded eyes that were like a bird's. She had you out one by one and you had to stand by the piano. She played a note and you had to 'la' the same note, and everybody laughed. Try again dear, Miss Cumming said and played the note again but it was no good and everybody giggled and Miss Cumming said poor dear you really are tone deaf aren't you and standing there by the piano looking at their silly faces, especially Woggy Robertson, who had the giggles, she was angry. They seemed to be ganged up against her, that was what it felt like anyway, and she decided then and there to show them, show them that she wasn't as stupid as they thought. Just because I can't sing in tune doesn't mean I'm thick, that's what she said, and she proved it too by coming top in History, top in French, top in Maths and top in Latin. They giggled and went about in groups. They had crushes on the sixth formers and sent them little love notes. There was Woggy Robertson's group and Vee Harper's group and Louise Ellworthy's group, and she didn't belong to any of them because she had come to the school a year later than them and anyway she was too tall and said things that they pretended to be shocked by. She was the one who read books in the library by herself, her knees hunched up under her chin, sitting on the oak window ledge with the rain pounding down outside. The one with the boxy fringe and a temper, who could shoot netball goals over and over again. She was the one who was always very nearly late and who dropped her books and spilt ink over her Joan of Arc project; the one who walked in her sleep and swapped her wristwatch for a rabbit she called Salazar, a rabbit with long bluey ears that lived in the animal hut which was the other side of the rhododendrons and overlooked the road where the boys from the grammar school went past at a quarter past four. She was the one who, in her first summer term, made friends with the new girl, Hilary Grear-Smith who had plaits and dirty finger nails and an adam's apple and who punched you if you didn't agree with her and they went around together for two terms before they had

218

an argument and nobody ever discovered why they had argued but Hilary said she was filthy and she said Hilary was beneath her scorn and after that they never even spoke to each other.

XIV

The boat sailed from Tilbury. Sometimes she went on the Highland Monarch and sometimes on the Highland Chieftain or the Highland Princess. On the first day when the stewards didn't know which passengers were travelling first class, you could get a deck chair and have beef tea on the sun deck and read a book. The Oporto crowd always sat together at the same table for meals: the two Randall boys who went to the Oratory, the Empsons, the Millets and the other Remingtons who came from Lisbon and whose father farmed cork in the Alentejo and who were very good-looking and knew it. Everyone behaved as badly as possible. Once she didn't like the boiled mutton and mushy potatoes that was served up so she opened the porthole and threw the whole lot – plate, food, knife and fork – into the sea. Another time they had a water fight and Marjory Empson put ice cubes down her neck so she retaliated by letting off a foam fire extinguisher and Nigel Millet, who was only nine, laughed so much that he did it in his pants. Usually the boats stopped at Vigo where they spent the night, before going by taxi to the border at Valença where they were met by parents who waited at the customs post. Then there was a picnic lunch on the way south and the arrival home, usually at tea-time, and the special feeling of arriving outside the gates, the deep bark of Ophelia the Serra mountain dog whose name was a play on the words 'O filha!' which was an exclamation of surprise to a girl. And when you got out of the car Ophelia put her paws on your shoulders and licked your face. Natália came out and kissed you, smelling of olive oil and sweat and onions, and Laurinda and Etelvina welcomed you and you went upstairs and Natália brought your luggage up and helped you unpack, chattering to you, taking away all the

219

things that needed to be washed so that the following morning she would be able to beat the dirt out of them on the cement slab, and you would feel shy because there was your bra for Eduardo to see and you wondered how on earth you had the courage to do what you did on the last night before you went off for your first term. And there were parties now, parties she went to with Stephen Randall who was very nearly as tall as her. Parties at which you drank fizzy lemonade and ate chicken rice and danced to Edmundo Ross and Glenn Miller or listened, solemnly, to the Rhapsody in Blue. These parties ended up with the Dashing White Sergeant or the Eightsome, the girls in cotton dresses, the boys in suits or dinner jackets that made them sweat, and bossy fathers who came in at midnight and sent everybody home. There were parties and picnics, tennis matches and lazy afternoons, and all too soon you were packing up all over again and going down to Lisbon to go on board the boat, back to Tilbury and the school and Miss Robson holding forth at Assembly and your rabbit, Salazar, who you sometimes put right up between your legs and felt him there, warm and pulsing between your just as warm and just as pulsing thighs.

XV

Colin was a bit flabby and he had sort of pink skin. He went to the grammar school and she had seen him walking past when she was in goal, and they had exchanged a Look. That was when she was in the fourth form, and two weeks later she met him properly for the first time on the Saturday of half term when she went down to the town with some other fourth formers. She saw him in Woolworths and she pretended to be interested in buying some electric plugs and he stood behind her and touched her behind with his hand as if by accident so she managed to separate herself from the others, which was against school rules, and walked out of a back entrance, going down by the canal and he followed her along a path and when

220

she turned up the hill, off the path, under the beech trees, he continued to follow her so she stopped and he came up and spoke to her and they smoked a cigarette. She arranged to meet him again and he climbed through a gap in the fence and they stood in the rhododendrons, and she made him kiss her with his tongue. After that they met almost every evening for a fortnight until eventually, the time they met after the time they lay down and nearly went the whole way, he said he didn't want to go on with it and she laughed and he got annoyed and she never met him again. That was Colin and he was very unsatisfactory.

Eduardo was different because he wasn't an experiment like Colin. Also, he was a proper man because when they were on the dunes and she let him touch her breasts underneath her swimming costume and tried to get him to lie down on top of her, he wouldn't because he said it would be very dangerous and she could see that he was right and she wanted that more than anything else in the world, however dangerous it was. She wanted it and thought about nothing else at all and the only way to stop thinking about it, or at least make the feeling go away, was to put it all down in a story, a story which sounded as if it wasn't true because she didn't say 'I' but 'she', a story which she wrote in a big exercise book that she kept hidden in a biscuit tin under the rhododendron bushes by the animal hut.

9

I

THE PRIZE-GIVING CEREMONY started at three in the afternoon.
The parents took up the rear rows of chairs in the big oak
panelled hall, chatting among themselves in subdued whispers,
some of the mothers fanning away the July heat, the fathers
trying to arrange their legs in adequate comfort between the
rows of wooden chairs which had been placed too close
together.

On the stage, the table was set, not unlike an altar, for the
proceedings that were about to take place. It was spread with a
baize cloth, and the cups, trophies, medals and glossy prize
books had been laid out in order of presentation. There were
two carafes of water, each with a glass upturned upon it, and a
microphone, from which a flex trailed to a bulky tape recorder
at the side of the stage.

And now the girls entered. In single file, wearing their
freshly-laundered pink and white dresses and straw boaters
they moved quietly, like a creeping tide of femininity, filling
the rows from the front, starting with the first formers and
ending with the lanky sixth formers. There they stood until, at
a double tap from the music mistress's baton, they all sat
down, and the grown-ups allowed a gentle sigh of appreciation
to escape at such discipline, such order.

Miss Cummings at the Selfridge Grand played the opening
bars of the school song, and having sat down only moments
before, the girls of Craybourne House rose to sing the well-
practised words:

> Once in these dear halls our founders
> Laboured for the truths we guard:

Earnest hearts once beat united,
Let their triumphs ne'er be marred:

Honesty! Sincerity! Purity!
O Craybourne keep us true to thee!

Stella Teape was in the seventh row back, among the fourth formers. She was just fifteen now, taller than most of her form mates still, but less conspicuous than she had been in earlier years. She had been asked by Miss Cumming to mouth the words of the school song only, as the sound of her voice was thought to mar the more tuneful effect of the majority; so there she stood, flanked by Vee Harper and Woggy Robertson, lipping the words but emitting no sound.

The last chorus was coming to an end. The word 'purity' occupied eight drawn-out notes, and a catch of the breath was required to continue with the last line, which seemed to deify the school itself, as if its spirit could keep a hundred and sixty girls of differing backgrounds and moral standards true to itself.

A rustle of ironed cotton, and the school sat down.

Miss Robson looked even more strained than usual at the end of a school year, and she now stood up as if addressing the crew of a sinking ship. To her right, a little man in army uniform sat, with shining Sam Browne and shining cheeks and shining shoes, which only just reached the floor.

'Major-General Rees-Soaper, ladies and gentlemen, members of the staff, girls of Craybourne House,' she began somewhat predictably. 'First of all, may I welcome you to this, our eighty-second founder's day since Craybourne House first opened in eighteen seventy-three. As is traditional on such occasions, I, as headmistress, will first give you a brief report on the activities of the school during the past year.'

Stella listened automatically for a few more sentences before her mind drifted away to more important things. The previous day, after breakfast, she had gone down to the animal hut to feed Salazar and had also paid a visit to one particular rhododendron bush, to collect her strictly private writings from the biscuit tin she had hidden there. But she had found

223

the tin open and her writings gone, and since that moment had spent most of her time wondering who had found them and what had been done with them. She was puzzled, alarmed, but above all, angry. She had calculated that she had written something in the region of eight thousand words in her large, alphabetically-indexed notebook, and it was her unannounced ambition to write three times as much: to make the total twenty-four, or even thirty thousand words; to complete a novelette, have it typed and send it to a publisher. It had been done, after all: wasn't the authoress of *The Constant Nymph* only fifteen? Wasn't there a writer called Françoise Sagan who had completed her first novel in her teens? Miss Robson's voice rambled on about the success of the hockey team, the university entrances, the building of a new science wing, while Stella Teape picked a scab on her knee and grew more angry by the minute.

'And now,' Miss Robson said, coming to the end of her speech, 'And now let us concentrate not so much on the achievements of the school but more on those of the individual. It therefore gives me great pleasure to call upon Major-General Rees-Soaper, who is himself an old girl, to present the prizes.'

In the moment of silent astonishment that followed, Stella looked up and remarked, quite audibly, 'This should be interesting,' which remark was followed by a moan of laughter and a few barely controlled titters from some of the girls and mothers.

'I'm so sorry,' Miss Robson said. 'I meant of course the *husband* of an old girl.' She turned to the Major-General, whose polished cheeks had turned the colour of his pink tabs. He rose to his feet, full of apple pie and cream and Nuits St George and spoke into the microphone as if by formula: 'Can you all hear me at the back? Good.' Then he put on a pair of spectacles, and in doing so seemed to undergo a metamorphosis from a man of blood to a comfortable old daddy, the husband of an old girl.

One by one, the girls were called, like first communicants, to receive their secular sacraments from the hands of this pinkcheeked, emasculate, military man. Each curtsied and

224

shook his hand, accepting his murmured congratulations and returning triumphant to her seat, clutching the book or cup or trophy as she sat down amid applause whose volume and frenzy were in direct proportion to her popularity.

But astonishingly, Stella Teape's name did not figure among the list of prize-winners. Though she had topped the examination lists in English, history and mathematics; though she had won the 100 yards freestyle; though she had been a member of the school tennis team in its several victories against other schools, she was not called out to receive so much as a commendation.

Frowns and whispers went up and down the seventh row, for Stella, known to her friends as Rozzy, had gained in popularity during the past year and had formed a loose association with Woggy Robertson and Vee Harper.

'You should have won that!' Vee hissed as Hilary Grear-Smith was called to the stage to accept the fourth form prize. Stella shrugged and looked straight ahead, and the prize-giving continued until the head girl went up to receive the complete works of Jane Austen in gold tooled morroco leather and Miss Robson announced, after the first formers realised that they could prolong the applause no longer, that tea was served on the lawns.

Parents and daughters hugged, kissed and mingled. Younger brothers hung about, scavenging rock cakes and éclairs from the tables. Mistresses were buttonholed and best friends introduced.

Stella stood apart from this, aware of the rapid glances in her direction as her acquaintances pointed her out. That's Stella Teape, over there. The one with a fringe. No, they aren't here, they live in Portugal.

Suddenly she wanted to get away from these gushing, hatted mums and pompous, suited dads. She made her way through the crowd and into the east wing, going along corridors and up wooden stairs to her dormitory.

Her suitcases were already packed. She would stay one more night at the school, and then the summer holidays would start. She stood at the window, looking out over the school grounds to the town beyond. In four days she would be home: home to sun and sand and swimming in the surf and in the evenings, waiting about on her bicycle in Valadares in order to meet Eduardo on his way home.

While nearly all the girls went home with their parents that afternoon, Stella remained in her dormitory, reading. In the evening, after an early supper with the few others whose parents lived abroad, she went down to the animal hut to say goodbye to Salazar, who was looked after by the children of the groundsman during the holidays.

She stroked his long, blue-grey ears, whispering intimately to him in Portuguese, enjoying the softness of his fur against her cheek.

A movement behind her made her turn. It was one of the first formers, a little girl with blonde plaits, the darling of the common room: Phoebe Something, whose parents lived in Egypt.

'Excuse me, Stella,' she said, out of breath from running her errand.

'Yes?'

'Miss Robson wants to see you.'

'Now?'

Phoebe nodded urgently, eager to be of service to Miss Robson, the school, Stella, Honesty, Sincerity, Purity, O-Craybourne-keep-us-true-to-thee.

'Where is she?'

'In her study.'

'All right.'

'Are you coming?'

Stella looked down at Salazar. 'Not exactly.'

'What?'

'Never mind.'

Phoebe hesitated, her brow furrowed. Stella had turned away from her and was stroking the rabbit's ears.

'I think you *ought* to go,' Phoebe said.

'I shall. In my own time.'

The first former hesitated further. 'What shall I say? If she asks?'

'Look, you've delivered your message, so just run along, see?'

Phoebe pouted. 'There's no need to be beastly,' she said.

Stella put Salazar back in his hutch and locked up the animal hut, pausing a moment outside the door.

She had half expected this summons. Indeed, she might even have been disappointed if it had not come.

As she made her way up the path between the rhododendron bushes, she reflected that it would be interesting to see how it would all turn out.

II

'You sent for me, Miss Robson.'

'Come in, Stella.'

The heavy oak door clicked shut. Miss Robson took off her glasses and arranged them so that they and her fountain pen lay exactly parallel to the edge of the leather-cornered blotter on her desk.

She looked up. 'Do you know why I have sent for you?' Miss Robson always laid great store by good diction, and considered that she set an excellent example to the girls.

'No, Miss Robson.'

The headmistress opened a drawer of her desk and took out Stella's large, stiff-covered note book. She held it up for the girl to see.

'Do you recognise this?'

'It's a notebook, Miss Robson.'

Miss Robson took up her glasses and put them on. 'Yes, Stella, I can see that it is a notebook. But do you recognise to whom it belongs?'

The girl took a step forward and looked at the book which Miss Robson had placed on her desk.

'It's mine,' she said eventually.

'Ah. That was what I wished to find out.'

Stella cleared her throat. 'Can I have it back?'

Miss Robson placed her white, ringless hands upon the lip of the desk, one upon the other. 'Oh no. That you may not.'

Outside, beyond the oaken door, one of the cleaners was

singing a Doris Day hit, imploring anyone who cared to listen to take her back to the black hills, the black hills of Dakota.

Miss Robson picked up the notebook and flicked the pages over, looking from them to Stella and back at the turning pages. 'That a girl from my school should be capable of writing such *filth!*' she said, and ejected the last word as if it were a morsel of the very filth that she regarded Stella's work to be.

'You didn't have to read it,' Stella said under her breath.

'I beg your pardon?'

'I said you didn't have to read it, Miss Robson.'

The headmistress's nostrils dilated with anger. She resembled a grey mare about to bolt. 'Impertinence will not assist your case,' she said.

Stella breathed in deeply so that her blouse tightened against her breasts. 'Am I on trial then?'

'There is no need for a trial when the evidence is as irrefutable as this.'

Outside, the cleaner had changed songs. 'I'd like to get you,' she wailed, 'on a slow boat to China, all to myself alone . . . '

Miss Robson's white finger tips fluttered a moment on the edge of her desk. 'And how much of this – this sordid account is factual, may I ask?'

In spite of her efforts to remain calm, Stella felt the lack of control that comes with anger. 'I don't see – I don't see why I should have to answer questions about it. If you want to punish me, why can't you get on with it? I put "Strictly Private" on that notebook – '

'No doubt,' Miss Robson cut in, 'to titillate the curiosity of those among whom you circulated it.'

'I did not circulate it! It was stolen. It's my private property, Miss Robson. I have a right to have it back.'

'A right? You have a right?' Miss Robson shook her head. 'You may think you have a right, Stella, but you should realise that I have something far more important. I have a duty. My duty to the school. My duty to the girls in my care. My duty to their parents. And even my duty to your parents.'

The headmistress looked down at her hands, and her eyelids blinked rapidly. It had been a long, hard term. She was physically and mentally tired. And she was genuinely offended:

she saw only one way of dealing with this bulky girl who stood before her, and that way was deeply distasteful to her.

'Do you have no vestige of shame? No embarrassment at being found out?'

There was a silence. The clock on the wall hiccupped and the minute hand moved on to twenty-two minutes past the hour.

Stella said, 'I don't see why I should be ashamed of something that took a lot of hard work.'

'In that case you have learnt considerably less during your time at Craybourne than I would have given you credit for.' Miss Robson frowned, subconsciously annoyed with herself at ending a sentence with a preposition. 'You have admitted to smoking, consorting with boys and behaviour of a kind that is totally unworthy of any girl from this school.'

'I haven't admitted to any of that!'

Miss Robson tapped the cover of the notebook. 'Are you suggesting that this is a work of fiction?'

'It's in the third person.'

'But you know, and I know . . . and what is more, as the reader, I am supposed to know, that the person all this sordid nonsense is about is you, Stella. Stella Teape. The fact that you chose to disguise your first person thoughts – '

'It was not a disguise! It was the way I chose to do it because it sounded right.' Suddenly Stella found that she no longer cared what she said: the words flowed out of their own accord. 'Anyway. What do you know about it? What do you know about real life? You told us yourself you went straight from school to university and straight from university back to school. And besides,' she added with a certain disdain, 'it's definitely had an effect on you, hasn't it? I bet you thoroughly enjoyed reading it.'

'That is where you are quite wrong,' Miss Robson answered. 'I have never taken pleasure in the failure of any girl at this school. For that's what we are talking about, Stella. Failure. All the time you were writing this, you were failing. Failing the school. Failing your parents. Failing your friends. And failing yourself.'

Stella's eyes darted downwards towards the notebook whose pages she had so carefully filled, evening after evening, in her wide-lettered, graceful hand, the words tumbling out close to each other, each page filled completely with words and new paragraphs starting only with new chapters.

'I may have been failing other people,' she said. 'But I was not failing myself.'

The room was very quiet. Miss Robson stood up, her finger tips splayed on the desk.

'Very well. I have no choice in this matter. I shall write to your father and send him what you have written. And I shall tell him that I cannot accept you back at Craybourne next term.'

Miss Robson looked steadily into Stella's eyes, and for the first time, Stella was unable to return that stare. She looked down at the floor, frowning. 'You mean – I'm going to be expelled.'

'I'm afraid so. Not that I gain any satisfaction from such a step, believe me. I had high hopes for you Stella, did you know that? A university entrance – perhaps even an exhibition or a scholarship. And I still hope – I mean this sincerely – that you will be able to put this behind you and make a fresh start. Do you understand?'

Stella nodded, still looking at the floor.

Miss Robson held out her hand. 'I shall wish you Godspeed. I hope you go on to greater and better things.'

Stella found herself shaking hands with the headmistress for the second time in her life. As she turned the door, a voice inside her said, I don't care, I don't care, I don't care, I don't care. It continued all the way upstairs to her dormitory and was with her intermittently throughout a restless night. She heard it as she sat in the taxi the following morning, looking neither left nor right as the car moved off, down the drive, leaving the school behind her for the last time. It returned to her frequently on her way to Tilbury by train, on the boat to Vigo, both when she was alone and in the company of friends.

She told no one: she kept what she knew to herself and the voice ran on, I don't care, I don't care, until the moment when she was met at the border by her mother and father and, after being hugged in turn by them both, she announced with her own particular brand of Stella Teape defiance:

'Guess what, I've been sacked.'

III

They knew already, for a telegram had arrived three days before saying MUCH REGRET YOUR DAUGHTER STELLA WILL NOT BE ACCEPTED AT CRAYBOURNE NEXT TERM. LETTER WITH FULL EXPLANATION FOLLOWS. ROBSON HEADMISTRESS.

In the car, Stella was obstinately cheerful. 'Somebody pinched my private notebook and gave it to Robson. She didn't like what she read in it. Silly old cow.'

'Stella!'

'Well! Who cares!'

'But what had you written about, darling?'

'Oh – me. Portugal. Us. Everything.'

'But was it a book?'

'Not really. It was private. I asked her for it back but she wouldn't give it to me. Trust Robson.'

The car sped south, the tyres singing on the hot tarmac and rumbling over the cobbles in the towns. They passed through villages full of dogs and widows and whitewashed cottages whose orange roofs blazed in the sun. They picnicked on fresh rolls, ewe cheese, tomatoes, melons and *vinho verdo*, and arrived at Quinta do Moinho Velho in time for tea.

She was in her room, later that evening, when Eduardo came home from work. She saw him enter the *quinta* by the side gate and walk down the slight slope past the water tank. He glanced up to her window, as she knew he would, when he came past. She looked down at him and he acknowledged her with a lift of his chin. Everything he wore was dusty, faded: his heavy boots, the grey trousers that were cast-offs of her father's and the collarless, pin-striped shirt that was open at the front to reveal the St Christopher medal he always wore. But in contrast, Eduardo himself did not appear dusty or faded: his skin was a splendid glistening brown, his hair nearly black, a little long,

231

unruly, and his teeth – which showed briefly as he smiled up at her – very white and uneven in a way that made his smile especially attractive.

She watched him go on, down to the cottage, and she heard the voice again saying, I don't care . . . I don't care . . .

IV

The letter from Miss Robson arrived the following Saturday:

Dear Mr Teape,

As I indicated to you in my recent cable, I have reluctantly decided that we cannot accept Stella back at Craybourne House next term. The reason for my decision will be found in the enclosed writings which were handed in to me by one of the girls who (I am glad to say) believed that literature of this nature should not be circulated within the school. I think it best that you should read what your daughter has written rather than for me to *précis* it: you will see the principal reasons for her expulsion thereby. As I believe I once made clear to you, I cannot tolerate certain types of behaviour at Craybourne House, and these include smoking, consumption of alchol, consorting with boys and behaviour of a lewd or underhand nature. As you are no doubt aware, I have to consider the moral safety of other children in the school, and to retain a girl of Stella's tendencies is, I regret, just too much of a risk.

Stella's reports have, I think, made it clear that she is a child of considerable intelligence with a personality that is forceful and in some (though not all) ways mature for her years. Thus she is regarded already as something of a leader within the school – especially among the younger girls. Clearly, by allowing her writings to be circulated within the school she has used her natural talents in a sadly misguided way. I have spoken to her about this and have pointed out that she has let *herself* down as well as other people: I hope this argument at least will strike home with her.

I appreciate that the expulsion of your daughter will have

232

come as a great shock to both yourself and your wife, and I would suggest that this time might be used to draw the family together and underline for Stella – in a tactful way – the importance of moral standards and self-discipline. I am hoping that the step I have taken will provide just the jolt she needs to teach her that the outside world really does demand certain standards of behaviour of her, and I think you would be wise to uphold and reinforce this point of view.

Finally may I emphasis that the step I have taken has been a difficult and sad one for me. While Stella has never been an easy child, I have always retained a certain admiration for her individuality – a trait which often shows itself as obstinacy, and which has placed my staff and me in difficult situations on more than one occasion. But in spite of this, there is something about Stella which I can only term lovable, and I believe that if this side can be developed and brought out, she may well become a powerful force for good, and surprise us all one day.

Yours very sincerely,
Margaret Robson
Headmistress.

Teape read this letter and Stella's word-packed secret journal in the privacy of his study. When he had done so, he went in search of Ruth.

He found her discussing the following week's menu with Laurinda. 'I'd like a word,' he said importantly, standing in the frame of the kitchen door.

She followed him into the study. He handed her Miss Robson's letter. She read it in silence, finally nodding in agreement.

'What a nice letter.'

'Yes. Now then – ' Teape picked up the notebook from the flap of the bureau. 'This.'

'Have you read it?'

He nodded.

'Is it very bad?'

'Bad enough.'

'May I read it?'

He shook his head. 'No need.'

'I think I'd like to, Bobby.'

'No. Most of it's filth. I'd rather you didn't.'

'Filth?'

'She's been mucking about with boys.'

'She is fifteen. Is that so very serious?'

He breathed out impatiently. 'Yes, it is serious. And kindly don't immediately leap to her defence. She has been expelled for very good reasons, you can take my word for that. The last thing I want now is for her to be able to set us against each other. We must be together over this.'

'Is there anything that I shouldn't see in it?'

He frowned. 'No. But I don't want you upset any more than is necessary.' He dropped the notebook back on the desk. 'There's one aspect of it that makes things damned tricky.' He turned to face her. 'She's started some sort of an affair with Eduardo.'

Ruth sighed a little. 'I'm sorry to hear it, but I can't say I'm all that surprised.'

'*Will* you stop taking her side?'

'Darling, if I could read what she's written I might be in a better – '

'There is absolutely no need for you to read it. You can take my word for that. Anyway. She's been carrying on with him.'

'What sort of carrying on?'

He champed his teeth, twice. 'She's let him touch her breasts.'

Ruth's eyes widened momentarily. She was in her late forties now, and her hair was streaked with grey. The difficult years of adjustment with Bobby after the war had left their mark: her eyes held a look of gentleness, and a certain sadness.

'What a pity,' she said quietly.

'I'll have to get rid of Eduardo, of course.'

'Oh, Bobby! Surely that's not necessary?'

'If you think I'm going to risk . . . Of course it's damn well necessary.'

He took back the letter from her and dropped it on the desk. 'Where's Stella now?'

'She was having a bath.'

'I might have known it.'

234

Stella's baths normally lasted at least half an hour, and often a lot longer. She lay in water that would parboil the average human being, and from outside the bathroom nothing could be heard except the occasional plop or gurgle as she shifted her position or added more hot water. 'What do you *do* in there?' her mother had once asked, to which she had replied, 'I soak. Figuratively and literally.'

Bobby Teape went into the hall.

'Stella?'

A voice, muffled, from upstairs: 'Yes?'

'Are you out of that bath?'

'Yes.'

'I want to talk to you.'

A moment's pause, and then a resigned, 'Okay!'

Teape walked up and down the hall, breathing through his mouth. At fifty, he was still remarkably trim: he had cut down on his intake of alcohol in recent years and had given up smoking except for the occasional cigar. Mornings at Moinho Velho started at seven o'clock, to the sound of his grunts as he did ten minutes of exercises.

'Stella!'

'All right! All right!'

He walked another length of the hall.

'What are you doing up there?'

No answer.

'Stella!'

Still no answer.

'Stella come down here, now!'

'I can't.'

His patience ran out. He went up the stairs two at a time, breathing like a charging bull. Her bedroom door was ajar, so he walked in saying, 'When I tell you to do something, my girl –'

He stopped in mid-sentence. Stella was at her mirror, naked except for her underpants, shaving an armpit.

She turned. 'Don't knock, will you?'

He backed away, angry, confused. He stood outside the bedroom door and said, 'Make yourself decent and come straight down.'

There was no reply.

'Did you hear?'

'I heard.'

He took a deep breath and let it out slowly. When she wanted to, Stella could rouse his anger in an almost diabolical way, so that the blood pumped round his system at high pressure and his breath came in gasps.

He returned to Ruth.

'She did that on purpose,' he said. 'Made me look a fool.'

'What happened?'

'She was undressed.'

'Darling, you *should* have knocked.'

He tried to relax. Before showing Ruth the letter, he had decided that he would keep this affair in as low a key as possible. He was determined to retain control of the situation throughout: to display a maturity and a restraint that would establish his authority as the head of the family once and for all.

'I want you to be here for this,' he told Ruth now. 'When she comes down, I want her to see it as a joint action by the two of us.'

'See what?'

'What I'm going to say to her.'

'But what are you going to say to her?'

'What do you think, Ruth? Do you suppose I'm going to pat her on the back and say never mind?'

They heard a door close upstairs. Teape straightened his shoulders. Ruth stared at him, bewildered.

Stella came to the study. Her brown hair was well brushed; she had put on a full skirt and blouse, and was fresh from her morning bath – as tall as Ruth now and like her to look at, except that the eyes were deeper set and more intense, and her shoulders squarer, heavier. She had grown into herself considerably during the last year, and looked closer to eighteen than fifteen.

'Good Lord!' she said. 'What's this? The Star Chamber?'

'Come in and close the door,' Teape said.

Ruth pushed the door to.

'I don't want the staff listening in, however little they

understand,' Teape said. He paused. 'Right. I've had a letter from Miss Robson, and I've read your – your journal.'

Stella smiled. 'Good. I hope you enjoyed it.'

He avoided her eyes. She seemed already to be laughing at him.

'Right,' he said again. 'Now. Do you know what I mean when I say *in loco parentis*?'

'I know what it means,' Stella said easily. 'But whether you mean what it means is a different matter, isn't it?'

Ruth glanced at her husband, aware that he was heading for trouble. It was like watching someone in a canoe without paddles, drifting downstream towards a weir.

Teape said, 'What does it mean?'

'Don't you know?'

He breathed out through his teeth. 'I want you to tell me what it means, Stella.'

She turned to her mother. 'Are we doing a crossword or something?'

'Very well,' Teape said, his anger beginning to show. 'I thought I could treat you as an adult, but as you are clearly intent on sabotaging anything I say, I shall treat you as a – '

'Saboteur?' Stella suggested. 'You're good at that aren't you? What'll it be, bamboo sticks? Or will you give me the water treatment?'

Ruth said, 'Stella darling – '

'Leave this to me, Ruth. Now. As I was saying. I have read what you've been circulating in the school, and I've come to the – '

'Wait a minute. Who said anything about my circulating anything? That book was stolen. If anyone circulated it, it wasn't me.'

He dismissed it with a wave of the hand. 'It makes not a whit of difference.'

'It makes a socking big whit of difference to me,' Stella objected. 'If it hadn't been pinched I wouldn't have been expelled.'

There was a silence.

'Would I?'

'Perhaps not,' Teape conceded. 'But the fact is – this rubbish

237

has come to light and Miss Robson has decided she cannot have you back at Craybourne.'

Stella looked out of the window, feigning boredom.

'And I want to make it quite clear to you, here and now, that I fully support her decision. She has acted as I would have wished.'

'How very pleasing for you.'

'Darling, we're not taking sides,' Ruth said.

'Oh no! Perish the thought!'

Bobby and Ruth exchanged a glance.

'Stella! Look at me.'

She turned, and her deepset eyes seemed to blaze into him.

'Yes, *Daddy*.'

'Learn this. Once and for all. There are certain basic standards of behaviour, and you must – at some time in your life – learn to respect them. If you think that this sort of filth –' and he picked up Stella's notebook '– is clever or can make anybody any happier, then you are sadly mistaken. Better to learn that now, once and for all. Do you understand?'

She stared directly at him, not moving so much as a muscle to acknowledge his question.

'Do you?'

'I understand what you are trying to say,' she replied, 'But I don't necessarily agree with it.'

He shook his head and turned to Ruth. 'I'm not going to waste any more time on this. He opened the notebook and turned back to face Stella. 'I'm going to *show* you what I think of this.' He took several pages and ripped them out of the binding. He tore them up and threw the pieces in the wastepaper basket. Then he took another lot of pages and did the same with them. 'The place for rubbish,' he said tearing up more pages, 'is the rubbish bin. I shall have to arrange a new school for you, though I'm not convinced you're worth the school fees.' He ripped the last chunk out of the book. 'And I'm not having Eduardo living here any more, either. So if that upsets him or Natália, you have only yourself to blame. Right?' He threw the last of the notebook into the wastepaper basket. 'There. And don't ever be tempted to write such dirty-minded drivel again.'

He was a little breathless now, and his hands shook. Stella had also lost some of her calm. 'That makes you feel better, does it?' she asked. 'That was father's example to his erring daughter was it? Destroying other people's hard work.' She turned to her mother. She wasn't really in control any more: her voice wavered with the coming of tears. 'Sometimes I don't know how you put up with him.'

This was her parting shot. She slammed the door as hard as she possibly could, so that the whole study seemed to rock, and the portrait of Rosalinde Teape in a silver frame that Bobby kept on his desk collapsed and fell to the floor.

'Oh dear,' Ruth sighed. 'Did you *have* to tear up her book?'

'Bit late to say that now.'

'I couldn't say anything at the time. We agreed that we had to be together over it.' She picked up the portrait of her late mother-in-law and replaced it on the bureau. Another door slammed upstairs. Ruth turned. 'I so hate these scenes.'

'I can't say I enjoy them, either.'

'Do you really think Eduardo will have to leave?'

'Not a question of thinking, Ruth. I've already decided.'

'Couldn't you have a word with him? Or Natália?'

'It takes two to tango, Ruth. I'm not risking having him living here. Not after reading that rubbish.'

'I wish I'd read it. I feel completely in the dark about what she's done.'

'Well if you feel like that you can always – ' He stopped, and they both knew what he was going to say.

'Yes,' Ruth said, in a rare moment of bitterness. 'Yes, I could always piece it together, couldn't I?'

'You didn't have to say that.'

'You were going to.'

'Yes, but I *didn't* say it, Ruth. Kindly credit me with a little tact.' He laughed, without humour. 'Altogether I've handled this business superbly, haven't I? I should have knocked on her door and said please, I should have let you read what she'd written beforehand, I should have given the book back to her, and I'm wrong in sending Eduardo away. And when I stop myself from saying something that just might have been a painful reminder for you, then I'm criticised for that and you open*that* old wound all over again and rub salt into it. Isn't that right? Would you say that was a fair assessment of my performance?'

Ruth shook her head. The tears flowed, and he found himself alone in his study, frowning at the carpet, wondering how and why it had all gone so terribly wrong.

V

Stella stayed out all day and came in late, going straight to her room and refusing supper. The following morning, a Sunday, she did not appear for breakfast. Ruth went to her room and found her reading on her bed.

'Ready for church?'

'I'm not coming.'

'Yes you are, darling. Be sensible.'

'I am being sensible, and I am not coming to church.'

Ruth sat down on the bed. 'Listen. What Daddy said yesterday – '

'I don't want to talk about what "Daddy" said.'

'Please come to church with us. If only for me. Please.'

Stella looked up from her book for the first time. 'I'll come if he doesn't.'

'That's a horrible thing to say.'

'I don't care.'

Stella returned to her book. Ruth knew her too well to turn the argument into another battle. Not for the first time she wondered, as she saw that strangely intense look in her daughter's eyes, whether she was entirely balanced.

She reached out and took Stella's hand. 'I care, even if you don't,' she said. 'So I'll say a prayer for you, and perhaps you could do the same for me.'

So Bobby and Ruth went off to church and people asked if Stella were ill and they said she was a bit off colour.

When they arrived back, just after noon, they were met by Natália, who was white-faced and upset.

'Ah my lady!' she cried, close to tears. 'The *menina* . . . down in the cellar!'

'What the hell has she done this time?' Bobby said.

They followed Natália into the house.

'Something's been spilt,' Ruth said, sniffing.

From the cellar they heard a crash and stifled sobbing. Teape led the way down. Stella had locked herself in.

'Stella! Unlock this door!'

Her voice, cracked and sobbing, shouted back, 'Fuck off!' and there was another massive crash.

'I'll get the spare key,' Ruth said. She ran back up the steps and returned a few moments later. Teape unlocked the door, and the fumes of spilt wine hit them as they entered.

Inside, Stella stood among upturned crates and broken bottles. Her face was blotched with tears and her hand was bleeding. Vintage wine lay in pools on the stone floor: rivulets of it crept about in the dust and a lake of it had formed in the far corner of the cellar. She had smashed nearly all of his most treasured years.

Stella pushed past her parents and went up the cellar steps, pausing to shout back at her father, 'The place for rubbish is the rubbish bin!' before going on up the stairs and slamming her bedroom door.

Teape turned to Ruth.

'Is *this* my fault?' he asked.

VI

Senhor Antonio Manoel Perdiz da Silva Pereira was a small pear-shaped man whose thinning black hair was brushed straight back over his sallow scalp in oily streaks, so that he had the look of somebody who had recently taken part in the hundred yards freestyle.

Like many Portuguese, he had the full ration of five names allowed by law: two forenames and three surnames. Each of these surnames had a special significance: the first, he had

241

inherited from his mother. The second, da Silva, came from his paternal grandmother; and the third, Pereira, was his father's name. This last name itself had a special significance, for at the time of the Inquisition, the Jews in Portugal were given a choice: either to leave the country or to abandon their religion and take new names. Many of those who opted to stay chose the names of various trees, such as Oliveira, Macieira, Pereira: Olivetree, Appletree, Peartree. One of Teape's favourite jokes, when the ladies weren't present, was to point out that his manager was the result of a Peartree in a Partridge.

Pereira was called to the Director's office on Monday morning. Teape spoke to him in Portuguese.

'Ah Pereira, *bom dia, com está? Bem disposto?*'

Teape always asked the Portuguese if they were 'well disposed'. It is a reasonable question, for the digestion plays a large part in Portuguese life and is regarded as important a subject as the weather is in England.

Pereira replied yes, he was indeed well disposed, and squeezed his jaundiced hands together.

'That's good. Now. I have a little matter I would like you to attend to.'

'*Sim*, Senhor.'

'It concerns the cooperage.'

'The cooperage, Senhor?'

'I have been looking at our production figures.'

Pereira looked sad. 'There has been a decline, Senhor. Over the past years. Since the war, as you know, we are bottling considerably more – '

'Exactly. There has been a decline. And yet we maintain our cooperage at the strength it was twenty years ago.'

'That is true,' Pereira began, 'but – '

'We are employing nearly twice the number of coopers we need.'

Pereira looked even sadder. 'Sir – as you know, many, if not all the coopers have been with the firm for a very long time.'

'Indeed. I well understand that. And I have no intention of reducing their numbers at this stage.'

The manager looked relieved. Even in 1955, trade unions operated in Portugal, and he did not relish a dispute over redundancy dismissals.

242

'However,' Teape was saying, 'I have decided that we really need not afford to continue training apprentices.'

Pereira's sallow forehead rippled to the hairline as his eyebrows went up. 'We have only one apprentice, Senhor.'

'Eduardo da Costa. Exactly.'

Pereira made a little blowing noise down his nose. Like many Portuguese who had lived through years of damp winters in damp houses, he suffered from chronic sinusitis.

'You are not suggesting –'

'I want to see him,' Teape interrupted. 'Personally.'

The manager took a deep breath and squeezed his hands together as if to extract the last few drops of tact. 'Senhor Teape,' he appealed, 'I should perhaps advise you that it would be a great shame to lose that boy from the firm. He has been here since he was fourteen, and has proved himself not only an excellent worker, but also one of intelligence. I have had it in mind, as it happens, to recommend to you that he be trained with a view to management. He is a lad of considerable ability and, what is more, he is exceedingly well liked by the other men in the firm. Only last week Mario Gomes was telling me –'

Teape held up his hand, and the flow stopped.

'I wish to see him, Pereira. Is that clear?'

The other became the dutiful manager once more. He bowed. 'Of course. I understand, sir. When would it be convenient for you to –'

'Now.'

Pereira gave his employer one last look of total incomprehension, and departed for the cooperage, where he found Eduardo marking out a stave for shaping. The boy wore a leather apron: he was dishevelled and sweaty, and the smoke from the fire where hoops were being heated had left smears of grime on his face.

'You're wanted,' Pereira told him.

'Me? Who by?'

'The *patrão*. In his office.'

Eduardo stared. 'What for?'

Pereira shook his head and placed a hand on Eduardo's shoulder. 'Don't ask me that, boy. Don't ask me.'

'He wants to see me now?'

Pereira nodded. 'Right away.'

Eduardo undid the lace of his apron and removed it. The manager watched him, but neither spoke further. Eduardo dropped the apron on a bench and made his way out of the cooperage, his heavy boots crunching on the earthen floor.

Teape was standing in his office. This was a place where he had always felt at ease. There were bookcases full of bound vintners' publications; a glass cabinet with his tennis trophies; two brass studded leather arm chairs, and several of his framed school and university photographs, pride of place being given to the one in which he figured as captain of the first eleven cricket team at Rugby. The window overlooked the entrance to the wine lodge, so that he could see visitors coming and going beneath the trellised vines. At the moment that Eduardo entered, an ox cart was being turned outside the window, and its driver was shouting and cursing at the team. The wooden wheels – of the same design as those used in Roman times – squeaked as the cart made its way off the property.

Teape turned to see Eduardo standing at the door. He immediately assumed the air of the Boss, the Senhor Director, the *patrão*.

'Come in, boy. Shut the door.'

Eduardo had often wondered why it was that Teape so often looked at him as if about to ask some searching question or make some surprising revelation. Now, having been summoned so unexpectedly, he wondered whether the question or announcement that had seemed imminent for so long was about to be made.

Teape came rapidly to the point.

'Do you know why I have sent for you?'

'No, your excellency.' Eduardo used the form of address that was common among the working classes to their masters even in the fifties and sixties.

Teape walked two paces away and two paces back. He clamped his teeth together a couple of times, and breathed out through his mouth.

'Right. Then I'll ask you a question.'

Eduardo's eyes narrowed under the thick brows.

'What started it?'

244

'Your excellency – I don't understand – '

Teape stared into the young man's face, and felt a surge of emotion that was half anger and half remorse.

'Was it you? Or was it – was it my daughter?'

Eduardo understood now: his nostrils dilated and his temples went white. Teape saw, and drew his own conclusions.

'You don't deny that you have interfered with her?'

'Your excellency – '

'Do you?'

Eduardo stood speechless, his mouth open.

Teape turned away. 'No, you don't.'

'It was nothing,' Eduardo said. 'I was – perhaps unwise. But I assure you that it was nothing, and will not happen again. If your daughter has any cause for complaint against me – '

Teape rapped his knuckles, once, on the desk top.

'I'm not listening to any hard luck stories. I shall give you one week's wages, and you will leave this firm. Is that understood?'

Eduardo looked from side to side as if appealing for allies. 'But, your excellency, there is no cause – '

'It's for me to decide whether there's a cause, boy, and for you to do what you're told.' Teape moved behind his desk, and they faced each other once more. 'Another thing. I'm not having you living on my property after this. So you'll have to move out.'

Eduardo's mind went back to that single occasion, four months previously, when Stella had guided his hand under her swimming costume and placed it on her breast. He remembered her lips, wide open over his, and her body, cold in the wet swimsuit, moving against him. How had her father found out? Had they been seen? It seemed impossible: it had happened on a deserted stretch of beach with not a soul in sight. So she must have told him. Done it deliberately to get him into trouble. All these years of little smiles, touching hands, little kisses – they had meant nothing. He should have known; he should have listened to his mother's repeated warnings about never touching anything that belonged to Senhor Teape.

'And if there's any trouble from you at all over this,' Teape was saying, 'I'll have your mother out of that cottage as well

245

and a new maid in her place. Do you want that?'

He shook his head dumbly.

'No, I didn't think you would.' Teape relaxed a little. 'Now then. If you're going to be sensible, I'll give you some advice. You'll be due for conscription in a year's time, won't you?'

'Yes, sir.'

'Good. Well – go along and volunteer now. You'll get a better deal than the conscripts. Work hard, and you might even get promotion. You'll have pay to send home and a roof over your head.'

Eduardo suddenly found himself shaking hands with Teape. 'I've told the manager that we can't afford to train apprentices in the cooperage any longer,' he was saying, 'and if you're wise, you'll accept that as the real reason. I'll give you a good testimonial, lad, so you won't be hard done by.'

It all happened so quickly that he was outside the office before he realised that he had been dismissed unjustly and blackmailed into keeping his mouth shut. He burst back into Teape's office and, abandoning the formal mode of address said, 'Whatever you think, I know that you have acted unjustly. I shall not complain, but I shall also not forget, and neither will you.' With that, he walked out of the office and off the premises, his heart beating wildly with anger as he descended the steep hill to the riverside.

Teape saw him go from his window. That final outburst had convinced him more than ever of his relationship to Eduardo, and he was oddly proud that the boy should have had the courage to say what he did.

He muttered inaudibly under his breath, and his mouth went crooked as he chewed his lower lip, alone with thoughts and memories that he had never, ever shared.

VII

When Rosalinde Teape invited Hugh Blunden to join the firm of Teape, Sons & Company, he accepted her invitation

246

because he decided that making port wine might prove amusing. Over the years he found that he had – by and large – been right. As the partner responsible for export and sales, he made it his business to travel the Continent, as often as not paying for the journeys out of his own pocket. Treating the work more as a hobby than a way of earning a living, he became widely known among the connoisseurs of good wine in most of the European capitals.

It was something of a privilege to be acquainted with Hugh Blunden. He was large, expansive and exceedingly generous. He wore an Eton tie and possessed the Etonian charm and confidence in good measure. At the dinner table, he delighted the ladies with his sensitive good manners and, when the men sat over the port, he entertained them with an inexhaustible fund of stories. These stories were often quite appallingly risqué, and if anybody else had tried to tell them, he would have been accused of bad form. But Hugh Blunden somehow managed to carry them off, telling them while taking gentle puffs at his cigar, which he would hold within an inch of his moist lips while he delivered the punch line in that half apologetic way of his that had you laughing even before you had seen the point of the joke.

As Dodger Remington had once remarked before the war, he may have been an ass, but you had to admit that he was also an asset.

He lived alone, in a bungalow just off the Boa Vista: that broad, straight avenue that runs from Oporto down the hill to the coast. The house was furnished in luxurious greens and golds: original paintings by some of the French Impressionists hung on the walls, and the bookcases revealed a love of music and the arts. Gramophone records occupied two long shelves in the drawing room, and until the early fifties he had played these records on a gramophone that was wound by hand and used needles made of wood which he sharpened regularly in a special machine for the purpose. Now, with the advent of the long-playing record, he had purchased the new Bush High Fidelity record player, and in the evenings when he was at home, works by Scarlatti, Chopin and Mozart would waft out through the open french windows and ease his mind as he

247

sipped a glass of chilled moselle before the maid served his dinner.

He rarely entertained at home, though he was an excellent cook, especially of omelettes and crêpes. But occasionally he would invite a close friend to spend an evening with him and they would talk, slowly and lazily, of the things that pleased them.

Over the years, Blunden's relationship with Bobby Teape had had its ups and downs. In the early days, when they were both unmarried and lived together in that same bungalow, they had not been much more than public schoolboys enjoying their first taste of freedom.

Slowly, their personalities had developed on diverging lines. Hugh didn't really give a damn what he ate, drank, said or did so long as he enjoyed it and so long as he suffered no unpleasant after-effects. But Bobby was not so relaxed. Hugh's apparent lack of discipline and lack of respect for the conventions of middle class respectability made him uneasy. The length of Hugh's hair, which sometimes curled over his collar, Teape felt was in some complicated way bad for the morale of the firm. And latterly, the size of Hugh's paunch had been the subject of frequent comment from Teape, and had spurred the latter into starting morning exercises. As for Hugh's enjoyment of the arts, this was something that Bobby could not even begin to understand, and so he felt suspicious of it instead.

In recent years, there had been rather more serious reasons for the two men to disagree. With the sharp decline in the popularity of port after the war years, Hugh had often expressed concern that the firm was being run inefficiently. On several occasions he had argued with Teape over the employment of a work force that he considered too large; also, he felt that too much emphasis was placed on the traditional aspects of port drinking and not enough on tailoring the commodity to meet the requirements of a changing market. When he suggested research into such things as the shape of a bottle or the design of a label, Teape repeatedly put the brake on and kept things exactly as they had been since the beginning of the century; and when he actually had the

248

audacity to suggest that Teape's port be advertised, Bobby replied haughtily that his family had never lowered itself that far and did not intend to start now.

Thus Blunden had become the progressive, and Teape the traditionalist.

Bobby had the edge over Hugh in one respect however: for it was he who could speak to the Portuguese in the way they liked to be addressed: it was he who was the real '*patrão*', the patron, the one the treaders toasted with the most gusto when the *bagaceira* was passed round during the time of the vintage. Teape was the man to whom they felt they could bring their troubles; whom they had, in many cases, known as a boy who trailed along after old Charlie Teape. There were even a few who remembered his grandfather, but that was going back a bit.

It was therefore all the more remarkable that the roles of the two partners should be reversed when the question of Eduardo's dismissal arose. For it was to Hugh Blunden that Senhor Pereira voiced his concern over the matter, and it was now Hugh Blunden who entered Teape's office to advocate the young man's retention.

He accepted a seat in one of the leather armchairs, and took a cigar from his inside pocket. He toyed with it for some time before lighting it, as if reluctant to consume such an elegantly manufactured piece of tobacco.

'I understand you propose to get rid of young Eduardo,' he said, after a little preliminary conversation about the sales of white port in France.

'Yes I do,' Teape said. He looked hard at Blunden. 'In the interest of economy.'

'Ah. Ah, I see.' Blunden busied himself with the preparations for lighting his cigar, taking a packet of Swan Vesta from his jacket pocket. 'Not a popular decision to have to make, I imagine.'

'Maybe not. But necessary.'

Hugh, to Teape's relief, at last lit his cigar. The blue smoke curled upward and the aroma filled the room. When it was fully alight, Blunden returned to the subject in hand, glancing at the smouldering end of the weed to ensure that it was burning evenly.

'I couldn't help wondering if there might have been some other reason, old sport. Would that be so?'

'Why do you ask?'

Blunden gave a little shrug, and held the cigar close to his lips, about to draw from it. 'Just a little hunch, you know.'

Bobby stood up. He felt better on his feet, more in control. 'In that case your hunch is quite wrong,' he said, and Blunden knew immediately thereby that it was quite right.

'I gather you had a little domestic crisis over the weekend,' he remarked. He blew a cloud of smoke and watched it rise and spread out.

Teape looked at him sideways. 'Where did you hear that?'

'Does it matter? Shall we say – a reliable source? That's what you fellows in the Corps used to call it, didn't you?'

'It was a family matter. I don't think it need concern you.'

'My dear fellow, I must disagree. When a family matter leads to the unfair dismissal of one of our most promising workers, I feel bound to insist that it does concern me.'

'Unusual,' Teape said. 'I never expected to see you taking up cudgels on behalf of the workers.'

'This worker is a little different though, isn't he?'

'I don't see why.'

Hugh laughed gently. 'Oh come on! He's a good-looking chap. And Stella's getting into a big girl. Do credit me with a little insight.'

Teape went to the window. 'I could say – ' he started, then checked himself.

'What could you say?'

There was nothing to look at outside the window, but Teape pretended to look at it, all the same.

'I could say the same to you.'

'Oh?'

'You don't know what I'm talking about, do you?'

'I must admit I don't.'

Teape turned back and looked down at Hugh. Seeing him so relaxed in the armchair he wanted, suddenly, to hit where it hurt.

'I'll explain, then. You see as far as I'm concerned, the fact that he's got a pretty face is neither here nor there. I'm not swayed one way or another by that sort of thing.'

Hugh, about to draw once more on his cigar, froze. Then, slowly, he rose to his feet: not as tall as Teape, but heavier and with a great dignity and presence.

'Would you care to explain exactly what you mean by that?'

Teape laughed. 'You know very well what I mean.'

'You're wrong there. I don't. At least – I hope I don't, if only for your sake.'

Perhaps, with skill, Teape could have avoided the ultimate clash, could have laughed it off or glossed it over. But it is a trait of the guilty that they need to accuse.

'I mean exactly what I said,' he replied, and for a moment the defiant way he moved his head could have been Stella. 'Just because Eduardo is – shall we say – personable, doesn't cut any ice with me. I don't have favourites.'

'You mean that I do?'

'I mean anything you like it to mean. If the cap fits, and all that.'

'What – cap?'

Teape felt carried away now, almost breathless. 'You know what I'm talking about. You know very well I'm right. You can't deny it. Can you?'

Blunden crushed his cigar into a heavy glass ashtray with controlled ferocity. When he spoke, his voice was like cold steel.

'So. I raise the subject of the dismissal of an employee and you, in the most roundabout way, imply that I have a homosexual attachment to him. Is that it?'

Teape reddened at the mention of the word. 'I never said anything about – that.'

'Not directly, no. You preferred to hide behind innuendo, didn't you? The sly suggestion. Perhaps you'll allow me to make a suggestion in return. How do you like the prospect of running this firm on your own? Eh?'

Teape blustered. 'For God's sake! Don't be ridiculous!'

'I'm not being ridiculous, Teape.'

Teape began, now, to realise the seriousness of the situation. 'Look,' he said 'I wasn't being entirely serious. I'm sure you realise –'

'I've been looking at the property market in the south,' Blunden cut in smoothly. 'I believe the Algarve has great potential, do you know that? I was talking to a young architect in St Tropez last month. He had some excellent ideas for that coast. If one built self-contained appartments, set back from the beaches – '

'Look here, old boy, there is absolutely no need – '

'I'm sure we can arrange things quite amicably. If you like to suggest a price for my share in the firm, that can be a starting point for our discussion. And once I'm out of the way, you can sack as many pretty faces as you like. Right?'

VIII

Eduardo arrived home in the evening, having taken the train to Valadares and walked from the village. He entered the *quinta* by the side gate and made his way along the path below the bamboo windbreak to the little whitewashed cottage. When he entered, he found his mother at the wood stove, cooking their evening meal of onions, beans, potatoes and pieces of smoked sausage that floated about in the oily mess. It was one of his favourite dishes.

Normally he would have kissed her on both cheeks, sat down by the table, poured himself some wine and talked easily about his day. Now, however, he stood in the doorway a moment, and she looked round at him, immediately aware that something was wrong.

'I'm out of a job,' he announced.

She stared at him.

'I am. They've given me the push. Today. One week's wages and – out.'

'It's not possible!'

Eduardo shrugged and came on into the room. He slumped down on the wooden chair, stretched his arm out along the table and slapped it once with the palm of his hand.

'Well. It's true. So I'll have to go looking for work.'

252

Natália glanced at the pot. The stew was beginning to seethe, so she pulled it aside from the hottest part of the stove.

'But what reason?'

'Oh – they say they don't need as many coopers. "Cutting back on expenditure", that's what they call it.'

'You'll find something.'

'Will I? Yes, maybe I will. But not as good.' He stared at the blackened cooking pot, tempted to tell his mother the truth, to force the issue so that they would both have to leave.

Natália stirred the stew. She was thirty-four now, sturdily built, with muscular arms and a certain pride in the way she held herself: not a fat woman, but generously built; a woman, as one of the locals described her, who would not slip easily through your fingers.

There was no doubt that she was attractive to men. When she went into the village to buy bread she was greeted affectionately by the pensioner who swept the road and the grey uniformed policeman who stood, revolver in holster, in the shade of the dusty plane trees. On market days she was popular with the traders who brought their wares to Valadares: they liked to joke with her and try their luck at catching her eye. But while she acknowledged these greetings and enjoyed the looks and attentions of men, she was content to remain unmarried. For her, men were creatures best kept at arm's length. Her life revolved round the Teape family and the Quinta do Moinho Velho. She had her work, her regular pay, her grown up son for company and the occasional visits from Pedro the *caseiro*, the other maids, the cook and their various relations.

She was very close to Eduardo. He was a good-looking young man, popular at work, and a loving son. Because of the small age difference between them they were in some ways more like brother and sister than mother and son. But this did not mean that she lacked any motherly pride in him: he had been doing well in the cooperage at Teape's, and she had done everything she could to encourage him to work hard. She wanted him to improve himself and gain a position in the world and not remain the *mó do baixo* or 'bottom millstone', as she sometimes called herself.

In that summer of 1955, it seemed to her that all the difficulties of her early life had been left behind. The memories of the wet, smelly fish harbour of Matosinhos were fading; she had not seen or heard of the Salsicha over ten years, and she had no intention of seeking her out.

Her days began at six o'clock and ended at ten or eleven. She fed the chickens, watered the Senhora's treasured potted plants, made the early morning tea, served breakfast, made the beds, cleaned the rooms, did the washing, served lunch, went shopping, served the tea, made the evening meal for Eduardo, served the dinner, fed the dogs, did the ironing, shut up the chickens and went to bed. On Sundays she had the afternoon off, and would occasionally walk the six kilometers to Arcozelo, to kneel by the preserved body of the local unbeatified saint in order to say a prayer for Manoel, the man she believed to have been her father.

Natália was not a religious person, but in recent years she had begun to feel the need for religious observance, and had taken to attending mass in the hot little church in Valadares, with its bleeding figure of Christ in a glass case and its heavy atmosphere of old wax, incense and sweaty armpits. And when, at high mass, the Kyrie Eleison and the Gloria and Credo were sung, Natália joined in as well as she was able, singing as many words as she knew by heart, for she did not know them all, nor was she able to read sufficiently well to make out the Latin.

Eduardo accompanied her to church only rarely. He preferred to use his free time by taking a fishing rod down to the coast and casting a weighted hook far out beyond the surf for the *linguado*, the flatfish that his mother could cook so well. But on the few occasions he did attend mass, he would from time to time join in the singing, and this was a special delight to her, for his voice had developed into a fine baritone, powerful and rich in texture, which she loved to hear.

During the post-war years, she had become slowly aware of the difficulties with the *menina*, but they did not often affect her directly and she was not troubled by them. She had overheard some of the battles that had taken place between Stella and her father, and had been saddened by them. For she loved Stella: she had cared for her as a baby and had looked after her on the days when Ruth had gone to the Factory House, during the war, to make surgical dressings to be sent to hospitals in England and at the front. From her earliest years, Stella had confided her secrets to the Portuguese maid who had become so much a part of the household.

Ruth, she adored. There were so many, many reasons. Ruth had taken her in, fed her, clothed her, given her and Eduardo a completely new chance in life. She had provided money for Eduardo's clothes, helped him with his lessons, encouraged him. And if ever there had been any difficulty with Senhor Teape or the other maids or the cook, it had always been Ruth who stepped in with her gentle, calm justice, her readiness to listen carefully to every side of a dispute and then to make up her mind.

'Why don't we both leave?' Eduardo asked suddenly, interrupting her thoughts. 'Why don't we go south, find something in Lisbon. The money's good, down there. If we both worked, we could save a bit of money. Maybe start a little *tasca*, even. A little kitchen. Tables and chairs. Good food. You could cook and I could wait at table.'

Natália regarded him sadly.

'Dreams,' she said.

He nodded, and the idea vanished as quickly as it had appeared. 'Yes,' he said. 'Dreams.' He thought again. 'Maybe I could get on a *traineira*. They say the pay's getting better, these days. Life at sea – ' He looked up at his mother.

She busied herself at the stove. 'Plenty of better things to do than go out fishing every night.'

He nodded. It was always the same. Whenever the possibility of following in his father's footsteps was suggested, his mother would become silent and aloof. He would have liked to know more about his father, to ask her what he was like, how well she knew him, whether he, Eduardo, took after him in any small ways. The absence of a father was a strange thing: it left a gap in your life, a gap that you wondered about and could never entirely forget. Natália had told him nothing more than that his father had been a big man, who went out in the *traineiras* and who was lost at sea. She had warned him, too, against trying to

255

find out more: had told him that such an investigation would be fruitless. She had shown him his birth certificate upon which, in the space for the father's name, was written the word *'inconhecido'*, 'unknown'.

Now, in the quietness of that August evening, after a long silence broken only by the gentle bubbling of the stew and the singing of the evening *grilos* outside, he said quietly, 'Well anyway. I'm leaving home.'

IX

Deirdre Romer, whose maiden name was Remington, wiggled her hips twice, kept her eye on the ball, swung the number three iron and sent her Spalding Spot soaring approximately eighty yards further up the fairway towards the seventeenth hole of Espinho golf course. She replaced the club in her bag and, accompanied by Joanna Remington, her sister-in-law, set out after it.

'The question is,' Deirdre said, continuing their conversation, 'What did they argue *about*?'

Deirdre was very like her mother had been in her mid-thirties: plump, auburn-haired, brisk and forceful.

'You heard that Stella had been expelled from Craybourne?' Joanna asked.

'No! Really? What for?'

'I'm not sure. Neither Bobby nor Ruth are too anxious to talk about it. But I think Hugh was mixed up in it somewhere.'

'That's interesting,' Deirdre said, stepping briskly along the sandy fairway, where grass had grown in the spring but was now all but gone. 'Because my cook – Ana – was telling me that there was some sort of rumpus at the Teapes' on Sunday. She said that Natália and the other maid – Paulina isn't it? – spent most of the afternoon clearing up the cellar.'

'Whatever for?' Joanna was slim and dark, the mother of four children and a most devout Catholic. Her husband, James Remington, was Deirdre's elder brother, and worked for Sandemans. Joanna was the daughter of Johnnie Millet, who had recently retired from Brothertons.

'Well,' Deirdre said, warming to her story. 'I gather Stella lost her temper over something and started smashing every bottle in sight.'

Joanna smiled archly. 'That certainly sounds like Stella.'

'Just what I thought. And another thing. Their maid's boy, Eduardo, has left the firm under something of a cloud and is also leaving home. I believe he's joined the *infanteria*.'

They had reached Joanna's ball. She took out her mashie. 'Gone for a soldier, has he?' she said, and whacked the ball a little unsatisfyingly into a bunker, just short of the green.

They walked a few more yards to Deirdre's ball. She sliced it, and it fell beyond and to the right of the green.

'Of course it puts Bobby in a difficult position,' Deirdre said as they approached the bunker. 'I mean he won't enjoy running the firm on his own for very long, will he?'

She paused while Joanna took three shots to scoop the ball and a large quantity of sand on to the green.

'Well done!' Deirdre exclaimed lightly, and walked to the line of eucalyptus trees, where her ball lay close to the rough. Her shot took it six yards beyond the pin. She walked on to the green and held the flag while Joanna made a nice putt, sinking the ball from three feet.

Joanna held the pin while Deirdre took two putts.

'Seven for you and six for me,' Deirdre said, marking her card.

They walked on to the next tee.

'Wouldn't James be interested in a partnership?' Deirdre asked.

'With Bobby Teape?'

'Yes.'

Joanna considered. 'He's certainly ready for a change.'

'Mother could buy him into Teapes at the drop of a hat,' Deirdre said. 'She's still got Dad's share of the firm.'

'I know,' Joanna said. 'But I'm not sure if James would be keen. He says Bobby's an awful stick-in-the-mud really. He welcomes new ideas but never does anything about them. I shouldn't be surprised if that's the real reason behind this business over Hugh.'

257

'I did hear another story, mind you.'

'Oh?'

'Promise not to repeat it?'

Joanna laughed. 'Of course!'

'Well, apparently there was something going on between Hugh and Stella *and* Stella and the maid's boy.'

'You mean Eduardo.'

'That's right. And when Eduardo found out, he had some sort of shindig with Hugh – '

'Oh I don't think that can be right,' Joanna said.

They had reached the tee.

'Why not?'

Joanna placed her ball, and Deirdre watched as she played a mis-hit, so that the ball dribbled twenty yards along the centre of the fairway.

'Oh well,' Joanna laughed. 'At least it was straight.' She waited while Deirdre played a reasonable shot, slightly hooked.

'Why can't it be right?' Deidre repeated as they set out again.

'Well I heard that Hugh's argument with Bobby was because he was *defending* Eduardo.'

'You mean Hugh was.'

'Yes. In fact – ' Joanna shot a mischievous glance at her sister-in-law – 'In fact, knowing Hugh, I wouldn't be surprised if something had been going on between him and Eduardo.'

They giggled for fifteen yards.

'Knowing Hugh,' Deirdre said. 'Yes!'

The sun beat down. They walked on along the fairway to the eighteenth hole, each looking forward to a long cool drink at the end of it and, after lunch, a quiet afternoon reading magazines in the clubhouse.

X

The gossip circulated and was embellished. Hugh Blunden and Bobby Teape agreed a price for Hugh's share of the firm, and Blunden moved south, investing his capital in Algarve property at precisely the right moment to take advantage of the boom.

Eduardo took Teape's advice and joined the army as a regular infantryman. He now lived in the Oporto barracks, and every other week Natália received a letter from him with some money. As Natália could not read, Ruth read the letters aloud to her, a practice which irritated Teape considerably.

That autumn, shortly after Stella went to her new school in Dorset, Ruth was admitted to the Oporto British Hospital to have a cyst removed. Bobby took her in by car one afternoon: he hated hospitals and anything to do with illness, so he spent as little time as possible in the building. He settled her in the private ward, expressed a vague hope that 'everything would go off all right', kissed her dutifully on the cheek, and left.

Alone in the city, he strolled down the hill to the waterfront and wandered for a while among the fish and vegetable stalls on the Cais de Ribeira, staring into people's faces as if in search of something or somebody. It was getting on for five: he did not want to go home, to the hostility of Natália and the emptiness of the house, and yet he had no wish to remain in the noise and dirt of the city.

He returned to the hospital grounds and sat in his car, wondering what to do. Ruth had been in hospital a couple of times before: she had never enjoyed really good health since having Stella. But during her previous visits, friends had always rallied round him. They had invited him out to dinner, looked after him. Their failure to do so now was the most pointed indication of his isolation. It was as if the members of the British colony, without actually saying anything to him directly, wished to make it quite clear that they disapproved of his action. For a man like Teape, who needed the companionship and reassurance of friends, the situation was almost unbearable. He was not a loner – never had been: and yet now he was being forced into the role of one.

He started the engine and drove out of the hospital grounds and up the hill to the centre of the city. He joined the stream of traffic going down the Boa Vista, and drove round the wide roundabout near Cheese Castle.

He had no aim in view, but drove automatically, going where it was easiest to go. The car seemed to choose its own route, turning off the main road and down the hill into Leça, the masts of ships and the cranes in the new dock at Leixões rising up to his left.

He stopped outside Number 154, Rua Ferreira and saw, without surprise, that the house was still unoccupied.

He got out of the car and stared for a moment at the ragged pines behind the wall. The tradesman's gate was nearly off its hinges, and he could see into the overgrown garden.

The house had been empty almost continuously since he and Ruth had vacated it sixteen years before. Rumours that it · was haunted had been circulated, and now it was not fit for habitation, even if a tenant could have been found.

He entered by the broken gate and stood in the wilderness of the garden. Frogs croaked in the pond and a grey cat, disturbed at his advance, leapt down from the balustrade by the front steps and ran off into the tangle of brambles and morning glory.

All the shutters were closed, and several roof tiles had fallen. Great smears of green damp streaked the outside walls.

Standing there, looking up at the house, he remembered how, when he returned to Portugal after becoming engaged to Ruth, he had promised himself that this would be their family home. In those brief months of separation between January and April, he had often imagined and looked forward to the happiness of having his wife and his children and his dogs in this house, and the sound of their laughter with which its rooms would be filled. He had foreseen children's parties, picnics, tennis afternoons, dances: and in each, this house had figured as the meeting place, the gathering point, the place where the Teape family lived and laughed and entertained.

He turned and went back into the road, making his way quickly down to the sea, unsure what he was doing or why, or whether whatever he sought even existed.

He reached the shore. This was the way he used to come with his dogs, Tagus and Minho. Along this track. . . .

He stopped abruptly, staring out to sea. The evening sun winked on the water and the waves broke evenly, cleanly upon the beach. He turned back, walking more slowly now, wandering into Leça and across the bridge into the dirtier streets of Matosinhos.

He sat down at a little metal table outside a bar and sipped a strong black coffee from a chipped cup. While he sat there, a funeral went by: an old-fashioned funeral, with four black horses pulling a black carriage with glass windows and an ornate coffin on display. The hooves of the horses clattered on the cobbles, and two cars of mourners, working people, followed on, nosing their way along the narrow streets towards the church.

He stared after them, reminded forcibly of the brief span of life, terrified suddenly that everything he was and wanted to be might prove worthless. He sipped his coffee and reflected that not many years would pass before time swallowed him up and he became less than a whispered memory that would be forgotten within a generation.

He paid, and got up to go. As he wandered along, a little boy came up alongside and hissed at him, clutching his arm. Teape looked down at him. The child wore patched shorts, a tattered shirt, no shoes. He gave that old, international invitation: the bent arm, the hand on the biceps.

He shook his head, pulling his arm away from the child's grasp. He quickened his pace, leaving the boy behind. He walked with no destination in mind, turning left and right at random, his hands in his pockets, his head down, seeing only the patch of cobbles immediately ahead of him.

He was aware, suddenly, of a voice calling his name.

'Bobby?'

He looked up.

'It *is* you!'

A black Morris Minor, the new sort, had stopped a little way ahead of him. A face looked back from the driver's window. It was Joy Remington.

'What on earth are you doing here?'

He shrugged. 'Walking.'

'I can see that!'

He was up with her now. She looked into his face, the engine ticking over, her hand upon the wheel. 'Ruth's in hospital, isn't she?'

He nodded.

She smiled. 'Come and have supper. You're not doing anything are you?'

'No, but –'

'I'll drive you. Hop in.'

'My car's in Leça.'

'Never mind that. You can pick it up later.' She reached across and opened the door. 'Come on,' she said. 'I won't take no for an answer.'

He hesitated no longer, relieved to be given a direct order. He sat down in the passenger seat. Joy looked across at him. When she smiled, she had a habit of bunching her top lip a little: she had always done it, even as a child. 'Good,' she said. 'Off we go, then.'

He dropped his glance from her confident blue eyes and watched, instead, as her hand gripped the black knob of the gear lever and thrust it firmly forward.

XI

She chatted happily all the way to her house which was further out, on the way to the airport. She had called on her sewing woman that afternoon, and had been delayed by a flat tyre.

'Wasn't it luck!' she commented.

She swung the car into the short drive outside the house and led the way in.

'Now. A drink. The cabinet's over there, Bobby, and there's beer in the fridge if you'd prefer it. I'll have a tomato juice.'

She gave him very little time to talk or think, and he was happy to have it that way. She set about cooking the supper immediately, explaining that she only had a daily maid, and was really much happier looking after herself.

When he brought her drink into the kitchen she was chopping tomatoes and onions determinedly.

'Lovely,' she said. 'Now if you'd like to light the fire, it'll be a lot cosier. It's already laid and there's more wood in the garage if we need it. All right?' She lifted her glass. 'Nearly forgot. Cheers. Nice to see you.'

'Well,' he mumbled. 'Very kind of you to –'

'Oh don't bother about all that, Rob.'

He hesitated. He hadn't been called 'Rob' for many, many years.

'The fire,' she reminded.

'Of course. Yes.'

He went into the sitting room and busied himself with paper and sticks.

'It's early to start having fires,' she called from the kitchen, 'but I do think it cheers the place up, don't you?'

He sat back on his haunches and smiled for the first time that day. 'Quite agree!' he called back.

The flames leapt up the chimney. She came from the kitchen and stood at the door. 'Are you any good at opening tins?'

'Certainly! Of course!' He got up from his knees and followed her into the kitchen, where she provided him with a tin of meat and an opener.

He had opened a tin before, once. He managed to pierce the can and proceeded to manipulate the opener awkwardly towards himself, making a jagged saw-toothed edge. Half way round, he got stuck. He wrestled with it for some moments until Joy came to the rescue.

'You're doing it back to front, silly boy,' she said, and took over from him, rapidly removing the top of the tin.

She was, it proved, an abominable cook. They ate a sort of stew, with underdone carrots and potatoes.

'I like them a bit scrunchy, don't you?' Joy said. 'So many people cook their vegetables to death.' She jumped up. 'I know. Let's have candles. Why not?'

She busied herself with wax matches which refused to light. 'Silly things!' she said. 'I can never get them to work.'

'Here – let me –'

'No, no. I won't be beaten.' She lit the candles. 'There. Isn't that nice?'

They raised their glasses. The candlelight sparkled.

'Only *vinho verde*, I'm afraid, but I didn't know you were coming. Here's to you.'

'Thank you.' He smiled a little lamely. 'You're very kind.'

They drank, and Joy's torrent of chatter suddenly ran dry.

They ate in agonised silence for all of twenty seconds, each wondering what to say.

Finally, out of desperation, Joy asked brightly: 'Well – how are things?'

He frowned over his plate.

'Not very "how".'

She laughed. 'I haven't heard that for years. Isn't it out of the Mumphie books?'

He shook his head. 'Pooh. Eeyore said it.'

'Of course!'

There was another silence. Joy put her knife and fork down. She frowned. 'I've felt so sorry for you Bobby. These past weeks.'

'Have you? I'm glad someone has.'

'One feels so powerless. I mean – I didn't know any of the reasons behind it all. And now you're right out on a limb.'

He concentrated on eating. A piece of gristle bounced between his teeth. He swallowed it whole.

'Aren't you?' Joy persisted.

'Am I?'

'Of course you are. Like this evening. Wandering about like some sort of – rogue elephant.'

He smiled. 'I've never been compared to an elephant before.'

'Well. You have now.'

He finished as much as he was prepared to finish.

'Was it ghastly?' she asked, meaning the food.

'It wasn't very nice,' he said then, realising what she had meant said, 'Oh – that is, I don't mean –'

She laughed. 'Never mind!' She collected his plate. 'Only fruit and cheese, I'm afraid.'

'That's marvellous.'

He peeled an orange.

'What *was* Stella expelled for?' she asked.

He explained about the secret journal.

'So what did you do?'

'I tore it up. In front of her.'

'Good for you! Just what I would have done!'

He felt a flood of gratitude. It was the first time anybody had given him any positive word of approval. 'I felt that unless I supported the headmistress, I would be flaunting the very authority I had paid to represent me. It would have undermined my own authority. Do you see what I mean?'

Joy was nodding her agreement.

'And – well, Stella, being Stella, didn't take to it.'

'Silly mixed-up little girl!'

'Of course she is. But you can't tell her that.' He shook his head, reliving the problem. 'But . . . for all that, there is something about her that – I can't explain. I love that child more deeply than I would have believed possible. Can you understand that?'

Joy experienced a feeling of elation. She had never ceased to regard Teape as her own private property, nor had she ever admitted to herself that she had finally lost him. Now, after all these years, he was once again confiding his innermost thoughts to her. It was a triumph which she savoured: he is still mine, she thought to herself, and I shall never give him up.

'Go on,' she whispered.

He stared into the candle flame. 'And I think – in some strange way – that she feels strongly towards me. When I came back, after the war, I expected that she and I would somehow be instant friends. But . . . it didn't work out. All the time I was away, I thought about her. Ruth used to send me snaps of herself and Stella. I kept them in one of those little Senior Service cigarette tins. They were with me in Tunisia, Sicily, right the way through. I used to pray – I used to pray that I would live to see Stella again. That was all I asked.'

He swallowed.

'I expected so much of her. Too much, of course. And I made the mistake of thinking that things would be easy and happy when I came home, when in fact they were – '

He stopped, and the silence lasted.

'They were what?'

'Just the reverse. A sort of eternal triangle with both Ruth and myself competing for Stella's affection, and Stella cashing in on the situation.' He smiled sadly. 'We spoiled her. It's as simple as that.'

In the following silence, Joy waited, confident now that

265

having started, he would go on. The hot wax from one of the candles dripped on to the table, but she ignored it. Bobby drew a breath.

'And this – notebook of hers. Well, it was a sort of "dear diary", written about herself as if she were someone else. Clever, for a fifteen-year-old, I suppose. A sort of stream of jumbled memories, all leading up to the romance she was having. Or thought she was having.'

'With?'

'Didn't you know? With Eduardo.'

'I wasn't sure.'

He nodded.

'And was that why you sacked Eduardo?'

'Partly.'

He looked at her quickly and then away, and she knew there was more. She said gently, 'I don't see . . . I don't see that it was altogether necessary to *sack* him, Bobby.'

'No. I didn't expect you would.'

'Was there some other reason?'

He surprised her then. He put his hands over his face and started to cry, as if she wasn't there. She stared at him: he was swallowing repeatedly, and his hands were shaking against his face.

'Oh!' she whispered. 'Tell me! Please tell me!'

When he removed his hands from his face, she was frightened by what she saw, for his eyes were red and puffy and he seemed to sway with pent-up feelings.

He spoke with difficulty. 'Don't you remember? That little girl on the beach? Who fainted? The day we broke it off?'

She gaped at him.

'That was Natália,' he said. 'And Eduardo –'

She understood, then. 'You mean – he's – your –'

He nodded. 'I couldn't let him stay on, could I?'

She let out a long breath. 'Does Ruth know?'

He shook his head. 'You're the first person I've ever told.'

'After all these years!'

He nodded. Tears streamed down his cheeks. She reached over and took his hand in hers.

'Oh Bobby!' she whispered. 'My poor darling!'

266

She held his hand tightly between hers, and they gazed silently at each other across the candlelit table.

Part Two

✤ 10 ✤

I

SAM NEVIN was one of those people you could never take very
seriously. It was not that he deliberately set out to make
himself a figure of fun, but simply that his idea of sound
commonsense tended to be regarded by others as bordering
on the ridiculous.

The Nevins had spent much of their time in India, where
Sam's father had taken an administrative post in the civil
service after retiring as a major from the Indian army. The
children (Sam was the youngest of four) had been brought up
in a rambling government house, and had led somewhat
sheltered lives, waited upon by servants in an atmosphere of
decaying grandeur. With the end of British rule in India, Major
Nevin brought his family back to England and settled in
Croydon, where Sam was sent to a minor public day school
that prided itself on its classical reputation.

When the boy announced his intention of taking the entry
examination for the Royal Air Force College, Cranwell, both
his father and headmaster did everything in their power to
dissuade him from his madness. But Sam had inherited a
certain determination from his mother – who had once played
hockey for Wales – and was not to be dissuaded. So, in 1952,
Samuel Jeremy Hetherington Nevin was admitted into the
Royal Air Force as a cadet officer. He was just eighteen.

Within days of joining Cranwell, he became regarded as an
eccentric. He was an ardent Catholic, and knelt every evening
at his bedside to recite a decade of the rosary. He wore
suspenders to keep up his socks. His mannerisms and way of
calling people 'old boy' brought howls of derision, and the
discovery that he played backgammon with himself set the
final seal upon his reputation.

271

But although he was regarded as an eccentric, he commanded a measure of respect, for he fought so violently to resist being de-bagged at the initiation ceremony that it was decided safer to leave him alone.

On his first day of flying he was saved from walking into the propeller disc of a Dragon Rapide by one of the instructors, who brought him down with a rugger tackle. On his air familiarisation trip he was sick into his helmet; and a few months later, when his Harvard Trainer caught fire and his instructor asked him if he could smell anything, Sam unhesitatingly replied: 'Yes. Butterscotch.'

But in spite of these anecdotes which caused such hilarity after flying hours in the mess, Sam earned his wings and was posted to a Meteor squadron in East Anglia. There, he was treated as something of a mascot, and was in great demand after mess dinners because of his impersonations. These included a recitation of The Railway Cat, a rendering of the Charge of the Light Brigade (complete with bugle calls, shouted orders and thundering hooves), a rendering of an aria from the Marriage of Figaro and a short piece of mime, reserved for very late at night, of a lady being sick from the carriage window of an express train.

Inevitably, he fell prey to the charms of a woman. She was a pouting debutante called Priscilla, and she knew a sucker when she saw one. She figuratively and very nearly literally gobbled him up.

They were married with great ceremony, pomp and spilt Veuve Clicquot in the summer of '57 when Harold Macmillan was on the throne and everybody was happy and the sun shone. The *Tatler* gave full coverage, including a photograph of Master Hare enjoying a joke on the stairs with Miss Hunt. A picture of Flying Officer Nevin and his new bride appeared on the front pages of the local newspapers, and the romantic barometer seemed to be Set Fair.

The marriage lasted only two years. The Honourable Priscilla found, after the first year as a wife of an RAF pilot, that there were better things in life than waiting for her man to come home from night flying, and these included going out to dinner – and other things – with a young, married and highly successful television producer who lived in a flat in Shepherd's Bush during the week. The two marriages were quickly and efficiently wrecked: Priscilla moved in with her producer, and Sam was left like a latter day Candide, puzzled that all did not, after all, seem to be for the best in the best of all possible worlds.

He was much more deeply hurt than he cared to admit, and when he was offered a posting to Singapore on all-weather fighters, he accepted eagerly, delighted to be able to put everything behind him.

During his time in the far east, he learnt a little more about women in a brothel called Tokyo Nights, in Johore Bahru. He also achieved a world record which is so far unbeaten. He did this inadvertently by taking off one morning from RAF Tengah in his very-nearly-faster-than-sound all-weather Javelin with the detachable cockpit ladder still bolted to the side of his aircraft. The ladder reached a maximum indicated airspeed of four hundred and twenty three knots, and a height of twenty-two thousand and seventeen feet before it flew off on its own and fell into dense Malayan jungle – to the surprise, no doubt, of the local pygmies.

Early in 1961, Sam returned to England and was posted to the Central Flying School at Little Rissington in the Cotswolds, to train for instructional duties. When, at the end of his six-month course, he won the low-level aerobatic trophy and emerged as a Qualified Flying Instructor, certain officers in light blue shuddered inwardly and predicted The End.

But it was not the end. Sam celebrated his success by growing a gingery moustache and purchasing an elderly Jaguar which he christened Daisy Bell. He arrived in this vehicle one afternoon at the gates of the Flying Training School, Sutcliffe, in the Vale of York, to take up his duties. His arrival was not without incident: upon being requested to produce his identity card by the sentry at the gate, Sam found it necessary to unpack his trunk and three suitcases in order to find it. The presence of his unpacked luggage (and in particular the colour of his pyjamas) amused a visiting Member of Parliament greatly, but did not amuse the Station Commander. Sam, being a tolerant man, forgave his commanding officer the

273

outburst of pent-up fury that followed the politician's departure, and settled down to the task of teaching enthusiastic young men like himself how to fly.

He did well. For in spite of his eccentricities, Sam Nevin had a certain warmth, a certain knack of establishing a rapport that induced his students to like him and actually listen to what he said. He brewed beer surreptitiously in a plastic dustbin, and took Daisy Bell for speed trials down the runways when the airfield was closed on Sundays. He began designing and making model jet aeroplanes, and took to composing verses about flying: in this way he tried to put into words the feelings of loneliness, power, fear and exhilaration he experienced in the cockpit of an aircraft. These poems were very private; he allowed no one even to know that he wrote them, let alone read them. Since his divorce, he had given up his Catholic faith, and now flying became his religion. One of the maxims which he instilled into his students was that in order to fly you must live, and in order to live, you must fly.

On a windy morning in April 1962 (Friday the thirteenth, to be precise) he set about demonstrating this maxim. He rose at half past six, breakfasted in the mess and attended an early briefing in the air traffic control tower in order to be ready to man his aircraft at a quarter to eight. He walked out over the wet concrete dispersal and carried out a rapid external inspection of the Jet Provost in which he was to do a practice session of low-level aerobatics.

He chatted amicably to the airman who helped him strap in, and having closed the cockpit canopy, ran briskly through the pre-flight checks and start-up procedure. He taxied out to the runway and took off, climbing up to five thousand feet before turning back towards the airfield.

Yorkshire spread out beneath him: he could see the city of York to the south, and the brown snake of the river Ouse winding its way north-west past the airfield of Linton-on-Ouse. To the north-east, the moors rose sharply at Helmsley, and to the west, smoke blew from the chimneys of the sprawling Leeds-Bradford complex. He opened the throttle fully, and dived down towards Sutcliffe, crossing the airfield boundary at three hundred and eighty knots and five hundred feet.

274

Outside the hangars, the instructors and students gathered with their cups of coffee to watch the display. The snub-nosed little jet trainer pulled vertically upward as it reached the air traffic control tower, and the onlookers craned their necks as Sam executed a faultless vertical roll followed by a stall turn. Whatever else anybody said about Sam Nevin, he certainly knew how to handle an aircraft.

Manoeuvre followed manoeuvre: stall turn, slow roll, Derry turn, barrel roll, wing-over, Porteus loop. In the cockpit, Sam Nevin had ceased, temporarily, to be an eccentric individual and had become instead a helmetted, gloved and visored set of complicated actions and reactions. His mind was full of speeds, engine readings, aircraft attitudes; his eyes were on the distant horizon as it fell away beneath him, surged up to meet him, or gyrated round him. His whole concentration was upon precision: precision of speed and height; precision of control movements, so that each manoeuvre appeared crisp and controlled from the ground; precision of position, so that the display remained in constant view of the spectators.

Towards the end of his sequence, when he was half way through an eight point roll, he encountered the birds. They were an odd mixture of seagulls and crows, and he ducked involuntarily as they whipped past on either side. He was aware that he had lost a hundred feet as a result of this instinctive reaction, and was cursing himself when the last seagull came into view. Its wings seemed to fold downward as it tried to evade: immediately he felt a heavy thump, and the whole aircraft began to vibrate.

He had very little time to think. He rolled the aircraft level, and looked at the engine instruments. The revs were winding down past the minimum, and the jet pipe temperature was climbing through the maximum. He pressed the radio transmit button and made a rapid emergency call: 'Juliet four-three, bird strike. Mayday, mayday, mayday.'

In the air traffic control tower, the local controller hit the crash alarm push with the heel of his palm. The siren wailed out across the airfield and echoed between the hangars. Children stopped playing outside the married quarters; wives hurried to windows and looked outward, upward. The red crash and rescue vehicles started up with a roar and started moving out over the grass, their wheels carving leviathan tracks as they sank into the damp ground.

In similar circumstances, the average pilot would almost certainly have reached for his face blind and ejected. But Sam Nevin was not an average pilot and he did not think in average ways. There was a runway four hundred feet beneath him and he intended to land on it. The only difficulty was that nearly all the runway was behind him, and he would have to reverse course before touching down.

He did what was obvious, but what few would have dared to do: he pulled the nose up nearly to the vertical, applied full right rudder, cartwheeled the aircraft round in what amounted to a stall turn and then, as the nose fell vertically downward again, pushed the button to lower the undercarriage and selected full flap. Almost immediately, the runway surged up to meet him: if he had been fifty feet lower on starting the manoeuvre, he would have flown into the ground. As it was, he had time to flare the aircraft and land, drawing to a halt in a remarkably short distance.

He shut down the engine, undid his straps and took his helmet off. The crash and rescue vehicles skidded to a halt alongside him, and the crews jumped out. He stood up in the cockpit and replaced the safety pins in the ejector seat, before jumping down to the ground to examine the starboard intake, which was splattered with the blood and feathered remains of the ingested bird. As he did so, one of the crash crew, wearing a fearnought suit, joined him. Nevin scratched his gingery brown hair. His moustache twitched in that rather foxy way of his.

The airman lifted the asbestos visor from his head and surveyed the aircraft.

'What happened sir?' he asked.

Nevin turned to look at the engine intake, out of which protruded a webbed foot.

'My aeroplane has unfortunately eaten a seagull,' he explained, 'and is suffering from indigestion.'

Inevitably, there was a party that evening to celebrate, and even more inevitably, the person to organise the party was Wilf Braintree. Wilf was an overweight flying instructor who lived in a bungalow in Clifton Without, on the outskirts of York. He was married but recently separated, and was going through a phase of intensive promiscuity.

As it was a Friday, the party started during an event called the TGIF. These letters stand for Thank God It's Friday, as every good RAF officer knows, and signal the excuse for the consumption of large quantities of draught beer at the end of the working week. The TGIF that week was well attended: Sam Nevin's aerobatic forced landing had turned him into an instant hero, and everyone wanted to hear all about it. The Watney's Red Barrel flowed freely: froth slid down the outside of tankards, stuck to upper lips, moustaches, carpets and sometimes the tips of noses. Nevin found himself surrounded by instructors and students, all anxious to hear in every last detail what it was like and how he had reacted.

'It was a piece of old doddle really,' he explained almost apologetically. 'It was abundantly clear that I was about to make like the proverbial gas-driven non-returnable boomerang, so I just pulled her up into a wing-over, popped the gear down and landed. Simple as that.'

While the beer flowed and Sam told his story a second and third time for the benefit of late arrivals, Wilf Braintree was busy in the telephone booth adjoining the bar. He was making a succession of calls to the colleges, polytechnics and hospitals in Harrogate, Leeds and York. Wilf Braintree held that no party was complete without Totty. And as he intended the party that night to be yet another party to end all parties, he organised a very large number of Totties and told each to bring a friend.

In due course the students fitted themselves into a communally-owned hearse and drove at a stately speed along the country lanes of the Vale of York, eventually parking outside Wilf Braintree's bungalow in Patterdale Drive. A succession of sporty flying instructors in equally sporty cars arrived and unloaded quantities of wine, beer, spirits, mineral waters, bags of crisps, tins of peanuts and a scattering of wives. Sam Nevin drew up in Daisy Bell and succeeded in bringing six bottles of Spumante to the front doorstep of the bungalow before dropping four of them.

The party then happened. The Totty arrived; the punch was mixed; the stereo was wired up and the first pop records played. Consignment after consignment of girls trooped in and began to drape themselves over the furniture and convenient aviators.

Wilf Braintree moved about the gathering throng, his antiperspirant still fresh, his round face flushed with success. 'Plenty booze, plenty music, plenty Totty,' he kept repeating as if it were a magic formula, adding: 'I like it. I *like* it.'

It is difficult to chart the progress of a party. There is no doubt, however, that Wilf Braintree's party on Friday 13 April 1962 was a success. One feature in particular made it a memorable occasion: this was the full performance by Sam Nevin of the Dam Busters' raid on the Ruhr Dams, which he gave with complete musical accompaniment and sound effects, simulating the low-level run-in over the reservoirs by lying full length on a table and shining two pencil torches on the carpet to represent the height-finding apparatus invented for that operation. Sam's ability to imitate aircraft noises had to be heard to be believed: his rendering of the bombers flying low over the water and pulling up over the high ground was something that nobody at the party would ever forget.

Shortly after this performance, when Sam was in the kitchen wiping a few glasses, he was accosted by a large and very forthright girl, whom he had talked to briefly earlier.

'I think you ought to come to the bedroom,' she said.

'Oh? Why's that?'

'It's Jonathan.'

'Jonathan Symes?'

'I don't know about the Symes bit, but I know he's your student.'

'What's the matter with him?'

'He's had a sort of breakdown.'

Sam Nevin followed the girl into the bedroom, where one of

278

the younger students sat on the bed in his shirt and underpants, weeping.

The girl said, 'I'll leave you to it.'

'Thank you very much,' Sam answered, a little hurt. He turned to Symes. 'What the hell's the matter with you?'

But the nineteen-year-old Symes was unable to explain that fear of flying, alcohol and the recent loss of his virginity had caused his lack of emotional control. After some rather ineffectual counselling, Sam eventually decided to take him back to Sutcliffe. He waited while Symes put his clothes on and escorted him out into the night wind. In the car, Symes remained silent except for one remark. 'She said I was bloody gorgeous,' he announced, and then relapsed into renewed sobs.

It took Nevin the best part of an hour to settle Jonathan Symes in his room and to ensure that he would report for further flying training after the week-end. In doing so, he felt like a nursemaid. They engaged in a rather Battle-of-Britainish conversation, in which Symes said he was sorry for making such a damned fool of himself, and was then sick into his wash basin. Nevin told him that the same could have happened to a bishop and left to drive back to the party.

Half a mile away from Patterdale Drive, he suffered the third misfortune of the day: his nearside tyre burst and he ended up nearly in the ditch. He swore for some seconds and then set about jacking up the car to change the tyre. However, the jack sank into the soft verge and made this impossible. As the car was off the road, he locked it and walked the remaining distance to Wilf's house to summon help.

All the cars had gone when he arrived, and the party seemed to be over. The front door was on the latch, however, and a light was on, so he went in. The debris of the party lay all about him: unwashed glasses, full ashtrays, cushions on the floor, bottles everywhere. He stood and looked at the ruins and then heard somebody coming out of the bathroom. He turned: it was the large girl.

'Somebody puked on my knee,' she explained, 'So I thought I'd have a bath. We're all going on to Phillida's.'

'Ah.'

279

'I'm going to purloin a pair of Wilf's trousers. Mine are all yukky. With you in a sec.'

She disappeared. He went into the kitchen and washed the oil off his hands. The girl appeared again in a pair of cricket trousers and floppy sweater.

'*Voilà*,' she said. 'Do you know the way to Phillida's?'

He shook his head. 'No, but – '

'I'll lead the way, then. Eggy bake and coffee. Shall we go?'

He explained about his car. She looked at him a moment: her eyes were rather deep-set, and unusually dark blue, or perhaps bluish-grey. 'We'll go in my machine then,' she said. 'Okay?'

She owned an Austin Healey Sprite: it was parked round the corner. As she drove off, he was immediately aware that she was a thoroughly competent driver. They went through the deserted streets of York and out onto the Tadcaster road, heading for Leeds. She didn't talk on the way until they were entering Leeds itself, and then she said, 'Look. Let's go to my place first, shall we? I feel like a proper nana in these pantaloons.'

They entered the city and she drove towards the University, parking outside some terraced Victorian houses.

'Come on down,' she said, and led the way down steps to a basement flat. He followed her in.

The room was a comfortable shambles: there were books and papers everywhere, and a collection of highly painted pottery roosters decorated a mantelpiece. There were too many pictures on the walls, and a small black fireplace was full of newspapers and soot.

She took off her duffel coat and threw it on the back of an old sofa. They faced each other for a moment, and in that moment he knew exactly why she had taken him there. Her eyes looked into his: the pupils seemed to dilate, and she breathed out suddenly, so that he wondered if she were all right. His mouth opened to ask the question, but that question remained unasked, for suddenly her arms were round his neck and her mouth was on his mouth and her body against his body.

He was taken by surprise: he had never been aroused so

rapidly before, never progressed so quickly to sexual intimacy. And although Sam Nevin was the son of a gentleman, although he was regarded as an eccentric and a muddlehead, although he was a person whom it was difficult to take seriously and who himself had difficulty in taking life seriously, he was also a man and subject to the same sexual desires as any less gentlemanly, less eccentric and less muddleheaded member of his sex.

He found himself involved in a struggle to possess and to be possessed. His hands made their way up, under her sweater, and she shed it for him. He undid her brassière and released her full, heavy breasts so that, when he held them and fondled them, she let out a long sigh of appreciation. He felt her hands searching, searching and finding. 'This is what I wanted,' she murmured. 'This. *This*.'

'I can't last,' he croaked. 'Please – '

'Come inside. Come on. Quite safe. Come on. Here. In. In.' She lifted herself for him, leaning back against the sofa. He felt her hands helping, guiding; he saw her hair falling across her face, the eyes, grey-blue, flickering open and shut. He saw and yet did not see, for he was overtaken by a wave of ecstasy and carried along by it, only dimly aware of her voice saying, 'Yes, yes, go on, go on, go on . . . ' until all he knew was that he was inside her and she was round him, warm, tight, deliciously pulsating; and the knowledge of the approaching orgasm was as sure as the sight of a runway coming up to meet him before a landing: the jolt of arrival was certain but still in the future; there was a sensation of almost unbearable anticipation, a strange blurring of all the senses until the muscle jerked and jerked and jerked again and he felt the flood surge into her.

Slowly, he regained an awareness of his surroundings. They were on the floor: the legs of chairs rose up beside them. She was smiling up at him, a look of triumph in her eyes as if she had been the one to win the battle for possession.

'You are bloody gorgeous,' she whispered, and reached up to touch his face.

He grinned, pleased with himself.

'I don't even know your name,' he said.

'Stella,' she replied. 'Stella Teape.'

III

They slept in late the following morning. She brought him coffee and ginger biscuits towards midday and sat on the bed in her dressing gown with nothing on underneath. She was not fat nor even overweight, but her body had a certain creamy solidity which he liked. She shook her head in mock despair.

'These men in my bed,' she said.

'It's a regular occurrence, is it?'

'Oh – certainly. I'm a devil for punishment.'

He reached up and slid his hand inside her dressing gown, and over her breasts. She breathed out in the way he now knew signalled her appreciation.

'Good?'

'Very.'

'I like to see you enjoy it.'

She looked away and laughed, perhaps a little bitterly. 'I do that all right. Too much, probably.'

They were silent for a while. He ran his hand downward over her smooth skin. 'Why do you say that?'

'Oh. Past experience. It never lasts, does it?'

'The enjoyment?'

'The relationship.'

'Some people manage it.'

'I don't.' She finished her coffee, put the mug to one side. 'Who was that woman? The one who turned sailors into pigs. In the Odyssey.'

'Ceres?'

'No. She was cornflakes. I know – Circe. Well, I'm like her. I turn men into swine.'

'Some people are swine already.'

'That was said with feeling.'

He thought of Priscilla. 'I was married,' he said. 'Once.'

'I know. I heard all about you from Wilf.'

'I'm not sure I like being talked about.'

'It's the price of fame, love. We can't all be heroes.'

He considered a while, then said: 'So are you going to turn me into a swine?'

'I expect so. Sooner or later.' She laughed suddenly.

'What?'

'I was thinking of that kid last night. Jonathan. Do you know he called me "Mummy" by mistake? Poor little boy.'

'We're all little boys, deep down.'

She came back into bed and he buried his face between her breasts. She writhed a little with pleasure. 'If you go on like that much longer you'll have to make love to me again.'

'That was the idea.'

'Bluff.'

'Not at all.' He guided her hand. 'Is that bluff?'

She laughed in that rather odd, gurgling way of hers and rolled on top of him. 'If a thing's worth doing, it's worth doing well,' she said. 'That's what my mother always says.'

He wondered what her mother was like, but said, 'I'm not a thing.'

'I know. But I'm not *doing* you.'

'What are you doing?'

'Don't ask,' she whispered, then added, 'Oh – bodies, bodies!'

'Yours and mine.'

'Especially yours.'

'On the contrary, especially yours.'

'I'm fat.'

'You're not. I'm scrawny.'

'I'd say hard.'

She covered his mouth with kisses, then drew back. He laughed gently and sang, 'She's broad where a broad should be bro ---- ad.'

'*South Pacific*,' she said.

'Right in one.'

'Do you always sing on the job?'

'Depends on the job.'

'I seem to remember talking rather a lot last night. I was a bit pissed.'

'We both were. Pissed with sexual desire.'

'Am I exciting you, Mister Nevin?'

'You are, you are, you are indeed.'

'Uncle Sid and Aunty Mabel fainted at the breakfast table.'

'Really?'

'All good children take this warning: never do it in the morning.'

'Proust used to wear white gloves in bed. 'Nough said.'

'How many times was it in the night? Three?'

'Four. You're a demanding woman. *Per ardua ad Stella*.'

'*Stellam*, love. I'm first declension.'

'Blow first declension,' he whispered, flushing. 'I'm on the fifth conjugation.'

IV

She was in the bath when he arrived at noon the following Saturday. He stood outside the black front door beneath the iron railings and knocked four times before she eventually let him in. She was swathed in a bath towel.

'You're early.'

'No I'm not, I'm exactly on time.'

'That's what I meant. You're early.'

She disappeared into the bedroom. The telephone rang.

'Shall I answer it?' he called.

'No!'

He stood in the room, which was in a slightly worse state of chaos than it had been the previous week. The telephone rang and rang, and eventually stopped. He picked a book off the floor: it was about Gestalt psychology, and a random reading of a few lines was enough to make him put the book down. Stella came in. The telephone rang again.

'Sod!' she said, and let it ring.

They waited.

'Don't you think you ought to answer it?'

'No. I know who it is, you see.'

The telephone stopped ringing. She relaxed. It rang again. She went quickly across to it and picked it up.

'Yes? Yes, it is. No. No, I don't want to. No. No. No, I thought I made myself clear on that. No. Look – I don't want to discuss it further.'

She looked at him. He mouthed, 'Would you like me to go?'

284

but she shook her head vigorously. A voice at the other end of the line spoke rapidly for some while. Suddenly Stella said into the telephone, 'Look, piss off!' and hung up.

'Let's go out,' she said. 'I don't want to be in if he comes round.'

'Who is he?'

'Oh – nobody. He no longer exists.'

She picked up her duffel coat and put it on. 'Let's go. My car.'

They drove out of Leeds and up into the Yorkshire Dales. They found a pub and lunched on veal and ham pie, and pints of Tadcaster ale. The telephone call had upset her, and only now did she begin to relax. He asked her about her week.

'Frustrating,' she said. 'I'm trying to find myself a job but don't seem to be getting very far.'

'What were you doing before?'

'Social work. It didn't work out.'

'You were at University in Leeds, I gather.'

'Who told you that?'

'Wilf.'

'God! That man! Yes, I was.'

'What went wrong with the job?'

'Oh . . . long story.'

'Go on, then.'

'Are you sure you want to hear?'

'Quite sure.'

She thought a moment, put out her cigarette. 'Perhaps it isn't a very long story. Just a bit sordid. I was working as a sort of trainee probation officer, and they gave me a man who'd been convicted of molesting boys. I – had a sort of affair with him.' She looked across the table at him. 'He committed suicide. Blew his brains out in a public lavatory. He was ex-army. Used a service revolver.' She smiled uncertainly. 'Sorry. I shouldn't have told you.'

'It must have been terrible.'

'It wasn't much fun. I went away and hid in the Black Mountains. Rather appropriate really.'

'Is that where you come from – Wales?'

She shook her head. 'Portugal.'

'*Portugal?*'

'Daddy brews port,' she said, and made a face. 'He's rather disgustingly well off, I'm afraid.'

'I don't regard being well off as something to be ashamed of.'

'I do. I hate it. I loathe . . . things. Possessions.'

'What about the car?'

'Oh, I know, I know. I'm a complete pseud, Sam. You'd better get that straight right from the word go.'

They walked on the moor after lunch and he talked about flying. When he was in the middle of an explanation of the difference between a slow roll and a barrell roll, she interrupted him. 'Tell me about your wife,' she ordered.

He was taken by surprise. They reached the top of the moor, and leant against a small cairn, out of the wind. She took his hand and put it with hers in the pocket of her duffel coat.

'What do you want to know?'

'Everything. How you met her. What she was like. What *it* was like.'

He launched into the whole story of meeting and marrying Priscilla, and the realisation that she was being unfaithful to him; the battles that had taken place, and the final, agonising break. And in telling her this, he learnt more about Stella, for she knew how to listen: there was, after all, a soft centre beneath the cynical exterior. So he talked, and the wind whistled through the grey stones of the cairn, and brilliant white clouds sailed overhead.

'What about you?' he asked at length. 'Have you ever approached the brink of matrimony?'

She laughed. 'Not me. I'm just a good lay.'

'You shouldn't say that.'

'Why not?'

'You undervalue yourself.'

She kissed him. 'Thank you.'

'I meant it.'

On their way down the hill, she said, 'I think I ought to warn you. What I said last week – well, I was partly serious. I do have trouble making things last. I don't know if it's me, or the sort of men I seem to attract. So if this – you and me – if you *do* regard me as a good lay, will you tell me? So that I know? Will you promise never to pretend you like me?'

They stopped. The wind blew her hair; her lips were cool. Curlews called to each other overhead. He held her hands and said, 'I promise.'

'I'm a crazy mixed-up kid,' she said, and smiled wryly.

'Aren't we all?'

'No. You aren't, for a start.'

They seemed to talk all afternoon and evening. He told her a great deal about himself, and she let out a few minute pieces of information concerning her own background. She seemed particularly cynical about her parents. 'It's pathetic,' she said. 'They don't really love each other, but they haven't the guts to separate. All Dad ever thinks about is the port wine trade. And my mother – she's in a sort of trap called Home. They both wanted more children, but they only got me. Awful. When I go back there we play a sort of charade called Happy Families. We pretend that we all get on as every family should get on, but underneath it all something festers. It'll erupt one day, and there'll be a nasty mess.'

They ended up, late at night, drinking Irish coffee in her flat and listening to nocturnes by Chopin, which she said she liked. 'I'm tone deaf,' she said, 'but I find this soothing.'

He took her hand: her fingers were short and stubby, and her fingernails spatulate. He had read somewhere that people with spatulate fingernails were unpredictable. It seemed true in her case, but he enjoyed her unpredictability. He closed his eyes and let the gentle piano notes flow by, wondering how on earth he had become so quickly involved with this girl. He still felt a little wary of her: he *had* regarded her as a 'good lay', but now, having told her so much about himself she inevitably meant more. He recognised a need to share himself with somebody, and detected in Stella a similar need, but he was still afraid of something about her which he did not understand and could not name. There seemed to be an element of danger in associating with her. It was, perhaps, this very feeling of risk that made her so attractive.

He had a bath and she offered to scrub his back. This led to other things: he found her tremendously attractive sexually, and the attraction was intensified by her uninhibited way of showing pleasure. He loved it when, reaching a climax, she would cling to him, crying out, convulsing.

But in the early hours of the following morning, after they had made love and she was lying in his arms, he became aware that she was crying.

'What is it?' he asked. 'What's the matter?'

She sat up in bed and put the light on.

'Oh sod!' she said. 'I may as well tell you everything.' She looked down at him: her breasts full and pendulous, the aureolas immense. Tears went down her cheeks; she swallowed in an attempt to control them. He reached up to her, pulling her down.

'Tell me,' he whispered.

'I enjoy it so much,' she said. 'Too much. I think I must be a nympho or something. It frightens me.'

He held her in his arms. Her sobs died down. Light began to seep in through the curtains, and he lay awake for a long time, listening to the morning traffic on the road outside.

V

They spent several weekends together, and in June he moved into the flat with her. She managed to get a job with the *Yorkshire Evening Post*, and he had a full programme of instructing during the week and giving aerobatic displays at weekends. At first, remarks were passed in the instructors' crew room at RAF Sutcliffe, but after a while Wilf Braintree and the other instructors accepted that Nevin was not merely 'in lust', and he was left alone. For several months, Sam and Stella presumed that the affair would not last: they treated it as a joke, telling each other to make the most of it because it would soon be over. But it did last: they had their first, second and third arguments, and emerged from them stronger and better able to understand each other. He was by no means her equal in wit: he needed time to think out what he wanted to say, whereas Stella could volley back replies at him that left him at a loss for words. But because he was slower and surer, he was able to give her the reassurance and dependability that she needed. He was big enough for her to lean on when she needed to lean, and slow enough to be outwitted when she needed to outwit. And he steadfastly refused to be turned into a swine.

They managed to arrange their leave and summer holiday so that they coincided, and he accepted when she invited him to drive out with her to Portugal. They arrived in her car outside the gates of Moinho Velho on a hot afternoon in early August. Stella sounded the horn, and Natália swung open the gates. The dogs barked and wagged, and a lady in a paisley dress came round the house to welcome them. Stella kissed her and said, 'Hullo, Ma. This is Sam,' and he found himself shaking hands with Stella's mother, whom he liked immediately. 'We're having tea by the pool,' she said. 'I expect you'd like a wash first, though. Natália will help you with your things.'

He was shown upstairs by the maid, who insisted upon carrying his luggage for him. Stella chattered to her in Portuguese, and Natália laughed and looked at him, saying something mischievous with a sidelong glance.

'She says you're very handsome,' Stella said. He bowed and said, 'Thank you very much,' and there was more laughter and chatter. He was shown to his room: the windows overlooked a valley that ran down to the sea, and over to the right there were people sitting by a swimming pool and children playing. He washed, changed his shirt, put on a cravat and was brushing his hair when Stella came to his door.

'Come and meet the folks,' she said, self-mockingly, and he followed her downstairs and out into the garden.

It was like walking backward in time: as he was introduced first to Stella's father, then to Miss Remington and finally to a slightly younger couple called Arie and Deirdre Romer, Sam could not help feeling that he had jumped back from the sixties into a pre-war era. The maid came along with freshly baked scones and another pot of tea. Mr Teape asked in a jocular way what sort of trip they had had.

'Where did you stay?' Miss Remington asked. She had neatly permed hair and was very precisely made up.

'We camped,' Stella said. 'Didn't you know?'

289

'That must have been fun,' Miss Remington said.

'It was,' Stella replied bluntly, and looked at Sam. 'Wasn't it?'

Sam sipped his tea, aware of undercurrents in the conversation but unable to identify them. 'Oh. Yes. Great fun.'

'And I gather you're in the Royal Air Force,' Mr Teape said.

'That's right, sir.'

'What sort of aeroplanes do you fly?'

'Jet Provosts at the moment. I'm instructing.'

'Good for you,' Teape said. 'Good for you.'

He felt like an unusual animal in a cage. Stella had warned him already that the colony would be intensely interested in him. 'They have so little to occupy their tiny little lives that any scrap of gossip is seized upon and worried to death,' she had told him. 'You'll be among the top ten topics for conversation for the next six months, more than likely. So don't give them too much to talk about.'

The Romer children splashed about in the pool, and Sam sat in the sun and answered the gently probing questions put to him by Miss Remington, who – he discovered later – was Stella's second cousin once removed.

'Let's have a swim,' Stella said.

'Do you think you should so soon after your tea?' Miss Remington said.

'I expect we'll survive,' Stella replied, 'And if we don't you can come and hoik us out, Aunt Joy.'

They changed into swimming things in the house. Stella came to his room in her bathing costume: they kissed, and he was immediately aroused. As they walked out to the swimming pool, he suspected that Miss Remington had guessed something: she looked at him in a way that might have been pleasant if it had come from a woman twenty years younger. He plunged quickly into the pool in order to hide what seemed very obvious, and was joined by Stella. She winked at him, and he looked quickly across at Aunt Joy, who looked away at the same moment.

The Romers left after tea, and Sam unpacked and changed for dinner. Below his window, Mr Teape walked up and down muttering occasionally to himself, and somewhere in the kitchens the maid sang while she worked. The sun began to descend towards the horizon. He went down to the patio.

'Ah,' said Teape. 'What will you have to drink?'

'A gin and tonic, if I may.'

'Try a white port.' Teape unstopped a decanter and poured a glass, adding a cube of ice. He handed it to Sam. 'There you are. You'll like that. A good, nutty flavour.'

They were joined by Mrs Teape. A large dog came along and flopped down at their feet. 'We're having some people in to dinner,' Ruth said. 'More Remingtons. James and Joanna.'

'My partner,' Teape explained.

'Is it a big firm?' Sam asked.

'Not very. But it happens to be the best. You must come to the lodge one day for lunch. I'll show you round.'

They were joined by Joy Remington, who was staying with the Teapes for a few days. She had changed into a midnight blue dress. Diamonds glittered on the fingers of her right hand. 'Well,' she said, accepting a glass of tawny port from Teape, 'Isn't this nice? Welcome to Portugal. Must I call you "Sam"? I think Samuel is so much nicer.'

'I don't mind much what I'm called,' Sam said.

'Samuel it is, then. How did you come to meet Stella?'

He told her about the forced landing, making it into a funny story, and half way through James and Joanna Remington arrived. James was rather military: ex-naval, Sam noted from the RNVR tie. Joanna was pert and talkative. Conversation tripped off her tongue like peas off a knife. She was inclined to giggle.

Stella arrived last, having had a very long bath. James Remington kissed her warmly, and Sam saw Joanna's smile freeze momentarily.

They went into the dining room, where the table was laid with silver cutlery and Edinburgh crystal. Ruth had arranged a silver bowl of flowers between the candlesticks, and the mats bore prints of old London.

'This is such a lovely room,' Joanna said.

'Isn't it,' Joy agreed.

They sat down. Sam was reminded of a mess dinner. He took the mitred napkin from the plate in front of him and spread it on his lap. Natália served onion soup with sippets.

Ruth said, 'I believe you lived in India once, Sam?'

'That's right. We left in 1948. I was fourteen.'

'Old enough to remember, then.'

'Oh yes. Certainly.'

'Did you like it out there?'

'It was a very easy life. Pleasant in its way, but rather narrowing.'

'Sounds like Portugal,' Stella remarked.

'And is your father retired?'

'He died. A couple of years ago. Mother lives in Croydon.'

'Do you have any brothers and sisters?'

'Three elder sisters. All married.'

'So you're very much the baby I expect,' Joy said.

'Oh, definitely,' said Stella.

'Stop quizzing the poor boy,' Bobby Teape said.

'Excellent soup,' said James.

Stella announced: 'We'd like to go to Saborinho.'

'So I understand,' her father replied. 'Aren't you going up next week, James?'

'Tuesday, yes.' James turned to Sam. 'We drive as far as Pinhão, then take the train. There's still no road.'

Ruth said: 'You'll love the Douro. It has a beauty all of its own.'

'Will you be going up too, Joanna?' Joy asked.

'Oh gosh yes,' Joanna said. 'I love it up there.'

'That's all right, then,' Joy said.

'What's all right?' Stella challenged.

'Well. You'll be properly chaperoned, won't you dear?'

Sam felt Stella's foot nudge his. 'Oh, silly of me,' she said. 'I should have thought.'

The conversation eased a little as the wine level in the glasses descended: they talked about maids and dogs and politicians. Joy told Sam what wonderful things Salazar had done for Portugal: how he had put the country on its feet and made its currency one of the most stable in the world, and how all the peasants really led very happy lives in spite of having to work unbelievably hard for breadline wages. James mitigated the effect of this somewhat by telling a story about how Salazar visited a small town and was introduced to the local dignitaries of whom the only one who seemed genuinely anxious to please was the undertaker, who doffed his cap and expressed the hope that he might be of service to his excellency the prime minister in the not too distant future.

When the ladies retired after the dessert, Sam and James moved up the table to sit on either side of Teape, and the three men worked their way through a decanter of Teape's '48. Sam talked about the future of the manned fighter and bewailed the recent abandonment of the Blue Water missile. He tactfully asked about the port wine trade, and was treated to a lengthy briefing on the problems of marketing port, and the reasons for the decline in its popularity – caused, according to James, at least in part by the connoisseurs themselves, who had turned the appreciation of the wine into a mystery, whose secrets could only be known to an élite. 'But that's all rubbish,' he said finally. 'We don't care how people drink port so long as they drink it, eh Bobby?' and Bobby Teape agreed, twirling his glass in his hand and saying, 'Absolutely, absolutely.'

Sam was over-full of good food, good wine and vintage port. He was glad, therefore, after they had rejoined the ladies and the conversation had tripped along for another hour, when the Remingtons decided to depart and a general decision was taken to retire for the night.

He lay in bed with the lights out and listened to the night insects singing outside the window. He hadn't heard that sound since he'd been in the far east. A dog howled in the distance: he allowed his thoughts to wander back over the evening.

He would never have guessed, when he first met Stella, that she could have come from such a colonial sort of background. It was odd, he reflected, how your surroundings affected your behaviour. It was as if the presence of real silver and cut glass actually induced you to behave in a more civilised way. Even Stella had seemed less provocative, less cynical that evening.

Then, silently, the door opened, and there was Stella herself, a dim shape in the darkness. She closed the door almost as silently as she had opened it, and came quickly into his bed. She wriggled out of her nightdress, and he welcomed her nakedness against his own.

293

In the next room, Joy Remington had heard Sam's door close, and was immediately alert. She lay tense, listening for the slightest sound and then, very quietly, got out of bed. She took a chair and placed it in the corner of the room and stood on it, listening intently at the ventilation duct. The sounds she heard were very faint indeed, but they were unmistakable: a stifled laugh, the creak of bed springs, a gentle sigh. She stood on the chair for a long time, and her fists clenched instinctively as she heard the bed springs squeak and squeak and squeak; she heard Stella – yes, it could only be Stella – let out a stifled cry, a cry that could only have been heard by the most careful of listeners. But Joy Remington heard and was glad that she heard, for it proved that she had been right in her suspicions about Sam and Stella, and she was filled with delicious disgust.

Later, when Stella slipped out of Sam's room to return to hers, she was unaware that Joy had opened her own bedroom door an inch and was observing her through the crack. Nor was she aware that her activities with Sam that night caused Joy to lie awake for a very long time, her mind full of indignation, anger and wild imaginings, and the desperate feelings of frustration born of many, many years.

VI

'I don't want to be a little wifey,' said Stella.

'You won't be.'

'Yes I will. I can just see it. I shall be plunged willy-nilly into matrimonial mediocrity.'

'So what do you suggest? Continue as we are now?'

They had found an expanse of rock beside the river Douro, a mile or two above Saborinho, and half an hour's walk from the Quinta das Rosas. The sun beat down upon them and waves of heat came off the cliff face on the opposite bank. At their feet, a deeper part of the river had formed a slow moving pool of water. They had bathed and picnicked and bathed again.

'I don't know,' Stella said. 'All I know is that I don't want to get married.'

'But you've said yourself that you're sick of relationships that don't last.'

'I am.'

'Well then.'

'No. It's not "well, then". I refuse to do what everyone expects me to do. I refuse to be so bloody – predictable. It's all so – clickety-clickety-click. I meet you, bring you out to Portugal, your name appears in the *Anglo-Portuguese News,* the whole colony speculates on when the engagement will be announced and – bingo! We announce it. A marriage has been arranged and will take place shortly. I'd rather live in sin and shock Aunt Joy.'

'I don't see where Aunt Joy comes into it.'

'Aunt Joy *always* comes into it. She gives me the screaming ab-dabs.'

'I noticed.'

'Anyway, I don't see why you should want to jump into matrimony again. After what happened to you.'

He rolled towards her, captured her hands. 'I need stability. We both do. We can achieve more together than we can apart.'

'Not chained together, though.'

'We shan't be chained together.'

'Oh no? Look – the way we are now, we're both free. It's not just that I don't want to be a little wifey. I don't want to turn you into one of those pathetic little men you see trailing round after their wives in supermarkets. That's what marriage does. One drags, the other trails. I'd go round the bend in either role.'

'What about children?'

'*What* about children?'

'Don't you ever want to have any?'

'Not really. What point is there?'

'You shouldn't be so defeatist.'

'I'm not. I'm realistic.'

They were silent for some time. In the distance, the Douro train sounded its whistle as it made its way up the valley.

'I'd like to have children,' Sam said eventually. 'But only with you. I just, well, I just like idea of a family. A *big* family.'

'I'm boiling,' she said. 'Let's go in again.'

They descended into the pool of brown water. Stella sat on the bottom, up to her neck. 'Delicious,' she said. She took off her swimming costume and threw it on a rock. He did likewise: the sensation of the cool water between his legs was oddly primordial.

'Look,' Stella said, 'My breasts float.'

They lolled about in the water and later climbed back on to the rock. 'Don't put them on,' Stella said. 'No one'll ever see us here. Come and lie with me.'

He sat with his arms round his knees. 'I feel very vulnerable like this.'

She reached across. 'You *are* very vulnerable. Beautiful ugly thing.'

She began caressing him. She knew exactly what to do, what to touch, how to touch and when to touch. She knew when to stop, how long to wait, when to start again, where to start again. She did it quite deliberately, almost at arm's length, it seemed: she went on and gently on, until he began to writhe and buck, trying not to pant, unable to look away from those eyes of hers which held him as surely as the light pressure of her fingers.

'Let me do something for you,' he whispered. 'Come on.'

'No, she said. 'No. Not this time.'

He gasped and his whole body began to shake. She was playing with him: controlling him, deciding for him the exact moment of relief. He hated it and yet loved it: he felt degraded by it and yet at the same time lifted into the heights of ecstasy. And when the moment came and he could not stop himself from crying out, even then she would not let him go. 'That's enough,' he almost sobbed. 'Please. That's enough.' He collapsed, exhausted, on the rock.

'Ah,' she said, and let go of him. 'We have a spectator.'

He tried to cover himself, and she laughed. She was looking at something behind him. He turned, and was in time to see a water snake slither down the rock face and into the river. It swam across the pool in a straight line, its head sticking up like a periscope.

They put on their clothes and made their way back along the river path to the Quinta das Rosas. They walked up the steep

296

track to the cluster of farm buildings that overlooked the river, and met the old muleteer, with whom Stella passed the time of day.

'This is Ayres,' she said, 'and he wants to show you the livestock.'

The old man grinned toothlessly at Sam and beckoned them to follow him. He led them first to the stables, where two mules were tethered. In the corner was an old mattress and some odds and ends of clothing. 'He sleeps here with them,' Stella said. 'Marvellous, isn't it? He's happier that way, apparently.' They followed Ayres on to the hen and turkey coops and finally to the pig sty. He talked to Stella at some length, the guttural Portuguese totally incomprehensible to Sam.

'This is Tomaz,' Stella explained, as they leaned over the wall of the sty and looked in on a large boar. The old man scratched the animal's back with his stick. 'And next door we have his wife Gertrudes and daughter Natália.'

'Why is he laughing?'

'Well, our Ayres is quite a merry wit. He's called the pigs after the president of Portugal and his family.'

The muleteer said something else, and Stella asked a question. The old man shrugged widely and laughed, and there was a further exchange.

'What was all that about?'

'He says they're going to kill Gertrudes tomorrow, so I asked if we could come and watch. He said it wasn't the sort of thing a lady should see.'

'How do they do it?'

'Haven't a clue,' Stella said. 'That's why I said we'd come along.'

VII

Joaquim António do Naxcimento de Jesus had been the farm manager at Quinta das Rosas for nearly ten years now, ever since old Bernadino died, and he knew exactly what was

297

required to be done before killing a pig. It was necessary, for instance, to insist upon a certain measure of discipline: if one did not, the occasion was inclined to lack dignity, and things went wrong.

He had spent an hour the previous evening sharpening his knives and oiling them, and now, at a quarter to eight, with the sun lifting clear of the mountain, he brought the wooden box containing them and placed it upon the stone wall opposite the sty. He opened the box and unwrapped the cloth from one of the knives, whose blade he tested. It was razor sharp: a thin weal of blood rose immediately from the ball of his thumb, and he was thereby satisfied.

Ayres and the farm hand Carlos brought a wide wooden bench and an enamel bowl from the farm buildings and set them on the flat ground between the sty and the wall. Carlos was a good-looking lad of sixteen: he had been taken on at Quinta das Rosas as a favour to his widowed mother, who was Joaquim's cousin. He was given the equivalent of two pounds a month and full board, and counted himself lucky.

A fourth man appeared: this was Pedro, who had come up from Pinhão with Senhor Remington. Pedro normally worked at the other Teape *quinta*, but occasionally accompanied the directors on their visits. He considered himself to be somewhat superior to Joaquim, so the latter was not greatly enamoured of him. However, a fourth pair of hands was welcome, for Gertrudes was a large and powerful pig.

'Where's the rope?' Joaquim asked.

Ayres turned to the boy. 'In the stable. Go and get it.'

Carlos ran off, and returned a minute later with a length of rope. Joaquim looked round to make a final check that all was ready. 'You two can take the back legs,' he said to Ayres and Carlos, 'And we'll take the front and rope the snout. Understand?'

Carlos grinned uneasily and glanced at the other two. Joaquim went on: 'We'll bring her straight out here and onto the bench. You can hold the bowl, boy.'

The sound of a woman's voice interrupted them. It was Stella and Sam. The men touched their caps respectfully.

'Good morning, Joaquim,' Stella said. 'We've come to watch.'

Joaquim took his cap off and held it in both hands. 'The *menina* shouldn't see this,' he said. 'It's not very pleasant.'

'Oh don't worry about that!' Stella said. 'You go ahead. We'll keep well out of the way.'

Carlos stared at her. You could see the shape of her breasts clearly under her yellow cotton shirt. Her denim trousers were tight round her buttocks and thighs.

Joaquim bowed. 'Very well,' he said. He cleared his throat, put his cap back on. 'Right,' he said to the men. 'Let's get it over with.'

They entered the sty. They had difficulty capturing Gertrudes, and Joaquim was embarrassed because the English were watching. He saw Stella smile and say something to her man friend, and his embarrassment turned to anger. They were laughing at him. He was losing face because of a pig.

Ayres and Carlos had captured the back legs now, and the old man put a noose round them pulling the rope viciously tight. Pedro did the same with another noose round the snout, and Gertrudes was dragged squealing to the bench. The four men gathered round her and heaved her up: she was tied down on her side, and the rope was pulled as tight as possible, so that she struggled in vain.

Pedro motioned to the boy, and Carlos fetched the basin, squatting down with it, ready for the blood.

Joaquim went to the wooden box that lay open on the wall and took up the knife. He bent over the pig, and massaged the throat with his hand. The skin was rough to the touch: rough, but also loose and warm. The animal grunted a few times. Her pale blue eyes darted back and forth beneath the pink lashes. He rubbed his fingers up and down the warm throat and the pig grunted and grunted. The sun shone down brilliantly through the thin foliage of olive trees. In the chicken coop nearby, a cock crowed repeatedly.

He felt with his fingers and found the right spot. The three men and the English couple watched, and waited. Quickly, but carefully, he plunged the knife into the throat and drew it across.

The blood gushed out over the boy's hands, and he moved the enamel basin quickly to catch its torrent. Gertrudes' mouth opened wide, the rope noose tight round her upper jaw, and she bellowed with the full force of her powerful lungs. This was not so much a cry of pain as one of outrage at the crime which had been committed. Suddenly the whole valley was full of her roarings, and a flock of doves flew up quickly from the eaves of the squat, whitewashed farm buildings. They flew in circles, rising and dipping, round and round in lazy, flapping formations that changed each time they swooped and climbed.

Except for the boy, who crouched holding the basin, the men now stood back, avoiding each other's glances, and watched with fixed and embarrassed stares.

The death seemed to last a long time, and went through definite stages. At first, the pig struggled violently, using every ounce of available energy. Later, it appeared to accept what was inevitable and lay groaning in pain, its breath coming out in great gusts of anguish and despair. Towards the end, the creature took two immense breaths: it let them out with horrifying moans, its whole body shuddering. Death literally shook the last remnants of life from the body: it convulsed violently for several seconds. And in those seconds, this death ceased to be individual and became universal: it was a death that every creature would one day have to experience.

The back legs twitched; a nerve jumped in the shoulder. The basin was full of blood, and a thick, scummy froth had formed on it. A dribble still came from the wound in the throat. The valley was silent.

When the cock began crowing, it was like a reveille: the men looked at each other again, and Ayres began to undo the rope. The sun shone down out of a blue sky. The doves wheeled and glided back to their eaves. Life started again. There was a carcass of pork to be shaved, gutted and hung.

On their way up the hill past the rows of vines, Stella remarked, 'It reminded me of you.'

Sam looked at her. 'How do you mean?'

'Yesterday. On that slab of rock.'

'Sorry,' he said. 'Not with you.'

She snorted with exasperation. 'Sam!' she said. 'Don't be so thick!'

300

VIII

Two days before they were due to drive back to England, and
had returned to Valadares, Joy Remington rang up and invited
Sam and Stella to evening drinks.

'I'm having some of the younger people,' she explained over
the telephone, 'and I thought it would be nice if they could
meet you both.'

Stella put her hand over the mouthpiece. 'What can we say
we're doing?'

'You must accept,' Ruth said. 'It would be very rude not to.'

So Stella accepted, but under duress. 'I can't stand her
parties,' she said when she had rung off. 'She's always setting
herself up as the Grand Old Lady of the British colony. She's so
bloody condescending.'

'She's been very kind to you in the past,' Ruth said. 'Think of
all those Christmas and birthday presents.'

'Nobody buys my affection with presents,' Stella said. 'Or
anything else, for that matter.'

Joy had inherited her parents' house in Foz. A neat, plump
maid opened the door to Stella and Sam, and they were shown
into the drawing room, whose french windows overlooked red
tiled roofs and, beyond, the entrance to the river Douro. The
usual crowd of young colony were there: the Millets, the
Randalls, the Hopkinsons and various Remingtons. Joy moved
among the groups of guests introducing Sam, prompting
conversation, encouraging people to eat the nuts and biscuits
and *pasteis de bacalhau* that another maid handed round.

In due course, she button-holed Sam.

'Well,' she said brightly, 'How do you find us?'

'Who do you mean by "us", Miss Remington?'

'The colony, of course.'

'Oh. Very pleasant.'

She put her head on one side and looked up at him. 'Now
you must be quite a bit older than Stella, aren't you?'

'A little over six years. Yes.'

'That's a good age gap, I think.'

He laughed politely.

'A young man should have time to sow his wild oats,' Joy

301

said. 'I don't expect Stella is by any means your first girl friend, is she?'

'By no means,' he said and then added out of sheer devilment, 'I've even had a wife.'

'I beg your pardon?'

'I was married. I'm divorced.'

'Oh,' said Joy. 'Oh I see.' She looked from side to side, and spotted an empty plate. 'Will you excuse me?' she said. 'I really must go and chivvy Custodia.'

On her way out of the drawing room, she waylaid Stella. 'Come and have a chat,' she said. 'I want to ask you something.'

Stella followed her into the blue tiled kitchen. Joy pushed the door closed. 'Now,' she said. 'I gather he's been married before, dear. Did you know?'

'Of course I knew, Aunt Joy.'

'You don't sound very concerned.'

'Why should I be?'

'My dear girl, isn't it obvious? Are you serious about him?'

'Depends what you mean by serious.'

'But have you discussed marriage?'

'I think that's my business, not yours.'

'Stella, I am your godmother. I have a responsibility for your moral welfare.'

'For God's sake! I'm twenty-two!'

'Maybe. But I still feel responsible. Have you told your parents about his previous marriage?'

Stella took a breath and her head went back in anger. 'I think I can leave that to you, Aunt, can't I? As you feel so responsible. In fact you'll be able to tell the whole colony. Why not put an entry in the *Anglo-Portuguese News?* "Flight Lieutenant Sam Nevin – divorcee – has returned to England with Stella Teape. They are sharing a small tent without a chaperone." How about *that?*' Stella turned on her heel and left the kitchen. She found Sam in a corner talking to one of the Randall girls. 'I think it's time we pushed off,' she said, so that everyone could hear. Sam looked at her and she looked meaningfully back. 'Let's go and thank Aunt Joy,' she went on. 'She's in the kitchen, brewing things up.'

He followed her to the door of the kitchen, where they met Joy coming out.

302

'We're off, Aunt Joy. Thanks so much. It's been a lovely party. Really lovely. Hasn't it, Sam?'

'Absolutely,' Sam agreed. 'Thoroughly enjoyed it.'

They left rapidly.

'What the hell was all that about?' he asked as they drove off.

Stella took a corner fast. The wheels screamed on the cobbles. 'Can't you guess? Who told her you were divorced?'

'Oh. Have I put my foot in it?'

'Yes, but I'm very glad you have.' She took another corner, revved to change down and accelerated hard to overtake a line of slower moving cars, reaching the traffic lights at the head of the queue and crossing them as they changed to green. She drove fast along the coast road and drew to a halt with a skid outside a bar, where tables had been placed outside in the shade of the plane trees. She switched off the engine and looked at him. 'Come on,' she said. 'I need a real drink.'

They sat outside in the evening sun and drank whiskies. 'Bloody woman,' Stella said. 'How dare she?' She looked across at Sam: he was wearing a pale linen suit that had been made for him by the Chinese tailor at RAF Tengah, in Singapore. During the holiday he had extended his moustache slightly: Deirdre Romer had said that she thought he looked rather like Douglas Fairbanks Junior. Now, they faced each other in the evening light. Trams clanked by along the water front, and a cargo ship was edging her way out of the harbour between the north bank and the sand bar.

'Bugger it,' Stella said. 'Let's get married.'

IX

'Don't you think I ought to ask your Pa first?' he asked as they drove off the bridge and up the hill, heading for Valadares.

'No I don't. They've been keeping their fingers crossed that we'll announce our engagement ever since you called Dad "sir" the first afternoon. You can do no wrong as far as he's concerned. He thinks the sun shines out of your backside.'

'Which of course it does.'

'And Ma thinks you're sweet. She told me so.'

'Which of course I am,' he said, and kissed her ear.

'You'll upset my sense of balance. I'll get the bends and we'll spin in.'

'The leans, you mean.'

'Well. Same thing.'

She swung the car off the main road, racing through Valadares, narrowly missed an oxcart loaded high with straw. She drove much too fast along the track to Moinho Velho, and the Sprite threw up a cloud of dust behind it. She braked to a halt and pressed the horn for several seconds. The cook opened the gate, and the car leapt forward into the courtyard. Stella got out and slammed the door. She went round to the back of the house.

'Ma!' she shouted.

'Hello!' Ruth called from the kitchen. 'Did you have a nice time?'

They went into Mrs Teape and found her helping Natália compose a letter to her son. It was a monthly event.

'We're engaged,' Stella said.

Ruth rose to her feet. 'Oh!' she said softly. 'What splendid news!' She came to them and kissed them both. She held Sam's hands. 'I'm delighted,' she said. 'Bless you both.'

Stella told Natália, and the maid enveloped her in a hug and kissed her on both cheeks, tears streaming down her cheeks. '*Ai menina, menina*!' she said, and dried her eyes on her apron.

'I'll go and fetch Daddy,' Ruth said, and hurried out of the kitchen.

Stella turned to Sam. 'You're in it now, buster. Up to your neck.'

They went into the sitting room. Bobby came in from his study. He kissed Stella and shook Sam warmly by the hand. 'Congratulations, my boy,' he said. 'Glad to get her off my hands!'

'Bobby, really!' Ruth said.

'Have we got any champagne?' Stella asked.

'Of course! Of course!' Bobby chortled. 'I'll fetch it up from the cellar. Not on ice, of course, but it'll be cool.' He winked at

304

Sam. 'Didn't want to anticipate the event, you know.'

Ruth rang for Natália and glasses were brought. Bobby arrived with two bottles of Moet Chandon. The wine frothed and sparkled in the glasses.

'Many congratulations, darlings,' Ruth said as she and Bobby raised their glasses. Bobby mumbled something about happiness, and when he had sipped his champagne his eyes were full of tears.

'Have you made any plans?' Ruth asked.

'What for?' Stella said.

'The wedding. Will it be a long engagement?'

Stella looked at Sam. 'Oh – I don't think so. I don't see why we shouldn't get married next month. What do you think?'

Sam shrugged. 'Don't see why not.'

Ruth asked, 'But I can't possibly organise a wedding as quickly as that! You'll want it out here, won't you?'

'Oh, Ma! No! We'll have it in England.'

'But where?'

'Leeds, I suppose. Good a place as any.'

'Leeds? Wouldn't it be very much nicer to have it here in Oporto? At St James's.'

Stella shook her head. 'We don't want a church wedding. It doesn't mean anything to either of us. Sam's a lapsed Catholic. And besides, he's a divorcee.'

There was a moment of stunned silence. Ruth said, 'I wish I'd known that earlier.'

Bobby looked down into his glass and shook his head.

'For goodness sake!' Stella said. 'It's not as bad as all that!'

'What sort of wedding will you have then?' Ruth asked.

'Oh – just a registry office do. We don't want any sort of fuss.'

'What a pity,' Teape said. 'What a great pity.'

Sam straightened his shoulders and said, 'Sir – I do apologise – ' and stopped, embarrassed.

'Well, I *don't* apologise,' Stella said. 'What was I supposed to do? Announce that Sam was a divorcee from the outset? Think what the colony would have done. The telephone wires would have been red hot. At least this way we get it all over and done with in one fell swoop.'

305

Ruth smiled. 'Never mind. It would have been nice to have a proper wedding. But if this is what you both want – '

'It is,' Stella said. 'Isn't it?'

Sam nodded. 'Yes. Very definitely.' He took Stella's hand.

'Come on, Dad,' she said. 'Say you approve.'

Bobby Teape put down his glass of champagne and looked from one to the other. 'How can I say that I approve when I don't approve?' he said, and went quickly from the room.

X

He lunched with Joy at the office the following day, and told her all about it. Since Hugh Blunden's departure from the firm in 1955, when James Remington had come in as a director, Joy had also started to take a greater interest in Teape & Co., of which she was a part owner.

They sat under the vine trellis sipping Dão wine and eating thin pork steaks. 'You must do something,' Joy said. 'There must surely be something you can do. If only for Ruth's sake. This will break her heart. A divorcee! An ex-Catholic! I sometimes wonder if Stella doesn't do these things deliberately in order to hurt. Besides – this may be the very last chance you have of asserting your authority over her. It may be her last opportunity to see sense.'

'But what can I do?' Bobby asked. 'I've shown my disapproval. The trouble is, I like the fellow. I think he may be the sort of chap that can steady her down.' He shook his head, and added: 'I do want her to be happy.'

'I wonder if she really is in love with him,' Joy mused. 'I mean – if they had to be apart for a few months, or if it could in some way be made difficult for them . . . You've said yourself often enough that you spoilt her. When she was a little girl. And this is just the same really, isn't it? Stella wants, so Stella gets. She's never known anything else. Ever.'

'What do you suggest, then?'

The servant brought coffee. Joy waited until he had gone,

then lit a cigarette which she placed in a short holder. 'Well,' she said, 'You could threaten to cut her off, couldn't you? That might make her sit up and take notice.'

XI

He found her in her room, packing. She and Sam were to leave early the following morning. 'I'd like a word with you,' he said, and shut the door.

She went on folding up clothes, wrapping shoes. He removed a towel and a pair of tennis shorts from the wicker chair in the corner of the room and sat down.

'Well?' she said.

'It's about Sam.'

'Surprise, surprise.'

He watched her continue to pack. She was like Ruth had been when he had married her, in some ways: large, deft, confident.

'I want to tell you something, first.'

She glanced at him. 'We've made up our minds, Dad. So don't think you can talk me out of anything, because you can't.'

'I haven't come to talk you out of it.'

'Well, what then?'

'I just – I just want to make quite sure you're doing the right thing.'

'The right thing!' she laughed. 'There's no such – *thing* as the right thing.'

'You know what I mean, Stella.'

'I think I know what you think you mean. How convoluted! Never mind.'

'Stop doing that and talk to me. Please.'

She looked at him and smiled. He felt the beginnings of rapport, and with it a surge of hope. She sat on the bed and stuck her feet straight out, like a little girl. 'All right, then. What do you want to tell me?'

There were so many things he would have liked to be able to tell. There were so many lessons from life that he felt she had not even begun to learn. Since unburdening himself to Joy some years before, he believed that he had found a new maturity, a new tolerance of life's frustrations. He was getting on for sixty now; old age was hull down on the horizon. He still played the odd game of tennis with Freddy Randall, still kept reasonably fit. Teape & Co. had come through the difficult post-war years, and business was improving. What remained now was to see Stella settled and – above all – happy.

'I don't think I've ever told you,' he started, 'what a great deal it meant to me when you were born.'

She stared at him in puzzled amazement.

'You see – your mother had had several miscarriages, and we both desperately wanted children. Ruth discovered she was pregnant just after the outbreak of war. And when you were born, it was like a chink of light in a dark tunnel. What I'm trying to tell you is that you were the reason for fighting. My whole war was for you.'

Stella sighed impatiently. 'The war, the war, the war. My God! Talk about "lest we forget"!'

'Maybe I'm just getting old and soft in the head. But I feel you ought to know, once and for all, how important you are to me.'

'Dad!' she said, and stretched out her hand to him.

'And when I see you making a very similar mistake to one that I made –'

She looked at him quickly. 'What's that supposed to mean?'

'Rushing into marriage like this.'

'We're not rushing. We've known each other five months.'

'But he's a divorcee.'

The rapport was suddenly gone. 'What the hell does that have to do with it?'

'A great deal. Have you any idea why his first marriage failed?'

She shrugged. 'It was nobody's fault. They just weren't suited.'

'You see the trouble is, everything has always been a little too easy for you, that's what I'm afraid of, Stella. Stella wants,

308

so Stella gets. That's the way it's been, hasn't it? Not that it's been your fault. I blame myself largely. We've had our battles, I know. But you've always got your way in the end. I've always weakened. Always given in to you. And now, now that you're taking one of the most important decisions in your life, well – I think it's my duty to put the brake on.'

She stood up and went to the window, her back to him. 'How do you propose to do that?'

'I'd like you to wait a year.'

'You're joking.'

'I'm not. You're very mature in many ways, Stella, but in some respects you're still a child. I think – if you wait a year as I suggest, you'll thank me for it one day. You really will. Whether you marry Sam or not.'

'Well, I'm sorry. But I'm not going to wait.'

There was a silence. During it, Teape thought carefully, determined, as he would have put it, to do the right thing.

'I didn't want to say this,' he said at length. 'but there is one way in which I could make you wait.'

She turned, looked down at him, her eyes very steady. 'There is *no* way in which you can make me wait.'

He felt his pulse quicken; he returned her gaze. 'But there is, Stella.'

'How?'

He champed his teeth twice, breathing through his mouth. 'I can stop your allowance. I don't intend to. But I could.'

She relaxed and smiled with a sort of evil triumph that frightened him. 'Ah!' she said. 'Now I understand! Now I see what all this has been leading up to!'

'I have not been leading up to it.' He felt a little breathless. 'I am trying to make you see, make you think twice. I'm doing it for your own good.' He stood up. 'I'm doing it because I'm your father. Because I love you.'

'But the love has to come on strings, doesn't it? Be a good girl and I'll buy you a bike. Pass your exams and I'll give you a skiing holiday. Get a degree and I'll give you a car.' She faced him. Her head went back: how often, during her tantrums as a little girl had he seen her do that! 'All right,' she said, 'You stop the allowance. I'll be happy to be off the lead.'

309

He felt his heart banging in his chest. 'You don't realise what you're saying.'

'On the contrary, I have never been more clearly aware of a situation in my life. If you think you can manipulate me with money, you can think again. Because it won't wash.'

'We'll see about that.'

'Will we?'

'Yes, we will.'

She turned away from him and said something he didn't quite catch.

'What did you say?'

'Nothing.'

'Yes you did – ' He stopped himself. They were back ten years: bickering as they had done when she was twelve and thirteen.

She whipped round. 'You can stuff your cheque book up your – your inside pocket. Sam and I are getting married. That's final.'

❧ *11* ❧

I

THE WEDDING took place at the Leeds Registrar's Office, in early November. Ruth travelled to England for it and stayed at the Queen's Hotel. It was bitterly cold: the sky was heavy with clouds that looked like beaten lead. She took a taxi to Stella's flat and found Stella having a whisky with a girl friend, whose mauve lipstick smeared her glass.

'Ma! Darling!' Stella kissed her. 'This is Phillida.'

'Pleased to meet you,' Phillida said.

'Like a drink, Ma?'

Ruth looked round at the bare walls and half-packed tea chests: Stella was moving out immediately after a three day honeymoon. 'No,' she said. 'I think I'll wait.'

'Just time for another *pinga*,' Stella said, and poured herself another whisky. 'Phil?'

'Thanks, love,' Phillida said.

Stella raised her glass. 'Well. Here's to whatever you're supposed to drink to on these occasions.'

'I don't think you should be drinking before your wedding in any case,' her mother said.

'Oh – blow that.'

Phillida laughed. Ruth felt a pang of sadness. Stella should be excited, apprehensive, jittery, dressed in white. But instead she was calmly finishing her second whisky, wearing a mustard yellow velvet dress and smoking a black cigarette.

The taxi arrived. The wedding was scheduled for eleven thirty, but Stella and Sam were third in the queue, and there was a delay. The wedding party waited about in a rather drafty hall. Sam was there, wearing a suit, together with his friends from the RAF station. His mother, an ardent Catholic, had

311

refused to attend. The only person of Ruth's age was an aunt: Mrs Hetherington-Jones. 'Such a pity they couldn't have had a proper wedding,' she confided to Ruth.

The ceremony was clipped and emotionless. Sam and Stella kissed three times for the benefit of the photographer, a friend of Stella's on the *Yorkshire Evening Post*.

Afterwards, there was a drinks party in somebody's flat. It could not possibly have been termed a reception: the bride and groom arrived last, having stopped at a pub for a drink on the way. There was a strange mixture of journalists, university graduates and Air Force officers, and nearly everybody seemed to be acting a part rather than being themselves. Ruth felt that Stella allowed herself to be kissed rather too amorously by several of the men. She felt totally out of things and stood, as if in a state of shock, with Mrs Hetherington-Jones.

At the end, when Stella and Sam were preparing to leave, she wanted to cry. She held Stella closely in her arms, not caring what anybody thought.

She kissed her and looked into her eyes. 'Goodbye, darling,' she said. 'God bless you. I do hope everything goes off all right.'

'It should do,' a male voice said somewhere in the background. 'They've had enough practice.'

The laughter that followed seemed to echo in her mind all the way south in the train to London.

II

She spent a week with the Blakelys in Hampstead after the wedding. Suzy was as warm, cheerful and bossy as ever, and Ruth was happy to catch up on her news. All the Blakely offspring seemed to be doing very well: Julian was lecturing at Durham University; Paul was finishing his houseman's year at the Middlesex; Tristram was taking a second degree at Harvard, and Jennifer was at Oxford, reading Politics, Philosophy and Economics.

'Sometimes I can't really believe they're mine,' Suzy laughed. 'I was quite hopeless at school. A bear of very little brain. But tell me about yourself. How are you?'

'Oh – very well, really. Getting older.'

'Well, now Stella's settled you should start thinking about getting *younger*, Ruth. It's high time you began to think more about yourself and less about other people.'

'That would be very boring.'

'I tell you what. While you're here, will you promise me to have a really good medical check up? Maurice can arrange one quite easily. An excellent chap in Harley street. You should. You owe it to yourself.'

'I'm perfectly fit,' Ruth insisted.

'Rubbish,' Suzy said. 'You haven't been perfectly fit since you had Stella. Why not take this opportunity. You're so rarely in England.'

After some further resistance, Ruth gave in. It was pointless arguing with Suzy once she had set her mind on something. Accordingly, Maurice arranged for her to go in for tests, and a few days later she was examined in a spacious second floor surgery in Harley Street.

The specialist was a young man, strikingly handsome, and he carried out a careful gynaecological examination. His youth and looks made her feel old and worn, but he was very gentle and kind. Afterwards, she sat by his desk and watched the snow falling outside as he looked through the results of the tests she had had a few days before.

He sat back and placed his finger tips carefully together. 'Well, Mrs Teape. I'll come straight to the point. You do have a number of small tumours in the musculature and the lining of the uterus. It's not an uncommon condition, and I would be very surprised indeed if they were not proved to be benign.' He looked through the reports again. 'Of course you do have a history of fibroids, and you are slightly anaemic.' He looked up and smiled. 'My feeling is that it will probably be in your best interest to have a hysterectomy.'

She had half expected bad news, but hearing him actually say this came as a shock.

'Is it entirely necessary?'

313

'Put it this way. If you have the operation, the chances are that it'll put paid to all these problems you've been having, once and for all. You'll feel enormously better.' He saw her hesitation, and added, 'If you were my mother, I would insist.'

'What about the tumours?'

'They can all be removed at the same time. We can kill two birds with one stone.'

She went back to Hampstead and discussed it with Suzy by a coal fire in the sitting room. Outside, the snow was settling. Sparrows perched on the gate, their feathers fluffed out for warmth.

'You must stay here, have the op and then convalesce with us,' Suzy told her. 'You could even stay over here for Christmas.'

'What about Bobby?'

'Bobby will be perfectly all right. It'll do him a lot of good to be without you for a while. And if he would like to come over for Christmas too, so much the better. We'll have a real family get-together at Laughton Hall.' Suzy leant across to Ruth and took her hand between her own. 'Besides, I'll enjoy looking after you. I'd like to build you up. Put colour back into your cheeks.'

Ruth hesitated.

'Look,' Suzy said. 'You've had the very best advice. You know you should have the operation. We can get you into a bed within the week. Why not have it now while you can? Why not ring up Bobby and tell him you'll stay over here for at least another month?'

'I'd certainly like to discuss it with him.'

'Ruth! Don't *ask* him. *Tell* him! Say you've made up your mind.'

'That's the trouble. I don't think I have.'

They booked a call to Portugal, and it came through eventually that evening. There was a short delay, and then Bobby's voice came over the line. 'Hullo? Who is it?'

She had to shout to make herself heard. 'Darling, it's me! Ruth!'

'Ah. How was the wedding?'

'Oh – it went off quite well. I'll tell you all about it when I see you. Listen: I rang up to tell you that I've been to a specialist, and he wants me to have a hysterectomy.'

'A what?'

'An operation. Hysterectomy.'

There was a silence at the other end, then he said, 'Oh.'

'What do you think?'

'Can't we talk about it when you get back?'

'That's the point. Suzy thinks I should have it in London.'

'What's wrong with the British Hospital here?'

'Nothing, but – '

'You'll be much better off out here. Much better nursing. And I gather it's damn cold in England right now.'

'Yes. It's snowing.'

'Well why the hell do you want to stay over there?'

'Suzy offered – '

'I can't hear! You'll have to shout!'

'Suzy's offered to have me here. To convalesce. After the operation.'

'There's no need for that. Absolutely no need. I'd far rather you had it out here.'

She hesitated, upset.

'Hullo?' he shouted. 'Did you get that?'

'Yes. Yes, I heard.'

'Well?'

Ruth looked at Suzy, who was shaking her head vigorously. 'All right,' she said. 'I'll come out.'

'See you at the airport on Wednesday then,' Bobby said. He sounded very cheerful, full of beans. 'Bye bye! God bless!'

She rang off.

'You let him talk you out of it,' Suzy said.

'Yes. But – I think he's right in a way. It's not really fair on you, expecting you to play nurse to me for three weeks. And the British Hospital in Oporto really is very good.'

Suddenly, and unexpected, she gave way to tears. 'I feel as though I shall lose the last shreds of my youth,' she said. 'I can never be young again. I shall have left all my childhood behind.'

III

There was the usual crowd of people at Oporto airport when Bobby Teape arrived to meet Ruth's plane. He found a parking space, and then went upstairs to the coffee lounge, where he sat in his overcoat and sipped a small black coffee.

He had mixed feelings about her return. There had been argument, before she had flown to England, as to whether or not he should accompany her to attend Stella's wedding. He had felt that having taken a stand over the allowance, it would be pointless and hypocritical to attend the wedding. So he had remained behind, and Joy had reassured him in his decision.

Joy was another reason for his lack of enthusiasm over Ruth's return. Although their relationship had not developed into anything even approaching an 'affair', he now confided more to Joy and felt more at ease in her company than he did in Ruth's. He knew, too, that Joy would have made a far more suitable wife for him. She was interested in the wine trade and had been brought up in it; she enjoyed entertaining and socialising far more than Ruth had ever done – however valiantly she had pretended otherwise. But while he now admitted this to himself, he was also very conscious of the fact that he had made promises to Ruth, and was bound to her by them. This he had discussed with Joy, and she had agreed wholeheartedly that it was their duty to avoid anything that might even approach infidelity on his part. Over the years, he had been particularly careful to hide nothing – at least, almost nothing – from Ruth: she had always known when he had lunched with Joy, and had never shown the slightest sign of jealousy or suspicion.

But still he had mixed feelings. This past week had been particularly enjoyable: he had lunched and dined with Joy. They had spent a great deal of time in each other's company, and he had begun to feel the need to reach out to her, to give her some of the love which he knew she would welcome if only –

He shook his head to himself, sitting there. It all came back to a big 'if only'.

He gazed out of the window at the low scudding clouds. The

316

plane was already nearly an hour late. He wondered about Stella. Had he been right to do what he had done? How difficult would it be to repair that damage? Perhaps he could write to her, in due course, and apologise. Start her allowance again. Or even settle some money on her. There were tax advantages, now, if one gave capital away. You could avoid death duties. How very depressing it all was. And how quickly life went by. Fifty-eight already!

The turbo-prop aircraft appeared out of the cloud and touched down, its engines roaring as the propellers were put into reverse thrust. He remained at his table, and watched it taxi in.

The doors of the aircraft opened, and the passengers descended the stairs to the tarmac. They walked across to the airport building, buffetted by the wind, the air stewardess holding on to her hat to prevent it blowing off.

He went down to the arrival lobby and looked through the glass. There was Ruth. She waved to him and he waved back. He saw that she had bought herself a new coat and had had her hair restyled. He wondered why, then remembered this operation she was going to have. Bolstering her morale, that's what it was. He felt impatient. Why did she always have to be ill? It was as if she enjoyed it. He sometimes wondered if she put it on in order to gain sympathy. Joy, on the other hand, had hardly spent a day in bed in her life. Disgustingly healthy. The thought of Joy made him smile in spite of himself, and then he saw that Ruth was looking at him again and smiling back, but in that brave way of hers which he had come to dislike.

He waited impatiently, wincing at a Portuguese who snorted repeatedly in order to clear his catarrh. Ruth came through the customs barrier. He kissed her on the cheek and took her suitcase.

'Well? How was it?' he asked. They were jostled by the crowd of people welcoming and arriving.

'Let's get outside,' Ruth said. 'I'll tell you all about everything in the car.'

They moved towards the main doors. A woman had dropped some money and the search for it was causing a hold-up. Ruth and Bobby were just going through the doors when they were stopped by a man.

317

'Excuse me,' he said. 'I think I know you.'

The man was tall, with gaunt features, and eyebrows that grew out in spiked tufts. He was well dressed in a Burberry raincoat and trilby hat; in his sixties, Bobby guessed.

'I'm sorry – ' Teape started, and glanced at Ruth. She was gazing at the man in amazement.

'It can't be,' she said.

The man smiled. 'I'm afraid it is.'

Ruth shook her head in disbelief. She turned to Bobby. 'Darling it's – Peter. You know. Peter Merriman.'

IV

The two men faced each other. 'I do apologise for accosting you in this way,' Merriman said, 'but having recognised your wife I really felt that I ought to make myself known.'

'Of course!' Bobby said.

Merriman looked back at Ruth. 'All this time,' he said.

She shook her head. 'I still can't believe it!'

He hesitated. 'You – er – live out here?'

'In the port wine business,' Teape said.

'Ah. I see.'

He was looking back at Ruth: Teape saw the way they looked at each other. He saw, and was angry.

'What are you doing in Portugal?' Ruth asked.

'It's my retirement year. My firm's had a certain amount to do with the hydro-electric schemes out here, so I thought I might come and have a look.'

'But – how long are you staying?' Ruth was almost girlish again. Bobby had not heard her speak with such zest for many years.

'Just a week,' Merriman was saying. 'I'm going on to Kenya after this.'

Ruth looked quickly back at Bobby then said to Peter: 'Where are you staying?'

He mentioned a hotel in Oporto. 'But I shall be travelling

318

about the country quite a bit. Down to Coimbra and up to Regua, you know.'

'You must come to dinner,' Ruth said, and glanced again at Bobby. 'You don't mind, do you darling?'

'Of course not!'

'Could you?'

'I'm pretty booked up,' Merriman said. 'But I'll be free on Sunday evening.'

'We live a few miles outside the city. A place called Valadares. Perhaps we could ring up and confirm.'

'That's very kind of you both,' Merriman said, and was careful to include Teape in his smile. 'Now I must rush. I'm part of a syndicate, and I think I see our coach over there. Wonderful to see you again. I shall look forward to Sunday.' He shook hands with Ruth; Teape saw her look up into his eyes, saw Merriman's intense stare beneath the tufted eyebrows, recognising instantly the momentary hesitation on each one's part. Then he was shaking hands with Merriman, and Merriman was saying, 'I do apologise once again for accosting you like that.'

'Not at all, not at all,' Teape said.

Merriman smiled. 'Well. Until Sunday, then.' He walked off towards another part of the car park.

Teape unlocked the car and loaded Ruth's luggage. As they drove off, he suspected that she was close to tears. A quick glance a few moments later confirmed his suspicion.

'Well, well, well,' he said as he drove along the straight stretch of road that ran southward from the airport. 'Well, well, well.'

'I wonder if I should have invited him,' Ruth said.

'What's the matter, having second thoughts?'

'Not really. Just – well, I was thinking of you.'

'No need to worry about me. No need at all.'

'Are you sure?'

He laughed. 'Of course I'm sure! Water under the bridge, Roo. Water under the bridge.'

She put her hand on his knee. 'You haven't called me that for ages.'

He grunted.

319

'Did you miss me?'

'When? Oh – you mean last week.'

'Well? Did you?'

'We muddled along. Natália did a very good *bacalhau* on Friday. Had supper with Joy a couple of times. How was the wedding?'

She sighed. 'Rather impersonal. But they seemed very happy.'

'No last minute hiccups?'

'None at all.'

He drove on, past Leça and Matosinhos, turning left up the Boa Vista and through the city to the bridge. The tyres hissed on the wet cobbles. 'What about this operation?' he said after a long silence.

'The specialist said the sooner I have it the better. I thought we might wait until the spring.'

They were crossing the Douro. Below them, to their right, the roofs of Vila Nova de Gaia announced the names of various brands of port. 'Why not have it right away?' Bobby said. 'I'm Honorary Treasurer at the Factory House next year. We'll be busy.'

'I don't know if the British Hospital could take me at such short notice.'

'Oh they can. I rang up yesterday. You can go in next Wednesday and have the op on Thursday. I made a provisional booking for you. We'll have you up and about for Christmas.'

It was raining hard in Valadares. The house felt damp after the Blakelys centrally-heated rooms. The dogs gave her a warm welcome, and Natália fussed around her, but she felt depressed, nevertheless. She went upstairs to change and unpack.

She stood in the bedroom and looked about her, aware suddenly how huge this house was for just the two of them. She could remember thinking, many years ago, how sad it would be to have too much money and to live in a house that was far bigger than one's needs. She had never promised herself not to let it happen to her, because she hadn't even considered the likelihood of such an eventuality. And when she and Bobby had moved into Moinho Velho, she still had hopes that they would have two or three children to enjoy the house and the grounds.

Meeting Peter like that had come as a tremendous shock, of course. She wondered whether she should have invited him to supper. Bobby seemed to have taken it reasonably well, but you could never be entirely sure with him: there had been many occasions in the past when he had suppressed his disapproval for a long time, only to let it out in a burst of anger during an argument about a totally different subject.

She felt suddenly pessimistic. The thought of the operation was behind it, she realised that. But all the same, she could not help feeling that her life was quite useless. What am I doing here? She wondered. Where do I belong?

She rested with a hot water bottle that afternoon, and got up for tea. Bobby had been for a walk with the dogs. His face was red from wind and rain; he helped himself to scones and blackberry jam from the tea trolley.

'I was thinking about Sunday evening,' she said.

'Oh yes?'

'Yes. I wasn't sure whether or not it would be a good idea to invite anybody else.'

'I'm easy.'

'I can't help feeling that it might be embarrassing if it's only the three of us.'

'Won't be embarrassing for me.'

'But what do you think, Bobby? Should we ask Freddy and Madge? Perhaps Joy, as well.'

'I don't know,' he said. 'He's your friend, not mine.'

'Bobby! Can't you be a bit more helpful than that?'

'You didn't have to invite him in the first place. Still. No going back, is there?'

'You sound rather pleased.'

He laughed. 'Well – I must say there is a certain irony about the situation, isn't there? You were the one to ask him, and now you're getting in a tizz over it.'

'I'm not getting in a tizz. I'm just anxious that the evening should be a success, that's all.'

He laughed again. 'Oh. I see. Of course.'

'Bobby, you don't think –'

'What?'

She shook her head. 'It's nothing. Never mind.'

'What were you going to say?'

'It wasn't important.'

'It doesn't look as though it wasn't important. Judging by the look on your face.'

'Please let's drop the subject, can we?'

There was a silence. He stood up and went to the french windows. He stood for some while like a sergeant major on parade, his hands braced behind his back. Then he turned suddenly.

'You've never really stopped loving him, have you?'

She took a long breath. 'Oh – no! You surely don't still think that!'

He laughed shortly. 'It was written all over your face Ruth. At the airport.'

She hardly knew what to say. 'But – in the circumstances, wouldn't you have been surprised?'

'I might have been surprised, but I doubt if I would have been reduced to tears.'

'That was unfair. You don't seem to realise – the sort of shock. Coming on top of everything else.'

'Everything else? What everything else?'

She was careful to keep control. 'Well, the wedding for a start. You didn't go to it. I did. That was our daughter, Bobby. And then this operation. It's a big decision – not like having your tonsils out. For a woman – it's like losing an essential part. I can't explain.' She turned away from him, in tears.

'For God's sake!' he muttered.

'I wish I'd never asked him!' she whispered.

'Well you have, so that's that.' He felt suddenly impatient. 'And it's no good putting up a smoke screen, either. Why the hell you can't admit the truth, I don't know. That man has dogged this marriage for the best part of thirty years. Why don't you face up to it? You've *always* loved him. Haven't you?'

She looked up at him. 'You may not believe this, but when I saw Peter this afternoon, I actually wondered to myself what I had once seen in him. I felt nothing for him. Absolutely nothing.'

322

'What about the tears then?'

'What tears?'

'The tears in your eyes. When we drove off.'

'It was – sort of shock, I suppose. I can't help my physical reactions. I felt confused. Upset. Can't you understand that?'

'And I suppose asking him to dinner was the same thing, was it? Shock. Physical reaction.'

'That's just childish.'

'All right. So it's childish. But at least I'm honest. At least I face up to things. If you'd been able to do that, instead of pretending the skeleton in the cupboard wasn't there, we'd have had a darn sight happier marriage.'

'I never pretended! I never *ever* pretended!'

'You're pretending now, Ruth. You've pretended ever since the first night of our honeymoon. We've never come to terms with this. It's always been in the background. We've never been really happy.'

She wept quietly. She felt crumpled, broken. 'I tried,' she whispered. 'I did try.'

He looked down at her. 'I shall be in my study until dinner,' he said, and left her to her tears.

V

The conflict remained unresolved throughout Thursday, Friday and Saturday. They had not had an argument like this for a long time: over the years, they had learnt to apologise and make good any damage done fairly soon after the petty disagreements that arose. But this row over Peter Merriman seemed to have set them back to the sort of tension that had existed between them in the first year of their marriage.

Ruth no longer had the will to do battle. She found herself frequently close to tears, and the prolonged silences at meals caused her mind to wander back to memories of long ago. She found herself remembering mornings at the village school in Yorkshire: wintry mornings, skating on a pond, holding hands with a little boy called Charles and wondering – at the age of sixteen – whether she would one day have children of her own; promising to herself that if ever she married she would devote her whole life to her husband and family. Such thoughts, and the sight of Bobby, red-faced, a little short of breath as he buttered his toast or piled cheese upon his after-dinner biscuits, brought on further waves of sadness, so that when he looked up he would catch her yet again with her eyes full of tears.

Inevitably, too, she began thinking of Peter Merriman again. She had very nearly forgotten him before that sudden meeting at the airport. He seemed to belong to a different world, a different lifetime. He had looked so old, so drawn and gaunt; and his skin had that yellowing look she associated with illness and approaching death. She wondered if he was ill. Perhaps he was suffering from cancer. Perhaps this tour he was doing was one last effort to be in the world before illness claimed him. And had he married? She doubted it. His rather precise manner had scarcely changed since the early thirties when she had known him. A wife would have cossetted him, softened him, instead of giving him that gaunt, lonely appearance. She looked at Bobby. They were in the middle of lunch. Had he changed? Had she changed him? She tried to remember him as he had been that very first night when he arrived at the Laughtons before Christmas. A cheerful, athletic-looking man in a tweed suit, with a twinkle in his eye. Those ridiculous conversations they had had. Tigger and Roo.

He looked and saw her face. 'For God's sake, Ruth.'

'I'm sorry. I was just thinking.'

'What were you thinking about?'

'Everything. You and me.'

'And did you reach a conclusion?'

She shook her head. 'I was trying to remember you as you were when I first met you. At the Laughtons.'

He grunted and went on with his lunch. She watched him. She wanted, even now, to be closer to him, to know his thoughts.

'Have you ever regretted not marrying Joy?' she asked, without even knowing why or how the question had formulated itself in her mind.

He looked up quickly. 'Why the hell do you ask that?'

'I just wondered. After all, she would have been a much more suitable choice than I, wouldn't she?'

'Rubbish!' he said, and coloured.

She was surprised by his embarrassment. 'Bobby, I know you're fond of Joy. It doesn't worry me.'

'I'm not ashamed of – ' he said, then stopped and frowned.

She smiled. 'Not ashamed of what?'

'I didn't mean that. I meant – I'm not ashamed of – of anything.'

'But you are fond of her, aren't you?'

'Just because I've made her a business partner doesn't mean to say that I love her.'

'I wasn't suggesting that you still love her. Or do you?'

His teeth champed twice. 'What the hell are we talking about Joy for?'

'For the same reason as we talked about Peter the other day, presumably.'

'That was quite different.'

'I don't see why. You accused me of pretending. Not facing up to things. Now, when I ask you a simple question about Joy, you go red as a beetroot and on the defensive. You can't blame me for jumping to conclusions.'

'You can jump to any damn conclusion you like,' he said.

'I don't want to jump to conclusions. I want to sort all this out. Once and for all.'

'I don't see how interrogating me about Joy helps to do that.'

'I wasn't interrogating you.'

'It felt like it. And all you're doing really is trying to transfer the blame. Joy has nothing to do with any of this. There was absolutely no need to invite that man to this house, and now you know you've made a mistake, you're trying to make *me* feel guilty about it. Well, it doesn't wash. I don't feel guilty. I *won't* feel guilty. You can damn well– ' He stopped. Ruth was getting up from the table. 'Where are you going?'

She went to the telephone. 'I'm ringing the hotel.' She found the number and dialled. '*Quero falar com Senhor Merriman*,' she told the receptionist who answered the 'phone. There was a short delay, and then Peter's voice answered.

'Merriman speaking.'

'Peter – it's Ruth.'

'How nice to hear your voice,' he said. 'I was wondering when you would ring.'

'It's about tomorrow night.'

'Splendid.'

She turned and looked at Bobby. Their eyes met: she looked steadily at him as she spoke into the telephone. 'I'm afraid I'm going to cancel. I'm awfully sorry. I think I was a little hasty in inviting you at the airport. Can you forgive me?'

There was a silence at the other end of the line. Then he said, 'Of course. Yes, of course.'

'I hope the rest of your stay goes well. And your trip to Kenya.'

'Is there no possibility of seeing you before I go?'

'I'm afraid not.'

'I see. Well in that case, in that case – I suppose it's goodbye.'

'Yes.'

There was another pause. He said, 'Hullo? Are you still there?'

'Yes.'

His voice had changed. He sounded very tired. 'I don't know what to say, Ruth. I think – all I want you to know is – I never forgot. And never will.'

She still stared at Bobby. He watched her like a great dog, his eyes fixed, unblinking.

'Goodbye, Peter,' she said. 'Godspeed.'

'Yes,' he said, and echoed, 'Godspeed.'

She put the 'phone down. 'Cutting off your nose to spite your face,' Bobby said.

She ignored him, and went upstairs to her room. She pulled out a lot of old clothes for the charity shop. She busied herself all afternoon, tidying her drawers, looking out old papers, throwing a lot of things away. And every time the thought of Peter came back, she quickly buried it by finding something else to do.

She kept busy on Sunday and Monday, as well. She made biscuits and a cake, and went out alone for a walk with the dogs on the beach. She walked further than she had ever walked before, and on Monday evening, feeling exhausted, she went to bed early.

Tuesday was cold and foggy. She packed her case for her stay in hospital, and gave Natália final instructions about the menu for the following fortnight. The next day, Bobby drove her out of Valadares and along the wide, undulating road that led into Oporto. Almost until the last moment, they maintained a curt silence. But as they were approaching the British Hospital, he made a slight detour and parked under the plane trees, whose yellow leaves lay damp along the gutters.

He put on the hand brake and switched off the engine. He turned to her, and stumbled through an apology.

'I didn't mean everything I said,' he told her gruffly.

She smiled sadly.

'And we have been happy, haven't we?'

'Of course we have. Will be again.'

He nodded. 'Yes.'

'Silly old Tigger.'

'Dear Roo.' He leant across and kissed her. 'Are things better, then?'

'Much better.'

'I'm glad. I didn't want – you know.'

He started the engine and drove up the hill, through the mist, and into the hospital grounds.

VI

He rang up on the evening following the operation and was assured that it had been a complete success. When he went in to see Ruth the next day, she was still under the influence of the anaesthetic, and looking weak, but the following afternoon when he visited she was sitting up and feeling a lot better.

He felt suddenly affectionate towards her, and a great deal more optimistic. 'I've had a splendid idea,' he said. 'How would you like to go away for Christmas?'

'Away? Where?'

327

'Somewhere warm and dry. I thought perhaps the Caribbean.'

'It's a lovely idea.'

'I want to get you really well. Put all this behind us. Start again.' He took her hand. 'I think it's time we concentrated a little more on enjoying ourselves. We can afford it, after all. Just a matter of pulling ourselves together and doing it.'

'Bobby! You can be so sweet sometimes.'

He felt tears in his eyes and wiped them away with the back of his forefinger.

'Sentimental old thing,' she said.

'Can't help it. It's the way I'm made. Anyway. What do you think?'

'I'll have to get over this, first.'

'Of course you will. But you'll be up and about in a fortnight. I was talking to the Sister. They don't believe in keeping people in bed too long after operations these days. You'll be prancing about like a young gazelle in no time at all. I say – that's a thought. What about Africa? The game parks?'

'I'm not sure I'll feel like bumping about in a landrover quite that soon.'

'Maybe not. Do that next year. Oh. A piece of news. Brothertons is being bought out by Associated Vintners. Poor old Johnny Millet very cut up about it. Still – there but for the grace of God, and all that. Another of the old firms gone to the wall. They'll keep the label of coure – that's what sells it. But it'll never be quite the same.'

He bumbled on about wine trade gossip, and eventually the Sister came along to tell him time was up. He held Ruth's hand between his: it felt frail and weak. 'Bye-bye, darling,' he murmured. 'See you tomorrow.'

He walked out of the ward and down the stairs. He met the surgeon in the hall. A first rate man: Portuguese, of course. They chatted about Ruth's condition, and Bobby walked out of the hospital five minutes later completely reassured.

It was getting on for six. He drove across the river and up the hill to call in at Teape & Co. on his way home. Joy was there: she came into his office. He told her about Ruth.

'That's splendid news, Rob,' she said. 'What a relief.' She wore a well-tailored suit; her hair was neatly permed, and her make-up faultless. It was nearly dark outside now. The office was lit by electric lamps which, because of the low voltage, cast a feeble light.

'I need to talk to you about her,' Teape said.

Joy put her head on one side like a bird listening for a worm.

'I feel I've been neglecting her somewhat. It's not that I don't enjoy your company, my dear. I do. You know that. But – ' He stopped and smiled uncertainly. 'Question of divided loyalties, I suppose.'

'Rob!' she said. 'Poor boy! We must be telepathic. I've felt exactly the same way about it all. And I'm doing something about it.'

'Oh?'

'I'm going to America. I've always wanted to. I've never met Mummy's side of the family. And I thought – now's the time. We're none of us getting any younger, are we? I'd like to see some of my relations before I get all doddery. So you see.'

'How long are you going for?'

'I shall take my time. Perhaps a year.'

'A year!'

'It's in a good cause, Rob.'

'You'll be away for my year as Honorary Treasurer.'

She put her hand on his arm. 'I know. But you'll be all right. You and Ruth. You'll do a marvellous job.'

She looked up at him and he felt suddenly drawn to her. 'I wish you weren't going,' he said. 'I shall miss you terribly.'

'Now now,' she said. 'None of that.' She became brisk. 'I must dash. I'm playing bridge tonight.' She kissed him on the cheek. 'Tell Ruth I shall be in to see her at the weekend, all right?' She patted his arm quickly and was gone.

He went home. It was strange how he could feel drawn to both Ruth and Joy in different ways within the space of an hour. He knew that Joy's trip to America was for the best, but at the same time hated the thought of a year without her to talk to over lunch or to go to for advice. She was such a positive person – so sure of her opinions. Of course Fay had been like that: a pillar of the colony, always organising, advising, encouraging.

There were letters for him when he arrived home, and

329

among them was the first from Stella since the wedding. 'Dear both,' it read, 'Well, here we are in a nasty little married patch which seethes with snotty-nosed children and folks in pale blue. Not a bad honeymoon, if honeymoon it can be called. Slight disaster on the way back: Sam rolled the car with all our stuff (and me) in it and it's a write-off. Pity. We got away with bruises and I broke a rib, but otherwise okay, except that it hurts to laugh still. But as we were only third party insured, neither of us have felt like laughing very much about it, so the Leibniz formula applies. Otherwise, things is just smashing, as you might say. We seem to spend a large amount of our time in a pub called The Jugglers. All good for the booze trade, eh Dad? Next Friday we have our (at least my) First Mess Function, which sounds quite revolting, doesn't it? (Ritualistic potty training?) A sort of militaristic rave-up, I gather, complete with all-steel band. Should be interesting. As no doubt you will have gathered from your assiduous listening to the BBC World Service, winter has come a trifle early this year and we are looking forward with growing horror to a White Christmas. Just got your letter, Ma. Very sorry to hear about the op. Still, *che sera* and all that, and I expect it's for the best. (Leibniz creeping in all over the place!) Not much more news. Sam sends love. I'm keeping the sting in the tail (ouch!) It is this: I am PREGNANT. Yes, in case you didn't quite get that, PREGNANT. And before you leap for your diaries and start counting up on your fingers and all sorts of other things, the monster is due in late May. Tell Aunt Joy that the gestation period for *all* graduates of Leeds University (Soc) is seven months. It'll cheer her up no end. Well. All for now. Tons of love, Ma, and get well soon. Stella.'

The letter had the same sort of effect on him as Stella's presence itself: an extraordinary mixture of surprise, disapproval, amusement – and love. It wasn't until he had read it a second time that he fully understood the implication in the announcement of her pregnancy. The baby would have been conceived out of wedlock. He wondered if she had known she was pregnant when they announced their engagement. He would never find out the answer to that, of course, along with many other questions about Stella.

A baby. He would be a grandfather. What splendid news! He wanted to share it with Ruth right away. He went to the telephone to call the hospital, but as he was about to lift the receiver, it began to ring.

VII

Stella was doing the last samba. She had started off trying to get Sam to do it, but he simply didn't have the rhythm, so she had settled for the West Indian who had been playing the marracas instead. The steel drum band, hired specially for the Winter Ball by the Mess Committee of RAF Sutcliffe, was playing 'All Day, All Night – Marianne' and the rhythm was reaching fever pitch. The tune clanged and pinged on the drums; beads of sweat stood on the brow of the West Indian, and Stella, in a yellow dress that plunged generously in the front, whirled and turned with such aplomb that several couples stopped dancing to watch.

On the sidelines, Sam Nevin watched his new wife, aware that she had already made a considerable impression on the officers and the mess staff. He was proud – of himself, as well as of her. She was a handful, no doubt of that, but at the same time he knew that a certain kudos attached to him as a result of the marriage. Stella was the sort of person people talked about: her latest remarks were repeated and misquoted; people were happy to be in her circle because of her outrageous conversation.

The samba came to an end: people clapped and cheered, and Stella pushed her way through the throng to rejoin him. The steel drum band players began packing up immediately: the ball was over.

They went to the cloakrooms to collect coats, and he waited for her in the lobby of the mess, where silver trophies were on display in a glass case and an oil painting of Halifax bombers landing after a night raid hung between the photographs of the Queen and Prince Philip.

331

On a mahogany table by the doors lay a leather bound visitors' book. It was open, and a single name had been signed on the left hand page: Philip. A few nights before, his Heron aircraft had been diverted into Sutcliffe with a minor engine malfunction, and he had been the guest of the mess for a few hours while the fault was put right. The Station Commander had invited the Duke to sign the visitors' book, and the royal signature had been the subject of considerable admiration ever since.

Sam was looking at it when Stella arrived from the cloakrooms.

'Coo-err, innit lovely?' she said, looking over his shoulder, and before he could stop her, she had taken the silver quill from the silver inkpot and, with a flourish, signed 'Stella' in the middle of the opposite page.

'Bloody hell!' he said. 'You'll get me shot!'

'Why?'

'Well – this is the VIP book.'

'I am a VIP,' she said, and dragged him out into the frozen night.

They ran back along Trenchard Drive to Number 8. They were both pleasantly full of alcohol: they leant on each other, giggling, as they went upstairs. In the bedroom, she stepped out of her dress, threw it on a chair, removed stockings, bra, everything. She danced the samba again, singing, 'All day, all night – Marianne. Down by the sea-side shiftin' sand. It's because she can screw like no one can. That's why de boys all love Marianne.'

Sam looked at her. 'How exceedingly crude.'

'Speak for yourself, baby.'

They fell into bed. Stella, impervious to cold, slept naked. She enveloped him: he fell asleep wrapped between her thighs.

An hour or so later he woke with a desperate need to go to the lavatory. He disentangled himself from her arms and legs and tiptoed out to the bathroom. He put no lights on, anxious not to disturb Stella, who still seemed to be asleep when he came back into the bedroom. He felt his way carefully round the double bed, and in doing so stubbed his toe badly on the castor. He winced aloud.

'What've you done?' Stella asked in the darkness.

'Stubbed my toe.'

She put the light on, and Sam was revealed naked, clasping his big toe. She gurgled with laughter. 'Clot!' she said. 'Why didn't you switch on the light?' She gave way to compulsive chuckles, which seemed to well up inside her and overflow. 'You've no idea how stupid you look, Sam.'

He limped to the bed and examined his toe, unable to share Stella's amusement. He was still half asleep, still a little drunk, and Stella laughed once too often. Something snapped: her neck was suddenly in his hands and he was banging her head on the pillow to emphasise his words.

'Don't – ever – laugh – at – me – like – that – again.'

He was not really aware of what he was doing. All he knew was that he needed to teach her a lesson, assert his authority over her; and the look on her face, the look of surprise and shock, seemed to justify his action. He was giving her something to think about.

'There,' he said, releasing her. 'Got the message?'

He could see his own finger marks, pink smudges, on her neck. She looked at him, controlling her breathing, her breasts rising and falling, her dark eyes unblinking, steady.

'Finished?' she said.

'Yes. I've finished.'

She reached out – he thought to switch off the bedside light. But she picked up the alarm clock that had been given to them by one of his sisters as a wedding present, and swung it at him as hard as she could, connecting with the side of his face.

The blow was like an explosion in his head, and he was dazed. He heard her voice: 'You use violence on me, buster, and you can expect violence back.' And then she mimicked him: 'Got the message?' She switched out the light and turned abruptly away from him. His head throbbed, and so did his big toe. It was some time before he got to sleep again.

He awoke towards ten, and got out of bed. Stella was still asleep, spreadeagled on her stomach, her arms out on either side of her head in a position that reminded him of a body being given artificial respiration.

He put on a dressing gown and looked in the mirror. He had

a black eye. He touched it carefully with his finger tips, reflecting a little ruefully that he would have to tell his friends that he got hit on the head with an alarm clock. Oh well, he thought. Make a good story.

He went downstairs. It was Saturday; freezing fog had hung a white tracery upon the trees.

In the kitchen, he sipped a mug of black coffee and tried to rehearse what he would say to Stella when she eventually surfaced. Just one of those things, he thought to himself. We were both a bit pissed. And the way she laughed. Okay, so I over-reacted. But there was provocation.

He was reading the newspaper over his third cup of coffee when the front door bell rang. It was a telegraph boy in woolly scarf, banging his feet on the doorstep to keep warm, his breath making clouds in the frozen air.

'Name of Teape?' he asked.

That annoyed Sam. Why couldn't whoever it was get the name right? He took the telegram, which was addressed to Stella Teape.

He thanked the boy and went upstairs. Stella had started her bath. She had lost her summer tan: her body was white in the steaming water. 'Telegram,' he said. 'For you.'

'Well, open it then.'

He read the contents aloud: 'Mother died Friday night. Funeral Monday. Please come. Love. Daddy.'

Her mouth opened and went crooked. She moved her head a little, and he saw in her eyes the same look of anger he had seen the night before. It was a wild, dangerous look that seemed to strike out against life itself: it was an anger that was always latent within her but which, when it showed itself, never failed to frighten him. She stared back, her mouth open, her eyes wide. Her nakedness made her seemed childlike, defenceless. He realised, then, that the anger was not a part of her but rather something that inhabited her, and in that moment he loved her in a deeper and more protective way than he had ever done before.

334

VIII

They were carrying her out of the church: the coffin swayed on the shoulders of the pall bearers as they stepped out onto the gravel, and a flurry of wind and rain billowed the vicar's cassock as he led the mourners to the grave.

Teape felt Stella's hand seek his. Their fingers interlocked and held tight, and as the words of the hundred and third psalm sailed outward and upward to the grey sky, he was aware of a sense not of unreality but surreality: each step he took seemed to last an eternity in itself; the branches of the trees seemed to sway in slow motion; the crunch of feet upon gravel sounded loudly in his ears, as if something were being slowly and deliberately crushed.

'Like as a father pitieth his children, so the Lord pitieth them that fear him. For he knoweth our frame; he remembereth that we are dust. As for man, his days are as grass: as a flower of the field, so he flourisheth. For the wind passeth over it and it is gone . . . '

As the voice continued, the events of the evening, the Friday evening, seemed to go round and round in his brain like an endless loop of film.

The words of the Sister when he answered the telephone: 'I'm afraid your wife has had a set-back, Mr Teape.' 'Set-back? What sort of a set-back?' The hesitation. 'She has had a haemorrhage.' The waver of uncertainty in her voice. 'I think it might be advisable for you to come to the hospital.' 'But is it serious?' The catch in her breath. 'Yes. I'm afraid it is.'

The drive back through the mist and drizzle, not willing at that stage to accept what 'serious' might mean. The electric light in the hospital entrance: a sort of half-darkness that held a foreboding which deepened when the nurse asked if he could please wait. And then the sound of footsteps: footsteps that sounded like the approach of a janitor to a cell. The surgeon, in white coat, his face damp with sweat. 'I'm afraid we've lost her,' in Portuguese. 'A massive internal haemorrhage. She went very quickly.' Other faces; the sensation that the world had somehow slipped sideways, the grotesque sound of human voices, babbling meaningless words of comfort in his ears. The

335

need, the desperate need to see Ruth. Ruth! Somebody shouted her name, and that person was himself. Ruth. Lying there in the bed as if asleep. Ruth whom he had seen, talked with only a few hours before. Ruth and yet not Ruth, for her stillness was absolute, final. Ruth whom he had loved from the very bottom of his soul but had never been able, while she was alive, to show that love. Ruth who had walked with him through the frost all those years ago; who had lain – perhaps even in this same bed – with his baby in her arms, and looked up at him with pride and love and gratitude in her eyes; and had said, 'I've decided. She's called Stella.' Ruth who had always forgiven, always cared, always tried. He bent over her, touched her brow gently, trying to brush away that last look of slight perplexity that life had bequeathed her. But the expression was fixed. It was as if she had died with a question on her lips: 'Do you love me?' That was the question, the only question that mattered, the only question he had never quite managed to answer completely. He had touched her brow and whispered 'I love you, I love you always,' until, gently, he had been pulled backward, away from her.

They were lowering her now on to the two wooden cross-pieces that lay across the grave. The mourners were gathering round the damp pit, and the vicar was reading the burial rite. Stella's hand was still in his: he glanced at her. She wore a mauve coat trimmed with black fur. She was staring unwaveringly at the coffin, tears going unheeded down her cheeks. There was anger more than sorrow in her expression: as if she felt that had she been told in time she might have prevented all this. And he too felt tricked: they should have told him. They should have warned him.

He began to feel weak: they were lowering her downward into the earth, and he suddenly remembered how she loved to be warm and dry between the sheets: how she would whisper, 'Come to bed,' to him in the early days of their marriage, and how her dark hair would be spread out on the pillow and her arms warm about him. He remembered, and the stark reali-sation that she was being lowered into a puddle of cold brown water was too much. The gravestones tipped and cried out. He felt arms supporting him, heard his own voice crack, heard

Stella speaking to him as if from a great distance.

And now, now he was in the car again, going he knew not where, the windscreen wipers banging to and fro.

It was over: he stared out at the passing scenery feeling old and weak and full of despair.

❧ *12* ❧

I

THREE WEEKS after the funeral, on a Sunday in mid-December, Natália paid a visit to the chapel of Santa Maria de Adelaide, in the village of Arcozelo, a four mile walk from Valadares.

The rain and fog of past weeks had given way to crisp blue skies, and there was a nip in the air. She had put on her best black dress and shawl, and now made her way along the narrow lane that led through the back of Enxomil, down the hill to the blue tiled church of Arcozelo, which stands among plane trees opposite the cemetry and the shrine. The church clock struck four as she approached, and the bell notes seemed to hang for a long time in the still air. A few coaches were drawn up in the car park, and the stalls that sold rosaries, picture frames and effigies of the Virgin Mary were doing a steady trade with the weekly flood of visitors. In the cemetry too, the families of the departed scrubbed marble slabs, replaced flowers and polished headstones. Such activities happen every week at Arcozelo: they are a part of the village life.

There was a queue of people waiting to pay their respects to the preserved remains of Santa Maria de Adelaide. Natália joined this queue, shuffling patiently forward a few steps as each pilgrim completed her (or occasionally his) prayers. While she waited, she said Hail Marys to herself, telling the beads of a rosary between her fingers, her lips moving silently, tumbling out the same words over and over and over again.

Slowly, she moved inside the shrine and up the steps beside the catafalque. And there was Santa Maria: she lay on her back in a glass-topped case, dressed in white satin and bedecked in golden bracelets, beads, necklaces. Her wizened brown hands were like claws: her face was shrivelled, so that her front teeth

338

protruded and her cheek bones were prominent beneath dark, stretched skin.

Natália knelt and crossed herself. She prayed for a long time: both for the Senhora and for her son Eduardo, who was now a corporal and had recently been sent to Africa.

Eventually, and rather reluctantly, she moved on to make way for another woman in black, who pawed the glass top of the catafalque, and sobbed noisily, keening in that particularly Portuguese way; 'Ai! Ai!' she sighed, and rapped her knuckles on the glass, as if trying to awaken the dehydrated body inside.

Natália made her way into an adjoining building, where hung the framed photographs of the hundreds and thousands of people for whom Santa Maria de Adelaide had been asked to pray. These photographs were suspended in lines from the ceiling, each with its own inscription imploring intercession. There were husbands, wives, sons, daughters; brides in wedding dresses, servicemen in uniform, children in cradles. Pale, faded people looked out at you from the past, each secure in his or her gilt frame, each the object of some other person's anxieties, hopes, love. Splints, crutches and leg irons were also propped up in this building, and at one end, a woman sat at a counter selling votive candles and plastic effigies. Such effigies catered for a variety of requirements: you could buy a plastic arm or leg or trunk in order to obtain intercession for a diseased limb, or to give thanks for a miraculous cure. You could buy a plastic baby to thank Santa Maria de Adelaide for a fruitful marriage, or to pray for one. There were even whole statues of indeterminate people to provide an outward and visible proof of the sincerity of your request or gratitude.

Natália entered this place and went to the woman at the counter. She produced a framed photograph of Eduardo, and made a donation so that his photograph could join the others. She followed the woman along a narrow aisle between the hanging frames, and watched as the picture of her son was attached at the bottom of a line. She stared up at it: the photograph had been taken when he was on garrison duty in Goa, a few months before the war in which the Portuguese had been so ignominiously ejected. He was standing at ease in his tropical uniform, laughing into the camera, a rifle cradled in his arms.

After saying one more prayer for him, she turned and went out again into the cold evening to start the long walk back to Valadares in the gathering darkness.

When she arrived at Moinho Velho, she went along the back of the house to the kitchen. She looked in at the drawing room window on her way past and saw Teape sitting as he so often sat by the fire with a book.

Just before Ruth had died, Natália had received a letter from her son, enclosing the photograph she had hung in the chapel of miracles. Had Ruth been alive, she would have gone to her that morning and asked for her assistance in reading and replying to her son's letter. Now, she was faced with the prospect of having to ask Teape to do this for her, and it was a prospect she dreaded.

She took out the letter, looking closely at the writing, but unable to make out the words. She had promised herself that morning that today she really would ask the Senhor to help her. She smoothed her apron and looked at herself in the old mirror that hung in the corner of the pantry, then went along the hall and stopped outside the door to the drawing room.

But she could not bring herself to knock. She returned to the kitchen, and went outside. She looked in on him again: he had not drawn the curtains, and seemed engrossed in his book. Since Ruth's death, he had hardly spoken to her, and whenever she approached him for his preferences for food, he would tell her simply to cook what she thought best.

She returned to the kitchen. It was impossible: she simply did not have the courage to approach him. Instead, she prepared potatoes and onions and put them on to boil to make *caldo verde*. She went down to the vegetable garden with a torch and selected three large leaves from the cabbage plants that grew shoulder-high along the borders of each patch, and put them through the shredding machine, winding the handle rapidly so that the leaves were transformed into thin shreds that looked, as Stella had remarked when a child, like seaweed.

She added olive oil to the boiling potatoes and onions, and leaving them to simmer, wiped her hands and had another look at Eduardo's letter.

Ruth had tried to teach her to read and write, years ago, and

340

she had made a little progress. But apart from reading the prices of goods in the market and the destination names on the local buses, she had never had much call to develop the skill; and by the time Eduardo was of the age to write letters to her, it was too late. She now stared at the two sheets of paper yet again, spending a long time on the words 'My dear Mother' and 'Your loving son', which she recognised.

Eventually, the desire to know the contents of this letter overcame her hesitancy to trouble Teape with it. She removed the pan of onions and potatoes from the hot plate of the range, and went a second time to the door of the drawing room.

A grunted reply answered her knock. She went in. He was standing at the window, his back to her. He turned.

'Yes, Natália?'

'Sir,' she said. 'I have a letter. From my son.'

His face was gaunt from lack of sleep and emotional strain. His eyes seemed sunken in their sockets: they looked through her more than at her. She was frightened by the change in him that had taken place in three weeks.

'What – you want me to – '

'The Senhora used to help me,' she began, and immediately felt a flood of tears. There was no hope in fighting them: they swept over her. 'Oh Senhor!' she wailed.

He frowned and shook his head. His mouth opened: he seemed to be struggling inwardly. Hesitantly, he reached out his hands to her, and she went to him for comfort.

He didn't really understand what was happening. She was weeping and he was holding her in his arms. All that mattered was that they had lost Ruth: this loss, he believed, brought them together, bound them together, so that holding her and comforting her was neither wrong nor dangerous nor indiscreet; rather it proved, once and for all, that she had finally forgiven him for what had happened on that beach so many years ago.

He comforted her like a child, and because she had regarded Ruth almost as a mother, she accepted his comfort in the same spirit. But as her sobs abated, Teape became aware that he was holding an attractive woman in his arms. In a confused way, he believed that she would not permit him to touch her as he was

341

doing unless this was what she expected, and that perhaps she was showing her love for Ruth by giving herself to him.

The very act of comforting her provided him with consolation, too: he stroked her hair, then moved his hand down, over her shoulders and down to her waist.

He looked into her eyes. 'My poor Natália,' he whispered, at the same time moving his hand up, over her breast; and when she offered no resistance, he presumed with an inward rush of pleasure and gratitude that she needed him in exactly the same way he thought he needed her.

Natália was surprised by this brief, intimate touch – so surprised that at first she thought it must have been a mistake. But when he ran his hand back over her breast, rubbing and caressing it, she quickly realised that this was no mistake, and she was filled with a growing sense of revulsion.

She tried to pull herself free, but he held on to her and bent to kiss her. She wrenched herself away from him and stood facing him, her nostrils flared, panting, mouth open.

'Natália,' he started. 'Don't be afraid. Please – '

She ran out of the room and back to the kitchen. She heard him coming along the passage after her and stood by the stove, wondering what to say or do.

He came to the doorway, flushed and angry at his loss of face. 'Wait,' he said. 'This was your fault. You caused this. All I did – '

But Natália had picked up the pan of onions and potato mush. She advanced on him and he backed away. Suddenly her tongue found all those words of abuse that had been flung back and forth in the fish market in the days of her childhood. She let fly at him, and he backed into the hall. She called him, among several other things, the son of a whore, and when she ran out of words she spat at him and threw the mess of soup on the black and white tiles at his feet, telling him to eat it up off the floor like the pie dog he was.

She ran out of the house and down the hill to her cottage. She stood alone in her kitchen, shocked at the enormity of what she had done, and frightened by the realisation that her life in the Teape household had finally come to an end.

342

II

When she had calmed down, she began to wonder what she should do. For nearly thirty years she had been housed and clothed and fed and regularly paid. The memory of her life in the tin-roofed shack, sleeping on a bed of rags, living on bread and cabbage soup, always hungry or tired or ill or all three had receded and dimmed over the years. Now it returned with frightening clarity. She knew she had to leave, but she had nowhere to go. She could, perhaps, find employment in Oporto or the surrounding towns; but she knew that the best way of doing that would be to call on the help of friends of the Teapes: the Remingtons or the Millets or the Randalls. And if she did that the whole story would have to come out.

The alternative was to move right away. She knew that there was a shortage of maids in Lisbon and the fashionable resorts nearby, and Eduardo, on his rare visits to her, had often suggested that she would be better paid if she went south. If only she could talk to him about it! But he was somewhere in Mozambique, and her only contact with him was a letter which she could not read.

She was unable to sleep at all that night. She sat up by her wood stove, thinking and worrying, and eventually, without quite knowing exactly what she would do or where she would go, she began gathering her clothes and a few treasured possessions together and packing them in an old suitcase that had belonged to Ruth.

She left the cottage for the last time a little before dawn. The hens were clucking and the new cockerel was making a half-hearted attempt at crowing. Mist lay in pockets in the valley, half covering the buildings, so that only the roofs were visible. The blades of the windmill were stationary and the house was a dark silhouette against the grey light.

She stopped at the side gate and looked back. Even now, she wondered if she should go into the house, make his morning tea, apologise. But then she remembered the sensation of his hands touching her and the smell of his breath in her nostrils: she remembered and despised him as she had despised him on the beach at Leça thirty years before. She went out of the gate

343

and pulled it firmly shut: she turned her back on the house and Teape and all that had happened, and walked quickly away along the path and on, down the hill to the railway station of Valadares.

While the thought of going all the way to Lisbon by train had seemed a fearful undertaking, putting it into practice turned out to be surprisingly simple. She bought a ticket at Valadares, caught an early train to Espinho and there, after an hour's wait, caught the morning express which rattled its way south and deposited her at Santa Apolónia station in the early afternoon.

She stepped down onto the platform, jostled by the crowd of people that surged towards the ticket barrier. She gave up her ticket, and found herself in the wide entrance hall.

For some reason she had not foreseen this moment. During the journey down, her thoughts had centred on how she would go about finding a job rather than what she would do when she arrived at the station. She carried her suitcase to the steps that descended to the street. Smoke from the ovens of chestnut vendors billowed in the wind. A blind man shouted to nobody, selling lottery tickets, which were clipped to his lapel. Newspapers were laid out for sale. Shoe shine boys sat on their heels or worked with cloths and brushes.

Natália looked out at this scene and felt the beginnings of panic. This place was like a foreign country to her: everybody seemed to be in a hurry and everything was completely unfamiliar. She didn't belong here. She had made a terrible mistake. She would have to go back, return to Valadares, beg to have her job again with Senhor Teape.

She picked up her suitcase and wandered into the entrance hall, considering whether she should buy a ticket back to Oporto. She was tired, confused and frightened. Unable to make up her mind, she took her suitcase and sat down on a bench near a kiosk that sold magazines and newspapers. Sitting there, watching the crowds of travellers criss-crossing about the hall, shivering in the draught of a swing door that banged to and fro, she gave way to tears.

And then she heard her name called.

'Natália!'

She looked up, and recognised Deirdre Romer, who was with another woman.

344

'What on earth's the matter? What are you doing here?'

She looked left and right, avoiding Deirdre's gaze. 'I – I'm visiting relations,' she said.

'Relations? I didn't think you had any relations!'

And already she was caught in the lie. She remembered how Ruth had always insisted upon the truth; telling this lie seemed like a disloyalty to her. '*Ai senhora*,' she said, 'I have come to find work in Lisbon.' She looked down at the litter of orange peel.

'But are you no longer working for Senhor Teape?'

She shook her head, stifling more tears.

Deirdre Romer turned to her friend and they spoke in English. Deirdre asked a question, and the other answered, nodding to emphasise her reply. There was a further exchange. Deirdre turned back to Natália.

'Why did you leave?'

She stared back, unable to answer.

'Oh – never mind!' Deirdre said. 'I'm sure it was a very good reason. Listen. We know somebody who wants a living-in maid. Would you mind working for a big family?'

'No, *senhora*, of course not. I would be – '

'Very well. Wait a minute. I shall give you an address.' She searched in her bag and produced pencil and an envelope. She tore the back off the envelope and wrote on it. 'There,' she said. 'They live in Cascais. I've given you a little testimonial, so with luck she'll take you on. They're good people. Now. We have a train to catch. Goodbye. And good luck!'

She watched them walk briskly away towards the departure platforms, then looked at the piece of paper. There was an address and a telephone number on one side, and on the other some writing in English, just a few words, starting with her own name. What was the name of the place? She couldn't remember, and she was unable to read the address.

She approached a woman who was waiting at the taxi rank. 'Excuse me,' she said, 'But I've left my glasses at home and I can't quite make out this address.' She showed her the slip of paper. The woman took it. She read the address out: 'Quinta de Luz, Estrada da Boca do Inferno, Cascais.'

'Are you sure that's right?' Natália said. 'Boca do Inferno?'

345

The woman smiled. 'Oh yes. I've been there myself.'

'Which way is it?'

'Cascais?' She pointed. 'Along the coast.'

'Is it far?'

'Too far to walk.'

Natália smiled proudly. 'Oh, I shall be all right. I'm strong, you see. I'm from the north.'

She thanked the woman and moved away. She rolled her scarf and made a circular pad out of it so that she could carry the suitcase on her head. She hoisted it up: it weighed about as much as a full basket of sardines. When she had it nicely balanced, she set out at a steady pace along the road, while taxis sped by over the cobbles, weaving their way between the clanking trams and the lorries that belched acrid fumes from their exhaust pipes.

As she walked, she repeated the address over and over to herself, still a little frightened by the name of the road: The Mouth of Hell.

III

The house stood well back from the road and its upper windows looked out over the Atlantic. Lights were on in the downstairs rooms, and several cars were parked in the drive.

Natália had been walking for six hours, and when she arrived she was on the point of exhaustion. Modern music was being played at high volume somewhere in the house, and as she went round to the tradesman's entrance, she caught a glimpse of young people through one of the windows.

She knocked at the back door and waited. Dogs barked, and the wind sighed in the pine trees. She knocked a second and third time, but no one answered. She carried her suitcase round to the front door and, summoning her courage, rang the bell.

It was opened by a figure dressed completely in black. The head was covered by a peaked hood, with slits cut in it for the mouth and eyes.

346

Natália started back, terrified. She screamed and turned to run. But the figure took off the hood and revealed itself as a grinning fifteen-year-old boy with fair hair and blue eyes.

'Thought you were somebody else,' he said in bad Portugese. 'Sorry. What do you want?'

She showed him the slip of paper. He turned it over, and smiled. Then he called into the house in a language that was neither Portuguese nor English.

A few moment later, a well-dressed woman came into the hall. The boy spoke to her and gave her the note, and when she read it she frowned at first and then smiled.

'You're Natália?'

'Yes, Senhora.'

The woman was also fair, with fine skin. 'And you're looking for a job?'

'Yes, Senhora.'

There was something about her expression that Natália could not quite understand: it seemed to contain a mixture of delight and amusement. It was a kind face, she decided.

'Where are you staying?'

Natália shrugged. 'Senhora, I came from the north today. I haven't had time to look round.'

'You'd better come in, I think. We're looking for a living-in maid.'

She stepped into the carpeted hall with a growing awareness that she had been incredibly lucky. And Brigitte Van de Eifel, Deirdre Romer's sister in law, also considered herself lucky, for the testimonial that Deirdre had written simply stated: 'Natália is the best maid in Portugal'.

❧ 13 ❧

I

TEAPE declined the duties of honorary treasurer at the Factory House that year. After Natália's departure, he took on a married couple, Júlio and Paulina, to live in the cottage. They came from the Upper Douro district: Júlio was a swarthy man, quiet and most respectful, while his wife was large and garrulous, complaining frequently of her stomach and suffering from chronic halitosis. Her style of cooking differed from that of Natália in that she was over-generous with the oil and garlic: she would bring boiled *bacalhau* to the table smelling strongly of these ingredients; indeed, in his lighter moments Teape was inclined to remark that he was unsure which he preferred, the smell of the *bacalhau* or the smell of Paulina's breath.

To get away from the loneliness of Moinho Velho, and from Paulina's cooking, he spent a lot of time at the Quinta das Rosas, in Saborinho. These were months of adjustment: after the first shock of his loss, he forced himself to manage by himself and continue with his life. In many ways, he was glad that Joy was out of the country: he needed nobody's condolences now; the wound had to heal on its own. He received a letter from Vermont, telling him that she had actually seen the grave of her great-grandfather, and later a colourful card from Monterey, where she was staying with another branch of the family.

Stella gave birth to twins in late May: two girls, whom she nicknamed Jawkins and Digby, but whose real names were Mia Ruth and Clare Rosalinde. She was not a frequent letter writer, and he found it difficult to judge whether she and Sam were settling down happily. As always, he wished that he could be closer to her, and now that Ruth was gone, this need for a link with her was all the stronger: she was his only close relation, and he longed for her confidence and love. But her letters retained their impersonal and cynical tone. He knew that they were living in a married quarter, and that Stella despised the coffee party gossip that went on among RAF wives; that Sam had passed his promotion exams and that there was a possibility that they might be moving to East Anglia the following spring. These, and other useless pieces of information filled her letters, and he looked in vain for something of the real Stella: something genuine, something sincere.

Joy returned to Portugal in August. During the weeks before her arrival, Teape caught himself having imaginary conversations with her, and he realised that he was looking forward to seeing her again with almost adolescent impatience.

She came to him in the tasting room one Monday morning. She looked younger: the Californian food and sun had given her a bloom that the Oporto diet and climate could never achieve. She wore a dazzling red suit and lipstick to match.

'Rob!'

He turned back from the window and saw her standing in the doorway. He had lost weight: his white overall coat was loose about him. He held two tulip glasses of tawny, and had been comparing their colour. He put the glasses down now and took her outstretched hands. She kissed him on both cheeks, and his nostrils were invaded by the smell of expensive scent.

'Wonderful to be back,' she said.

He shifted awkwardly. 'It's splendid to see you.'

'How are you?'

'Oh – muddling along. You know.'

She gazed up at him and squeezed his hands very tightly. 'I've been so looking forward to seeing you again.'

'Did you have a good holiday?'

'Wonderful. Quite wonderful.' She let go of his hands, glanced round the room at the shelves of samples, the empty coffee cups, the unwashed glasses, the racks of test tubes. She went to the wide window and looked out over the river to the city and the seething slums of the Cais de Ribeira.

'Has it changed?' he asked, standing behind her.

She shook her head. 'It never changes. Do you know they

349

tried to persuade me to retire in California? I was quite tempted for a while, but every now and again I remembered this view.' She pushed her hands outward. 'All *that*. And I knew however inefficient and noisy and dirty Portugal and the Portuguese are, I could never be happy anywhere but here.' She turned to him. 'This is where I belong.'

He had forgotten how brisk and go-ahead she was. Since Ruth's death, he had put off several major decisions regarding the running of the firm: James Remington had been pressing for some time to purchase modern fermentation vats at Pinhão; plans to connect Quinta das Rosas by road were ready for approval, and an addition to the board of directors had been proposed: this last was Martin Laughton, a nephew of Suzy Laughton and Stella's second cousin. Martin had recently completed a short service commission in the Fleet Air Arm, and had expressed an interest, after working for a year with a wine and spirits distributor in England, in entering the port wine trade. At a board meeting a week after Joy's return, it was proposed that Martin be taken on as a trainee manager with a view to becoming a director in due course. Teape would naturally have liked a son to continue the family name in the firm, but Martin seemed the best available alternative, and the proposal was agreed to without opposition.

Now that the port wine trade was emerging from the doldrums of the fifties, Teape & Co. began a little cautious expansion, and Bobby finally agreed to a modest advertising campaign, which paid dividends almost immediately in the shape of a contract to supply port to a chain of international hotels. But just as the trade began to look forward to a time of prosperity, Salazar's chickens began coming home to roost. Riots broke out in the universities; guerilla wars flared up in Angola, Mozambique, and later Guinea Bissau, and the anti-Salazarist voices began to multiply.

The army, smarting from its humiliation at Goa in 1961, now found itself waging war with outdated weapons on an ever-increasing scale. Within a few years, the eight million people of Portugal were paying out taxes to keep two hundred thousand soldiers in the field.

Eduardo was one of these soldiers. He had been at Goa at the

350

time of the withdrawal, and after a few months in Portugal for retraining, had been sent out to Mozambique.

Every month, he wrote a letter to his mother in Cascais, where she continued to work for the Van de Eifels; and from time to time he would receive a rather pathetic scrawl back, dictated by Natália to the cook, who prided herself on her literacy.

The world paid scant attention to the guerilla wars in Africa, largely because Salazar's censorship of the press prevented any worthwhile information getting out. Most of the British colony paid more attention to Westminster politics in the pages of their airmail editions of the *Daily Telegraph* than to the 'news' printed in the state-run Portuguese papers which, if they were bought at all, were bought for the entertainment guide and sports reports. Portugal was slowly becoming a political pressure cooker: as the vapour of discontent built up and began lifting the escape valve, more and more people found the quality of life and the lack of political freedom intolerable. Hundreds of thousands of them gave up waiting for the liberty that people like General Delgado and Mario Soares struggled for, and emigrated illegally to France and Germany: finding themselves unable to vote electorally, they voted with their feet.

Joy Remington gave up waiting for a different reason, and she did so in April 1964, proposing marriage to Bobby Teape under the vine trellis after an office lunch.

'Rob,' she said. 'We can't go on like this.'

He looked blank. 'Like what?'

'Like a pair of gauche school children. We're old enough to speak frankly.'

'I'm sorry, but I haven't the foggiest idea what you're talking about.'

She put her hand over his. 'Haven't we waited long enough? Aren't we wasting time?'

'I'm very sorry, I – '

'Wouldn't we both be much happier together?'

He stared at her, amazed. 'Are you suggesting marriage?'

She laughed and laughed. 'Yes, you idiot! What do you think I was suggesting?'

351

'You're really serious?'

'Of course I am! We should have got it over and done with months ago!'

He shook his head. 'I didn't realise . . . why didn't you say?'

'Wasn't it obvious?'

'I didn't really think about it. I mean – at my age – '

'Oh, rubbish! Life in the old dog yet!'

'I don't know what to say.'

'How about yes?'

He could hardly believe that Joy, the neat, well turned-out, brisk and cheerful Joy should actually want him as a husband. It made him feel happier than he had for many years.

'Well?' she prodded.

He blinked and smiled and tears came to his eyes. 'Well! Yes. Yes, I think it's a wonderful idea.'

'Are you sure?'

He felt dazed. 'Yes. Quite sure.'

Joy felt the deeply satisfying thrill of achieving a lifelong ambition. 'Excellent,' she said. 'Let's call in at the vicarage this afternoon and fix a date. A nice quiet wedding, as soon as we can. No point in waiting. After all, we don't have to go through all that nonsense of being engaged again, do we?'

II

She came into the hotel bedroom and closed the door behind her, feeling suddenly apprehensive. She crossed to the window: the room was on the fifth floor and looked out over the harbour of Funchal. The view was almost too perfect, as everything had been that day. Nothing had gone wrong. Everything – every single detail had been just right. Her dress, her small bouquet, the flowers in the church; the quiet reception at the Randalls' and the ordered departure for the airport. The arrival at Madeira, and the drive by taxi to the hotel; the walk that afternoon in this city of flowers, with the breathtaking mountains rising up out of the sea. Rob, fitted out in a new lightweight suit, his white hair neatly cropped and his new shoes (she had chosen those for him, too) beautifully polished. Dinner at the hotel: delicious prawns and chilled Moselle; crepes suzettes, Stilton cheese, and Teape's '27, probably the finest port that had ever existed.

And now, and now . . . She stood at the window and looked out at the sweep of the harbour, the glittering lights that thinned out to ones and twos in the mountain heights. The moon was up, and cast a pale light that made the peaks visible against a backdrop of stars.

She drew the curtains and turned to the mirror. She had chosen to wear her favourite colour – midnight blue – for this first evening, and the sight of herself earlier on, with Rob in his white dinner jacket, had given her a great lift of pride and happiness. Now, she removed the sapphire pendant that had been Rob's wedding present to her, and the real pearl earrings which her own mother had given to her for her twenty-first birthday. She stepped out of her dress and stood in her slip, wondering and worrying a little what he would think of her, and whether he would be disappointed. She would know instantly if he was: his eyes would give him away. She prayed a little. Please let him not be disappointed. Please let him like me.

She ran the bath, took off her underclothes and looked down at herself. Her breasts: she had always worried about them, because she felt they were too small. Years ago, when she had been engaged to Rob the first time, it had been something of an advantage to be flat-chested, but now she would have liked a slightly fuller figure.

She lay down in the bath and washed meticulously, as she always washed. She dried herself in the huge pink towel provided by the hotel, and put on her pale blue nightie. When Teape entered, after a discreet knock, she was brushing her hair at the mirror.

She turned: this was the moment. He closed the door behind him.

'You're early,' she said. 'I'm not ready.'

He looked crestfallen. 'Oh – I'm sorry. Shall I – '

'Oh Rob! Silly boy! I was only joking! Go and have your bath!'

He hesitated. 'Would you prefer it if I undressed in the bathroom?'

'Why? Are you nervous?'

'Of course not! Well – a bit, perhaps.'

'We've got to get used to each other some time,' she said, and held her hands out to him. 'Thank you for a wonderful wedding, Rob.'

'Thank you for making it possible.'

'Am I all right? Will I do?'

'I should be asking that. Not you.'

She dropped his hands. 'Off you go. Bath.'

He took off his dinner jacket and unknotted his bow tie. He was just a little short of breath. She got into bed. 'I won't look,' she said. 'Not tonight, anyway.' She turned on her side and immediately saw his reflection in the mirror. She saw him lower his trousers, saw his white legs, almost hairless now, and remembered the days of picnics on beaches, tennis parties, bicycle rides, when his legs had been suntanned, muscular, covered in pale ginger hairs. She remembered and was saddened. All those lost years! She lay and listened to the sound of running water, the splashes as he washed, and then the water draining out. She wondered what Ruth had been like with him, whether she had been a good wife in this particular respect; the thought of her caused a little surge of anger.

He was coming out of the bathroom in his silk pyjamas.

'May I join you?' he said with a little bow.

'Please do, sir,' she said. She sat up beside him. 'I have a little confession to make.'

The blood drained from his face and his eyes opened wide. 'What?' he said quickly. 'What's happened?'

'Rob! It's not as serious as all that!'

'Well, tell me what it is, then.'

She was taken by surprise by his manner. She had meant it all as a little joke.

'Kiss me first and promise not to be cross,' she said.

'Joy please – '

'Come on! Do as I say!'

Their lips touched. 'Well?' he said.

'Well, I'm not sure if I should have told you this before, Rob, but I think you ought to know one thing.' She gave a little tinkling laugh at his face. '*Please* don't take it so *seriously*, darling!'

He shook his head. 'If you'd just tell me, instead of keeping me in suspense like this – '

She threw her arms round his neck. She felt twenty-two again: young, fresh, innocent. 'I've never been to bed with a man,' she whispered. 'I may be fifty-five, but I'm still a virgin.'

She pulled away from him to see his face, and she knew then that he was not disappointed.

III

When the honeymoon was over, she set about turning him into the sort of husband she had always wanted: she threw out his old clothes and chose new ones for him; she moved him out of Moinho Velho and into her house at Foz; she ordered him about, she scheduled, timetabled and domesticated him, so that within quite a short space of time he wondered how on earth he had ever managed to get along without her.

14

I

DURING THE FIVE DAY PASSAGE from Lisbon aboard the troopship *Uige*, Sergeant Eduardo da Costa heard a lot about what to expect in Guinea-Bissau, and very little of it was optimistic.

'It's a bit like the Alentejo,' Sergeant Lopes had told him. 'About as big and about as flat with about as many trees, only they're palm trees instead of cork oaks. The only real differences are, the people are black, it's twice as hot and most of it's under water.'

Sergeant Lopes was a large, goodnatured fellow who ate a lot and laughed a lot and talked a lot. He had already served three years in Guinea, and now took great pleasure in painting as grim a picture of it as possible. 'If you don't get malaria, you'll get ring worm or hook worm or snake bite, and if you don't get those, you'll get VD from the girl who washes your clothes. And if you daren't risk that, you'll probably go mad. You might get shot, of course. Or blown up by a mine. Cheer up, boy, you'll enjoy it!'

The ship berthed at Bissau, and the new arrivals disembarked to the military base. Two days later da Costa and Lopes, along with fifty others, loaded their kit and weapons on to the high wheel-base Berliet lorries and set out on the ninety mile journey to the support company headquarters at Bafoto, in the southern part of the province. It was July 1970: the rainy season had started. The lorries bumped and splashed over mile after mile of dead flat plains where tidal canals and wide tracts of flood water steamed in the pelting downpour. Apart from a few small villages and the occasional glimpse of women working in the rice paddies, the countryside seemed utterly forsaken.

When they arrived at Bafoto in the late afternoon, it had stopped raining. The jeeps and lorries entered the village via a sentry post, and proceeded slowly between huts made of mud and straw where children stopped playing to watch the vehicles go by.

They drew up outside the whitewashed buildings of the company headquarters, and the men jumped down from the lorries and stretched their legs.

Eduardo slung his Uzi sub-machine gun over one shoulder and hoisted his kitbag over the other. As he walked across to the Sergeants' mess with Lopes, he said, 'Well. Could be worse, I suppose.'

Lopes laughed. 'You won't say that in a year's time.'

The following morning, they were interviewed by Captain Almeida, the Company Commander. He was a neat, polished officer, with beady brown eyes and a smile that displayed even, white teeth. He stood up to talk to the two sergeants, and Eduardo was able to look down upon his bald head.

'I rely very heavily upon my sergeants,' he said, walking up and down. 'Most of us here are amateur soldiers, as you well know. So we can use all the experience we can get.' He stopped and looked up at Eduardo, a powerful looking fellow, with thick eyebrows and dark, wavy hair. 'How long have you served?'

'Just on fifteen years, sir. I was in Goa and Mozambique before this.'

'You were, were you? Well we wage a different sort of war here. We're not trying to conquer them so much as cultivate them. We capture hearts and minds, not dead bodies. So you can forget all those punishment tactics the Pink Panther taught you. General Spinola does things differently.'

Eduardo knew what the Captain was talking about. 'The Pink Panther' had been the nickname given to General Kaulza de Arriaga, whose merciless tactics had become legendary in Mozambique. It had been the Pink Panther who had made no bones about destroying native villages and executing guerilla sympathisers. Eduardo had been involved in such punitive operations himself: he had seen women and children weeping while their huts went up in flames, and once supervised the

357

digging of a mass grave for the corpses of FRELIMO activists who had been summarily shot.

The duties that Captain Almeida outlined represented a radical change from what da Costa had been used to. 'We want to show them we can help and that the guerillas can only make life worse for them,' he said. 'We're encouraging them and assisting them in a variety of projects: irrigation, farming techniques, building new schools and hospitals. "For a better Guinea". That's our motto. Don't forget it.'

Later, in the mess, they were questioned by a thin streak of a man called Coelho. 'Don't tell me – he gave you the old hearts and minds routine. "Don't kill – cultivate". That man gives me the shits! Ever since he was commended by Spinola he's been brainwashed by all those candy-floss bulletins they send back to Lisbon every day. I tell you this war is impossible to win. And who the hell wants to hang on to this godforsaken swamp, that's what I'd like to know.'

'Just because you've been detailed off to go to Mudanda!' said Tavares, one of the older sergeants.

Coelho whipped round. His eyes held a dangerous, wild look, and a tic jerked repeatedly at the corner of his mouth. 'We'll see about that,' he said.

'What's special about Mudanda?' da Costa asked.

'It's a *tabanca* near the border,' he was told. 'Been several attacks on it in the last few weeks.'

Tabanca was a much used word in Guinea-Bissau. It meant 'village', and usually referred to the defended collections of huts that were part of the anti-guerilla strategy. Most of the *tabancas* were manned by platoons consisting of twenty-four men. In this way, the army lived in close contact with the native population throughout the country, and good relations were fostered between the Africans and the Portuguese.

The other word that was used a great deal was *bajuda* – girl. In bigger villages and towns, some of the girls now wore blouses to cover their breasts, but elsewhere they wore only cotton shifts tucked round their waists. Many of them were very attractive: their skin was soft and smooth, and they took pride in plaiting and parting each other's hair. A lot of them worked as wash girls – *lavandeiras* – for the officers and men, and if you gave your *bajuda* a coloured headscarf or a bracelet or a bead necklace, she would let you have sex with her. Such relationships were encouraged by the parents of the girls, especially if the soldier concerned was in a position of authority: the liaison could often be used to good effect, for columns of military vehicles passed back and forth along the dirt roads every week, and it was sometimes useful to be able to persuade a corporal or sergeant, via his *bajuda*, to fix a truck for a load of peanuts or goatskins. Thus there was an unofficial aspect to General Spinola's 'Hearts and Minds' policy, which probably had as much effect on the population as did the agricultural and building schemes, and the lectures in public health.

The rain came down every day for hours on end. Sometimes it rained continually for periods of twenty-four hours or more. The sentries in the elevated look-out positions stood in their poncho capes and stared out through the steaming air, searching for any sign of movement beyond the wire. Thunderstorms flickered and crashed all night; the tracks turned to quagmires, and vehicles became easily bogged down, and had to be dug out. The canals overflowed and the mosquitoes multiplied. Daraprim tablets were put out on the tables every day at lunch time, but many of the men scorned them as being worse than useless. Some said that if you took Daraprim and then caught malaria, you would have a much more serious dose of it.

When the rain stopped, and often when it didn't, the women went out into the paddy fields and planted rice, while their menfolk stayed at home and smoked pipes, sitting and talking in the doorways of the huts. Every day, patrols were sent out to protect the women working in the fields and to prove to the guerillas that a constant guard was maintained. This was something that Captain Almeida insisted upon: he said that the villages that were attacked were the ones which failed to send out patrols regularly. From time to time, military convoys were ambushed or a lorry blown up by a mine. One young soldier found a newspaper lying by the canal. It blew up when he tried to pick it up, and he was killed.

In the sergeants' mess, it became increasingly clear that Sergeant Coelho was prepared to go to any lengths in order to

359

avoid duty in the *tabanca* of Mudanda. He repeatedly requested to speak to the company commander on a 'personal matter', and it was rumoured that he had written a personal letter to the president of Portugal, Admiral Tomaz. The other sergeants regarded him as a 'nut case', and his continual complaints and arguments began to get on people's nerves. Second Lieutenant Cardoso, a small, moustached officer who played the guitar and liked dogs, made no attempt to disguise the fact that, as officer in command of number three platoon, he would rather have no sergeants at all than have Coelho under his command.

The matter came to a head on a day in mid August when the platoon was mustered outside the headquarters prior to departure. The full number consisted of three sergeants, three corporals, eighteen soldiers and Second Lieutenant Cardoso. They fell in in full kit, the soldiers armed with G3 rifles and carrying hand grenades slung on their belts, and the sergeants with sub-machine guns over their shoulders.

Cardoso looked absurdly young and small to be in charge of these men. He had left Coimbra university only a year before; his guitar was already in the lorry. He waited while Sergeant Tavares fell the men in and sized them, aware that Coelho was absent. The night before, Coelho had tried to bribe Eduardo da Costa to go to Mudanda in his place, but Eduardo had refused.

Now, Captain Almeida came out of his office, and Cardoso called the platoon to attention and made his report.

'Number three platoon mustered, sir. One man not accounted for.'

'Who? Coelho?'

'Yes, sir. Coelho.'

'Have you sent for him?'

'Not yet, sir.'

Almeida snorted impatiently. 'Do so.'

Cardoso turned. 'Sergeant Tavares!'

'Sir!'

'Find Sergeant Coelho and bring him here immediately.'

'Sir!'

Sergeant Tavares went off at the double. The soldiers remained at attention, glancing sideways at each other, and

360

shifting their weight from foot to foot. A minute passed, and then the sound of shouting came from the direction of the sergeants' latrines. A moment later, Coelho appeared dressed only in underpants that hung slackly from his protruding hip bones. He ran towards Captain Almeida shouting incoherently, and took him by the lapels of his dolman. He shook him back and forth, and burst into tears, babbling and screaming hysterically.

Almeida remained rigidly at attention. 'Restrain this man!' he shouted. 'Put him under arrest!'

Sergeant Tavares and two soldiers seized Coelho by the arms and tried to drag him off. There was a tussle, during which Coelho managed to grab a hand grenade from the belt of one of the soldiers. He wrenched himself free and held the grenade high above his head. He was so tall that no one had a hope of reaching it.

'Hands off!' he shouted, and withdrew the safety pin. 'Look! Look!' he screamed. 'The pin's out! I can put it back or I can let it go! It's up to you, Almeida! You'll have to make a decision for a change! It's up to you!'

Coelho's face was mottled white and red. Sweat stood on his forehead in large beads. There was so little fat on his narrow torso that his rib cage showed through. During the struggle, his pants had been pulled half off him, and he now displayed a long, thin, white penis that dangled slackly between his legs.

Almeida was a courageous officer. He was married with three small children whom he loved and looked forward to seeing again when his tour of duty in Guinea was over. But at the same time, he believed in firm discipline.

'Put the pin back in, Coelho,' he said. 'You aren't frightening any of us.'

There were a few moments of silence. The Portuguese flag, green and red, hung motionless in the still air. In the trees beyond the huts, a parakeet squawked once, and was silent. Coelho laughed, and his voice cracked. 'All right, all right, all right, all right!' he yelled. 'If I go on this trip, you come with me, Captain!' He lunged at Almeida and grabbed him by the neck.

Then he dropped the grenade.

361

Somebody shouted, 'Down!' and several soldiers started running. The explosion rent the air: Almeida and Coelho were literally blown apart. People came running from the office and accommodation buildings. The ground was littered with bodies.

Coelho, Almeida and one of the soldiers were killed instantly. Tavares lasted sixteen hours, recovering sufficient consciousness to call upon Jesus, Mary and Joseph to pray for him. He died in agony, most of the lower part of his abdomen having been blown away. A further four soldiers were injured, one severely.

It was as a result of this incident and the consequent reshuffle of sergeants that Eduardo da Costa and Rui Lopes received orders to report for duty with number three platoon, at Mudanda.

II

The *tabanca* consisted of forty-three circular huts with thatched roofs and mud floors. Two of these huts provided the sleeping quarters for the members of the platoon: each contained four two-tier bunks and four singles. The men decorated the walls with pictures of their wives, families and girl friends, as well as the inevitable cut-outs from magazines. Everybody – including Cardoso and the sergeants – lived and ate and slept in surroundings that allowed virtually no privacy at all.

Food was a continual source of complaint, and a lot of time was spent bartering for extra sweet potatoes or goat meat to supplement the meagre supplies that arrived each week in the military convoy. This convoy also brought the mail, and its arrival was eagerly awaited. Letter writing took up a major part of everyone's spare time.

A travelling cinema show came to the village every six weeks or so, and for a couple of hours a dream of another world sparkled on the screen that was rigged up under the branches of an orange tree that grew by the platoon huts. During the love scenes, the soldiers would hoot and whistle and cheer, and the villagers, clustering in a crowd at the back, would sigh and grin, muttering to each other, their eyes wide with avid attention.

The orange tree itself was a source of discussion at first. It stood on a slight rise in the ground, which was sufficient to make it conspicuous from quite a distance. As Mudanda was close to the Guinea-Conakry border, where the PAIGC guerillas were known to have their bases, some of the men were convinced that the tree must serve as a useful landmark, and may have contributed to the accuracy of the guerilla attacks in the past. Rui Lopes was all for chopping it down, but Cardoso would not permit it: it was the only orange tree in the village, and he was afraid that if he cut it down the villagers would be offended.

But Cardoso himself offended the people of Mudanda in another way. When the platoon first arrived, the village was overrun by sick and mangy dogs. They were everywhere: they licked and scratched their sores; they queued up to copulate with the bitches on heat; they produced miserable little puppies, many of which starved or drowned. The sight of these dogs upset Cardoso so much that eventually he rounded up a large number and shot them to put them out of their misery. This caused an outrage among the villagers, for to kill a dog was considered very unlucky. The village headman made a formal complaint, and for a week an uneasy atmosphere prevailed. The ill feeling ended, however, when Cardoso invented a public shower, which he made out of an empty dried milk container with holes bored in the base. It was a means of saving water in the dry season, and was to prove very popular with the local girls.

In October, Eduardo da Costa went down with his first bout of malaria. He was sent to the *enfermaria* in Bafoto, and was given the standard medication and treatment. He recovered after a fortnight, but felt considerably weakened for some time afterwards. He also gave up smoking: as is often the case, the disease left him with a strong aversion even to the smell of tobacco smoke.

In the dry season, the harmattan brought dust from the Sahara, and there were fewer mosquitoes. Fresh water became scarce, for the canal water in this part of Guinea is tidal, and therefore undrinkable. What well water there was had to be filtered and boiled before consumption.

On carnival night, the soldiers put on a show for themselves and the villagers. Extra wine and beer was allowed, and everyone relaxed for a few hours. An oil lamp swung from the branches of the orange tree, and Cardoso played his guitar. The men sat drinking and smoking, some with their *bajudas*, some joining in with the songs they knew. A few volunteered to sing solos, and among these was Eduardo.

He stood in the lamplight and sang a song called '*Numa Casa Portuguesa*' – 'A Portuguese House'. The lantern cast a gentle light, in which moths and winged insects fluttered. The tune was well known, and the words evoked memories they all shared:

> 'Four whitewashed walls,
> The scent of rosemary;
> A bunch of golden grapes,
> A blue tiled figure of St Joseph;
> The sun in springtime,
> A promise of kisses:
> Two arms awaiting me –
> It's a house in Portugal, you can be certain;
> You can be certain it's a house in Portugal.'

Eduardo had more than just a good voice: he had the gift that is only given to a few of being able to move hearts and minds with song. And as he sang, he knew that the words somehow conveyed more than their immediate meaning, as if the light of the lantern, the notes of the guitar and his own voice worked a magic of their own rather than one of his or Cardoso's making. The experience was oddly exhilarating: far back in his childhood memories, he retained the image of his mother also singing by the light of a lamp, and he now remembered and recognised in his own performance the same magic that she had wrought all those years ago.

364

In April he went down with malaria for the second time. He took longer to recover from this bout, and when he returned to Mudanda he was noticeably thinner.

If anybody in the platoon had had any high-flown ideas about creating a better Guinea, such ideas had by now been abandoned. The newspapers reports about the miracles Spinola was working which reached them from time to time were greeted with cynicism and hollow laughter: they often wished that the editors of the newspapers containing such reports could experience for themselves the feeling of stalemate and fear that protracted guerilla warfare engenders.

The time went slowly by. They went out on daily patrols close to the village; they kept watch in the sandbagged bunkers inside the perimeter wire; they played cards, wrote letters and listened to records on battery-driven record players. When the weekly delivery of provisions, newspapers and mail arrived, they caught up on the war gossip and news from home. Sometimes, in the evenings, they would argue whether Portugal should even be trying to hold on to her overseas possessions at all. Cardoso, fresh from university, had particularly radical ideas.

'If I were Guinean, I'd be fighting on the other side,' he said.

'Why are you here then?' Lopes asked.

'Because I was a fool, like everyone else, that's why. We believed what they told us at school. We were brainwashed from the cradle. These people are no more Portuguese than the Algerians were French or the Indians British. But it takes time for people to realise it, that's the trouble.'

Eduardo was due for leave at the end of July, and he had saved enough money for a flight back to Portugal, which he booked for the 29th. The effect of approaching leave produced an end of term feeling among the half dozen soldiers who were due to go. The drab monotony of life in the *tabanca* suddenly had a visible end: you could 'see' the week after the week after next, and the prospect of Portugal, beautiful, carefree Portugal, brought about a surge of optimism.

The rains were late coming that year, and the latter half of

July was unusually hot. Because of the cramped conditions in the huts and the fetid atmosphere caused by twelve sweaty men, da Costa had taken to sleeping on an air bed under the long straw eaves, which nearly reached the ground.

There were only ten days to go now: he lay awake, an hour or so before dawn and looked forward to his leave. A slap-up meal, that would be the first thing: thick soup with fresh bread and butter, good *bacalhau* with olive oil, a thick steak, pudding flan; a bottle of *vinho verde* to wash it down and a cup of real coffee with a glass of brandy to follow. And of course he'd ring up his friends: Zé Oliveira, Nuno Gomes, Luis Carvalho. He lay on his back, thinking about it all. They'd paint Lisbon red, all right. The bars and night clubs in the Bairro Alto. *Fado* until five o'clock in the morning. Walking back to your room in the first light of dawn, down the Rua da Rosa, where half the people were just going to bed and the other half just getting up. Afternoons on the beach; pretty girls: Portuguese girls, tanned as golden as the beaches, girls that spoke your own language, shared the same sense of humour, enjoyed good living, good loving. Then he thought of his mother. He would spend a bit of money on her, too. Perhaps he was looking forward to seeing her more than anyone else. He would go in at the back door of the house where she lived and worked, the big house on the sea front. He would go in and sit down in the kitchen and he would tell her all his news, listen to all of hers, laugh with her, tease her about her man friend, Fernando Palmeira, who drove a taxi and had already proposed to her twice. He would watch her bustling about, working and talking at the same time, and he would feel the warmth of her love again. And on her night off, he would take her to a little *tasca* he knew, and they would eat *caldeirada*, good stew, and her very special favourite pudding, which was *toucinho do ceu*, 'heavenly bacon'. He would treat her like a guest of honour: she would be waited upon for once, instead of waiting upon others. He would make her feel as important as a good mother should feel, instead of the 'bottom millstone', the *mó do baixo* which she sometimes called herself.

He shifted his position and lay on his back. The night insects whistled and rang in the darkness. His thoughts became jumbled as he dropped back to sleep again. He dozed for a while, and began half dreaming, half thinking about the girl who washed his clothes.

She had come to him a few days after the carnival night, when he had sung in the lamplight to Cardoso's guitar. One morning, she brought his clothes to him instead of his regular *lavandeira*. She was the daughter of the headman, about thirteen or fourteen. She stood before him and laid out his shorts, his shirts, his pants and his singlets. She wore a green and orange cotton shift round her waist; her hair was carefully parted in three lines, and her breasts were almost fully developed. She was like a tender fruit that will be ripe within a few days.

But although he had wanted her, and although her eyes had often looked up into his in a way that left no doubt that she wanted to be his *bajuda*, he had never taken advantage of her silent looks of invitation. He had made her little presents from time to time, and had paid her promptly for the work she did for him, but never once had he so much as touched those breasts or kissed those lips.

He shivered a little, and images of the girl invaded his mind: he half dreamt, half imagined that she lay with him and that her body was in his arms, her breasts against his lips. The desire rose in him like a tongue of flame: his body demanded relief, and his imagination conjured up pictures that compounded and intensified the need.

It would be so easy. He could get up, now, and go to her hut. He could wake her, gently, by touching her foot. And it would not even matter if her father or mother awoke: it was probably they who had sent her to him in the first place. She would come out of her hut, and they would lie together under the eaves. She would be anxious to please him. Her lips would be on his, her body supple and ready.

He was damp with sweat. He rolled over on to his side, felt the hardness of his sub-machine gun, and moved it aside.

Why not? Why not!

The insects that had been trilling almost continuously all night had fallen silent. He looked out from under the over-hanging eave. There was no moon, but an electric storm flickered silently on the horizon. To his right, the sentry in the sandbag bunker was invisible in the darkness. To his left, beyond the orange tree, was the perimeter wire; beyond that, the flat savannah stretched out towards the foot hills of Guinea-Conakry.

The night had become oddly still. A mosquito whined close to him: he had discarded the net over his head, and when it settled on his neck, he squashed it quickly.

Still silence. It was too quiet: he began to imagine things. Was that a movement, somewhere over to his left?

The faintest waft of a smell reached him. He lifted his face into the night air and sniffed. Yes, there was a smell: faint, but distinctive. Human sweat.

He reached backward and closed his hand over the metallic hardness of the sub-machine gun. He picked it up and edged forward, out of his sleeping bag. He had been sleeping naked; there were clothes close at hand, but putting them on would make too much noise. He crept forward like a leopard, carrying the machine gun in his right hand, feeling ahead with his left.

He edged his way slowly away from the hut, so that his track converged with the line of the barbed wire perimeter fence. He felt a thorn or sharp stone penetrate his knee, and paused a moment, wincing silently. And in that moment, he heard a metallic click that came from only a few yards away.

It was enough. Quickly, he took the safety catch off the Uzi and assumed a crouching position. He felt sweat breaking out all over his body: it trickled down his flanks and was salt on his tongue when he licked his lips. He was convinced now that somebody was out there on the other side of the fence, but he knew that if he opened fire first he would give away his own position.

He did not have to wait long. He heard a sudden movement and the grunt of a man who has exerted himself. Something sailed overhead and behind him there was an explosion as an incendiary grenade burst into flame beneath the orange tree.

He saw them then: three or four figures, one standing up, about to throw another grenade. His reaction was instinctive: kill or be killed. Holding the machine gun close into his body

368

he fired in bursts of three and four rounds, keeping his aim as low as possible so that the bullets whipped out barely a foot above the ground.

The night filled with shouts and confusion. Another incendiary grenade had been thrown and one of the huts was on fire. Soldiers ran out into the night, some naked, some in singlets and shorts, their bodies illuminated by the flames. Over to the right from the bunker came the crack-crack of a G3 rifle and beyond the wire forms were running bent double along the path that bordered the canal.

He ran towards the perimeter wire, stopped, and fired four more bursts. On the fourth the magazine emptied. He ran back to the huts, shouted orders, detailed men to reinforce the *tabanca* defences. He grabbed two more magazines for the Uzi and, fitting one, ran back to the wire. He emptied the magazine in bursts in the general direction he reckoned the guerillas had taken, then fitted the other magazine and lay down to wait.

Behind him the confusion continued as attempts were made to put out the fire. The hut blazed like a torch and the figures moving round it looked like actors in a shadow dance. Eduardo remained where he was: if the guerillas returned he reckoned he would have a better chance of seeing them by the light of the blaze before they saw him.

The flames died down and a dark pillar of smoke rose vertically in the still air. At first light, he stood up and made his way back to the huts. He was met by Cardoso, who wore a pair of pyjama trousers and was grimy with smoke and dust.

'We got one!' he said, unable to hide a certain boyish excitement. 'Just outside the fence.'

They went down to the perimeter wire together. Beyond it, a body lay huddled as if trying to get to sleep and feeling the cold. Ants were already trooping in a black line over the bare stomach to the bullet wounds in the chest.

On their way back to the huts, they saw some of the village women watching as the soldiers threw buckets of water over the smoking remains of the hut. Cardoso glanced at Eduardo, who was still naked. He grinned.

'Better put that weapon away now, boy. We don't want to frighten the natives.'

369

But as he looked up his grin faded, for Eduardo's face was bathed in sweat, and he was shivering uncontrollably.

IV

General António Spinola, officer in command of Portuguese forces in Guinea-Bissau, and civil governor of the province, emerged from a side door of the governor's palace on the outskirts of Bissau at precisely seven o'clock in the morning and walked briskly out to the awaiting Landrover, accompanied by his adjutant. The vehicle drove off immediately, turning right out of the palace grounds and speeding northward along the palm avenues of the outer suburbs of the city to the military airport.

The general didn't believe in having a personal helicopter. He preferred to demonstrate his confidence in the pilots and aircraft of the Portuguese Air Force by travelling in the most readily available machine. What he did insist upon was punctuality: lack of it had already cost one or two officers their careers.

The Landrover took the last corner onto the aircraft dispersal with a squeal of tyres and came abruptly to a halt. The pilot of the Alouette was already strapped into the cockpit and ready for start-up. He watched the general and the adjutant make their way across the dispersal: Spinola, tall, erect, in combat gear but wearing a monocle; the adjutant a lean officer, who carried a small case with a few of Spinola's personal things. The duty major saluted, and a moment later the aircraft shook as the two passengers got in.

'Know where we're going, boy?' the general asked.

'Mudanda, sir!' the pilot replied.

'Right. Let's go then. What are we waiting for?'

The pilot gave the wind up signal to the ground crew and initiated the starting cycle. The rotor blades moved round, gathering momentum, and the turbine whined as the revs mounted. A few minutes later, on a radioed clearance from air traffic control, the helicopter rose from the ground, turned, dipped its nose to gather forward speed, and climbed away heading south-east. It flew at a thousand feet over the wide stretch of brown water which was the Geba estuary, and on, passing over the villages of Tite, Fulacunda and Buba.

Spinola looked down at the featureless terrain that sped past, beneath him. It was three years since he had been put in command in Guinea. He'd told Salazar that these wars were like chasing fleas in haystacks: the fleas got fat and the soldiers died of exhaustion. But the old dictator had talked him into going out for a trial period of six months, and he'd used that time to formulate a plan involving revolutionary techniques to wage this guerrilla war.

A lot had happened in those first six months. Salazar's deck chair (made in England, so they said) collapsed under him one summer afternoon, and the old man hit his head on the stone patio of his summer residence. A month or so later, suffering from headaches and blurring vision in one eye, he was taken into hospital, where an exploratory operation revealed a blood clot near the brain.

That was the beginning of the end for Salazar, but he took a long time going. Week after week, his ministers hovered by his bed, waiting for him to emerge from his coma and whisper his instructions to them. The president, old Admiral Tomaz, agonised and dithered and delayed until, with the government of the country grinding to a halt, he reached the decision that everyone else knew was a foregone conclusion: Marcello Caetano would have to take over as prime minister.

There was a lot of gossip, that autumn, about Salazar's housekeeper, Senhora Maria. In fact the Portuguese people seemed to find her more interesting than the new prime minister. Was she actually Salazar's wife, or was she merely a devoted servant? The ordinary people, chattering about it in the markets and shops, displayed an unconscious political shrewdness by asking these questions; in doing so, they were asking a much more important question, for Senhora Maria was a woman, the only woman in the dictator's life. Portugal – the mother country – was also a woman, and the real question being asked was, should Portugal be the unquestioning servant of a dictator, or should a prime minister be the devoted husband of his country?

The helicopter was altering course now, and the adjutant was pointing out signs of progress in a land drainage scheme in which the general took a special interest. Spinola leaned forward to look out of the open door, nodding his acknowledgement to the adjutant before sitting back and returning to his train of thought.

When he returned to Lisbon in November 1968 to meet the new prime minister and report on his six months of fact finding, he had taken care to move his family and all his personal belongings back to Portugal with him. It was a deliberate move: he was able to go to Belem and tell the bespectacled Caetano that he was prepared to return to Guinea Bissau only if he was given a completely free hand to fight the war in his own, very personal way.

He didn't have a great deal of time for Caetano, whom he regarded privately as a yes man. Salazar was still being kept alive and still believed, in his brief moments of consciousness, that he ruled the country. Because Caetano had been reared and fed on Salazarist policies, he was now frightened of doing anything that might meet with his master's disapproval. Spinola, having been appointed by Salazar in the first place, knew that Caetano would have to say 'yes' to his demands, and after a short period of indecision, Caetano did just that.

Now, Spinola looked back over his three years in command and reviewed the policy of total commitment he had demanded from his officers and men. He had not spared himself during that time, flying about the country daily, visiting danger zones that lesser officers would have avoided, weeding out those whom he considered lazy, overfed or gutless; exhorting everyone under his command to believe totally in the struggle and to give every last ounce of energy to it.

It had been a long haul, and he was beginning to wonder if even more radical changes were necessary to keep the Ultramar under Portuguese sovereignty. Taking the larger view, he believed that given imaginative leadership, Portugal could be great again; he even dreamt of a union of Portuguese-speaking peoples including those in Brazil, Africa and the possessions in the far east. Already he was collecting thoughts and ideas for a book: a book that he would call *Portugal e o Futuro*, 'Portugal and the Future'; a book that would either lever Caetano into positive action, or push him right out of the way.

The helicopter was circling now, and the adjutant again pointed downward. He could see a meandering waterway, and beside it a small collection of mud huts, encircled by a wire fence. As the Alouette passed low over the *tabanca*, soldiers and villagers could be seen looking upward. The helicopter climbed, banked and made another low pass, on the General's instructions. He noted that the soldiers were running about: the platoon commander had clearly guessed who the visitor was, and was making haste to receive him. He knew that his unexpected appearances in the most unlikely places caused alarm and confusion, and considered it very right and proper that they should. A leader who was not feared and respected was not worthy of the name.

The helicopter reduced forward speed and descended slowly, approaching a clearing within the *tabanca*. Its rotor blades chopped the air and sent a cloud of dust flying upward and outward. It lowered itself onto the ground and the rotor noise decreased as the blades went into fine pitch and the pilot shut down.

Spinola and his adjutant stepped out into the searing heat as the rotor blades slowed to a stop, and Second Lieutenant Cardoso came forward to meet them. All his personal belongings had been burnt in the hut, and he wore shorts and shirt that were rather too big for him.

He saluted. 'Welcome to Mudanda *S'or General*,' he said.

Spinola looked down at him with a baleful stare. 'You're Cardoso, are you?'

'Yes, sir.'

'What happened to your uniform?'

'It was in the hut that went up in flames, sir.'

They were walking over to where the platoon was fallen in. 'Tell me about the attack,' the General said.

'They tried to surprise us in the early hours,' Cardoso said. 'Fortunately one of my sergeants was too quick for them.'

The men had been called to attention by Sergeant Lopes,

who now reported: 'Number three platoon for your inspection, sir.' Spinola looked at the lines of men. Few of them had complete uniforms; none of them were overweight, and several of them looked dangerously thin. He had been briefed about the attack within an hour of its taking place: he had cancelled the inspection of a company headquarters in order to make this visit. He turned to Cardoso. 'Which sergeant?'

'Da Costa, sir.' Cardoso indicated with his hand. The General strolled over and the two men faced each other. This man was as tall as he: they looked directly into each other's eyes. Eduardo's teeth were clamped together and he was drenched in sweat.

'What's wrong with you?'

'Not sure, sir. Touch of malaria, I think.'

'Had it before?'

'Twice, sir.'

'How long have you been in Guinea?'

'Nearly a year, sir.'

'Due for leave?'

The sergeant's face broke into a grin, and revealed two broken teeth at the front. 'Next week, sir.'

The General nodded. 'Good. Sounds as if you've deserved it.'

'Thank you, sir.'

Eduardo's teeth chattered momentarily. In the village, boys were banging a syncopated rhythm on an empty oil drum.

Spinola looked along the line of faces. He liked meeting men like this: he liked their loyalty, their resilience, their humble obedience that was mixed with pride. He believed firmly in the idea of being born to lead; as a cavalry officer he was imbued with the stylish off-the-cuff mannerisms of Portugal's élite regiment.

He stood before them, a little bow-legged but otherwise very upright. In repose, his face resembled that of a solemn monkey wearing a monocle. When he spoke, every man in the platoon listened.

'You men are part of the flower of Portuguese manhood,' he said. 'You are fighting in conditions that are scarcely fit for animals, with weapons that are inadequate for the task you

374

have been given. As your commander-in-chief, I want you to know that I am aware of the difficulties you face. I am aware that the life you lead is not only dangerous but also unhealthy. And I also want you to know that I represent your case in the strongest possible terms on each occasion that I return to Lisbon.' He relaxed a little. 'Well, boys, I've heard about what happened. I reckon you were lucky to have a sergeant on the alert. Next time you may not be so lucky. This war doesn't go away, you know. You have to fight it twenty-four hours a day, seven days a week. Remember that.'

The men were fallen out, and the General made a rapid tour of the village and the defences. He talked with the headman, the sentries and the chef, and looked at the burnt-out remains of the hut.

'You'll have that sergeant hospitalized?' he asked Cardoso on the way back to the helicopter.

'Yes, sir. He'll go to Bafoto tomorrow.'

The General turned to his adjutant. 'Is there a medical officer there at the moment?'

'No, sir. He's at Fulacunda.'

'Have him transferred. I'd like to give that lad the best chance of being fit for leave.'

The adjutant made a note. 'I'll see to it, sir.'

'Good. One other thing.' He turned to Cardoso. 'Have that orange tree chopped down. My chopper pilot used it as a landmark, so the guerillas will as well. And it stands out like a donkey's dick.'

He gave Cardoso no time to reply. The adjutant followed him into the Alouette, and the starter whined.

As the aircraft lifted clear of the ground and climbed away to the north, the adjutant opened a bottle of Agua de Luzo, the General's personal water supply, especially imported from Portugal. He handed it to the General, who drank gratefully, pausing to look downward at the collection of huts as the *tabanca* slipped out of sight beneath the fuselage.

V

The medical officer arrived at Bafoto a couple of hours after Eduardo da Costa. He was a young man, fresh from medical school, and had been in Guinea only a month. He examined the sergeant very carefully, and having diagnosed malaria prescribed Commel tablets to ease the symptoms and an injection of Nivaquina to combat the disease.

'I had tablets before,' Eduardo said when confronted with the needle.

'Well you're having a shot this time. It's new stuff. More effective.'

'I hope so. I've got a flight to Lisbon on the 29th.'

'This should do the trick.' The doctor rubbed ether on Eduardo's arm and prepared the vein. He injected Nivaquina, withdrew the needle and held the cotton wool swab against the arm for a second. 'Right. Get yourself turned in, Sergeant.'

Eduardo did as he was told. He lay down between sheets in the *enfermaria*, his ears singing, sweating profusely at first, shivering later, burning later still.

As the light faded and it grew dark, he began to realise that this was the worst bout of malaria he had had so far. His whole body ached: he writhed about for hour after hour. The bed seemed to float about the room and the humming in his ears sounded as if some huge insect were trapped inside his head and was trying to get out. As the night wore on, he became aware of new and disturbing pains: his heels ached and his foreskin became tight and painfully tender. His mind descended into delirium: he became convinced that Second Lieutenant Cardoso was going to perform a circumcision operation on him, and was frightened because Cardoso had had very little experience of medicine. In his moments of consciousness, he suffered from a raging thirst, and he realised that his sheets were completely soaked in sweat.

The doctor came to see him in the morning. He gave him another injection of Nivaquina and took his temperature. Da Costa babbled incoherently. 'Where's Cardoso? My heels ... aching ... thirsty. Is Cardoso any good? So tight ... it stings ... it'll have to be circumcised, won't it? Won't I? And my heels ... do something ...'

376

The medical officer began to suspect that this sergeant was not suffering from malaria after all. His temperature was forty degrees centigrade: the equivalent of a hundred and four fahrenheit. He took a blood count, and the result of that was equally alarming. He had no plasma at Bafoto and very little blood. He had been sent here on the personal orders of General Spinola, and was frightened of making a mistake and prejudicing his future career. He looked down at the flushed face and made a decision. 'Right. I'm getting you evacuated to Bissau. I'll radio for a helicopter. The sooner we have you out of here, the better.'

Da Costa vaguely took this in. He lay in the bed all day and eventually a medical attendant asked him if he could walk to the helicopter. He said yes, he could. But when he stood up, the pain in his heels shot up his calves and the room spun round him. The attendant caught him as he fell, and he was carried out to the aircraft on a stretcher.

He felt as if he were in a dream. His mind seemed to have detached itself from his body, so that he could watch them carrying him out of the infirmary and across the stretch of ground to the awaiting helicopter.

He had never travelled by helicopter before, and as it rose into the air above the company headquarters, some dim interest drove him to try and pull himself up off the stretcher and look out of the window.

He put his hands on the metal surround and heaved. But instead of seeing the view and being interested by it, the sight of something else caused a dull shock: the backs of his hands, wrists and arms were covered in a rash of purple, watery blisters.

VI

He was taken from the helicopter by stretcher into the military hospital in Bissau and dumped in a treatment room, where he lay for two hours. He dropped in and out of consciousness, sometimes hearing his own voice and sometimes the voices of others. His thirst became unbearable. He cried out for water over and over again and eventually managed to attract the attention of a medical attendant in the corridor.

'Water. I must have water. And a doctor. Quickly.'

The water came in five minutes; the doctor took an hour. But when he did arrive he took one look at Eduardo and had him transferred immediately to the intensive care unit. He was given a blood transfusion and put on a plasma drip. He was visited by doctors at hourly intervals: they discussed his case, but he was unable to concentrate sufficiently on what they were saying.

Days merged into nights, and he lost track of time completely. He still knew, from time to time, that he was due for leave, and in moments of consciousness he reminded whoever happened to be present in the room of the fact. The plasma drip continued into his left arm for eighteen hours out of the twenty four, and he was given blood twice a day. He lay immobilised, sweating a lot, often thirsty, often troubled by a dizzy disorientation that caused a dull realisation that he must be close to death. But death, being so close by, did not seem nearly so frightening. He felt as if he had already died once or twice. The experience was not alarming. You slipped quietly out of life and had some rather strange visions on the way. You saw your mother washing clothes in the cement tank outside the kitchen. You heard her voice singing. There was a man whose face was in shadow, but you knew that he was your father. You heard people talking: people you had known years and years ago. There were other noises, too: cocks crowing, the metallic whirring of a windmill, the squeal of a rabbit. You saw your watery reflection, relived another death. Sometimes there were long, erotic dreams about half forgotten or nameless girls: a mulatto in Lourenco Marques, a Goan prostitute, an English girl with wet, white breasts. Then, drifting back into consciousness, you revisited life. There were white-coated people near your bed, people who talked interminably but whose talk was quite incomprehensible.

One of these looked down. You saw his eyes looking directly

at you. 'How are you feeling?'

'I – don't know. Will I be fit to go on leave? My flight's booked –'

'I've got news for you, Sergeant. You're going back to Lisbon a day early. And you won't be paying for the flight.'

'I don't understand. Who's paying?'

The doctor chuckled. 'The army. You're being sent back. You'll do no more fighting in Guinea-Bissau.'

The mists in his brain seemed to clear. 'I haven't got malaria, have I?'

The doctor shook his head.

'What is it then?'

'You've had a disease of the blood. A form of purpura. We've had a couple of other cases in the last few months.'

'Did they get free trips back as well?'

The doctor shook his head. 'No. They weren't as lucky as you. You're on the mend, you see.'

'You mean – '

'Yes. You're the first one to pull through.'

VII

For a month, he lay bandaged like a mummy in the Lisbon military hospital. His legs, arms and trunk were swathed in dressings and were changed every day. When the bandages were removed, the stench from the suppurating spots was atrocious. 'Just imagine I'm an over-ripe *serra* cheese,' he would tell the male nurses who attended him. 'I may smell a bit, but I'm not all bad.'

After a few weeks his skin turned dark brown like the sodden skin of a rotten potato. He tried to keep making jokes about it, but the smell and sight of himself caused an inward shame and disgust that gave rise to periods of mental depression.

When his mother visited him the first time, they both wept. His illness had weakened him emotionally as well as physically, and he saw in her eyes the shock and fear caused by his own appearance.

379

She tried to kiss him, but he pulled away. 'No, Mother. Wait till I'm better, all right? I'm not nice to know, right now.'

Natália had come up in the world a little: she was better paid now than she had ever been, and had bought some good quality clothes at a second-hand shop in Carcavelos. She stood by his bed and looked at him, dabbing her eyes. She called him by the diminutive of his name she had used when he was a little boy. 'What have they done to you Eduardinho?' she said. 'You were so big, so strong! And look at you now!' She shook her head and struggled with fresh waves of tears.

On the day that they took the dressings off for the last time, he made his first attempt at walking since he collapsed at Bafoto six weeks before. Lurching unsteadily from bed to bed down the ward, he made his way to the mirror and looked at somebody he hardly recognised in it. The eyes had sunk into their sockets and the cheek bones, once well covered and rounded, now protruded. A grey streak had appeared in his hair, and his beard, once dark and thick, grew in a few pathetic little tufts.

He went back to bed. The dead skin over the blisters itched infuriatingly. He began to pull at it and tore it gently off strip by strip, to reveal soft pink skin underneath. For a fortnight he lay in bed pulling the old skin off and revealing the new baby tissue.

'Look, mother,' he said, and pulled his pyjama sleeve up to reveal the soft skin. 'Your new son.'

She had brought a wicker basket of things for him: some fresh milk, some cheese biscuits which she had made, a quantity of grapes, and a thin bar of chocolate.

'Mother! Chocolate! You shouldn't!'

'If I want to buy you a bar of chocolate I'll buy you a bar of chocolate. You're my only son, after all.'

She told him about her daily life at Quinta de Luz with the Van de Eifels and gossiped about the lavish dinner parties and entertainment that went on and the crises that arose in the kitchen. She never ceased to be amazed at the amount of food that was eaten.

'But they don't waste very much, I will say that. Madame is very careful.'

'Madame? What's wrong with "Senhora"?'

Natália blushed a little and adjusted her dress over her knees. 'Well. Nobody says "Senhora" down here. They only say that up north.'

A little while later, he started physiotherapy. The illness and the prolonged inactivity had reduced him to a pitiable state of weakness: he was unable to walk without support and his left arm was almost useless, having been kept in a bent position to receive plasma for so long. He had lost the tissue from his heels, and Doctor Mendes, who was in charge of his case, broke the news to him that he had in all probability suffered a loss of sexual potency. The news did not jar him at first, but as the weeks went by and he had nothing to do but think or read or listen to the radio, the realisation that he would never be able to have children of his own and perhaps might never be able to enjoy sex with a woman again caused a creeping despondency which was difficult to combat. When his mother visited he forced himself to behave like a man even if he didn't feel like one. But sometimes he would lie awake at night for hours at a time, wondering what would happen when he was declared fit. Life would never be the same again, he knew that. And he wanted, now, to leave the army and start again. Perhaps put his savings into a little *tasca*, and set up business with his mother cooking and him waiting at the tables. But these were only castles in the air: he had several years to serve yet in the army. Anything might happen: he might be sent out to Guinea again. The very thought of it made him shudder.

In the new year, he underwent several operations to graft skin from his legs to his heels, and this weakened him again. But gradually, through continued physiotherapy and improved diet, his muscles regained some of their former power, and he began to put flesh on the eight stone frame to which he had been reduced.

Cardoso paid him a surprise visit in June. He was on a month's leave, and was looking suntanned and fit after a fortnight in the Algarve.

'So you're still here!' he said. 'When are they going to let you out?'

'Oh – it'll be a month or two yet.'

381

Cardoso laughed. 'All on full pay and African allowances too, I bet! You'll be a rich man!'

'I don't know about that.'

'Any idea where you'll go when you get out?'

Eduardo shrugged. 'The medic says they may invalid me out.'

'Invalid you? What for?'

'Well. Various things. It's knocked it out of me a bit, you know.'

'So what'll you do?'

'I haven't an idea. Sell chestnuts on the streets, I expect.'

'If you're invalided, they'll have to give you a pension.'

'Some hope of that.'

Cardoso went to the window and looked out. 'That's cheerful. You've got a cemetry right under your window.' He turned. 'I don't see why you shouldn't get a pension. Wasn't your fault you got sent out to that stinking swamp. If they insist on hanging on out there they should bloody well pay the people who do the dirty work for them.'

'Getting them to pay up's a different question.'

Cardoso thought. He looked at Eduardo quizzically. 'You never know. I might be able to pull strings.'

'Strings?'

'No promises. But I'll have a go.' He took out his wallet and produced his card. 'Here. Just in case you get stuck when they chuck you out of this place. I'll be out of the army in another year. I might be able to help.'

'Thank you, sir.'

'For goodness sake! I hate being called "sir". And anyway, I should be thanking you. I reckon you saved a few lives that morning. It came out in service orders, you know. You got a commendation.'

'I never saw that.'

Cardoso shook his head. 'Typical! Still. It's the deed that counts, not the commendation, eh? That's what this country needs right now. A few more deeds and a lot less talk. This man Caetano's a dead loss. At least you knew where you stood with that old devil Salazar. But our Marcello's trying to play both ends off against the middle. One moment he's a pseudo-liberal

382

and the next he's dismissing the union leaders and playing at being a dictator. Still. I won't bore you with my theories. See you around, eh?'

They shook hands and Eduardo was left on his own again. He thought about what Cardoso had said. He had already heard a lot of rumours about industrial unrest and sabotage. Such incidents were not reported by the media, which was still heavily censored: the news was passed by word of mouth. It was known, for instance, that rising inflation was forcing the poorly paid industrial workers to turn to the only organisation that was prepared to champion their cause: the outlawed Communist party. By refusing to recognise opposition and by suppressing the truth about it, Caetano, like Salazar before him, was effectively strengthening and motivating that opposition. A growing feeling of impatience with the prime minister and his vaguely optimistic pronouncements about the African wars and the financial situation was producing a broadening base of determination that – one day – Caetano and all the trappings of his dictatorial government would have to be overthrown.

Eduardo sat on his bed and thought about all this, dimly aware that there were massive changes on the horizon: for himself as well as for Portugal.

VIII

He went before the medical *junta* at the beginning of August, just over a year after being admitted to the hospital. He put on his sergeant's uniform and found that the tunic and trousers were too big. It was like wearing another man's clothes. He waited for a quarter of an hour outside the office before he was called in. The Principal Medical Officer was there, together with Doctor Mendes, the physiotherapy specialist and a couple of civil servants. They sat behind a table and conferred together, passing Eduardo's papers back and forth. Eventually the Principal Medical Officer looked up.

383

'Very well, sergeant. We have examined your case, and it is our decision that you are no longer fit for any form of military service. As of today, you will cease to be a member of the armed forces. And in view of your record of service to Portugal and the disability you have suffered, it is the decision of this *junta* that you be recommended for the award of a disability pension. Do you have any questions?'

Eduardo shook his head, numbed by the suddeness of the news. One of the civil servants pushed a piece of paper across the table towards him and held out a ball-point pen. 'Sign here, please, to certify that you understand the decision of this *junta*.'

He signed.

The civil servant took back the piece of paper and handed it to the Principal Medical Officer.

'That's all, sergeant. You may go.'

Eduardo stood up. 'Er – may I ask a question, sir?'

'Yes?'

'Can you tell me how much pension I'll get?'

The Principal Medical Officer looked at the civil servant. The civil servant shook his head. 'It'll be the minimum, pending a further decision.'

Eduardo saluted for the last time in his life, and a few moments later found himself outside in the corridor.

That afternoon, he went out into the city and walked slowly among the crowds of Lisbon, staring into people's faces, trying to adjust himself to his new situation. He had been in the army for nearly seventeen years and now, wandering along in the heat of the afternoon, standing at corners, looking at the passers by who went up and down the Avenida de Liberdade, he felt like an alien in his own land.

He walked slowly back to the hospital: he had been allowed to stay on there until he found accommodation for himself. He returned to the ward where he had spent the last twelve months and sat on his bed, frightened and bewildered by the very independence and freedom for which he had so often longed.

384

15

I

THE NEVINS were on their way back to RAF Sutcliffe after nearly nine years. They were heading north from London in the family car, Stella at the wheel, Sam at her side and the twins, Mia and Clare, sitting in the back with Bovver.

Bovver was a black mongrel with a curly tail, who had been a member of the family since the twins were a year old. He was sitting with his slobbery chin on Stella's shoulder and keeping up a continuous mournful whine.

'Bovver's popping,' Mia said.

'Well he'll just have to pop. I'm not stopping here.'

They were travelling along a stretch of dual carriageway, and Sam was on the look-out for a stop for a picnic lunch.

'I shall be popping soon, as well,' Clare announced, a few miles later.

'You should have gone before we left,' Sam said.

'I didn't feel like it.'

Her twin sister looked at her with contempt. 'You should think, stupid.'

'I'm not stupid.'

'Yes you are.'

'For God's sake!' Stella said. 'Give it a rest.'

A turning appeared ahead.

'How about here?' Sam suggested.

Stella nodded and swung the car off the main road and along a narrow lane between fields to woodland. She took a track that led into a copse and stopped the car. 'Right, everybody out,' she said. 'This is it.'

Bovver leapt out and was followed by the twins, who ran off

385

over the leaf mould. Sam got out in slower time and stretched his legs.

'We can sit on that log,' he said. He opened the tailgate and extracted the basket with the picnic from between suitcases. Stella remained in the car, smoking a cigarette.

'You'll have some lunch?' he asked.

She waved her cigarette. 'Don't bother about me.'

He went to her. 'Let's at least put a good face on it, Stella. After all, it isn't as bad as all that.'

She turned and looked at him. 'No?'

'No, it isn't. So I'd be most grateful if you'd join us. Please.'

She got out of the car. He called the twins back. They were alike, but not identical: tall for their age with short brown hair that gave them a tomboy look.

They sat on a felled beech tree and ate hardboiled eggs, cheese and ham rolls, tomatoes and lettuce. Sam talked nonsense to the dog and made him give a paw for the ham rind. He chatted to the children and tried to include Stella in the conversation. But she was careful to make it as difficult as possible for him: she did not wish to be included.

'Would you like me to drive the rest of the way?' he asked when they were preparing to set off again.

'If you want to.'

'But would you like me to, Stella?'

She threw down her cigarette. 'It'll look better, won't it? More in keeping with the image. The new Squadron CO arrives at the wheel of his Triumph Estate, complete with dog, children and little woman.'

'All I'm asking you is whether or not you want to drive. I have no ulterior motive, and I don't give a stuff about my image.'

She shrugged. 'Do what the hell you like. You usually do.'

'Very well,' he said quietly. 'I shall drive.'

'Clare's fallen in cow muck,' Mia announced when the twins came back to the car.

'I didn't fall, you pushed me.'

'I did *not* push you!'

'Never mind,' Sam said. 'It's done now.' He collected handfuls of grass and wiped the worst off Clare's trousers. He found a newspaper for her to sit on; Bovver was persuaded back into the car, and they drove off, up the Great North Road.

He thought about himself and Stella as he drove, trying to identify the cause of the antagonism that had grown up between them. Was it his own fault? He didn't know, and in any case, he disliked the concept of 'fault' in such a situation. But all the same, he did feel that he was being forced, over and over again, to choose between his own set of ideals and Stella's increasingly radical outlook. There seemed to be a sad inevitability about it all, as if their lives were like two roads that converge and run side by side for a while before gradually diverging and separating.

Perhaps the fact that they had never had a house of their own was a major factor in the process of their gradual estrangement: it had not mattered, in the early days of their marriage, that they lived in a married quarter. Indeed, very little had mattered in those Beatle years, those all-you-need-is-love years. Sam had been the best aerobatic pilot in the RAF and Stella, having published articles in *She*, looked forward with confidence to a career in freelance journalism. On Saturday nights, they filled the house with her university and journalist friends from Leeds. There had been parties that lasted until dawn, at which large quantities of spaghetti bolognaise had been washed down by even larger quatities of cheap Italian wine. They had been able to laugh, then, at the petty gossip of the married patch, because they did not regard themselves as part of it. The Nevins, they were sure, were destined to go onward and upward.

After their first tour in RAF Sutcliffe, they had gone to RAF Bittersfield in East Anglia, where Sam was a flight commander on a Lightning squadron. In order to avoid the strain and extra cost of a long drive to work every day, they chose once again to live in service quarters. Then, three years later when they were posted to Gütersloh in Germany, there was no question of living off the camp.

It was while he was at Gütersloh that Sam won the Air Force Cross. He did this by delaying his ejection from a Lightning that was going out of control to the last possible second in order to prevent the aircraft crashing into a built-up area. When he came back from the presentation ceremony at Buckingham Palace he was suddenly aware that his opinions counted for more among his equals and seniors. It began to dawn on him that perhaps he might make a real success of his career in the Air Force. But this realisation sowed the seed of dissension between himself and Stella, for he now laughed less and less at himself and the system and instead began to take both more seriously.

Stella reacted against this new tendency in him: she took an increasing pride in flouting mess rules and shocking neighbours. In the early days of their marriage he had been proud of her outlandish behaviour and healthy disrespect for authority. Now, it began to get him into trouble: mess presidents took him aside and advised him that his wife should modify her language. Next-door neighbours complained about her sometimes embarrassing way of telling their children the whole truth, and on one occasion he was presented with a bill for ninety pounds because Stella had painted the Ministry of Defence furniture in their married quarter white – over the French polish.

They went to London in 1970 after their tour in Germany. By now, they had been overtaken by the property boom, and Sam could not afford a mortgage without accepting a massive drop in their living standards. They went into married quarters at Stanmore.

The news of Sam's posting back to RAF Sutcliffe had come as the last straw to Stella, and at first she had told him that he could go by himself. He had managed to talk her out of that attitude however, and she now accompanied him in a state of smouldering rebellion.

As they drove north, the sky became overcast, and a little drizzle set in. They by-passed Newark-on-Trent, Pontefract and Doncaster, and Sam talked to the twins about slag heaps, liquorice and horse racing. They turned off the trunk road and drove along familiar roads through Tadcaster to York and on to RAF Sutcliffe.

Their address was 16, Brabazon Avenue. It was drizzling when they arrived, and they were welcomed by their new next-door neighbour, Wendy Cheetham. She came out to them wearing a red anorak and electric blue trousers.

'Welcome to sunny Sutcliffe!' she said.

She gave them the key to the front door and they let themselves in. There were trunks and tea-chests in the hall and downstairs rooms, and the house had that dead smell of distemper and polish that can only be experienced on taking up tenancy in a service married quarter. In the kitchen, all the pots, pans, crockery and kitchen utensils had been laid out as if for inspection. In the living room, the curtains and covers and carpets were of identical designs to those of the married quarter they had vacated in Stanmore that morning.

Clare was made to change her trousers, and the twins went outside to explore. Bovver also went out. He trotted up and down, leaving his card here and there on the gateposts of neighbouring houses.

When Stella and Sam had been unpacking for nearly an hour, there was a knock on the door. It was a woman in a sheepskin coat with a silk scarf over her head.

'I'm sorry to trouble you when you're settling in,' she said, 'but I think you're the owners of a black mongrel, aren't you?'

Stella nodded. 'Yes. We are.'

The woman smiled unhappily. 'I'm Mary Benwick, the Group Captain's wife. I'm afraid your dog has got at ours. She's on heat, you see, and – ' She turned. 'I don't know how she got out, but they're doing it. I tried to catch them, but they ran off.'

Sam said, 'Where are they?'

'In the field. She's a pedigree cocker, you see, and we really don't want – '

He was already on his way out of the house. He ran along the road, past 8, Trenchard Drive where they had lived when they were first married. He saw children playing in the field and beyond them the dogs.

When he reached them, they were locked. Something seemed to snap inside him. He kicked Bovver hard, in an attempt to separate them, but was unsuccessful. He kicked again, and again, and again. They separated, and the cocker bitch screamed with pain. He was shaking with anger. He took

389

one last running kick at Bovver, then grabbed him by the scruff of the neck and dragged him all the way back to Brabazon Avenue. He shut him in the tool shed, then returned to the living room.

'There was no need to kick him like that,' Stella said.

He was sweaty and slightly out of breath. 'How else was I to separate them?'

'If you can't separate them without using force it's too late anyway,' she said. 'Besides, I bet you wouldn't have laid into him like that if it had been a corporal's cocker spaniel, would you?'

'I don't know about that.'

'I do.'

They returned to the task of unpacking. Outside, the drizzle turned to rain. Stella called the twins in and they were sent up for their bath. When they came down in their dressing gowns, Sam was changing the plug on a fan heater and Stella was reading the *Guardian*.

'Have you let Bovver out yet?' Mia asked.

'Not yet.'

'When will you?'

'Tonight, probably. Or possibly tomorrow morning.'

Clare said: 'It wasn't really his fault, was it Daddy?'

Stella looked up. He was aware of the three of them watching him, waiting for his answer.

'Okay, okay,' he said. 'Let him out, I don't mind.'

The twins rushed out and he heard them open the shed door. Then Mia called, 'Mum!'

'What is it?'

'He's ill!'

They went to the shed together. Bovver was lying on his side, his eyes dull. He had vomited a quantity of blood.

Stella turned to him. 'Satisfied now?' she asked.

II

16 Brabazon Avenue
RAF Sutcliffe
York.
21st September 1972

Dear Phil,

I've been trying to get you on the phone but no joy, you're always out or lecturing or at a conference, so hence this note.

Well. Guess what, we're back at dear old bloody Sutcliffe. It's all happened rather suddenly. Sam has been smooth-talked into accepting command of a squadron here because they're telling him that providing he keeps on using Old Spice they'll make him a Wingco, and of course that's an offer he can't refuse. So here we are and here we are and here we are again. We have this really nice semi-det. res. (ha!) with nice furniture and nice mock-regency curtains and nice shit-coloured carpets. We have a nice stretch of lumpy lawn and nice hardy annuals that are doing nicely in the nice clay amid the nice groundsel and buttercup.

Our neighbours? You've guessed, haven't you. They're really nice. Mike and Wendy Cheetham (air traffic control) to the right of us and Bob and June Veal (Tech. wing) to the left. And lots of lovely kiddies that play mothers and fathers and tell tales and catch colds like every well brought up service kiddy is supposed to do. The social life: no change from Bittersfield, Gütersloh or Stanmore. Classified by function: mess functions, instructors' functions, students' functions and (say it softly) Other Ranks' functions. Not forgetting the private functions of course, which include Tupperware mornings, Avon mornings and dear old come-for-coffee mornings.

I'm afraid I'm not a very good wife. Good Wives attend coffee mornings and give better coffee mornings in return. They chat at the NAAFI shop and bring their second-hand clothes (which never look second-hand) to the Nearly New. They talk about kiddies and batwomen and the price of Weetabix, and sometimes they have babies, which always turn out to be Gifted.

There are, I regret to say, Bad Wives. Bad Wives drink Cyprus sherry for elevenses and have nervous breakdowns. They wear dark glasses when it's raining and their husbands smell of dirty dishes (that's because they're married to them). They have nearly

empty bottles of Valium hidden behind the cough mixture in the
bathroom, and everybody knows all about their problems, which
are discussed behind their backs at great length at all the better
coffee parties.

Got the picture?

Well anyway, anyway. You know how I hate writing letters. The
whole point of this one really is to say 'hi' and 'c'mon over' in the
best mid-Atlantic tradition. Perhaps – to be a little less pseud for a
change – it is a sort of cry for help. The voice of one crying in the
wilderness, as you might say. I won't bang on, but would like to
share your wit and intellect over a spag bol one of these evenings
when Sam is doing airborne circles in his red and silver Noddy car.
Our tel. no. is Sutcliffe 6314, so give us a ring, love. Okay?

Duty is about to call. I have to go to York to collect Mia and
Clare. (Remember Jawkins and Digby?) They're getting big now:
private school/grey flannel uniforms/stripey hatbands/little fiends
(sic) to tea, etc.

There's lots more news but I won't bore you further. We had to
put my best beloved bog dog down the other day. Family tragedy,
but it was all for the good of the Service, so that was nice.

See you sometime, I hope. I am up to my tits in trivia, Phil.
Come and unwind me: your calming presence is urgently needed.

Luv,
Stella.

III

'What you've failed to grasp,' Phillida Davis said, 'is that Stella
needs to escape from the whole middle-class conformity bit.'

'You mean she's fed up,' Sam said.

'No I *don't* mean she's fed up. That's a typically masculine
reaction. Just because she's a woman, you have to belittle her,
don't you?'

They were in the married quarter sitting room. Sam had
come back unexpectedly early from night flying, and was
eating cottage pie off a tray. Stella was listening to the
argument with inner amusement, not contributing very much
to it, but happy to let Phillida take her part.

'So what do you suggest I do?' Sam asked. 'Buy a guitar?'

392

'Isn't he witty!' Stella said. 'That was a real corker!'

Phillida leant forward in her chair. 'You can't help revealing yourself, can you? You see, the reason you're grinning like that is that you're completely immersed in the ethic of male dominance. At the end of the day, women don't matter to you, do they? That's what this is all about.'

Sam took a gulp of beer. 'Aren't we just talking about the frustrated wife syndrome?'

'No we're not,' Phillida said. 'It goes much deeper than that. You see you're quite happy as you are. You don't feel trapped the way Stella does. You've never experienced the frustration of knowing that you want to change and yet having to suppress and drive back that need.'

Sam turned to Stella. 'Have I ever prevented you from doing anything you wanted?'

'The family has,' Phillida said. 'And your whole attitude indicates that you consider it right and proper that it should.'

'But then you've always been anti-marriage, haven't you?'

'When it means the abdication by the woman of the right to become herself, yes. And that's what's happening to Stella.'

'Who said anything about abdication?'

'Your whole attitude says it. In your eyes, Stella is a piece of property. *Your* wife. Everything you say indicates a willingness on your part to regard her as a thing. And in order to be what you regard as a "good wife" she has to accept that role.'

Sam topped up his beer tankard. He glanced at Stella. You didn't have to get married in the first place,' he said. 'And I seem to remember it was you who suggested it.'

'That's a totally invalid argument,' Phillida said. 'You are now making the woman responsible for her own predicament – a predicament that is forced upon her by a male-dominated society. You only have to look at your own married life to see that. Stella is forced to play a satellite role. She has no option but to remain within your orbit. She is tied to you.'

'Shackled,' Stella said. 'With links of high-tensile steel.'

He looked from one to the other. Stella sat in an arm chair, her legs drawn up under her, nursing a glass of whisky. Phillida sat like a farmer, knees apart, the smoke from her cigarette rising in a long trail. He had had brief meetings with her during the previous months. She had founded an organisation called 'Refuge' in aid of the underprivileged, and Stella had been helping at the headquarters in Leeds twice a week since the beginning of October. Since that time he had become increasingly aware that she was deliberately drawing away from him, and he had no doubt that Phillida was giving her every encouragement. A tension had built up between them so that it was now a relief to get out of the house in the morning and away from the silent hostility she used against him. He knew, now, what real loneliness was: as the commanding officer of a squadron he found it difficult to be on intimate terms with anyone: he was a god to the students, 'Boss' to the instructors, a competitor with other squadron commanders and a loyal subordinate to his seniors. Service life had forced him into what Phillida had called a structured existence, an existence which ran happily along on the camaraderie of the crew room or bar, but one which provided little outlet for the strain of a marriage going out of control.

'Look,' he said gently, striving to get the conversation back to amicable terms. 'When we got married, we agreed that we would make a life together. There was never any question of any sort of abdication. Ever.'

'There never is,' said Phillida, the light by the television reflected momentarily in her glasses. 'That's what's so shitty about marriage. It brainwashes the innocent into an acceptance of what is, quintessentially, a confidence trick.'

He controlled a sudden impulse to argue more forcefully. 'I was under the impression that we loved each other and wanted to share our life together.'

'No doubt you were. And it's worked very nicely for you, hasn't it? You've been able to sublimate your achievement urges by flying aeroplanes upside down, taking charge, giving orders. The trouble is, you're not content with that. Once the ego becomes inflated, and our society is geared to the inflation of men's egos, its appetite becomes voracious. And in order to satisfy the craving for ego-satisfaction you destroy Stella as a person by forcing her to be subservient to you.'

He finished his supper and put the plate back on the tray. 'Well,' he said. 'All I can say is – I haven't been to university,

394

nor am I versed in the intricacies of modern sociology, but it seems to me that women are better suited to bringing up children and making homes than men are, and when they accept that role they're usually a lot happier for it. So are the children, for that matter.'

'Big Daddy has spoken,' Stella said. 'They gave him the AFC, you know. It stands for Awfully Fine Chap.'

He smiled. 'I'm not quite the ogre you make me out to be, Stella.'

'Aren't you?' Phillida said. 'In that case, when are you going to do something for Refuge?'

He shrugged. 'I don't know. I haven't been asked.'

'What if I ask you now?'

'Try me. I'm always open to suggestion.'

Phillida stubbed out her cigarette and lit another. 'We're organising a sponsored walk,' she said. 'Next Easter.'

'You want me to join in?'

'Not necessarily. But we want you to get other people to walk.'

'Lots of other people,' Stella said.

'Like – the whole of this place. All those students of yours.'

'What is this? Am I being manoeuvred into a corner?'

'You said you were open to suggestion,' Phillida said. 'You don't have to do much. Just encourage people to participate. It's a very good cause.'

'I might be able to fix something,' he said. 'Have to get the go-ahead from the Station Commander first, of course.'

'Oh – of course,' Stella echoed.

'It could be very good for your public image,' Phillida said. 'If you could get it off the ground. I mean – the RAF would actually be seen to be doing something useful for a change. For the community.'

'Instead of roaring around at two hundred feet frightening minks and making admirals eat their young,' Stella added.

Sam grinned. 'Where's this walk happening?'

'Are you interested?'

'I don't see why not.'

'It's nation-wide,' Phillida said. 'We're calling it "Walk for Refuge". It'll be a really big thing.'

395

'Have you asked any of the other RAF stations?'

Phillida looked quickly at Stella. 'Could we?'

'I could,' Sam said. 'Given the necessary clearance. I could send out letters to every single RAF station in the country.'

'That'd be great!'

He was flattered by her sudden enthusiasm. 'No promises of course, but I could try. I'll have a word with Benwick.' He stood up. 'Look – I've got an early start in the morning, so if you don't mind I'll leave you two to it. I know you'll want to talk into the small hours. So if you'll excuse me, Phil – '

'Oh – sure – '

He kissed Stella on the cheek, then picked up the supper tray. 'I'll wash this lot up,' he said. 'You can chalk it up as another victory for Women's Lib.' He hesitated a moment, looking in vain for a hint of warmth from Stella. 'Well. Goodnight, both.'

After he left the room, Stella drained her whisky and poured another. There was silence, during which they exchanged a glance.

'Are you making it with him these days?' Phillida asked.

Stella laughed shortly. 'Christ, no!' she said. 'We haven't slept together for yonks!'

IV

Group Captain Bruce Benwick, the Station Commander of RAF Sutcliffe, was a tall, narrowly built officer with eyebrows that looked as though they might have been plucked and facial skin that appeared to have been given a daily treatment of wet-and-dry emery paper.

He was in almost every way a meticulous officer: his confidential reports referred to him repeatedly as an excellent staff officer and one who expressed himself with great clarity on paper. Certainly, a split infinitive was as abhorrent to him as an untied shoelace or an airman who failed to salute. His aim in life was to be the ideal officer, and he gave the impression of always acting a part: when he was at home, he acted the part of perfect husband, father or host; when at work, he became a model Group Captain, and when at the helm of his twenty-six-foot yacht, he became the sort of yachtsman that every yachtsman should aspire to be.

His office was at the end of a highly polished corridor in the administration block of RAF Sutcliffe. Its sash windows overlooked the neatly trimmed lawns and freshly painted white kerbs, the well-hoed rose gardens and the main gate, where an RAF corporal in white belt and gaiters stood on duty.

'Come in, Nevin,' he said when he saw Sam at the door. 'What can we do for you?'

Sam Nevin said good morning and accepted a seat.

'An unusual request, sir,' he said.

'Oh?'

'I don't know if you're aware of the fact, but my wife does voluntary work for an organization called "Refuge".'

'Does she indeed? Good for her.'

Sam outlined the proposal of the sponsored walk. Benwick listened to him with studied attention. When he had finished, the Group Captain remained silent for several seconds.

'I see,' he said carefully.

'I thought it might provide a useful link with the local population, sir. Handled properly, it might be very good for the public image of the service, too.'

'Indeed it might, Sam.' Group Captain Benwick pushed his chair back from the wide, teak desk and went to the window. 'I think we would do well to get clearance from Group HQ before going ahead,' he said carefully. 'Would you agree?'

'Entirely, sir. I was going to suggest it.'

'Right you are, then. Put it on paper and we'll submit it through the proper channels. Fair enough?'

'Certainly, sir. Thank you very much indeed, sir.'

Benwick nodded to dismiss him. 'Excellent,' he said. 'Well done.'

Nevin departed. It was eleven minutes past ten. In four minutes time, Benwick reflected, his corporal would bring him a cup of coffee and he would take a few minutes off to read the latest *Flight* magazine. He listened to Nevin's footsteps recede down the passage. In five days' time, his daughter would be home from boarding school for the Christmas holidays. If he looked diagonally out of the window, he could see his own front door: No. 1, The Green. His wife's red mini was still parked outside, which meant that she had not yet departed for her weekly hair appointment. Ah. There she was now. He watched her put the shopping basket in the back, get in behind the steering wheel, drive off. Then he heard a movement behind him.

'Coffee, sir.'

'Ah. Thank you corporal. Excellent. Well done.'

He sat at his desk and took out the magazine. He stirred his coffee slowly and evenly, reflecting that all in all, life was very pleasant indeed.

V

Sam took great trouble over the wording of the written proposal that was to be forwarded to Group Headquarters. He made several drafts of it before having it typed. He submitted it under cover of a formal letter to the Station Commander whose obedient servant he had the honour to be.

He heard nothing until the new year, when he was rung up by the station adjutant. 'This charity walk do of yours, Sam,' he said. 'We've had a call from Group. The Air Vice Marshall's happy for you to go ahead, but he doesn't want you to mention the fact that he's given his blessing, okay? Otherwise the press might latch on to it as an officially sanctioned function, which of course it isn't. Got the message?'

He bore the news home in triumph that evening. 'We've got the green light,' he told Stella. 'So the next thing is to send out letters to the world and his wife.'

She was cutting up meat for a stew. She threw the cubes of beef into a saucepan as she cut them. He watched her for a moment.

'Well,' he said. 'Aren't you pleased?'

'What am I supposed to be pleased about?'

'The fact that we're going ahead with it. Doing something.'

She snorted. 'I find it rather pathetic that you had to ask permission in the first place.'

'Och! That's the RAF, Stella. We have to live with it.'

'Yes. Don't we just.'

'I thought you'd show a little more enthusiasm,' he said. 'After all – I'm doing this more for your sake than anything else. Had you realised that?'

'Oh – sure, sure. Let's hope you pick up a few Brownie points on the way. Tax-free bonus.'

She finished cutting up the meat, and now shook flour over it to prepare it for frying.

'Don't you want to improve things between us?' he asked.

She took the saucepan of stewing steak to the electric cooker and switched on the electric ring. 'We're on that again, are we?'

'Yes, we are. Maybe it sounds stupid, but I still love you, you know.'

She stirred the meat with a wooden spoon. 'It does sound a bit stupid, yes.'

'Do you actually hate me, or is it just dislike?'

'I find this conversation boring,' she said. 'After all, we've had it so many times before, haven't we?'

He went to her, put his arm round her. 'I'm not going to give up, Stella. I *do* love you. I'm going to bring you through this, and we'll both be stronger for it.'

The electric ring glowed red hot, and the meat sizzled. She turned and looked at him with her steel-blue eyes.

'Look,' she said, 'If you want to make yourself useful, you can lay the table. Okay?'

VI

She hated him for his perseverance, his tolerance and his willingness to forgive; and she hated herself for treating him the way she did. She hated the RAF for preventing him from becoming what she wanted him to be, and she hated him for upholding all that was good and right and traditional about

399

service life. She hated his uniform, she hated his short haircut, she hated his moustache. She hated his ties and his suits, his RAF cufflinks which his mother had given him and his electric razor which shed bristles on the washbasin every morning. She hated his aftershave lotion and his brush and comb, his polished brown shoes and his worn Hush Puppies. She hated it when he said how much he enjoyed the food she cooked, the way he said 'that was excellent', and the way he offered to wipe up. What had happened? What had gone wrong? Was there such a thing as 'wrong'? She didn't know, she didn't understand. They were out of touch, no longer able to communicate. She had dreamt, only a few nights ago, that she was trying to climb a steep hill which started to slip down beneath her feet. She had looked back, while rocks and earth gave way under foot. She was nearly at the top, but the top itself seemed to be crumbling, slipping down. She had looked back, and seen Sam and the twins, far away below her. They were standing, waving to her, shouting to her to give up, come down. That was how it was. The dream needed no analysis. She was on her own private landslide.

VII

He went ahead with the arrangements for the Refuge walk with unabated enthusiasm during the early months of 1973. He sent a letter out to every RAF station in the country inviting officers in command to look favourably on the project and to encourage volunteers to take part. He visited the Refuge office in Leeds to meet Phillida and to discuss the distribution of 'Walk for Refuge' stickers and the sponsorship forms. He made himself personally responsible for drumming up support at RAF Sutcliffe, and the list of volunteers and sponsors lengthened steadily as the weeks passed.

By mid-March, over three thousand pounds had been pledged for the walk as a result of his efforts. And because he and Stella had not had a verbal battle for a week or so, he began to believe that their relationship was improving.

He came into her room one morning before he went off to work. He sat on the double bed in which she slept alone. 'Things are getting a bit better, aren't they?' he asked.

She gave a little laugh of disparagement.

'I've had an idea,' he said. 'I thought we might buy the twins a puppy for their birthday. What do you think? One of those English setters.'

She shook her head. 'I'm not having another dog.'

'Stella! Why not?'

'Why not?' she repeated. 'Because I don't want to, that's why not.' She got out of bed abruptly and put on her dressing gown. She drew the curtains back a little and looked out into the half light. She was nearly thirty-three now, and had gained weight over the past few years.

'If only you could let go,' he said. 'Love and be loved. It would make life so much easier.'

'That's all you think about, isn't it? "Making life easier".'

'You know what I mean.'

'Yes,' she replied quietly. 'That's the trouble. I know exactly what you mean.'

Later that day he received a message from the adjutant to say that the Station Commander wanted to see him.

Group Captain Benwick bade him enter and shut the door.

'I've just received a rather disturbing piece of information from Group,' he said, and twirled a silver propelling pencil between his finger tips. 'It's about this charity walk affair.'

Nevin sat on the edge of his chair. 'Sir?'

'Do you know a woman called Phillida Davis?'

'Yes, sir. She's a friend of Stella's.'

Benwick's sparse eyebrows rose to two points. 'Is she indeed? I understand she's the driving force behind Refuge.'

'She founded it, sir.'

The Group Captain put his propelling pencil down and folded his hands together. 'Were you aware that she is an active member of the IMG?'

'IMG, sir?'

'International Marxist Group.'

Nevin's mouth opened then closed again. The colour drained from his normally reddish cheeks. 'No, sir,' he said. 'I hadn't realised that.'

'Well she is. We have it on good authority.'

Benwick allowed his words to sink in, and for several seconds neither spoke. On the airfield, a Jet Provost was having an engine run; the sash windows vibrated as the revs went up to full power.

'We're going to have to call off this walk of yours,' Benwick said. 'For reasons which I hope are obvious.'

Sam nodded. 'Yes, sir. I see that.'

'How deeply committed are we?'

'Well, sir, I've had replies from a large number of stations. And we've got over sixty volunteers to walk here at Sutcliffe.'

Benwick put finger and thumb to the bridge of his nose and squeezed. Then he opened a drawer of his desk and took out a piece of paper. He turned the tip of his propelling pencil until the lead appeared, and prepared to write.

'Let's see,' he said. 'We must put out another letter.' He spoke the words aloud as he wrote, as if dictating to himself. 'Owing to a misunderstanding, it is regretted that support for—what's this walk called?'

' "Walk for Refuge", sir.'

'. . . support for the Walk for Refuge is no longer considered to be in the best interests of the service.'

Benwick paused, looked at the ceiling, at Sam and at the picture of a Vulcan bomber that hung upon the wall. Then he continued: 'For this reason, officers in command are advised that any support given to the walk should not be as a result of official encouragement. While individuals remain at liberty to take part, it must be emphasised that they do so on a private basis and as a result of their own volition. Broadsheets and advertisements concerning this function should be removed from noticeboards, and no further information should be provided from service sources.' Benwick paused, then added a second paragraph: 'Individuals who have already volunteered to walk or to sponsor walkers, should be advised that if they still wish to participate, they should make their own private arrangements.'

He looked at what he had written, and added a capital letter here, a comma there. 'Now,' he said, 'I want this letter sent out over your signature. We must keep it in a low key, you understand?'

402

'Yes, sir.'

'Good. And show me the letter before you actually send it out.'

'Will do, sir.'

'Very unfortunate, this. But there we are. Of course your wife's involved with this Refuge business herself, isn't she?'

'To a certain extent, yes, sir.'

'Mmmm. Well if I were you I'd steer her out of it. No need to say anything about this Davis woman's political inclinations. Just say – just say there are political ramifications. Something like that. I'm sure she'll understand.' The Group Captain handed Sam the letter. 'There we are. Let's get it out as soon as possible.'

Nevin took the piece of paper with Benwick's even copperplate writing on it and walked away down the polished corridor and out into the March wind. He walked past the rose gardens between the white kerbs and up the steps to the officers' mess.

In the entrance lobby, he stopped and looked up at the portraits of the Queen and Prince Philip; he stared up at them, as if they might be able to tell him how to break the news to Stella.

VIII

When he arrived home he found Stella reading the *Guardian*, which was spread out on the kitchen table. He came in at the back door wearing his uniform overcoat and carrying a brief case. He took off his cap.

'Hi,' he said, sounding deliberately casual.

Stella did not look up. 'Hi,' she replied without the slightest trace of warmth in her voice.

He paused a moment, then went upstairs to change. When he came down she was still reading the paper.

'Twins at Brownies?' he asked.

'Yes.'

'Bad news,' he said. 'We've hit a snag over the Walk.'

She continued to read. 'What sort of snag?'

'We're going to have to play it down.'

'Who's "we"?'

'Well. Me, basically. Benwick had me into his office. Group's getting cold feet. I think they're getting concerned about the publicity angle.'

'Too much or not enough?'

'The wrong sort. Political ramifications is the okay phrase.' He produced Benwick's letter. 'I'm going to have to send this out.'

He put the letter down in front of her. She took her time reading it, eventually saying, 'Who wrote this?'

'Benwick.'

'I thought you said you were going to send it.'

'I am.'

'So it's your idea, is it?'

'No. The objection came from Group, originally. But we want to keep it low key.'

'Wait a minute. You mean *you're* going to sign this?'

He nodded, yes.

'You're going to sign a letter drafted by your boss, who drafted it because he was told to by his boss. Is that right?'

He shrugged uncomfortably. 'It's the way the system works, Stella.'

'Bugger the system,' she said. 'Why didn't you tell him to get stuffed? Sign his own bloody letter.'

'I'd have liked to. But I didn't have very much choice in the matter, did I?'

'You mean you didn't have the guts to exercise any choice.'

He felt his temper beginning to rise. 'I don't think this was a question of guts.'

'Wasn't it? If you weren't so shit scared of not getting promoted to Wing Commander I bet you'd have argued the toss soon enough.'

She returned to her newspaper.

'All right,' he said, 'I'll admit that promotion is a factor. But I happen to believe, unlike you, that loyalty and obedience don't necessarily add up to a lack of guts.'

She turned a page and began reading the editorial. 'I'm not talking about loyalty and obedience,' she said. 'I'm talking

404

about sycophancy and being a yes-man.'

In a strange, almost frightening way, he enjoyed this argument: it was as if the differences between them were at last being laid bare, like the backbone of a filleted fish. He experienced a slightly breathless feeling of elation, an awareness that he actually believed in what he was saying.

'I appreciate that my career is unimportant to you,' he said. 'And I appreciate that authority in any form is anathema to you. Perhaps you might do well to understand that my career is important to me, and that because I have authority over others, I am able to respect it in those above me.'

She said nothing. His pulse was racing now. He wanted to force her to understand, make her see how he felt.

'Stop reading that damn newspaper and listen to me,' he said.

She ignored him. His heart beat thumped in his chest. 'You see you could just be wrong,' he heard himself say. 'There may be factors in this business that you know nothing whatsoever about. It is just possible that Stella, the infallible Stella, may have made a mistake. It may be that I am not quite as gutless as you think. It may even be that you should have had your bottom smacked a very long time ago.'

'Ah,' she said, still appearing to read the newspaper. 'The old bottom-smacking bit. The authoritarian streak coming out again. When in doubt – '

He snatched the paper away from her, tearing it where her elbow rested on it. She looked up.

'Please don't do that.'

It was as if somebody else were doing what he did, saying what he said. He balled up the newspaper and threw it down. 'Shall I tell you something? Shall I?'

She looked amused. She shrugged. 'Please do.'

'All right. I shall. There are good reasons for backing out of this walk. Reasons that I'm not prepared to tell you about. And if that makes you think the less of me, well – so be it. Because I'm beginning to care less about what you think. You're not the bloody marvel I once thought you. I am beginning to realise that it does not take a superior intellect to stay up until three in the morning drinking cups of coffee. I am beginning to suspect that perhaps a degree in sociology is not the be all and end all. I am actually beginning to realise that I prefer my own sense of values to other people's trendy ideas. So if you want to go and be a women's libber with your lefty friend Phillida, I'll wish you the best of luck. Because if you think I'm going to be your fellow traveller, you're wrong.' He paused for breath.

She stood up. 'I'm going out,' she said. 'Do I have to ask your permission?'

He was standing between her and the door. 'Stella,' he said. 'Wait a minute. I'd like to talk this out.'

She laughed. 'Christ! You mean there's more of that crap?' She shook her head, tried to push past him.

He caught her arm, but she flung it aside and went out of the kitchen and upstairs. He went after her, caught her as she was entering the bedroom. He felt shaky now, out of control. He wasn't entirely aware of what he was saying. He had hold of her by the arms and was trying to make her listen to him. He was saying, 'Stella! Listen!' and his voice sounded oddly high-pitched to himself. He was shaking her, gripping her arms as tightly as he could. And then, without giving any warning, she brought her knee up hard into his groin and the pain made him gasp and double up.

She left the room very quickly after that. He was still sitting on the bed and recovering from the pain when he heard the car drive off.

IX

'Make the break,' Phillida said. 'Do it. You know you won't regret it. You'll be free again. Able to be yourself.'

They were sitting in Phillida's living room, which was lit by candlelight. A record played softly in the background.

'I know it sounds trite,' Stella said, 'but I'm concerned about the kids. I don't want them hurt.'

'Why don't you ask them? Talk to them about it. Tell them. They're old enough. Christ! It's a marvellous opportunity to get on their wavelength. They'll thank you for it. You'll have paid them the compliment of treating them as adults. You can give them the choice: to stay with their Pa or go with you.'

Stella put her head back on the corduroy covered sofa and closed her eyes. 'When you actually come to the decision it's – more difficult than you expect. It shouldn't be, I know. But somehow it's like taking out a knife and cutting your own flesh.'

'In order to arrive there, to arrive where you are,' Phillida quoted, 'to get from where you are not, you must go by a way wherein there is no ecstasy.'

Stella opened her eyes. 'Thank you. Yes.'

'You can't seriously believe that you can continue the way things are. Or can you?'

Stella stared at the ceiling and said, half to herself. 'I think it has to be the end of the road. I mean – even if he did achieve his ambition, can you see me as a Group Captain's wife? We disagree on everything. His career. Politics. The kids. He's even started going to church again.'

'Yes, and the next thing he'll be doing is taking Mia and Clare with him.'

'We had our first real argument over them, you know. When they were a few months old. He objected because I had them in bed with me. You know how sensual babies are. How they love body contact.'

'And how they need it.'

'Exactly. Well, Sam the Ham didn't like it. Offended his instincts, he said. Wasn't quite on, don't you know. We bloody nearly came to blows over that, as well.'

Neither of them spoke for some while. The record came to an end and Phillida, in a long loose dress, padded barefoot across the room to change it. When she had done so she turned and Stella looked up at her.

'You've made up you mind, haven't you?'

Stella nodded. 'Yes. I've decided.'

The voice of Bob Dylan filled the room. Phillida got out the whisky, and they drank to the future.

He made his own breakfast the following morning and left the house early, before Stella and the twins were awake. He had a full day: one of the flying courses was ending, and he was involved in three final handling tests – flights that required a lot of preparation and debriefing. During his lunch hour, he managed to visit the Administration Wing to have the letter typed, and it was ready for collection that evening before he returned home.

He walked back across the stretch of grass between the airfield and the married quarters, and along Trenchard Drive to Brabazon Avenue. He let himself in by the back door.

Stella was out: she had presumably gone to collect the twins from school. He made himself a cup of tea, and ate a piece of toasted brown bread and honey. It was a relief to have the house to himself. Life had become an unending battle. He finished his tea and washed up the cup and saucer, the knife and the plate. He put away the milk, the honey and the butter, and wiped up some spilt sugar from the kitchen table, before going into the sitting room to watch the six o'clock news on television.

It was then that he found the letter. It was propped up on top of the television set and was addressed simply, 'Sam,' and read:

> I've decided to pull out. No need to state reasons, is there? Just– I've had enough and don't want to drag things out. I talked to M & C this morning and asked them whether they would like to come with me or stay with you, and they chose to come with me. So there we are. We're going to Oporto for a few weeks and after that, well, we'll see. Please don't do the pleading bit, will you, because it won't work. Better to make a clean cut now. It was good while the good part lasted, but no hope of getting that back.
>
> Goodbye
Stella.

He stared out of the window.

It had happened again: for the second time in his life, his wife had walked out on him. He felt a heaviness, a drooping of the spirit. What would happen to Mia and Clare, he wondered.

He turned away from the window and sat down on the sofa. He put his head in his hands and stared at the carpet. His thoughts went round and round. He remembered odd little moments of love and happiness: moments when he had considered himself to be so lucky to have Stella as his wife and those children as his children.

When the tears came, he did not try to stop them. They flowed silently for a long time. But that did not matter: there was no one to see the Commanding Officer of number one squadron weeping in his married quarter sitting room, nor would there be, for a long time to come.

XI

Stella and the twins had gone by taxi to Leeds, where they had spent the first night at Phillida Davis's flat before going down to London. Stella sent a telegram to her father saying 'ARRIVING PM SATURDAY WITH TWINS DON'T BOTHER TO MEET EXPLANATION LATER LOVE STELLA,' and now, after a five hour delay at Heathrow, they were going through immigration at Oporto airport.

Stella led the way out to the taxi rank. It was a windy night: the blown clouds made the stars seem to move at great speed and Clare, looking up at them, was nearly left behind.

'Come *on*!' Stella said. 'Why must you always lag behind?'

The taxi driver cleared his nose and spat out of his window before driving off. Clare held her Panda up to the window as the night rushed by. They descended towards the sea, and you could make out the lights of fishing boats a few miles out. The taxi swayed as the wheels became stuck in the tram lines, and to the right the entrance to the River Douro came into view.

The taxi turned off the main road and up into the suburb of Foz do Douro. Stella grumbled. 'He's come the long way,' she said. 'We could have gone up the Boa Vista.'

They turned right down a drive that was lined with pine trees that made an arch overhead, and pulled up outside an imposing building with dormer windows in the top storey and ancient wisteria that clamboured round the front porch and clung, like a huge gnarled hand, to the stucco walls.

Joy welcomed them in the hall. Clare was a little bit scared of Joy. She was always very neat: she wore a blouse whose sleeves were loose and creamy; her hair looked like a silver wig, and when she kissed you her pearls swung forward and hit you on the chest.

'My dear girl!' she said to Stella, looking at the pile of luggage the taxi driver had brought in. 'You look as though you've come to stay!'

'We have,' Mia said. 'Didn't you know, Gran?'

Having been kissed, Clare looked about the hall. She could just remember it from her last visit, nearly three years before. It was a dangerous hall – in fact the whole house was dangerous – in that you had to be very careful not to knock things over. Anything you knocked over was almost bound to be extremely valuable. Last time, she had knocked a blue vase off a stand and there had been a terrible atmosphere of tight-lipped tolerance in the house for some time afterwards because the vase had been Ming dynasty and quite irreplacable.

At the end of the hall was a large portrait in oils with a little light over it which Joy always switched on when it got dark and switched off when she went up to bed. The portrait was of Rosalinde Teape, and Clare knew this, because she had been named after her. The painting portrayed Miss Remington at the age of twenty-seven: this was in 1888, the year the Suez Canal was completed, and the young lady looked down out of her picture with that massive self-confidence in the rightness of things that Victorian England bestowed upon the sons and daughters of the privileged classes.

The others had gone on into the drawing room, and Stella was calling her in. She entered the large room with its cabinets and glass and porcelain, its Persian carpets, its furniture with curved legs and clawed feet, and there was Grandpa, his hands stretched out to greet her, his hair close-cropped and completely white, his breath whistling even more noisily in his nostrils than she had remembered. He pressed her cheek to his, which was excitingly bristly. He put his hand round her waist and pulled her towards his chair on one side, doing the same to Mia (who resisted) on the other.

'How are my favourite girlfriends?' he asked. 'Eh?'

Stella and Joy had been talking about something else, and Joy now turned and said, 'I expect you'd like to get these two straight off to bed.'

'I'm not a bit tired,' Mia said, as quick off the mark as usual. 'I slept on the plane.'

But they were ordered up for a bath and bed. Stella came up with them and showed them where everything was. The lavatory was up two steps and had a huge polished wooden seat. Mia came out of it looking guilty. She had pulled the paper holder off the wall by mistake, and Stella pretended not to be angry.

In the bedroom where they were to sleep were two identical beds, high beds with thick mattresses, and sheets that smelt of lavender. On the wall opposite the beds was a large water colour of oxen pulling a cart with a barrel on it, somewhere in the Douro region, and below this picture was a stand with a blue patterned jug and basin on it, and underneath a large jerry pot that was decorated with pink roses. You had to pull a cord in order to draw the curtains, and the brushes and mirror on the dressing table had silver angels and cherubs on the backs.

The bed was the most comfortable bed Clare had ever been in. You sank into it, right down: it was impossibly comfortable, and between it and Mia's bed was a small table with a big bedside light on it which had been made out of an oar, or at least part of an oar, and Stella explained that the oar had been Grandpa's when he was at university.

Stella kissed them both goodnight and said, 'Don't touch *anything*,' and went out, shutting the door, because the year before they had given up having the door open and the landing light on.

Now, lying in that extraordinary bed that made you feel like a princess, it suddenly seemed as though the adventure of leaving home, leaving England and coming out here to Portugal had reached a pause, a breaking space, and there was a question that had remained unasked, a question that Clare now needed to ask.

411

'Mi?' she said.

'What?'

'I was thinking.'

'What?'

'About Dad.'

'What about him?'

'Well. Do you think he will be very unhappy?'

There was a silence. The wind swished in the pines and rustled in the wisteria. Mia said, 'Yes. Probably.'

Clare thought for a long time. There were other questions she would like to ask: questions about what would happen next, where they would live, where they would go to school.

She reached out and just managed to catch hold of the curtain. She pulled it aside and saw, through the window, a ragged sky of racing clouds. From far away came the murmur of traffic in the city. She let the curtain go, and immediately another question asked itself before she had time to stop it.

'Do you think we'll ever see him again?'

'How should I know?'

'But do you *think* we will?'

Mia sighed impatiently. 'I don't know and I don't care. Shut up and go to sleep.'

Clare shut up, but she could not go to sleep. The bed was too comfortable for that. She lay on her back and listened to the wind and remembered the morning – it was only yesterday, but it already felt like weeks ago – when Stella had come up to their room and had sat on Mia's bed and talked to them about her and Daddy, and told them about how they didn't really enjoy living together any more, and how everybody would be much happier if they lived apart. She remembered how Stella (she liked them to call her that, and Daddy hated it) had looked at Mia more than at her, and how when she asked them what they would rather do, stay with Daddy or go to Portugal with her, Mia had replied with a hardly a moment's hesitation, 'Go with you.'

Then she began thinking about her father. If she tried, she could almost hear his voice in her mind and see him the way he was when he came back home in his uniform at the end of the day. She had been ill a few months before, and in the evenings

412

he had come up to the bedroom and read to her. It wasn't that she needed to be read to: she was quite good at reading (she was nearly ten) and had read all the Famous Five books already. But all the same, she liked it when he read to her. She liked the sound of his voice and the way it went up and down, making the sentences interesting; she liked watching his face as he read, his eyes going back and forth along the lines, and glancing across at her when he turned a page. The story didn't matter at all when he read to her; what mattered was that he was sitting there, close beside her, doing something just for her, in his own particular way.

She couldn't imagine having a nicer father. She had compared him with other people's fathers, and she was quite sure that he was the best. Sometimes he talked to her about God, and this was almost a secret between them because Stella didn't like it. He said that it was a good thing to talk to God – just to say hullo to Him quietly, or to thank Him if you'd had a nice day or to ask Him to help you if you were lonely or afraid or had something difficult to do. He said that sometimes he talked to God when he was flying, and that although it sounded silly, he always asked Him to keep him safe before he took off.

Downstairs in the drawing room, Stella had broken the news. She, Joy and Bobby were for a moment frozen into a tableau: Stella at ease on the sofa, Joy sitting forward in her chair, her hands joined together upon one knee, and Bobby standing up, warming the backs of his legs at the dying embers of the log fire. And the entire meaning of the whole of the conversation that took place that evening was encapsulated in one exchange:

'Is there no hope of a reconciliation?'

Joy had asked the question. She sat in her chair like an attentive and extremely well turned out bird, Stella thought. Probably a hen, a hen with painted finger-nails and a sharp beak. And her father, she likened mentally to a cock that has forgotten how to crow.

'No,' she said emphatically. 'There's no question of that. None whatsoever.'

XII

Clare woke up very suddenly.

The light was on: a harsh yellow light that made her blink. It was pouring with rain outside, and you could hear the water cascading off the roof and splashing onto the ground below. Mia was crying, and Stella was coming into the room in her nightdress.

'What's the matter? What is it, love?'

'I – had – a – a – dream – and – ' Mia sobbed.

Stella bent to comfort her, but Mia's sobs grew all the more uncontrolled. Her words came out in great gulps.

'I – I – I – I – wet – wet – my – '

Stella pulled Mia's bedclothes back and her face darkened. 'Oh God!' she said.

'I'm – I'm – sorry – ' Mia said, hiccupping and shaking with fresh waves of tears. 'I'm – sorry – Mummy – '

Clare watched as Mia was made to get out of bed, and the bed was stripped, and Stella swore under her breath (bloody hell, that was what she always said) and then pulled Mia's wet nighty off; she saw Mia standing there, naked, weeping, ashamed, in the harsh glare of the electric light; and it was seeing her thus that Clare knew with an inward certainty that she wanted to be at home again with her father, and that if Stella had asked her as well as Mia, if she had asked her, and she had known that this was going to happen – something that had never, ever happened before – then she would have said no, no, I want to stay here, I want to stay with my Dad.

What had gone wrong? Why did all this have to happen? Why couldn't they be happy as they had been happy once, a very long time ago, when she had the skirt with giraffes on it and Mummy and Daddy had been friends, and happy together?

She turned away from the light, from her sobbing sister and from Stella. She crammed the crisp white sheet into her mouth so that no one would know that she too was crying.

Her tears made the pillow wet and warm under her cheek, and were salt on her tongue when they leaked in between her lips, and she prayed, prayed fiercely, saying – O God, please make us happy again.

24 May 1973

Phil, love. I don't know if I'll ever even send this to you, because I'm using you as a sort of imaginary listener. It's going to be a bit of a splurge I'm afraid, because I've got to start somewhere and get the wheels turning, so to speak, after all these unproductive years. Trouble is, you have to sort yourself out, don't you, before you can sort anything else out, so what I'm going to do, or at least try to do, is put down an accurate description of my attitudes to certain of my 'kin folk and own'. Am I capable of doing so without cynicism? We shall see. Maybe it'll be therapeutic to get rid of it this way. I'll try not to bewail my lot too much, but it may be necessary, from time to time, to give details of what is afoot. Happening, even.

We'll kick off with Dad. He'll be sixty-nine in October. Soixante-neuf. What do I think of him? He is like a very well-trained, well-kept, well-trimmed, well-shampooed, well-dressed, well-heeled, well-wined, well-dined, well-everything'ed Pavlov Dog. Who is Pavlov? Joy, of course. She has him eating out of her hand. When she rings the bell, there he is, breathing heavily, salivating a little, one ear cocked cheerfully, head on one side, waiting for her command. 'Yes dear. Yes dear. Yes dear,' he says, and off he goes, his metaphorical tail waving contentedly in the metaphorical breeze. Do I resent his authority? No. For the simple reason that he has no authority left. She has taken it away from him like a prep school matron takes tuck away at the beginning of term; she has locked it away for safe keeping, because he has no more need of it. He is her prisoner; for him, the war is over. Poor Dad? Not at all! He loves every minute of it. No more decisions to take. No more

415

responsibility. He even asks her if he can go to the lavatory. (No, that is not an exaggeration. I have heard him do it. 'All clear is it, dear?' he says. Perhaps we ought to have a siren.) And yet surely there must be something left, something deep down there inside him. He hasn't actually said anything to me about my 'problem'. It always comes via *her*. ('Stella dear, I think I ought to tell you that your father is most concerned . . . .') Sometimes I detect in his expression, those eyes that water at the slightest provocation, a certain sadness. I don't know. Wishful thinking, maybe. He's still very involved in the wine trade of course, and I heard somebody (one of the Randalls, I think) say that he was still the best taster in the business. That was a surprise: I hadn't realised he had ever been regarded as such. And – I'm prepared to believe that there are aspects of which I know nothing at all. For instance: he never says anything about what he actually did in the war. Also, I never found out what was wrong between him and my mother. But that's all history, isn't it, and I'm not concerned with history. Unfortunately, I'm more concerned with Joy.

She likes dark blue and cream, these days. I remember that a long time ago she used to wear pink and white, or sometimes brilliant red. Now it's blue and cream, navy and Devonshire. She likes her hair to be exactly so, and her lips are carefully accentuated with deep red lipstick. She says 'Right-ho!' in a cheerful, WW II way. I suppose that is her 'period' really – about 1944. Her humour comes from Wilfrid Pickles (She knows *all* the words to the 'Have a Go' signature tune) and Tommy Handley. She adores a nice little crisis. 'Never mind, dear. Let's see what we can do. Right-ho.' She is a professional Tower of Strength. She and millions like her Won the War. And she is still winning the war. For her, the war will *never* be over. It is her life: it symbolises those years in which she was forced (oh – we all were, dear) to fend for herself, make the best of a bad job, etc.

Does she 'lurve' Dad? She loves him in the same way as an elderly spinster (which she still is, essentially) loves a poodle. Am I being cruel? Maybe, but I think this is accurate. If he shat on the drawing room carpet, he would have to be Put Out.

Sam? I feel very little. A sort of numbness. There may be –

416

somewhere in here – a feeling of regret that it had to happen. Yes, of course there is. I am 'sorry' that it had to happen. And yet it did have to happen, and I am not 'sorry' that I am not with him now. Therefore, presumably, I am not sorry. How complicated. I can imagine a day – no, I can imagine that there could be a day in the future when I would not object to meeting him. But never with a view to 'getting back' as he puts it in his letter. There is no point even in considering that. I am grateful to him, I suppose, for the continued financial support. But at the same time I suspect his motives. This is his way of keeping me on a string. Let him think that: it won't do anybody any harm, and it makes life easier for M & C. Sam will no doubt revert to what I suspect he was before we were married: a thoroughly 'nice', and thoroughly boring 'chap'. Excellent officer-like qualities, these, and no doubt they will assure him a bright future, with many gold-embroidered oak leaves on his hat. But – but – there is still, isn't there, a chink of regret? It was good. There were good times. Come back Nevin, all is forgiven. The concept of 'good times' is part of the trouble, of course. Part of my 'prarblem'. I don't want 'good times'. Or a Good Time, for that matter, either. I want a time that is worthwhile, not a wasted, frittered-away time.

The point of all this, as I said, is supposed to be therapeutic. A gentle rinsing out of what is left of my mind prior to actually using it. (Tch tch. What you mean is 'prior actually to using it'. Prior Actually, that well known metaphysicist and emetic. Ah! Discovery! I *can* say 'prior to actually' because 'to using' is not an infinitive, is it Malvolio? and *ergo* no infinitive has been split). So – prior to actually using my unrinsed mind (still sounds wrong, Norman) it is necessary to have a quick flick round with the old metaphorical feather duster.

But all these words are just excuses, verbal manoeuvres to avoid or at least delay putting anything down that actually hurts *me*. Like my attitude to Mia, for instance.

Almost impossible to write this, and I am immediately afraid that she might read it. I can see so much of myself in that kid, and I am continually worried that she may lose out because of the me in her. I admire her tremendously: I wish I could have been so controlled, so direct, so graceful when I was her age (and older). I admire her, also, for ignoring Dear Joy's little sallies in condescension: that step-grand-parental omniscience of hers. This bedwetting: it is almost certainly a symptom of over-control. Joy says it's *lack* of control; Joy would. I have talked to M about it all and explained that leaving home and her dad is a traumatic experience, and she asked what that meant, so I explained about the word *trauma*, and we talked a little about psychology – a subject which I would, in retrospect, have preferred to do. The soc. world has been somewhat discredited in the past few years. We are the Hams and by God, have we ever Hammed it up. (Sorry about this Ham fixation I seem to have.) She is too 'big' for this school, I'm afraid. If I can scrape up enough of the necessary, maybe I'll send her off to boarding school next year. She wants that. Unlike Clare.

People love Clare because she's so dreamy, so cuddly, so soft. She will amble her way twenty-five yards behind life for another seventy years and no doubt she will be an Aunty, one day. Is that cruel? Do you have to accept the risk of being cruel in order to be accurate, or can you be accurate without being cruel? Extraordinary that they should be so difficult, having slithered out of me in such quick succession. If I am frightened that Mia will suffer because of the 'me' in her, I am frightened that Clare will not 'suffer' (note inverted commas, please) enough. It is necessary to suffer in order to progress. Steel has to be tempered, and all that. Mia may be over-, Clare under-tempered. Mia too brittle, Clare too soft.

Difficult to write about yourself if you aren't yet where you 'are'. I am not 'there'. To even consider staying here in this latterday colonial mansion is unthinkable. Perhaps that's the trouble. I look down at this body of mine (which in its way is another sort of latterday colonial mansion) and I think 'Eeugh! You great big ugly flab!' But you can't get out of it, can you? (Yoga? 'Tis a thought. But all those straining thighs, dot-dot-dot) I cannot be the person I really am, here. The difficulty is, I don't know where to go in order to find myself. And I suspect that it is necessary to go alone. One is weighed down with such a welter of unnecessary bric-a-brac in this life isn't one? If M & C had opted to stay behind ... things would have been different. And I saw the look on your face, Phil, when we all

418

turned up on your doorstep. You could hear it drop. Bonk. You've brought the kids. Idiot. Fool. Dolt. You have broken your chains but brought them with you, sort of thing. No doubt we would have had a 'relationship' if I'd turned up *sans enfants*. Certainly that would have been an easy way out, and as you said, a splendid way to raise two fingers at the entire male sex. But . . . no. Doing that, *becoming* that would have been exchanging one form of slavery for another. Taking off one label and slapping another straight on. Of course you did advocate giving them the choice, didn't you? Maybe you felt that was what I wanted to hear. Dunno. But where am I? Where *am* I? In transit, as you may say. Living in the transit mess. Between two stages. It is an uncomfortable phase, but a necessary one. However much it hurts people, I know now that I must have independence: I must be at liberty to go in and come out as I please and to have relationships with whoever I want. I cannot, ever again, accept that anyone else has any right whatsoever to tell me how to behave, what attitudes to display, who I may mix with, what clothes I should or should not wear. (For the record, Sam did all these in various ways and at various times). But this is not a record, is it, Rosalinde? No, Stella, no. I'm breaking out in a schizophrenic sweat here. Think I'd better stop. There is an ideal, however, and I reserve the right to aim for it. I want to be a real person. I *will* be a real person. I will not be a 'member of the colony'. (! What would H. Pinter say?)

So – there we are, there we are. Has this been worthwhile? A whole morning at it, and Custódia has just come out into the garden to pick mint for the new potatoes. A positive note to end on, perhaps: I *do* love this country. I am *right* in coming out here. I can put up with all Joy's little ways and Dad's bumbling bonhomie provided I can be here for a while, ease down, let go. And this is a start: if I can do a bit every day . . .

Lunch.

25 May
My dear Aunt Joy and I have been having a 'serious talk', and in order to prevent myself from running round the garden

tearing out my hair by the handful, I reproduce it here.

'I think it's time we had a serious talk, dear.'

'What about?'

'About what you plan to do. You can't just live off your father, you know.'

'I don't intend to, Aunt.'

'Well what *do* you intend?'

'I have a few ideas. Nothing definite.'

'Was that a letter from Sam you had yesterday?'

'It was.'

'What did he have to say?'

(Bit of a nerve that, I thought.)

'Nothing of great importance.'

'But is there any hope of – of – '

'No, Aunt.' (This is me being patient) 'No, I did say there was no question of that, if you remember.'

'What about money?'

'Isn't that my business?'

'Not when it begins to worry your father, dear.'

'I don't see why it should worry him.'

'Of course it worries him! He's terribly concerned about you. He hasn't been sleeping well for weeks. I don't think you have any idea–' (No, I think she used the word inkling) 'I don't think you have any *inkling* how much you mean to him, do you know that? If you did you wouldn't hurt him as much as you do. He's not a young man any more, you know. He's splendidly fit for a man of his age, but he is getting on.'

'That isn't my fault. We all are. I am, for that matter.'

'You know precisely what I mean.'

Then she sort of changed gear. She had trapped me in my room–I was writing to the bank–and she looked meaningfully down at the bank statement by my typewriter. 'Now,' she said, and clasped her hands together under her chin like a Mother Superior. 'I think I ought to tell you that your father is seriously considering settling a sum on you.'

I said something like, 'He is, is he?'

'He feels he'd like to see you secure. Settled.'

She blinked at me. When she does that she reminds me of an elderly parrot with blue feathers and a slash of scarlet, gripping

420

her perch with knobbled claws. How nasty can you get? A lot nastier, rest assured.

'All contributions gratefully received,' I said.

'Is that all you can say?'

(What was I supposed to say? Go all of a flutter, I suppose. 'Oh Aunt! How wonderful!')

I shrugged, wordless.

Then she explained all about it. Apparently he has a bit of spare capital sloshing about in an external account which he doesn't know what to do with. 'In the region of thirty thousand pounds.' Well, nice work if you can get it, say I (but not aloud of course). I asked if it was some sort of tax dodge and she got very ratty, so I presume that it is. It is also the thin end of a very thick wedge, I suspect. I am being offered a large mess of pottage for my 'soul'. I would have to stay out here in order to receive the benefit of it. Mind you, it would solve one or two *problemas*, as you might say. Also it would be a handy way of being quite independent of Sam. It occurs to me, too, that I would not necessarily have to stay in the north. I could hoof it off to the Algarve, for instance. Ho-hummm. I don't think they've thought of that.

Anyway – I've skipped what 'happened' (not that it's very important). She became ratty because I asked if it was a death-duty dodge (dig the alliteration?) and we got into one of those breathless staring matches and she said she would say nothing about this conversation to 'Robert' and then she added, 'But I think that if your father does bring it up, I think you ought to make an effort at least to appear grateful.' Then she asked me if I understood.

I said yes, I understood all too well, and she hopped off, squawking gently. I don't think we're hitting it off, know what I mean?

28 May

Twins' birthday on Saturday last. Lunch at Martin & Penny's. Odd to be back in Moinho Velho. Martin has a large number of fierce white teeth. When he laughs, the lower set disappears and the upper ones stick out at thirty degrees to the vertical.

He has thin black hair and fiery red cheeks with a lot of vein endings in evidence. Likes his gin and tonic, thank you very much, which Dad feels is a bit off for a port wine shipper. He's a forthright 'bloke': deliciously masculine, every inch a naval officer. Penny is muddleheaded, sexy, with lovely heavy boobs and a sluttish way of dressing which I like, and which scandalises Aunt J. They barbecued chicken legs for us and we sat round the pool. The tank's gone, and so has that cranky windmill. They have a filtration unit and changing rooms instead. That's progress. Also, they have *bought* the house from Dad, and I understand that's where this influx of cash has come from. They have also (as part of the deal) bought all the furniture, which makes me spit blood. How Dad can blithely get rid of all those beautiful pieces that Mum so lovingly collected and cared for completely beats me. Aunt J says it wouldn't have 'gone' in the Foz house, and I guess she's right there. None of it is pretentious: it's beautiful chunky furniture, and the only consolation is that Penny is the sort of person who will appreciate it. Does, in fact.

Chat, chat, chat. I hadn't intended this at all, Phil. Is it of value? I fear the the sun is weakening my resolve. It is so very easy to soak it up, putting off the evil moment when work must start. I talked to Penny quite a bit on Sat. afternoon. She has great ideas for the firm, and is frustrated at being the 'junior wife' so to speak. She obviously regards Dad, Joy and even James as being stuck-in-the-mud traditionalists, and is aching to get her hands on the redecoration and refurnishing of Quinta das Rosas. She said that Martin had already managed to improve working conditions at the Lodge and the *quinta* considerably. Really quite a refreshing person – an ally, I felt. Never had the opportunity really to get to know her before.

Martin's on the school committee apparently, and we dished the dirt on that subject. So really I've strayed from my way like a lost sheep, haven't I? Gossiping with the best of them, I am.

30 May
This isn't working out. Another incredibly petty row with Aunt J. I am *not* going to go and work in some coffee-stained

little estate agency. So she reckons I'm irresponsible, ungrateful, spoilt, you name it, that's me. And the irony of it all is that Dad likes me staying here and wants to keep me within his reach, as it were. So the whole set-up is becoming counter-productive.

14 June
Well. There has been a certain amount of water under the bridge since I last slotted paper into typewriter. How the hell it started I don't know but any way . . . dot-dot-dot . . . There was a dinner party with Penny & Martin and afterwards a bit of dancing: they have some rather swinging Latin American stuff and a couple of grossly nostalgic Ella Fitzgeralds. Anyway, anyway. One thing led to another, as they say. Maybe I did slightly over-egg the pudding (what an obscene expression that is!) Dunno. Nice while it lasted (it usually is, I find). Don't blame Penny, either. Poor girl, she practically pinned me to her kitchen tiles and said 'hands off my man' which I suppose I would have done in her place. So it's goodbye from him and it's goodbye from me. Joy is in a right old tizz-wozz about it being 'all over the colony' and all the usual crap. But the really big laugh is that I have now accepted the money (instead of opening the box, as you might say) and am therefore a woman of means. Nice.

Even nicer, I've decided to move south. Haven't told them yet but will do so tomorrow. That should be good for a laugh, too.

17

I

THE HARBOUR FOGHORN was sounding when Natália set out to do the shopping. Coastal mist lay in a shallow bank over the Tagus estuary and along the Costa do Sol, that stretch of coast that runs westward from Lisbon. As the sun rose and burnt away the mist, the upper part of old Cascais cleared, and the jumble of crusted tiles and whitewashed buildings was suddenly brilliant against a blue sky.

She was in her fifties now, and ten years of service with the Van de Eifels had given her a certain dignity that was far removed from the countrified mannerisms she had brought with her when she came down from Oporto. Seeing her walk down the hill towards the harbour, you would hardly have guessed that she was in service: she was neatly dressed in a grey skirt, grey pullover and white blouse, and had recently given way to the vanity of a colour rinse from time to time to conceal the white hairs that would otherwise have appeared. As a combined Christmas and birthday present (her birthday was on Christmas Eve) Eduardo had given her a locket shaped like a heart, which she wore round her neck on a silver chain. Only by looking at her hands could you be led to suppose that she was accustomed to menial work.

The sardine trawlers were appearing like ghosts out of the damp air. They were anchoring a hundred yards or so off the small stretch of beach, and dories were already being rowed ashore. The fishwives waited on the sand for their menfolk, and helped to unload the trays and boxes of fish, and carry them up the steps to the esplanade.

Natália hated fog. That morning, she had awoken to the sound of a big ship's siren, and in her mind's eye she had

424

witnessed yet again the scene which she had so often imagined: a massive liner, thundering through the night, its bow wave all but capsizing a sardine trawler; and the horrified face of an old man as he was sucked under water and down into the milling propellers.

Perhaps it was the fog and the sight of the trawlers coming in to anchor that caused her to stop on her way along the esplanade. Usually, she took no interest in the goings-on of the fishing community. But that Saturday morning in late July, she stood for a few minutes and watched as crates of fish were manhandled and dories dragged up the beach. She looked into the red-rimmed eyes of the fishermen and listened to the cackling repartee of their wives and daughters.

She paused, she watched, and she remembered.

Then, pulling herself together, she walked briskly away along the main street towards the vegetable market.

II

The mist disappeared rapidly as the sun climbed higher, and the streets of Cascais became thronged with tourists. There were English ladies in pastel dresses and white cardigans, their hair neatly prinked for the package holiday, their shins and forearms reddened by two afternoons on the beach. There were American husbands, paddling along after their hatchet-faced wives, in big sandals, big trousers and big, loose shirts. There were hitchiking Scandinavians in short shorts and long sneakers, weighed down by their rucksacks, accompanied by the earnest American college girls they had met on the camp site the previous day.

These, and many subtler types, wandered about the shopping precincts, sat outside cafés and told each other, from time to time, the difference between *obrigado* and *obrigada*. They dodged in and out of the traffic, licked icecreams, gazed in wonderment at the grilling of sardines on charcoal stoves and spent their money often, and often unwisely.

425

The beaches swarmed with nearly naked humanity. Middle-aged men took their pot bellies for walks up and down Carcavelos beach; lustful couples lay face to face, their pulses racing, and grannies in black satin sat where they had been plonked. A gentle swell crashed and crashed upon the shore, and the people in the water rose and fell with each succeeding peak and trough like basking seals. In Cascais bay, a speed-boat cut a white gash in the sun-glittered water, and a girl in a white bikini sent up a feather of spray as she zigzagged behind it on a mono-ski. Further out, a flotilla of racing dinghies bobbed and surged, their spinnakers opening one by one as they rounded a mark and bore away before the northwesterly breeze.

It might have seemed, on that sun-soaked day in July, that all was well in Portugal. Wherever you looked you could see evidence of prosperity – or at least, almost wherever you looked. Sleek German cars slipped in and out of Estoril; hotels and luxury apartment blocks were being built with almost indecent haste; the restaurants and night clubs were doing a roaring trade. Vast sums of money were being borrowed, and nobody seemed to care very much how or when they would be repaid. Many of them never were.

These outward signs of prosperity were in fact the results of a boom that had been deliberately engineered by Caetano to provide a veneer over the deepening cracks within the system he had inherited from Salazar. Already, the outside world was beginning to see through that veneer: the scandal of the massacre at Wiriamu had brought the African wars into the limelight, and when Caetano appeared on British television and dismissed them as 'internal matters', insisting that Angola, Mozambique and Guinea-Bissau were not colonies at all but part of Mother Portugal, his words were taken with rather more than a pinch of salt.

But it was in the army that the situation was becoming critical, and particularly so among the conscripted officers, known as *milicianos*, most of whom were well-educated young men who had been through university and had no military ambitions at all. They found themselves being sent out to the worst areas with minimal training and maximum responsibility;

many had done two or more tours of duty in Africa, and they were losing patience with the candyfloss appeals to their patriotism – not to mention the diet of goat meat and rice, the ennervating heat, and the continual dangers of disease, maiming or death. Morale was draining away at an alarming rate, and something had to be done quickly.

What was needed, General Rebelo, the Minister of Defence decided, was to have a larger core of regular officers within the army. Regular officers were much easier to handle: they did what they were told because they were usually afraid of stepping out of line and prejudicing their careers. So the solution to the crisis of morale and manpower seemed to be to persuade some of these ex-university *milicianos* on to the regular promotion ladder. Once there, they would not only be obliged to display that unswerving loyalty that was traditional in the regular officer corps, but it would also be possible to make it conveniently difficult for them to leave.

General Rebelo thought it was a good idea, and his mandarin generals quite naturally thought it an excellent one. A scheme was worked out to offer ex-university conscripts the chance to become regular officers under very attractive terms. Instead of spending four years at the military academy they would only have to spend one. And to put the icing on the cake, they would be allowed to count their conscript time as seniority for promotion. So a young man who had left the army after four years of the 'draft' could – if he was fool enough – jump back on to the military career ladder a rung or two above regular officers of his own age.

Unfortunately for General Rebelo and all those senior officers who had agreed what a splendid idea it was, this scheme, known as the 'Rebelo Decree' was not quite such a splendid idea after all: first, the morale of the *milicianos* was already so low and their contempt for the Ministry of Defence such that they felt insulted by it; secondly, the regular officers were outraged by the duplicity of their top ranking officers, and thirdly, for the first time, both regulars and *milicianos* were now united in their disapproval of the Caetano regime: at the stroke of a pen, the Portuguese government had provided them with a common grievance – a grievance that was to serve

427

as a long-awaited catalyst for revolution.

While the sun blazed down, captains and majors and lieutenants sat over their lunches in the military messes up and down the country – and in the Ultramar – and discussed this new humiliation that had been meted out to them. Many already feared that withdrawal from Africa was inevitable, and that the army would be blamed for the defeat, just as Salazar had blamed it after Goa. Nearly all the regular officers had joined the army after taking fiercely competitive examinations and interviews, and they now saw younger men being offered the same rank and seniority as themselves.

What course of action was open to them? How could they protest? How could they organise themselves to take effective action for redress?

There was hurt and disillusionment in the air: they were the servants of the politicians, yes, and were bound by a common oath of loyalty. But when a master humiliates his servant, they argued, he abdicates his right to that servant's loyalty.

III

Saturday was nearly always a busy day for Natália. The Van de Eifels were sociable people, and enjoyed entertaining their friends to barbecue lunches and afternoons round the pool. And as she was the only living-in maid and the daily woman didn't come at weekends, any work that had to be done had to be done by her.

She was preparing a salad in the kitchen when she heard a car arriving and the sound of voices in the drive; a few minutes later, Brigitte Van de Eifel came in and said, 'Here's someone to see you, Natália.'

For a moment, she didn't recognise the woman who now came to the door with her two daughters. She had not seen her for several years, and that moment of non-recognition caused an exclamation of surprise.

'*Menina* Stella!'

They kissed on both cheeks, and the twins were introduced. Natália fussed over them and saw family likenesses. 'Are you staying for a holiday?' she asked.

'No,' Stella said. 'We've come to live in the south.'

'And your husband? Is he in Portugal also?'

Stella explained that he had remained in the England. 'He's in the Air Force,' she added.

Natália understood. As far as she was concerned, people in the armed forces were rarely at home. And there was nothing strange in Stella's decision to live in Portugal. She patted Mia on the head and allowed her hand to rest on the child's shoulder. Mia moved away.

'And how are you?' Stella asked.

'Very well, very well. A few aches and pains, you know, but that's old age creeping on, isn't it?'

'And Eduardo?'

'He was very ill, you know. When he came out of the army. But he's got a job now. A garage in Estoril.'

'Really? That's good.'

And then there was nothing to say except how good it was that Stella should come to live in Portugal again and how happy Natália was and how the climate was much better, much drier, in the south.

Stella and the twins withdrew, and Natália returned to the preparation of the salad. She cut the outer leaves off crisp lettuces and made flowers out of radishes by slicing them half through and leaving them to soak in a bowl of water. She cut tomatoes into rosettes and made patterns with slices of green pepper and cucumber. While she worked, other cars arrived and the sound of voices and laughter drifted across from the swimming pool where the English and Dutch were sitting in deck chairs and sipping long glasses of iced sangria.

Later that evening, she was still in the kitchen when a squeal of bicycle brakes announced Eduardo's arrival. He often dropped in to see her on his way past, when he went fishing at the weekends. She turned to greet him as he entered through the bamboo fly-screen that hung across the doorway.

'Guess who's here,' she said, when they had kissed.

'Who?'

429

'*Menina* Stella.'

He looked away. 'Oh, her. What's she doing in Portugal?'

'I've no idea. She's brought her children with her. Twins, they are.'

He grunted.

'I expect she'd like to meet you,' Natália said. 'I could go and tell her you're here if you like.'

'No thank you. I don't want to see her.'

'Eduardo! You used to be such friends when she was small!'

'That was a very long time ago.'

She turned away from him to work at the sink. He watched her washing glasses and rinsing them for some moment, then said: 'I've heard from the pension people.'

She stopped working immediately. 'You haven't! What did they say?'

He grinned; he had aged in the last year or so. His hair had thinned out and his face was harder. 'They've decided to give me the full amount. Any idea how much that is?'

She shook her head.

He was unable to hold back his pleasure. 'You won't believe this, but it works out at just over four thousand *escudos* a month.'

'Four *thousand* – '

'Four thousand. Four *contos* a month. And you know what? It's linked to a regular sergeant's pay, so every time the army gets a rise, I do too. And another thing – they're giving me all my back pay since last August. Best part of thirty-five *contos*.' He began to laugh. He took her in his arms and hugged her. 'And it's for the rest of my life, mother. The rest of my life!'

Natália sniffed and wept.

'Now what's the matter? What is there to cry about?'

'I'm happy, *filho*. I'm happy for you.'

He put his arms round her shoulders to console her. She found a handkerchief in her apron pocket and dabbed at her eyes. When she had calmed down, he paced up and down the big kitchen, thinking aloud. 'You know what I'm going to do? I'm going to move out of that room and get myself a decent apartment. We'll share it.' He looked round at the pinewood cupboards, the white formica worktops, the electric appliances.

430

'We'll have a cooker and a freezer and a washing machine. And a television. What do you say?'

'I don't know what to say.'

'Don't say anything then. Leave it all to me. We'll have a balcony facing south, and potted geraniums and deck chairs, and in the evenings we'll sit out in the sun like – like that lot out there. We'll have a bit of luxury. Agree?'

She shook her head. 'I can't share a place with you, Eduardo.'

'Why not?'

Natália struggled inwardly, avoiding his stare. She had never been able to rid herself of the memory of one who had taken her into his bed when she was still a child: the man who, even now, she believed to have been her father. It was this secret memory that had made her determined never again to share her home with a man, any man – not even her son.

Looking quickly back at Eduardo she said, 'Well, I can't leave here, can I? They won't want me if I'm only a daily.'

'Find another job then.'

'No. I'm happy here. Madame is very good to me – '

'Madame, Madame! I'm sick of hearing about Madame!' He smiled sadly. 'You don't really want to do better for yourself, do you? You want to stay like this for the rest of your life. That's the truth, isn't it?'

'Maybe. I know when I'm well off. I've got regular work here and a fair wage. A roof over my head and good people to work for. So. You go and find yourself a place. It's better you should be on your own. Have a bit of independence. You never know, you may want to marry one of these days. Make your own family. You won't want me round your neck then.'

'Not much chance of that happening,' he said.

'*Filho*! Why do you always say that? Why shouldn't you get married? What about that girl – the one in the *farmácia*, what was her name? She was getting really fond of you, you know that?'

He went to the kitchen door, his back to her. He remembered what the doctors had told him in the military hospital at Lisbon. He had promised himself that he would never tell his mother, never share with her the hurt and anguish that his loss

431

of sexual potency had caused. So there was a long silence between them during which she returned to the sink and he stood in the doorway, listening to the voices and laughter that came from the people who sat round the pool.

'Are you going fishing tonight?' Natália asked eventually.

'No. I meant to tell you. I've been invited to a party.'

'Oh yes?'

'Rui Cardoso called in the other day. His uncle's got a place up behind the Guincho. I'm going there.'

She had finished washing the glasses and was drying her hands on a towel. 'Isn't he an officer?'

'Yes. But he's not a regular. Only a *miliciano*. He doesn't go in for all this yes-sir no-sir rubbish.'

'What sort of party is it?'

He shrugged. 'I don't know. A barbecue, I think.'

'Well. That'll be nice, Eduardinho.'

He sat down on the kitchen chair, and they chatted for a while longer. Eventually he got up and kissed her goodbye. He went out of the kitchen and collected his bicycle, which was leaning up against the house. He wheeled it along between the house and a slatted wooden screen which had been put up to conceal the swimming pool from the casual glance.

He stopped, and looked between the slats at the Van de Eifels and their guests. Passion fruit hung, pendulous, from trelliswork, and cultivated bougainvillaea cascaded overhead. The water was a brilliant blue and the people who reclined in deck chairs heavily suntanned.

Stella was there. She wore a yellow bikini and huge circular sunglasses. Her hair was swept back into a single, thick plait. She lay on a canvas bed, reading a paperback novel.

He stared through the slats for several seconds before mounting his drop-handlebarred bicycle and riding off down the drive and out onto the coast road.

IV

He rode north, with the cliffs and sea to his left and the Sintra

432

hills rising up ahead. It was evening now, and the homegoing traffic streamed past in the opposite direction on the way back to Lisbon and the dormitory towns. At the roadside, the people who sold carpets and tablecloths and goatskin rugs were packing up their vans. Further on, where the road ran along beside the long sweep of Guincho beach, women and girls held out packets of biscuits to the cars as they went by.

It was too early to go to the party. Instead, he turned off the main road and onto the track that led to the Praia do Abano. He locked up his bicycle and left it in the bushes that grew by the track before walking along the path to the cliffs.

He often fished here: it was a less frequented stretch of coast and he enjoyed the solitude it offered. The wind off the cliffs was hot in his face and bore the scent of cistus and rosemary. He sat on a ledge and watched the sea crashing and surging on the rocks below. The sun sank into a hazy horizon, and the unending succession of waves crumbling into white foam on the volcanic rocks began to have a mesmeric effect.

Life had not been easy since leaving the military hospital. In the early months he had lacked the energy and will to hold down a job for any length of time. He had worked as a warehouse night watchman, a delivery van driver and a checker in a beer bottling plant and had then been unemployed for several weeks before accepting the job as a pump attendant in the Shell garage at Estoril. It was not a job he enjoyed, but it was regular money, and it offered a degree of independence.

He had been determined to regain some of his physical fitness after leaving hospital, and it had been for that reason that he had bought the bicycle. Weekend after weekend, he forced himself to go for longer and longer excursions, and gradually the muscles began to come back and the sun tanned the new skin and reduced the mottled appearance of which he had been so ashamed. Gradually too, he had begun to feel a little more at ease in the company of other people, a little less of an outcast.

Cardoso had turned up unexpectedly one afternoon two weeks before. He had been posted to the barracks at Santarem for the last few months of his national service.

'Twenty litres of super,' he had said, before recognising his old platoon sergeant.

He got out of the car – it was a white Triumph TR4 – and shook Eduardo warmly by the hand. He introduced the woman in the passenger seat. 'This is Jacinta, my cousin,'

She looked like a Greek goddess to Eduardo, who excused himself for not shaking hands because his hands were covered in oil. He felt ashamed of himself, but Cardoso seemed not to notice. He talked in his usual breezy way, and was shocked to hear that Eduardo's pension had still not been settled. 'It's nearly a year!' he said. 'We'll have to see about that.' Then, out of the blue, he invited Eduardo to a barbecue party.

Eduardo's instinctive reaction was to refuse. He was not the same class as Cardoso and he could not but be aware of Jacinta's eyes on him, looking at his dirty hands and face, the rag hanging out of the pocket of his overalls. But Cardoso had insisted: the barbecue was to be held in the garden of his uncle's house; all his friends were going, and he wouldn't take no for an answer.

Now, with the sun gone, leaving a pale glow behind it in the sky, Eduardo stood up from his ledge and made his way back along the path to his bike.

He found the house without difficulty. It was built on rising ground and commanded a panoramic view of the beach and the Atlantic. Cars were parked under the pines, and a fire flickered making silhouettes of the people who stood about talking and drinking.

He hesitated before entering the grounds, suffering from last minute nerves. Then a car drew up behind him and he found himself in its headlights. There was no question of turning back. He walked up a path between oleanders and was welcomed immediately by Rui Cardoso.

There were no formal introductions, but he was made to feel at ease: he found himself in an unusual circle of people – people who talked about art and books and music instead of the interminable conversations about football and food and women that he had been used to all his life. He was able to contribute little to such conversations, but was interested by them, nevertheless. People wandered about eating chicken legs and drinking wine from earthenware mugs, and later on Cardoso and a few others started playing guitars and singing.

434

Jacinta came up to him. 'I believe you sing?' she asked.

'Well – only a bit.'

Her eyebrows were pencilled into a peak that gave her a look of permanent surprise. 'What do you sing?'

'I enjoy *fado*.'

'Have you ever sung in public?'

'Not really. Only at army concerts. That sort of thing.'

'You have to start somewhere.'

They watched Cardoso and a few others doing a takeoff of the Rolling Stones. When it was over, Cardoso came over to them, full of late night bonhomie.

'You're going to sing,' he said to Eduardo, pointing a finger at him and digging him in the stomach. 'You – are – going – to – sing.' Then he turned and spread his arms wide. 'Silence! Silence please!' he shouted, and continued in the formal style as the general conversation died down. '*Excelentissimos Senhors e Senhoras*,' he said, and there was much exaggerated shushing. He continued amid asides and laughter. 'Most excellent gentlemen and ladies! I want you now to imagine yourselves three thousand kilometres away in the sweaty swamps of Guinea-Bissau.'

'I am in a sweaty swamp!' a girl said in the darkness.

Cardoso continued. 'The mosquitoes are whining all around, and an oil lantern hangs from an orange tree. Gathered round, the humble soldiers are enjoying a quiet evening. And with them, the dark natives gather, their eyes glinting in the lamplight as they listen to a song which to them means nothing but which, to the brave servants of the Republic, means home and love and friendship.' He looked round. 'Where's my guitar?'

Somebody handed it to him. He walked into the candlelight by the barbecue and jerked his head to Eduardo. 'Are you ready?'

Eduardo grinned. 'What for?'

'To sing, of course.'

'I don't know –'

Jacinta whispered to him. 'Go on. Please. Don't pretend to be shy.'

Cardoso was playing the opening bars of the song he had

sung on that night over two years before at Mudanda. At first, the atmosphere of lightheartedness prevailed among the audience that stood and sat in the shadows under the trees. But as the introductory notes came to an end and Eduardo stepped forward to sing, the magic was suddenly there again, and the words of the song – which were so well known, so trite – came alive:

> Numa casa Portuguêsa fica bem
> Pão e vinho sobre a mesa,
> E se a porta humildemente bate alguem . . .

His voice floated up into the night, and behind him the surf on the beach made a white line that bordered the darkness of the ocean. At the end, the applause was tumultuous. He was embarrassed by it. Jacinta came up to him and said, 'That was very, very good.'

They demanded that he sing again: Cardoso handed his guitar to a man called Nuno Freire, and as soon as Nuno began to play, Eduardo knew that he must be a professional. He sang twice more and each time was given applause that he felt was embarrassingly overgenerous. He declined to sing a fourth time, and the guitar was handed on to somebody else, who did not have anything like Nuno's skill.

After the party, it was nearly three in the morning when he arrived at Alvide. He padlocked his bicycle and went up the litter-strewn concrete stairs of the tenement block where he lived. His room was part of a flat, and had been sub-let to him. On the floor above, an alsation dog was imprisoned; it started barking soon after he let himself in, and within minutes all the dogs in the neighbourhood were barking.

He stood at his window and looked out across the road at the other tenement buildings. He felt suddenly pessimistic. The pension – it wasn't all that much. Would he ever be able to afford his own apartment? And why had his mother been so unwilling to consider sharing it with him?

The dogs barked and barked. He hadn't sung all that well, in fact. What had happened, no doubt, was that Cardoso had told them he'd had a rough time, and they had been sorry for him:

that was the reason for their enthusiastic applause.

He turned away from the window and lay down on the bed. As dawn came up, he dropped off into a fitful sleep from which he awoke to the sound of a baby crying in the next door room and the howl of a Japanese motorbike in the road outside.

V

It was late August before he saw anything of Cardoso again. He drove up one afternoon looking crisp and cool in a red aertex shirt and belted blue jeans.

'I think I've found you a job,' he said. 'How would you fancy working in a *restaurante típico*?'

'You mean as a waiter?'

'Barman. But there's an opening to sing *fado*.'

'I'm not good enough for that.'

'*Bolas*! There are plenty of singers worse than you who are coining it in. *Fado*'s a big tourist attraction these days. And with a talent like yours, well – you'd be stupid not to use it.'

'All the same, I'm not so sure. I haven't got much of a repertoire – '

'That's no excuse, is it? Look. I tell you what I've done. I know the owner of this place. I said I'd bring you along one evening so they could hear you sing. If you like the place and they like your voice, well – you'll get the job. What do you say?'

He made excuses. He said he thought he was too old to start a career as a singer, that he didn't have the experience to compete with professionals and that having found himself a place in Alvide he didn't want to move back into Lisbon.

'Who said anything about Lisbon?' Cardoso said. 'This place is in Monte Estoril. Just up behind the Cruzeiro. Pinginhas. You probably know it.'

'Pinginhas! That's a snob place! I can't go there!'

'Yes you can. Listen, if you get this job you'll be on full barman's wages plus tips, and you'll get extra for singing, too.

437

It's up to you, *rapaz*. If you want to go on working in greasy overalls for the rest of your life, well, that's your business. But I know what I'd do if I were in your shoes. I'd seize the opportunity.'

A queue of cars had formed, and the driver of the Volkswagen behind Cardoso's TR4 was beginning to show his impatience. He slapped the side of the car with the flat of his hand.

'Well?' Cardoso asked.

'I'll give it a try,' Eduardo said.

'Good. How about next Saturday then? Come at about midnight. There's a better *ambiente* later in the evenings. They even let me play sometimes. Don't look so scared! They're a friendly lot!'

'What shall I sing?'

'I don't know! Whatever you're good at. A couple, maybe. One with a bit of passion, the other with a bit of *allegria*.'

'What about the accompanists? How do I know they'll be able to play the tunes I know?'

The driver of the Volkswagen started tooting his horn. 'Look,' Cardoso said, 'Nuno Freire and Zé Armando have been playing at Pinginhas for the best part of twenty years. If there's a tune they don't know it isn't worth knowing. So you needn't worry about that.' He started the engine. 'Midnight on Saturday, okay?'

'Okay.'

'*Ciao*.' Cardoso revved and drove off with a squeal of tyres and a growl of exhaust.

The Volkswagen moved up to the pumps and the driver leaned out of the window. 'I hope you've had an interesting conversation,' he said. 'Now would it be possible to sell me a little petrol? I believe that's what you're paid to do.'

VI

The bicycle headlight threw a jerky patch of light on the road ahead as he pedalled up the hill through Monte Estoril. This

438

ahead as he pedalled up the hill through Monte Estoril. This was a wealthy district: six-bedroomed houses stood in their own grounds, and guard dogs hurled themselves in paroxysms of fury at the railings as he went by.

Pinginhas Restaurant had been a private house itself, and it, like its neighbours, stood back from the road. There was a carved wooden arch over the entrance to the drive and an illuminated sign announced:

PINGINHAS
Restaurante Típico

Fados

He propped his bicycle against a palm tree in the car park and approached the entrance. The windows were of coloured glass, so he could not see in. He had put on his best suit and a clean white shirt, and was feeling hot and nervous.

He pushed at the door and went in. Just inside, a waiter stood with his back to him. He turned and held a finger to his lips as Eduardo entered. The sound of stringed instruments came from the lower level of the restaurant which was dimly lit, and a woman began to sing. He edged forward in order to see.

It was Jacinta. She wore black and stood in the classic pose of the *fado* singer: her hands clasped before her, her head thrown back. Behind her, Nuno Freire and Zé Armando played a contrapuntal accompaniment on the *viola*, which is a guitar, and the *guitarra*, a twelve-stringed instrument similar to a lute.

He had been to many *fado* sessions before and the scene was familiar to him. But seeing Jacinta there and hearing her sing when he had been unaware that she was a *fadista* came as a surprise. He listened with appreciation: she had a powerful contralto voice and sang with that passion and force which is peculiar to the *fado;* she seemed to pluck the words from the very depth of her soul.

Sou tua!
Como o luar é da lua,

439

como as pedras são da rua
e, p'ra ser tua, nasci!

Sou tua!
Deixa-me dizer ao vento
p'ra que o vento, num lamento
diga ao mar, a terra e ao ceu . . .

I am yours!
As the moonlight is the moon's
and the stones are of the street
and, to be yours, I was born!

I am yours!
Let me tell this to the wind
so that the wind, lamenting,
may tell earth and sea and sky . . .

I am yours,
and let these eyes of mine
live just to look at yours,
although you are not mine!

As she reached the last lines, she seemed overtaken by a
climax of passion, and the applause started before the final
words had been sung. The lights went up, and Eduardo saw
Cardoso sitting with an older man at a table on the far side of
the room. He went over to them, and Jacinta joined them at
the same time.

He was introduced to the older man, Narcisso Oliveira, who
was Jacinta's father. He wore thick-lensed glasses, and suffered
from a peculiar tic that caused his right shoulder to jerk
upwards from time to time as he spoke. Jacinta seemed
drained of energy after her performance: she sat back in her
chair and closed her eyes for several minutes. Oliveira turned
to Eduardo after his drink had been brought and said, 'I
understand you were a soldier for some years.'

'Yes, sir,' Eduardo said, for Oliveira was obviously wealthy,
and probably came from an aristocratic family.

'How long did you serve?'

'Nearly seventeen years.'

Oliveira sipped a glass of mineral water. His shoulder jerked. 'You're from the north?'

'Yes, sir.'

'What part?'

'Valadares.'

'They don't sing much *fado* up there. Where did you learn?'

'I left home when I was eighteen, sir. There was a group in my battalion – in Goa – we used to sing *fado*. I picked it up.'

'In Goa were you? When was that?'

'Right at the end. We spent three months in a prison camp before they shipped us out in the old *Patria*.'

A waiter brought drinks, and a short while later the lights went down again. Nuno and Zé played a duet which involved intricate and rapid fingering: their performance was greeted by enthusiastic applause from the audience, which contained several groups of tourists: German, English and Canadian. The lights remained dim, and the accompanists started the introductory bars to a *fado* which Eduardo recognised. He looked round for the singer, but none appeared, and it seemed as if a mistake had been made. But as the introduction came to an end, Narcisso Oliveira stood up and began to sing:

> You cannot escape
> Your fated destiny
> An evil star may dictate:
> You can lie
> To the rule of your heart
> But – *ai*! – like it or not,
> You must comply
> With fate.

'I can't possibly sing here,' Eduardo said to Cardoso as the applause died down.

'Why not?'

'I'm not nearly good enough.'

'*Bolas*!' Cardoso said, and lit a cigarette.

'Is the owner here?'

441

'I can't see him.'

'Not much point in my singing in that case.'

'Suit yourself,' said Cardoso.

He relaxed a little. Cardoso made sure his glass was never empty, and by two in the morning he felt pleasantly hazy. Several more of Cardoso's friends had arrived, and they sat together in a group. They talked and drank and ate salted nuts between the *fado*-singing sessions, and eventually Jacinta turned to Eduardo and asked him when he was going to sing.

He laughed awkwardly. 'I'm not going to,' he said.

'But you must! We all do. Everybody who can, that is.'

'That lets me out, then.'

'You don't mean that.'

He shrugged and looked into his glass.

'Don't you enjoy singing?'

'I enjoy it very much.'

'Well then.'

He shook his head. 'There's a difference between singing at a barbecue party and singing in Pinginhas.'

She said nothing for a while, then returned to the attack.

'You disappoint me,' she said. 'Rui talked so much about you. He said you had one of the finest natural singing voices he had ever heard. He said that if he could get you to sing in Lisbon the way you sang in Guinea-Bissau, you'd be a hit overnight. No, that's the truth. A hit overnight. All right, maybe he does exaggerate, he's like that. But when I heard you the other evening, well – I agreed with him. And now that he's gone to the trouble to introduce you here, now that you've got the chance to sing to two of the best accompanists in the business, don't you think you might have the good grace to sing? Don't you?'

He stared downward. It was easy for her to say all that: she came from a wealthy family; she had been brought up to expect success as a birthright. She didn't know what it was like to wear secondhand clothes that didn't fit and to have broken fingernails and hands ingrained with motor oil.

One of the waiters was preparing to sing, and the lights were dimming. The singer had a shock of dark hair and striking good looks. He sang about the windows of the Alfama district, a part of old Lisbon.

442

'What did you think of that?' Jacinta asked when he had finished.

'It was very good.'

'It was terrible,' she said quietly. 'And you know it. But still, if you're determined to bury your talent under your pride, I suppose that's your privilege.'

She turned away from him. He felt angry and suddenly determined to prove himself. The conversation went on around him. I don't belong here, he thought. I should never have come. I don't fit. Maybe I am a *mó do baixo*. A nobody, a never-has-been, a never-will-be.

He drained his glass quickly, and went over to Nuno and Zé.

Nuno was small and tubby with thin black hair plastered over his bald head.

'*Então, que quer cantar?*' he asked. 'Right, what do you want to sing?'

They discussed what would be suitable, and Nuno identified the melodies, picking them out rapidly and quietly. They agreed on a *fado* about the sorrow of parting and that almost indefinable emotion called *saudade*, from which the Portuguese are chronic sufferers. For *saudade* is the spirit of *fado*; it is that emotion which is experienced when the inevitability of destiny is mingled with a yearning of the soul for better times, better places, and the knowledge that what has been can never be again. Eduardo stood up, aware of the faces looking at him. He breathed deeply, wished that his heart would stop thumping, and concentrated on the meaning and spirit of the words.

> The memory of your face
> When we said good-bye
> Is always with me:
> I see you standing at your door
> The night the north wind blew;
> I see you standing there,
> Your face, your eyes, your smile of sadness:
> Ai – *saudade*!
> You are always beside me,
> And I know you will remain thus
> Until I die.

Sitting at a long table near the door was a party of English: three families, out for the evening with their teenage children. Eduardo became aware that they were laughing at him during his performance; it had happened before in *fado* houses, and would happen again; the passion that is expressed often appears and sounds ridiculous to those who have been brought up in less romantic latitudes.

The knowledge that he was being laughed at wrecked all the feeling and depth that he had wanted to put into his performance. There was polite applause, and he returned to his table angry, and ashamed.

'Well done, I like it,' Cardoso said.

'Kind of you to say so. Some people obviously thought it funny.'

'You mean those come-ons over there? You don't need to take any notice of them.'

Eduardo sat in silence for some while, then stood up abruptly. 'I'm working tomorrow,' he said, 'So I think I'll be on my way. Thanks for everything.'

He left quickly and went out to the car park. He collected his bike and pedalled fast out of the gates and down the hill towards the main road. The night air was pleasantly cool in his face; he was glad to have left. He'd made a fool of himself. He wouldn't go back.

He freewheeled on, and was nearly at the coast road when the car came up behind him, overtook and screeched to a halt in front of him. He jammed on his brakes and just managed to avoid going into the back of it.

It was Cardoso's white sports car. The door slammed as Jacinta got out.

'Right,' she said, angry. 'Do you want this job or don't you?'

He stared at her.

'Make up your mind,' she said. 'You won't get another chance.'

Cardoso was getting out of the passenger seat. He strolled round to the back of the car.

Eduardo looked from one to the other. 'You mean – *you're* offering me the job?'

'Yes,' Jacinta said. 'And I'd be grateful if you'd make up your mind.'

444

'But – do you own the place?'

'A fifty per cent share. With my father.'

Eduardo looked at Cardoso. 'I thought – you said – '

'I had to say something, didn't I? Otherwise you wouldn't have sung at all.'

'Probably a good thing.'

'Look,' Jacinta said, 'You don't have to sing if you don't want to. All we need is a barman. We're doing you a favour. There're plenty of people who'll leap at the offer if you don't. So do you want this job or not?'

'Of course he wants it,' Cardoso said. 'Don't you?'

Eduardo grinned suddenly. 'All right. Yes.'

'*Optimo*,' Rui Cardoso said. 'Let's go back and clinch the deal before he changes his mind.'

VII

He was given a month's wages in advance, and used it to buy the barman's outfit he was required to wear. When his disability gratuity and pension came through, he bought a second hand Vespa motor scooter and moved into a seventh floor flat whose windows overlooked Cascais and the Tagus estuary. Within a space of a month, his whole life changed. He was the barman at Pinginhas. He was Eduardo da Costa, who sang *fado* in a new intriguing way that made you feel that he was confiding his innermost hopes and sorrows. He was the man in Flat 714 whose mother came every Sunday to cook his lunch, and who kept potted geraniums on the staircase outside his door.

🔉 18 🔉

I

IT WAS on the second Sunday in September that the first large scale meeting of officers took place. There was no single leader, no individual who could be named as the instigator; but since the promulgation of the Rebelo Decree in July, a dozen or so junior army officers had been sounding out the opinions of their contemporaries and compiling a list of those they felt were prepared to take action.

The list of names was then turned into a guest list: each officer was invited by personal invitation to come to a special barbecue at a country farmhouse. They were told that the farmhouse was a little difficult to find, and that they should therefore *rendez-vous* at the Temple of Diana, in the old town of Evora.

There were a hundred and thirty-six of them in all. They drove out independently from Lisbon, crossing the River Tagus by the Salazar and Vila Franca bridges, and heading eastward along country roads that ran between rolling hills of cork oaks and sun-baked land.

Each officer was met on the steps of the Temple of Diana, and each was invited to continue his journey to the farmhouse in another car. It was a sort of magical mystery tour: nobody knew where he was being taken, but each had a shrewd idea that this was more than just a barbecue lunch.

It was difficult, on arrival at the farmhouse, to discover exactly who the hosts were; pork and hazel nuts were served, but the meal did not drag on into the afternoon. The last carloads of officers arrived, and the meeting was called to order.

The organisers were quick to point out that there was no

446

political purpose to this gathering; that would have been illegal. No, they were there to air and discuss the grievance all of them felt over the Rebelo Decree.

But inevitably, it went much further than that. Although the officers who attended this five-hour marathon represented a wide range of political persuasion, all were agreed that radical changes were necessary in the African policy of Caetano's government.

All four divisions of the army were represented: the infantry, traditionally radical; the cavalry, conservative; the engineers and artillery, argumentative; and the parachutists – out of their depth. While officer after officer spoke, notes were taken on each one's attitudes and political leanings: embryo alliances were formed, and those men with special talents earmarked.

The product of this meeting was a document of protest. It was drafted and agreed before the guests departed, and within a few weeks it was backed by nearly three hundred signatures. It dealt largely with matters of career structure, pay and prestige, and only touched on the deeper, political issues. It was presented to Marcello Caetano, whom it angered, and who did nothing about it.

Two days after the Evora meeting, the Chief of Staff of the army, General Costa Gomes, represented a similar case direct to the prime minister, saying that he would resign if the matter were not properly resolved. If ever there was a time for forthright action, this was it: the army had presented Caetano with a clear warning that trouble lay ahead. But instead of heeding the warning and doing something about it, Caetano vacillated and put in hand a token enquiry.

His indecision served only to enrage the lower echelons of the armed services further, and to strengthen their resolve to seek redress.

More meetings followed. The *Movimento das Forças Armadas*, or MFA, was now in being, and its slogan 'For the good of the State and the Army' was to be found at the foot of the declarations and circulars that it issued. A co-ordinating committee of eight officers was formed, one of whom, Vasco Gonçalves, was a full colonel. His presence on the committee

447

added respectability as well as weight to the protest.

The autumn months passed, and although there was a succession of meetings in private houses in and around Lisbon, nothing very much was achieved. Mass resignations were discussed and the shades of legality studied and argued. Then, out of the blue, Lieutenant Colonel Banazol stood up at one of the many meetings and said he was sick of the paper war and proposed that the only real way of sorting things out was to have a coup.

It was the first time that anyone had actually suggested a takeover by force, and it was discussed again as one of three options at a meeting in the walled town of Obidos, a two-hour drive from the capital.

Lisbon was suddenly full of rumours. While Caetano was away in Madrid, General Kaulza de Arriaga – the 'Pink Panther' – tried to whip up support for a coup from the right, but he hadn't bargained for the popularity of Spinola, whom he distrusted, and his plan was quickly betrayed. The political situation by the end of the year was now comparable to a pan of milk being slowly heated: a skin had formed on the surface, but the milk was seething underneath it, and it was only a matter of time before it boiled over.

On the recommendation of the Portuguese Secret Service – the DGS – a large number of army officers were moved to new posts in the new year. The aim of this move was to break up cells of dissension, but its effect was just the opposite: by being moved from barracks to barracks, officers were able to make new friends, new contacts, and to spread the gospel of protest throughout the army. Then, towards the end of February, Spinola's book *Portugal e o Futuro*, 'Portugal and the Future' was published. Its sentiments collided head-on with government policy for the conduct of the wars in Africa, and Caetano was later to admit that when he read it, he became aware for the first time that revolution was inevitable.

At the time, however, the prime minister tried to take a tough line. He ordered his minister of defence to call a meeting of the heads of the three services, at which they would be invited to endorse the African policy. Two generals and a rear admiral – Gosta Gomes, Spinola and Bagulho – refused to attend this meeting, saying that only in totalitarian states did politicians ask generals for public endorsement of their policies. Once again, Caetano misjudged the mood and intensity of feeling in the army: Costa Gomes and Spinola were dismissed from their posts, and a further twenty-three officers were sacked or transferred. Thus the army's most respected leaders were seen to be humiliated because they chose to voice the opinions of those whom they commanded. Portugal took another step towards the precipice of rebellion.

Events seemed to come to a head in the early hours of 16 March: a handful of junior officers, backed by two hundred men, mutinied at the headquarters of the 5th infantry battallion at Caldas da Rainha, a town eighty kilometers north of Lisbon, known for its pottery. They locked up their commanding officers, commandeered a squadron of armoured vehicles, equipped themselves with small arms, and set off down that abominable road that links Oporto and Lisbon, the N1. On the motorway leading into Lisbon, they were stopped by a roadblock set up by units of the 7th cavalry division and the National Guard, and after a bloodless confrontation, they returned to their barracks.

A lot of people thought, then, that the scare was over.

II

In Oporto, the members of the British community were aware of the unrest but were more concerned with the news they heard about Britain on the BBC World Service. Heath's government had fallen, the miners' strike had practically brought the country to a standstill, the oil crisis had sent inflation rocketing and share prices were back to the levels of the early fifties.

By comparison, Caetano seemed to be steering Portugal rather cleverly through dangerous waters. 1973 had been a boom year, and most of the port wine firms were expanding. Teape & Co. was no exception.

449

'You can buy Teape's Port in Tokyo, Texas and Toulon,' Bobby said over lunch at the British Club one day in April. 'And in a couple of years we'll have them drinking it in Taiwan, Tahiti and Trieste as well.'

But the day after he made that boast, Martin Laughton brought a disturbing piece of news back with him from his sales visit to Germany, which warranted immediate discussion by the four directors.

They gathered in Teape's office: Bobby, Joy, James and Martin. Bobby sat at the big mahogany desk, and the others in arm chairs. Formal board meetings at Teape & Co. were unheard of: business was conducted in a deceptively informal way.

'Right,' Teape said when they were ready to start. 'Let's hear the worst, Martin.'

Martin Laughton was in his thirties now: he had returned from Germany that morning and was armed with a file of papers and notes. He wore a blue pinstripe suit and a naval air squadron tie, and looked a little out of place in the rather musty atmosphere of Teape's office.

'It concerns a test of radioactivity made on our products in Germany a year or two ago,' he said. 'The aim of the test being to discover the age of individual ingredients.'

'Trying to catch us out on our vintages, I suppose,' James Remington said. At sixty, he was a slightly larger version of his father at the same age: sunburnt from recent weeks in the Douro mountains, nearly bald, with blue eyes and tufted eyebrows.

Martin Laughton shook his head. 'No. It's not that. The test they've been doing – it's called the C14 test – reveals whether or not any of the ingredients are synthetic.'

'Surely there's nothing to worry about in that case,' Joy said.

'I'm afraid there is. You see – the result proved that the brandy content in our port was of prehistoric origin.'

Bobby snorted. 'What the devil does that mean?'

'Quite simply that the brandy wasn't made from grapes at all.'

There was a shocked silence. Outside, empty barrels were being rolled along the cobbles to an awaiting lorry.

'What was it made from?' Teape asked.

'They can't say definitely. Probably coal. Or oil.'

'So what you're saying,' James said, 'is that the port that's got this stuff in it isn't port at all.'

Martin Laughton nodded. 'Technically speaking, yes. It contravenes the definition of the product. It is not "wine made from Douro grapes the fermentation of which has been stopped by the addition of grape brandy".'

'So where did this stuff come from?' James asked.

'It was brought in from Yugoslavia, but nobody knows exactly where it was manufactured. Possibly France.'

'Do we know which years are affected?' Joy asked.

'Some of our '71, more of the '72 and all of last year's. The only consolation is that all the port wine firms are affected in the same way.'

'Small consolation!' Teape said. 'This could put the port wine trade back twenty years.'

'What about the taste?' James said. 'Is that affected?'

'Not yet,' Bobby said. 'Otherwise we'd have spotted it. Don't know about the future, though.'

'I asked about that,' Martin said. 'They said there should be no difference. They also said that the radioactive level of the synthetic brandy is actually lower that that of grape brandy. So there's no question of the stuff doing anybody any harm.'

'Tell that to our French customers,' James said. 'Or worse, the Italians. They've been waiting for something like this ever since the Chianti scandal.'

Teape shook his head and put his chin in his hands. Joy looked across at him, worried for him, thinking how old he looked.

'What about our whites and tawnies?' he said, more to himself that anyone else. 'Every time I blend a new port, I'm going to have to worry about whether or not there's some of this rubbish in it.'

James Remington was taking out a slim cigar and lighting it. 'Of course we're under no obligation to reveal what years we use to make a blended port,' he said. 'So it'll be impossible to tell.'

'You mean wink at it? Carry on as before as if nothing had happened?'

451

'It's either that, or pour the affected stuff down the drain.'

'It makes one wonder,' Joy said. 'I mean – do you think this was a deliberate move? To discredit the port wine trade? What do you think, Martin?'

'I don't know. It was purchased by the Casa do Douro at a pretty low price, so maybe they should have smelt a rat then. But on the other hand we bought it cheaply too, so you could say that we should have asked questions.'

'Disagree,' James said. 'The government holds the monopoly for fortifying brandy. We have to buy what they give us, and no questions asked.'

'This is beside the point,' Teape said. 'The question remains – what should we do about it?' He looked round at the other three. 'James?'

'I propose we lie low and say nothing. Play it right down, and let the Casa do Douro do all the talking if it leaks out.'

Teape looked at Joy.

'I feel we ought to consult with other firms,' she said. 'Whatever action we take should be part of a common policy for port shippers – or at least, British port shippers.'

Teape nodded. 'Yes. I agree with that. Martin? Anything to add?'

'Nothing much. Except that it might be an idea to push as much as possible of the affected port into our cheaper blends and sell it off on the home market as quickly as we can.' He grinned. 'Sounds bad, I know. But it's business.'

'I'd go along with that,' James Remington said. 'Good sense.'

'Very well,' Teape said. 'I take note of your comments. I don't like the idea of selling port that is even technically speaking synthetic, but on the other hand I don't think we can afford to lose the best part of three vintages. I'll sound out the opinions of the other firms, but in the meantime I'd be grateful if you said as little about this as possible. The less said, the fewer the rumours, as I'm sure you'll agree.'

There was no need to take a vote: Bobby Teape ran his firm autocratically, as his father and grandfather had done before him, and although marriage to Joy had turned him into a mild and obedient husband at home, in the office he was still very much in charge.

452

It came as no suprise, a few days later, to learn that the other British port wine firms had decided on a similar course of action, for the nature of the Oporto British colony is in some ways a microcosm of the British national character: while individual firms compete quite ruthlessly with each other, when they find themselves under attack from a common enemy, they act as one.

III

Captain Otelo Saraiva de Carvalho came from a colonial background in Mozambique. He had served with Spinola in Guinea-Bissau, and had studied the guerrilla tactics of the PAIGC. He was a student of the revolutionary theories of Che Guevara and Fidel Castro, and had once nursed an ambition to become an actor. He was in his late thirties now: a stockily built officer, with close cropped, greying hair, a ready smile and a somewhat self-important manner.

As the principal architect of the revolution, he chose the classic design.

He had working with him a group of young, determined and war-toughened officers who had everything to gain from the overthrow of the Caetano regime and very little to lose. In the fiasco of the Caldas da Rainha uprising, he had a ready-made dress rehearsal that provided him with some useful lessons and also served to lull the security forces into a false sense of having the situation under control.

The date for the coup was set for some time between 22 and 29 April. Melo Antunes, a member of the coordinating committee, completed a draft political programme for the MFA to follow when the revolution had taken place. It covered the major actions that were to be taken immediately, and a long term policy. It included the disbanding of the hated DGS, the abolition of press censorship, and the removal of all existing civil governors from their posts overseas. But most important of all, it promised free, democratic elections within one year of the revolution.

453

The last days passed very quickly. The plan was simple: in the early hours of the morning, the bridges and access roads to Lisbon would be sealed by army units. The communications centre at Pontinha barracks, to the north of the capital, would be taken over. The national radio and television centres would be occupied and the airports closed. The operation would be initiated and controlled by the playing of certain prearranged tunes and songs on the radio.

At six o'clock in the evening on 24 April, Otelo Carvalho held his last briefing. Code words were issued and last minute questions answered. Then, after a final word of encouragement, the members of the coordinating team were despatched to their units.

A few hours later, the engineering regiment at Pontinha barracks rebelled. It was the first move: Carvalho now had at his disposal the central communications network of the Portuguese army, and was immediately able to transmit coded messages to key positions all over the country.

The pan of milk had finally boiled over.

IV

Revolution cannot be encapsulated or made into a vignette: it is not a single entity that can be picked up or examined. Its character is different for every individual, so that it might be said that there was not just one revolution on 25 April 1974, but nine million, one each for every member of the Portuguese population.

Revolution was the sound of tanks clattering down the Avenida de Liberdade in the early morning, a grey, overcast dawn coming up. It was the nervous announcement at six o'clock on the radio that told people a coup was in progress and that shops should remain closed. It was the rush to buy petrol and groceries, the listening to the radio, the exhilaration that was mixed with apprehension and fear.

The press made it into a revolution of flowers, of carnations

454

stuck in gun barrels and laughing soldiers accepting packets of cigarettes from excited civilians. But it was more a revolution of blue jeans: of thousands of students marching arm in arm through the city centre chanting 'Down with Fascism!' It was a revolution of strangers hugging each other, banners waving, people climbing on lamp posts, beating drums, playing their transistor radios at full volume.

For Stella, the revolution was four spools of 35mm film and the brief glimpse of Spinola coming out of the Carmo barracks having formally taken over the power from Caetano. It was the shouts of the ten-thousand-strong crowd chanting 'Victory! Victory!' It was the distorted voice of a young army captain standing up in an armoured car and addressing the crowd over a loud hailer. It was supper in the back streets of the Bairro Alto, and all night in a bar watching the television and drinking *bagaço*.

Joy's revolution was a succession of telephone calls. It was, 'Is that you dear? Are you both all right?' 'Yes, yes, we're fine.' 'I just thought it would be a good idea to keep in touch. Bye-bye, then.' It was telling Bobby, who was pacing up and down in time with the military music on the radio, to stop worrying and sit down. It was worrying about him because he was worrying, which was silly.

Revolution was Natália weeping into her apron and saying, 'Ai, Madame! What will become of poor Portugal now?'

I

FOR A WEEK OR SO after the revolution a strange, almost heady atmosphere prevailed in Portugal. People made way for each other in shops and public places where formerly they would have elbowed their way to the front. In bars and restaurants strangers struck up conversations with each other, as if it were everyone's duty to break down all the old social barriers. People wore carnations in their lapels in those early days: there were a lot of late parties, laughter and celebrations. At work, the traditional suits and ties in the city offices were replaced by blue jeans and leather jackets, and it did no harm to look in need of a haircut and shave.

Soon after the first Labour Day celebrations ever held in Portugal, Sr Rodrigues, the manager of the Teape wine lodge in Vila Nova de Gaia, called on Bobby Teape in his office and asked that he and the other directors attend a meeting of the employees, to be held in the canteen that afternoon.

'What's this for?' Teape asked.

'Sir,' said Sr Rodrigues, 'It is in order that we may discuss the policy of the firm in the light of what has happened in the country,' and Teape, seeing which way the wind blew, agreed that he and the other directors would attend.

Teape, Remington and Laughton lunched together at the Oporto British Club that day, and afterwards gathered in Teape's office where they waited until the manager reported that the employees were assembled.

'Let's hear the worst then,' Teape said, and led the way out of the old panelled office and down the sloping cobbles to the whitewashed canteen where the workers sat on rows of benches.

456

They rose to their feet as the three directors entered, and Sr Rodrigues told them all to sit down again. The directors were invited to sit at a table facing their employees, and the chatter subsided. A shop steward in flared jeans and knitted cardigan then stepped forward and proceeded to read a speech, in which he assured Teape of the continuing loyalty of the work force and the collective approval of the way in which the firm was being run. While he spoke, cloth caps were turned round and round in hands, and many of the people looked at the floor. Although the speech was complimentary, the fact that it had to be made and that the directors should be sitting in their midst was embarrassing.

Teape then stood up and thanked the shop steward for his kind remarks and hoped that the good relations which had always existed in the firm would continue in the future, and with that, the directors filed out of the canteen.

'What a waste of time that was,' Teape said when they were back in his office.

James Remington took out a penknife and cut the end off a cigar. 'Better than a long string of demands,' he observed.

'No doubt those'll come later.'

They lounged in the leather arm chairs under a daguerreo-type of Edward Teape, the founder of the firm, which looked severely down upon them.

'Of course we could forestall their demands,' Martin said.

Bobby looked round at him. Young Laughton was a bit too full of bright ideas. 'How?' he asked.

'We could put in hand an immediate programme of improve-ments in working conditions for a start,' Martin said. 'And if we announce a pay rise straight away, before they ask for one, we'll immediately put ourselves a lap ahead. We'd be calling the tune still, and that might provide us with a useful advantage.'

'Damn funny way of calling the tune,' Teape said.

Remington lit his cigar and looked at the end. 'He may have a point, Bobby. We can't hope to beat this revolution, so we may as well join it.'

'We could find ourselves nationalised within the year, though,' Bobby said. 'In which case it'll be money down the drain.'

457

Martin sat forward in his chair. 'What worries me is – what was the real reason for this meeting? I can't believe it was simply to tell us what fine chaps we are. I think they wanted to set a precedent. Face-to-face meetings with the workers. We had to agree to see them, I'll admit that. But it could be the thin end of a wedge. Next time they ask to see us, maybe they won't be so complimentary.'

Teape reported the discussion to Joy that evening; he was in his seventieth year now and was inclined to puff and blow between his sentences. He walked up and down on the terraces at the back of the house, muttering to himself and slapping his right fist into the palm of his hand.

'Stop worrying about it,' Joy told him. 'Worry never saved the Roman Empire.'

'All very well to say that.'

They stood together and looked down the garden and out over the entrance to the Douro.

'What would you do?' he asked.

'I think Martin may be right this time. I think it's better to spend money on them now, before they ask for it, than to wait for a demand.'

He stood in silence for a while.

'This could be the end of the firm, you know. They may take us all over. Amalgamate us into one big national combine.'

'You mustn't think that. There's no reason to yet.'

'Exactly. Yet.'

'Don't be so pessimistic, Bobby! It isn't the end of the world!'

'I wonder. This country could go commie within the year. They're talking about farming cooperatives already.'

She took his hand. 'You don't have to blame yourself for anything, do you? You've been a good *patrão*. You've always dealt fairly with your people. They won't forget that. See?'

He smiled a little sadly and raised her fingers to his lips. 'You're very kind to me,' he said. 'I don't deserve it.'

His eyes were watering a little. She squeezed his hand. 'Silly boy,' she said.

He wondered what would happen. There was so much to look back on and so little to look forward to.

'What are you thinking?' Joy asked.

'I'm going to retire,' he replied. 'After the *vindima*.'

II

Stella bought a small terraced house in old Cascais after moving south. It had high ceilings and creaky wooden floors, and she hung her collection of Aubrey Beardsley prints on the whitewashed walls. In the winter, the draughts whistled through the cracks in the window frames. From an upstairs balcony, you could just glimpse the sea over a jumble of roofs.

Mia and Clare now went to school at St Julians, five miles away in Carcavelos. Stella took them in by car every day before going on to her language teaching job at the British Council in Lisbon. Sam was making difficulties over the divorce, and from time to time she received wordy letters from her solicitor explaining the position.

The euphoria of the revolution had largely evaporated by early July. Spinola and his *junta* were at loggerheads with the Armed Forces Movement, and the country was running out of money. Lisbon and the surrounding towns were plastered with political posters and daubed with slogans, and the streets were littered with handbills advertising the latest rally or meeting or *manifestacão*. In Cascais, as in almost every other town in the south, there was now a Communist Party headquarters, complete with red flag over the door and the well-worn exhortation to the workers of the world. In the capital, there were brilliantly coloured murals of Marx and Lenin, of victorious workers brandishing impossibly large revolutionary flags, of brave new people marching arm in arm towards a brave new horizon and of fascist rats being crushed under the dainty heel of a virtuous maiden called Portugal.

When Phillida Davis came to stay for ten days in July, she revelled in it all.

'It's invigorating,' she declared. 'There's no other way to describe it.'

459

They sat outside the Baía hotel and drank capitalist scotch on revolutionary rocks. The sun beat down upon them, and Phillida urged that it was right and good that censorship should be relaxed and pornography made freely available. Of course there was a rush to see *Last Tango In Paris*. Of course 'morals' in the conventional sense were bound to decline. But wasn't this better than the falsely propped façade that the Portuguese had presented to the world in the days of Caetano and Salazar? Of course it was.

'It is necessary to reduce the whole edifice to rubble first,' she explained. 'Then they will be able to build.'

Stella was going through a period of self-appraisal, and was more interested in herself than in Portugal. Having escaped from Sam, from England and from her father, she now felt adrift, aimless.

'I'm not achieving anything,' she said one evening when the twins were in bed. 'I seemed to have exchanged one captivity for another. What a bloody world it is.'

'But do you know what you want to achieve?'

'I've thought about it. Endlessly. And you know what I always come back to? Don't laugh. What I need, really need, is a deep, lasting relationship.'

'Don't we have a relationship?'

'Not a complete one. Or a sexual one.'

Phillida stretched out her hands. 'Stella, love – I know you said no the last time I asked you, but have you changed your mind? Would you like a sexual relationship with me?'

Stella went to the window and looked out over Cascais bay to the lights of Estoril and Carcavelos.

'It might be the answer, you know,' Phillida said. 'It may be that you're denying yourself something that – well, that you need.'

'It would be fun, I suppose,' Stella said. 'To experiment. But it would only louse things up between us. In the long run. And I can't risk that. No. I think I need a man.'

Phillida lit a cigarette. 'Plenty around. Go and grab one.'

'That's what I used to do. But it always ended in tears, didn't it?'

'You know why, don't you?'

460

'Why?'

'Well, I know this may hurt, but you've never really succeeded in throwing off the parental influence. I know you think you have, but you haven't.'

'All very well saying that. But how do I "throw it off"?'

'You need to go back to root causes, love. From what I know of you, I'm convinced that your relationship with your father is the key. He's always there, isn't he? Between you and the person you want to be.'

Stella snorted. 'He's always come between me and everything.'

'Maybe you should review your childhood experience, try to identify the areas which caused the deepest conflict. Wasn't there something about a boyfriend when you were in your teens?'

'Oh, yes. That was one of many battles. He's living around here now.'

'Do you ever see anything of him?'

'From time to time. But we never speak. It's a sort of mute agreement. We cut each other dead. He has good reasons to loathe my guts, like every other male I bump into on this planet.'

'Why should he loathe your guts?'

'My father sacked him. Didn't I tell you about it ages ago?'

'Perhaps you did.'

'He was the first really. The first of a long line of heterosexual disasters.'

'Has he married?'

'No. He had some sort of disease in Africa. He's a bit disfigured.'

'You should go and befriend him,' Phillida said. 'He could well be part of your guilt complex.'

'More likely I'm part of his.'

'All the more reason for trying, in that case. He'd probably welcome an advance. You should do it, Stella. Honestly. For your own sake.'

III

She acted on Phillida's advice a week later. She had seen Eduardo down by the harbour from time to time over the past weeks, and he was there again one afternoon when she was walking back to her flat after taking the twins to their judo class. He was watching a fishing trawler being hauled out of the water by a winch operated from the stone esplanade. She stood on the far side of the road, aware that the decision to go and talk to him was entirely hers, and that in taking such a decision she could alter both their lives.

The thought of it pleased her, giving her a sense of power which she had not experienced since the early days with Sam. A number of people were watching the winching operation, and she walked across to join them, moving close to Eduardo so that she stood almost beside and slightly behind him.

It was strange to see him at such close quarters again: he wore a check shirt and flared blue denims; his hair was thinning and lank, and she remembered how it had once been thick and wavy. In a perverse way, the very fact that he was not particularly good-looking made him all the more attractive.

The mechanical winch revved and strained and the trawler, which had been badly holed, came slowly out of the water. The people watching exchanged remarks, and in due course Eduardo turned and saw her.

She smiled and said hullo, being careful not to feign surprise. She made him shake hands; he was clearly embarrassed, and she was pleased to feel that the situation was hers to control. He made a move to go, but she kept him talking, asking him about his mother and what he was doing. Her Portuguese had been rusty when she had come out to Portugal the previous year, but it had improved now, and she was reasonably fluent again.

'I hear you've been making a name for yourself as a singer,' she said.

He smiled awkwardly, and his broken front teeth showed. 'Not any more. That's over.'

'Oh? Why?'

'The restaurant closed down. I'm out of a job.'

They watched the winching operation for a while.

'I'm glad I bumped into you,' she said. 'I've seen you in the town, but I never had the courage to say hullo.'

He grinned and avoided her eyes. She enjoyed his self-consciousness: it was a relief that he was not at ease, not making small talk. She asked him where he was living, and he told her about his flat.

'Look,' she said, 'Why don't we go and have a coffee?'

He hesitated.

'Or would you rather not be seen with me?'

'No it's not that,' he said quickly.

'What's stopping us then?' She moved a little closer, smiled and blinked at him, inwardly amused at herself for using such a blatant technique. 'Let's,' she said. 'I'd like to talk. Wouldn't you?'

'All right,' he said, and they walked together along the sea wall and into the shopping precinct, where jeans and shirts hung outside the shops and a gipsy sold trinkets and a cripple hawked lottery tickets to the passers by.

'Why did Pinginhas close down?' she asked when they were seated outside a café in the sun.

'There was trouble with the staff. They wanted to take over the business, but the *patrão* wouldn't agree. He closed the place down, and a week later there was a fire.'

'So what are you going to do now?'

'Look for another job.' He stirred his black coffee and she saw his big blunt hands and the burn-like scars on his wrists and forearms.

'I gather you had a bad time in Africa,' she said.

'It wasn't a holiday for anyone.'

'You were in Guinea, weren't you?'

'At the end, yes. Mozambique before that. And Goa before that.'

'So you've seen quite a bit of life.'

'I suppose so.'

'You never got married.'

He shook his head, and their eyes met for a split second before he looked away in embarrassment.

There was a lengthening silence. Eventually she said, 'It's

almost twenty years, isn't it? Since you left Moinho Velho.'

He looked at her steadily now, and she felt his antagonism.

'Did you hate me for that?'

'I didn't like you for it.'

'Do you hate me still?'

He considered. 'I don't know you, do I?'

'You never heard the real story about what happened. I often wanted to explain. Afterwards.'

He said nothing. He picked up his coffee cup and drained it.

'Would you like me to explain now?' she asked.

'If you want to.'

'Would you like a brandy?' She saw his face, and added: 'Don't worry. This is on me.' She beckoned to the waiter and ordered. Ridiculously, sitting with him at the table under the gaze of the pedestrians walking up and down the precinct made her feel as though she were breaking rules. Fraternising with the enemy. Phillida was probably right, she reflected. This is what I need to do.

The brandies arrived and she raised her glass to him. He grinned cautiously and she thought to herself, I'm winning, I'm winning. She put her elbows on the table and leaned slightly towards him, aware of his glance down her cheesecloth shirt, and fizzling inwardly once again at the excitement of the chase.

Eduardo sat and sipped his brandy, listening to her talking about herself, glancing from time to time into her eyes, enjoying the feeling of being with a woman again. She told him the story behind his dismissal from Teape & Co. and of the battle she had had with her father over the diary.

'So – you didn't tell your father about it at all?' he said. 'It wasn't your fault.'

'Did you think it was?'

'Of course. I thought – I thought – '

'You must have hated me,' she said. 'My God!'

But he explained that he had not hated her so much as what she had stood for: he had hated her wealth and her position; above all, he had come to despise, through her, the English as a nation.

She told him how she had often toyed with the idea of

464

writing to him, to explain what had happened; but their lives had headed off in different directions and keeping in touch had seemed futile and pointless. 'And anyway,' she added, 'I doubt if you would have believed me.'

'Perhaps not,' he said, and for a moment she recognised in his roguish smile the Eduardo she remembered. She allowed her hand to touch his as if by accident. He looked down quickly and then back into her eyes. 'And now you're married, and have a family.'

She told him about Sam and her life on the various air stations. She talked about her friends, her children, her impending divorce. He could not understand why she should confide so much in him, but was flattered by it nevertheless, and happy to listen to her and to be seen with her. Eventually she looked at her watch and said that she had to go and collect the twins.

'I'm glad we've met at long last,' she said when she had settled the bill and they were leaving. 'Aren't you?'

He nodded in his rather awkward, jerky way. They walked together down the precinct.

'I'm off every Wednesday afternoon,' she said. 'So what about lunch?'

He agreed, and they arranged a time and place. They reached the main road and shook hands to say goodbye. He watched her go away towards the older part of the town, and then walked up the main street and on, to his flat.

When he arrived home, he stood on his seventh floor window and looked out over the coast line towards Caparica, feeling more confidence in himself than he had for a very long time.

IV

They lunched at a *tasca* near the Gil Vicente theatre the following Wednesday, and shared a bottle of wine. They ate *caldo verde* soup, grilled squid, and 'heavenly bacon', and had coffee and double brandies afterwards. Stella insisted on

465

paying. 'I'm not out of a job,' she said. 'Yet.'

He began to contribute a little more to their conversation. He asked her what she thought about Portugal's revolution.

'It had to happen, didn't it?' she said. 'Those wars in Africa were bleeding you white.'

She asked him what he thought of Spinola: he said he was a great soldier, but not a great politician.

'Did you ever meet him?'

He grinned. 'Oh yes. I saw him all right. Everyone did. He made quite sure of that.'

They sat opposite each other in the crammed little restaurant, and around them other people talked and ate a great deal, the waiter hurrying back and forth between the tables and kitchen and shouting orders to the chef.

'Looks as though he's run into trouble now,' Stella said.

Eduardo opened his hands. 'He won't last long. This time next year Otelo Carvalho will have taken over.'

'Will you be glad about that?'

He shook his head. 'If the communists get in, they'll rape this country. He'll have us all working for Moscow within a few months of taking over.'

'So you're not a Communist?'

He shook his head.

'Who do you support?'

'Mario Soares. There isn't anyone else, is there?'

'So you're a socialist?'

He nodded. 'I suppose so.'

'That makes two of us,' she said, and reached across the table to shake his hand.

They sat over their coffee until nearly three, and then he sat beside her in her mini as she drove through the town and up past the market along the road which had been recently renamed 'The Road of 25 April'. She turned right after the Oxford cinema, following his directions, and up the hill to the new estate of high-rise flats that towered above the Ribeira das Vinhas.

'Can I come up?' she asked.

They stood in the lift, aware of each other. They got out at the seventh floor and she admired his potted geraniums.

466

He led the way into the flat: the walls were rather bare and the furnishings cheap and new. There was a Japanese stereo music centre on a shelf, and a few records.

He apologised for it. 'I haven't been in it all that long. I'd meant to do it up better.'

'You've got a nice view, haven't you?'

'It's not bad. Trouble is, I don't expect I'll be here much longer.'

'Why not?'

'Can't afford it.'

'But you'll get another job!'

'I don't know about that.'

'Have you done any singing at all since leaving Pinginhas?'

'No.'

'Well you must try. You must make the effort.'

'I haven't really got the talent, that's the trouble.'

'I heard you were very good.'

He shook his head. 'I'll show you something.' He went to a drawer and took out a press cutting from the *Diário de Notícias*. It was headed 'New Voices at Pinginhas' and mentioned several names. Eduardo da Costa was one of them, and the commentator dismissed him as a singer with a nice voice who lacked the depth of feeling or passion to sing really good *fado*.

'See what I mean?' he said when Stella had read it.

'But this is only one person's opinion,' she said. 'You mustn't take any notice of this.'

'The trouble is, he's right. I've always known it, really. With *fado* – you've either got it or you haven't. And I haven't.'

'That's not what I heard. Besides, you've only just started professionally. You can't give up because of one critic's remarks.'

He shrugged and put away the press cutting. 'We'll see,' he said, and when he turned back she was close to him, taking his hands. 'I'd like to help, Eduardo. And I think I can, if you'll let me.'

'How?'

'Well, any artist needs encouragement. Everyone knows that. I'd like to see you make a success of singing. And if you let me help you – it'll help me, too.'

He smiled and frowned at the same time. She pulled his head down to hers and kissed him.

'There,' she said. 'I've been wanting to do that all afternoon.'

He stared down at her, tongue-tied.

'Shall we help each other?' she said.

She drove away from the flat with a feeling of elation: she would set him on his feet, give him the self-confidence he so obviously lacked. She would forge a bond between them, reach out to him, get really close. She could make him love her; she would teach him; she would mould him into her man, the man she needed, the man that would fill the blank void of aimlessness in her life.

V

They met again twice at the weekend, and the following Wednesday drove out to a secluded beach. Stella lay on a flat rock in her yellow bikini, and Eduardo sat beside her, too self-conscious to take off his shirt. The waves rattled on the pebbles at their feet and the heat of the sun came off the nearby cliffs in sudden warm gusts.

She asked him all about his life in the army and he explained how it had been possible to make a bit of money on the side in Mozambique. He drew a diagram of the *tabanca* at Mudanda and explained how the defences had worked and what sort of life they had led. He told her about the time when Cardoso shot all the stray dogs, and of the night when the guerillas had attacked. She asked him if he had ever seen anyone killed and he told her about an officer in Goa who had refused to surrender and had died while actually firing a machine gun. He told her about the mass burial of guerillas in Mozambique, and the death of Sergeant Coelho and Captain Almeida.

He found suddenly that it was easy to talk to her and that he needed to talk: she seemed genuinely interested in what he had done, what he had enjoyed, what he had hated. He told her about his *lavandeira*, the young girl who had offered herself to him, and when he looked back at Stella, he saw that she had removed the top half of her bikini and was lying back on the flat rock, her eyes looking into his.

'Do you mind?' she asked.

He grinned and his crooked front teeth showed.

'You could do me a favour,' she said. 'There's some sun tan lotion in my bag. Could you get it for me?'

He opened the bag and found the bottle. He handed it across, but she shook her head. 'You do it.'

'Where?'

'Where I need it. On the white parts.'

He started.

'That's lovely, Eduardo. You do it very well. Have you had lots of practice?'

He smiled sheepishly, shook his head.

'Do you know the difference between a girl in a bikini and a roast chicken?' she asked, mock serious.

'No?'

'Can't you guess? There's no difference. The white meat's better in each case.'

It took him a moment to understand.

'Relax,' she said. 'We won't get into trouble this time. Why don't you take your shirt off?'

He shook his head.

'Are you shy?'

'Perhaps.'

'What are you shy about?'

'I'm not as nice to look at as you are.'

'I won't mind. Honestly.'

He hesitated further. She reached up and undid the buttons of his shirt, put her hand up, over his chest. 'Come on, boy,' she whispered. 'Take it off.'

So he took it off, and it was difficult to hide her feelings when she saw the pattern of scars that had been left behind.

'Isn't that better?'

'Perhaps.'

He lay down on the rock beside her, and some time later she said, 'Never be shy with me, Eduardo. Will you promise that?'

They lay face to face and she began kissing him. She ran her

469

hands over his chest and arms and legs, and he looked troubled.

'What is it? What's the matter?'

'There's something you ought to know.'

'What?'

He seemed to struggle inwardly, avoiding her eyes. 'I can't – do it,' he said. 'I'm impotent.'

'Since when?'

'Since my illness. It did something to me.'

'Are you sure?'

'Yes. The doctors warned me about it.'

'But have you tried?'

He nodded. 'It didn't work.'

'You probably tried too hard.'

'I don't think so.'

'They might be wrong, you know. Doctors sometimes are.'

'I don't think they're wrong.'

'Look at me.'

He looked into her eyes.

'It doesn't make any difference,' she said.

'It does to me.'

'Of course it does. You're a man. Men always have to prove themselves. What you must do is forget you're a man for a while. Just enjoy things the way they are.'

He smiled and looked away.

'Like that,' she said. 'Isn't that nice?'

It was much easier than she had expected.

'There you are,' she whispered. 'I said they might be wrong, didn't I?'

VI

Bobby and Joy gave a small dinner party in early August. They invited Freddy and Madge, James and Joanna, Martin and Penny. Custódia made a mistake with the soup which had to be watered and tasted like superior dishwater, and the boiled potatoes were slightly hard in the middle, but otherwise everything went off very well.

Bobby was in particularly good form. He helped everyone to rather more white wine than they wanted, and had a long humorous argument with Freddy Randall about their bachelor years. The ladies withdrew at the end of the meal and left the men to sit over the Teape's Special Reserve.

'This is going to be Bobby's last *vindima* before he retires,' Joy confided when the drawing room door was shut. 'So I'm planning something rather special for him. I thought it would be nice to hold a really big lunch party in his honour at Quinta das Rosas.'

'What a lovely idea,' Madge said.

'But I shall have to enlist your support,' Joy went on. 'I hope to invite all Bobby's old friends, so that it becomes a real occasion.'

'When will you have it?' Joanna asked.

'That was what I wanted to discuss. If the vintage starts some time late next month, probably the best time to have it would be on the first Saturday in October, which is nice and close to Bobby's seventieth birthday.'

'What about children?' Penny asked. 'Are they invited as well?'

'I thought not at first, but I know Bobby will want Stella to bring the twins up, so really I don't see why everyone else's children shouldn't come along too.'

'You'll have hundreds!' Joanna said.

Joy went to the bureau and took out some papers. 'I've got fifty-eight names so far, and possibly another thirty or so children. But of course they won't all be able to come. What I'm anxious to avoid is hurting people's feelings by leaving them off the list. So I've made a couple of carbon copies for you so that you can have a look at it and add any suggestions.' She handed the copies to Joanna and Penny and showed the original to Madge. 'The other thing is the problem of putting people up for the night. Most of them will be up for the vintage in any case, and staying at their *quintas*, but we shall have to find extra beds, all the same.'

'Does Bobby know about it yet?' Joanna asked.

'No. I thought I'd talk to you about it first, and get your agreement.'

'I think it's a marvellous idea,' Penny said.

Madge looked at the list. 'I see you've got Hugh down here. Do you think he'll budge from his Algarve villa?'

'Well there's no harm in asking him. It's about time that old axe was buried.'

'Hugh?' Penny asked.

'Blunden,' Joy replied. 'He was a partner until the mid-fifties. There was a silly argument, and he left.'

'When will you tell Bobby?' Joanna asked. 'Because once you start sending out invitations, it'll be difficult to keep it a secret.'

'I thought I'd just say I was planning a little celebration for him. He'll have no objection to that, and the numbers of people who come will be a tremendous thrill for him.' She looked round at the others: her sister Madge, looking more and more like an old lady these days; Joanna, nearly fifty now; and Penny, just pregnant again but not letting it be known yet in the colony. 'It's rather exciting, isn't it?' she said.

In the dining room the men were talking politics again. Only a week before, Spinola had gone on television to announce that he now recognised that the African territories had an immediate right to independence. Guinea-Bissau would be the first to be released from colonial rule, and Angola and Mozambique would enter a transitional phase almost immediately. At home, there were growing fears of a wage explosion and industrial chaos.

'It hasn't even started,' James Remington was saying. 'These last three months have been the honeymoon.'

'I've given up worrying about it,' Freddy said. 'We're too old to get worked up about a revolution here or there, eh Bobby?'

'You speak for yourself!'

James carefully detached the ash from his cigar and turned to Martin. 'I see they've given your wall the treatment.'

'*Morte ao fascistas*, yes. The trouble is, I can never quite make up my mind whether or not I'm a *fascista*.'

'They've limited themselves to a red hammer and sickle on ours,' Freddy said. 'Madge suggested painting in a background of miniature swastikas. But then she always was rather artistic.'

'Time we made a move,' Teape said. 'I don't know about anyone else, but I know where I'm going.' He opened the french windows and went out into the garden. He was joined by the others and they relieved themselves into the shrubbery.

In the drawing room, Joy was saying, 'Do you know what Custódia found in the garden today? Quite horrible. A frog with its mouth sewn up. Would you believe it? Aren't they despicable?'

'But why should anyone do that?' Penny asked.

'Oh, it's an old trick. These people have never really thrown off superstition. Custódia chased some boys out of the orchard the other day. I expect one of them did it. It's supposed to put a curse on you, you know.'

'How very frightening,' Penny said.

Joy gave her little laugh. 'Not a bit. It could be, if one didn't have a belief in a greater power than witchcraft. But as it is, these things really don't worry me at all. Mind you,' she added, hearing the men's voices in the hall, 'I haven't told Bobby about it. I think it might upset him.'

'You're all very quiet,' Teape said as they came in.

'Bound to be up to no good,' Freddy laughed.

They settled down in armchairs and the conversation tripped along. Bobby was quieter now: it was getting on for eleven o'clock, and he was tired and rather too full of Custódia's lemon meringue pie. He listened to James and Martin swapping stories about their naval experiences, and his mind wandered back over the years, remembering so many other evenings he had spent in this house, first as a bachelor and suitor to Joy, later as a guest of Fay and Dodger when Ruth was alive, and now as host and master of the house. Of course it was much too big for them now and when he retired they would almost certainly sell it and move into something smaller. He and Joy had discussed the possibility of spending their last years in England, but that seemed a terrible break to have to make. He wondered about Stella. She hadn't written for two months now. He wished he could see just a little more of her. But she had a life to lead, and he was lucky to have her in Portugal at all. If only she and Sam could settle their differences . . .

The guests were going. He got to his feet and went out to see them off. The headlights of their cars went away up the drive between the pine trees; he came back into the hall and shut the front door.

473

'Right,' said Joy. 'You go straight up and have your bath. I could see you were nearly asleep just now. Off you go, there's a good boy.'

He went up the stairs, and Joy went into the kitchen to make sure Custódia wasn't putting the bone-handled knives into the dishwasher. That done, she returned to the drawing room, plumped up the cushions and collected a few ashtrays. She heard the hum of the dishwasher as Custódia switched it on, and went back into the kitchen. At the same time, she heard Bobby call from upstairs. She put the ashtrays down on the kitchen table and went up to him.

She found him on the landing. He was on all fours.

'My dear man, what are you doing?' she asked, but then she saw that his face was racked with pain and that a stream of saliva hung from the side of his mouth.

'Feel sick,' he managed to say. 'Feel very – '

His whole body shook. She went to him, holding him. The attack passed: his breathing was rapid and shallow, and when she felt his pulse it was irregular and weak. She kept very calm. She made him lie down there on the landing and ran to fetch the pillows off all the beds, in order to prop him up. She covered him with a blanket. He looked up at her, his eyes wandering, his face grey and damp with sweat. There was no doubt in her mind what had happened. She must get hold of a doctor straight away.

She hurried down stairs and flipped open the telephone book, dialling the number three times before it rang properly. Eventually, after a long pause, Doctor Reis answered it.

'It's very inconvenient,' he said when she asked him to come.

'I don't care how inconvenient it is or how much it costs, doctor. I want you to come immediately. Now. It is very urgent.'

He agreed. She rang off and went upstairs. Custódia was outside the bedroom. 'I've turned the bed back, my lady.'

'Thank you, Custódia. Now if you'll just help me we'll get the Senhor into bed. Come along.'

His dressing gown was not properly tied and he was naked underneath it. Custódia tried to help lift him while looking the other way.

474

'Never mind what you see, girl,' Joy said. 'Put your hand under his legs here. And the other one round here. That's the way. Now give me your hand. Up we go.'

They carried him into the bedroom and lowered him gently into the double bed.

'Now go down to the kitchen and put a kettle on to boil. Stay there until I call for you.'

'Yes, my lady.'

'And when the doctor arrives, bring him straight up here.'

'Yes, my lady.'

She turned back to Bobby when Custódia had left. She put another pillow behind his head and ran her fingers gently through his thin, white hair.

'Does it still hurt, my darling?'

He tried to smile. 'Not quite so much.'

She took his hand. 'Don't be afraid, Bobby,' she whispered. 'Please don't be afraid.'

VII

Foz do Douro
12th September 1974.

My dear Stella,

I have now confirmed the date for the lunch party at Saborinho for Saturday 5th October, and I really do feel that it is your duty to attend: your father has continued his improvement since I 'phoned you last week, and went into the office today for the first time since his little stroke. He is being very brave and determined about it all, insisting that he will continue at the firm until the vintage is over. I have told him that I am planning a little celebration for him, and his very first question was, 'Will Stella and the twins be there?' so you see how important it is to him that you do come up for it. I know you have already planned a holiday at that time, but I'm afraid I must insist that on this occasion your family has to come first. As to your suggestion that the twins come

475

up and stay from the Thursday, I have spoken to Penny and she is happy to meet them at the station and look after them. But please, *please* make sure that you come up – at least for the day, and preferably longer.

I am enclosing your father's letter to you. As you will see he is a little wobbly with his writing still, but he is coming on well and in good heart.

With love,
Aunt Joy.

Dearest Stella,

Only a very short note I'm afraid, as I have difficulty in controlling this damn pen which keeps jumping about in my hand. It was splendid to hear your voices on the phone last Sunday. Mia sounds so grown up now, what with her judo and her reading. It only seems like yesterday that you were burying your nose in books up in your room, in just the same way.

I am thinking of you lots and lots, and looking forward to seeing you very soon.

Your very loving,
Dad.

⚜ 20 ⚜

I

THE VINTAGE started on 26 September that year. The grapes were of good average quality: somewhat light in colour, but otherwise perfectly sound.

James and Joanna Remington arrived at the Quinta das Rosas a few days before the picking started so that James could tour the surrounding farms and discuss quality and prices, while Joanna put in hand the considerable catering arrangements that would be necessary during the following three weeks.

The pickers and treaders began arriving from the surrounding villages at about the same time. Some of them had come to Saborinho every vintage of their lives: they had been brought up by their mothers while still taking milk from the breast, had played in the dust as toddlers and had grown up with the rhythm of the seasons that produces olives, almonds and small dark grapes in the extraordinary terrain of the Douro valley.

In the old days, the men and women had slept wherever they could find room to lie down under shelter: in stables among the animals or in sheds provided by a magnanimous *patrão*. Now, at Quinta das Rosas, they were housed in a whitewashed building that overlooked the Douro valley where once the river had flowed swiftly along but where now, since the building of the dams, the mountains were reflected in wide stretches of still water. They slept in bunk beds, crammed together in dormitories which they regarded as comfortable in comparison with those provided at other, less luxurious *quintas*. Their food was cooked in big black three-legged cauldrons over an open fire in the farmhouse kitchen: they ate sitting on benches at trestle tables amid much laughter and

477

talking and the drinking of young red wine.

Now was the time that the young people started new romances and the old rekindled friendships born of many vintages. This was the time of working together, the women chattering among themselves as they moved slowly along between the vines, the young men grunting as the heavy baskets of grapes were hoisted onto their shoulders and sweating as they ran down the steeply sloping paths.

There was a new road to the *quinta* now so it was no longer necessary to leave your car at Pinhão and come the rest of the way by train. The sound of the *paciência*'s siren still echoed between the mountains as the train moved inland, but it was a diesel train now, and it no longer heralded the arrival of the English.

Bobby Teape's arrival was heralded in a different way: towards four o'clock, a pale cloud of dust appeared on the skyline and crept along the ridge a thousand feet above the chalet. Slowly, it crawled in a wide zigzag down the mountainside until you could see the car as it approached.

On the terrace behind the chalet, Joanna brought out a handbell and rang it until the noise echoed and re-echoed. Dogs began to bark down at the farm, and the people began to make their way up the hill to welcome the *patrão* for his last *vindima*. James and Joanna walked out, under the arch of vines, and waited as the car negotiated the last hairpin bend and drew up outside the chalet.

Bobby looked thinner and older, but he wore the same straw hat he always wore, and he managed to get out of the car without assistance. Old Ayres, toothless and in his ninetieth year, croaked '*Viva patrão!*' as he had every year, and Etelvina, the new maid, held up her baby for him to admire. The manager and the *caseiro* came forward to welcome him, and Joy looked on proudly as he shook their hands and asked them about their families.

The Remingtons and the Teapes went into the chalet, and the servants brought in the luggage. Tea was served on the terrace in the shade of the vines. James hoisted the British and Portuguese flags. Teape was in residence. The vintage had begun.

Joanna poured the tea, and the men started talking about the quality of the grapes almost immediately.

'We're getting SGs of ten and a half and eleven at Terra Nova,' Remington said, 'and I would say that ours here would be better than that.'

'What about the people?' Teape asked. 'Are they happy with the astronomical wages we're paying them?'

'I think so. But they're not saying so.'

Teape laughed. 'I suppose that would be asking too much.'

'What sort of journey did you have?' Joanna asked.

'Not bad at all,' Joy said. 'But this new road really is the limit, isn't it? Goodness knows what it's done to the springs of my car.'

'Oh – I nearly forgot,' Joanna said. 'There's a letter for you.' She went inside and brought out an envelope. The address was typed, and so was the letter inside.

It was from Stella.

Dear Aunt Joy,

Thank you for your letter about the *vindima* arrangements. I've changed my dates to fit in and now plan to return from the Algarve on Thursday 3rd and drive up to Saborinho on the 4th. I have to be back at work on the Monday, so will have just the two nights with you. I am sending the twins to the Van de Eifels while I'm away, and they will put them on the morning train to Oporto on Thursday as planned.

I think now is the time to give you some information which may not entirely meet with your approval. It's this: for the last few weeks I have been seeing a lot of Eduardo, Natália's son. As you know, he and I were very friendly a long time ago, and we have now re-established a relationship. As I detest secret affairs, I have no intention of hiding this from the colony, and I therefore propose to bring Eduardo up with me when I come on the 4th. You may as well know from the start that we have been living together for the last fortnight, so we could quite easily share a room at Quinta das Rosas. But if this is too much for the colony's over-developed sense of propriety, then I suppose we could pretend we were 'just good friends' this time round. Whatever – I thought I'd let you know in advance so that you could tell Dad and avoid any unnecessary big surprise. Now that he's so much better, I'm sure it'll do him no harm; you might tell him that meeting and getting to know Eduardo has been a tremendous relief (and release) for me, and that I feel happier and more settled inside myself than I have ever done before. So even if you do object I'm afraid he *will* be with me when I arrive on the 4th. You will just have to face up to this. By the way – Mia and Clare already know all about it, so you can talk quite openly about it to them.

I shall send this to Saborinho as there may not be time for it to reach you at Foz before you go up the Douro.

See you on Friday, and give my love to Dad.

As ever,
Stella.

'Who's it from?' Bobby asked.

Joy looked up. 'Stella. It's just a note to confirm that she's arriving on Friday week.'

'Can I see?'

'I'd rather you didn't, Bobby. There's a little surprise in it. Something I don't want you to know about.'

She felt herself colouring. She had never kept anything from him, nor had she ever deceived him. That had been something she had promised herself that she would never do.

'Oh – very well, very well,' he said goodnaturedly.

She forced herself to smile. 'She sends you her love and says she's looking forward to seeing you.'

Later, behind the closed door of the bedroom, Joy read the letter again, and was filled with a grim determination to bring about the end of Stella's affair with Eduardo and to ensure, above all, that he would not on any account be with her when she arrived for the *vindima*.

II

Being with him was like finding a different part of herself that she had never known before. He was not her intellectual equal, but nevertheless he was her superior in other ways. He was possessed of a certain integrity, an inner calm which she needed because it was complementary to her own unending sense of the futility of all existence. He gave her back things that she thought she had lost for ever: her belief in people, her belief in friendship, her belief in life itself. When she talked about herself, which she did far too much, he would simply nod and grin and remain silent. Did he understand what she was trying to say? It didn't matter, because he was content to listen and to be there with her and to do what she wanted to do. There had been a disagreement about money and it had been necessary to overcome his reluctance to allow her to pay for almost everything, but what was money except a means to an end? Why should he feel obliged to share expenses when he was already giving so much of himself? Friendship, affection, love – they could not be totted up and balanced between two people. Love is a river, she said, and it must find its own level. It cannot be permanently dammed or conserved; it must move down the valley to the sea. And it did move: it moved that morning when she collected him in the car and they drove out of Lisbon and across the Tagus and over the rolling plains of the Alentejo. It moved when they arrived the first afternoon and swam together in the Atlantic rollers. It moved when she made love to him in the dunes, with the sun smashing down and the white grains of sand whispering along in the wind that blew them against the pale green sand-holly. They asked each other why it had happened, and what the other had thought that first day, the day she approached him on the harbour wall in Cascais. They wondered if it would last and told each other that they would make it last, promising that every morning they would say to each other, 'It lasts and will last because we shall make it last.' It would last because they loved each other's weaknesses as well as strengths. It would last because she had to talk about herself a great deal, and because of her depressions and her feelings of guilt. It would last because he was afraid that he might not be able to please her with his sex and because he was shy of those terrible marks on his body, the marks that he would not have had if he had not joined the army, the army he would not have joined if she had not been expelled from school, and the school from which she would not have been

481

expelled if she had not been the way she was and had not needed him so much because she had hated her father. It would last because it seemed fated from the start not to last. It would be permanent because it was so obviously ephemeral, passing, transient. And there was no fear now: there was no fear, because the decision had been taken between them to tell and admit and talk. His mother knew already; she had objected but her objections had been overruled. No one would be allowed to stand in their way this time. They were the masters of their fate, and it no longer took courage to admit what had happened; rather it was something to be proud of, for a great barrier had been broken down, and a ghost laid. This was what it all meant, and the effect of it was obvious and visible to each in what they saw in the other and what they felt in themselves. For it was not fresh air and sunshine that caused this inward feeling of wellbeing but the love that poured back and forth between them, that was shared by them every day. She had been frightened by such love at first, but he gave her back the belief that such a thing could exist, so that now she could sit with him eating *conquilhas* and drinking wine, with a harvest moon reflected on the oyster beds below Cacela Velha; she could sit and take both his hands across the table and lean across and kiss him full on the lips, and what was happening was no longer make-believe love, a story she told herself before going to sleep, but a reality, for the thing flowed between them and would always flow because she believed it. And when they went back to the whitewashed bungalow under the almond trees, when she stood with him under the shower, when she lay with him, exhausted after lovemaking, and listened to the sounds of the night, it was as if two people had been fused into one, as if the whole universe revolved round this new being that they had created. So this was love: this was what she had deceived herself about so often, with Sam as with all the others, who seemed to take it from her like an indigestion pill after meals. So good, so good, so good, she said sometimes in the frenzy of lovemaking, but words were not enough to express all that she felt. And the 'so good' was not just the high point, the moment the sky jolted, it was the continuing knowledge of belonging with each other, a know-

482

ledge that could not be prevented or destroyed by anything that anyone, including Aunt Joy, could say or do. It was the knowledge that whatever happened, *whatever* happened to either one, the other would understand, would care, just as he cared on that last night, the night before they went north, when she woke up in the hour before dawn and heard an animal shriek in the darkness somewhere near the window: it shrieked and shrieked, and she clung to him, waiting for it to die. And the shrieks became softer and softer, and when they finally stopped there was a silence that brought a great release and she lay with her head against the warm hardness of his body and let the tears go out of her. And he was solid and whole: he was hard and complete and entirely her Eduardo.

III

They were starting the cut. The men stood with their arms over each other's shoulders like a chorus line of tramps: old men and teenage boys, their shirts tucked into shorts or underpants and their legs already stained by the dark juice of the grapes in which they stood. In the middle of the line, an old man with a wall eye began a slow, rhythmic chant. The line swayed left and right as the treaders marked time, and the making of another batch of Teape's port began.

The rhythm was that of a slow march, and the voice of the old man echoed in the semi-darkness of the building. This was the most exhausting part of the treading: although the grapes had been broken on being loaded into the granite tank, it was now necessary to squash the juice out of them, and this required a positive downward effort with each step. Nor did the treaders move forward immediately: instead, they marked time for several minutes before a prolonged yell from the leader indicated a half step forward. Thus, very slowly, they made their way across the *lagar*.

'*Um*! . . . *dois*! . . . *um*! . . . *dois*! . . . '

The shouts went on and on in a rhythm that was like that of a grandfather clock ticking slowly, majestically. Some of these men had trodden the wine before at Teape's; one or two would not live to see another vintage; for some it was the first experience of the cut, an event that has taken place year on year, back through the centuries, beyond the memory of man.

This was the culmination of the seasons, the high point in the cycle of work. These twelve men, moving in almost funereal rhythm, were the focus of all that the vintage meant. Every person in the valley, hearing that single voice shouting the time, was inevitably one with them. For the Douro exists for the wine, and the wine would not exist without the Douro. Every activity that takes place is linked in some way to the steeply soaring mountains, their terraces of stone: each vine, each dark cluster of blue-black grapes contains within it the labour and care and sometimes even love of the people who live or have lived in that remote, rugged country.

The swaying men in the line that crept forward through the darkly glistening mass seemed in some way aware of the role that they played, for the older men wore serious, almost tragic expressions, and the boys glanced about self-consciously, their eyes red and watery from the recent drinking of *bagaceira*, their lips and teeth blue from the tasting of grapes that day, their thighs crimson from the must they trod.

Afterwards, after the cut was finished, there would be the *Liberdade*, and the men would dance thigh deep in the trodden grapes. There would be ridiculous games of blind man's whack; they would sing ribald songs and boast to each other of conquests they had made or would make. Later, the girls who had been picking all day would join in, their skirts tucked up round their thighs, their eyes bright, excited, embarrassed. There would be the evening meal, men and women jammed in together under a low roof, sitting hip to hip along the benches, eating their fill of rice and meat, fresh bread and wine. There would be listening to the older ones, telling the stories heard at the last vintage and the vintage before that. There would be the slow exchange of looks, the heavy, heart-stopping sensation of shared desire, and – for a few – the moment of ecstasy under the stars, the mountains towering overhead and the pale clouds reflected in the sheen of the Douro.

This was the reality behind all the posturing and solemnity of those who speak of 'colour', 'nose' and 'body', who forget when they raise a glass of port and admire it that they are admiring the sweat of the common people, their laughter and their tears, their hopes, their loves, their tragedies. This was the real magic, the real taste, the real bouquet. This was the vintage.

IV

The sound of those rhythmic shouts was still echoing about the valley when the Laughtons arrived in their new Range Rover. They brought Suzy and Maurice Blakely with them, as well as Mia and Clare and their own three children. Bobby and Joy welcomed them: the Blakelys had flown out from England the previous day, and Teape had not seen his cousin since Ruth's funeral. Suzy was white-haired now, but still full of energy and talk; but Maurice, after two operations for cancer, looked thin and tired.

The chalet was suddenly full of people and children: there would be thirteen for dinner that night, and thirty-six for lunch the following day. Joy had insisted on taking over the catering from Joanna. 'It's my last *vindima* as well, dear,' she said. 'Don't forget that.'

Now, with people milling about from room to room and the maids bringing out the tea things to the terrace, Joy said, 'Why don't you all go down to the *lagar* and watch the cut, and by the time you get back tea will be ready.'

They filed down the hill, Clare holding Bobby's hand, because she was very fond of her grandfather, and Mia talking to Martin, whom she fancied.

Joy remained behind and went to the telephone in the sitting room. She had tried several times to contact Stella during the day but without success: she had not been able to discover where she had been staying in the Algarve, and it seemed from her letter that she and Eduardo would spend a night at Cascais before coming north.

She dialled the number three times before she achieved a ringing tone and then, almost immediately, it was answered by Eduardo.

V

They had arrived back only twenty minutes before, and Stella had gone out to the Pão de Açucar to have the heel put back on her shoe.

'It's Tia Joy speaking,' the voice at the other end of the line said in Portuguese. 'May I speak to Stella?'

'She's out at the moment. Could you ring back in ten minutes or so?'

'That's you is it, Eduardo?'

'Yes.'

There was a pause at the other end of the line. Then Joy said, 'I understand you plan to come up to Saborinho tomorrow with Stella. Is that correct?'

'Yes, that's right.'

'The line isn't very good. You'll have to speak up.'

'I said yes. I am coming up with Stella.'

She sounded upset: 'Well, listen. I may as well tell you right now. You and Stella can't go on the way you are, do you understand?'

Stella had warned him that Joy would make objections, and had silenced all his own misgivings about staying at Quinta das Rosas. They had talked about it at great length, and she had said that if he didn't accompany her, she wouldn't go at all.

'Stella's written and told me all about it,' Joy was saying, 'So I know. Eduardo – you and she *cannot* go on as you are, and you must *not* come up to Saborinho tomorrow. Do you understand? Can you hear me?'

'I can hear you but I don't understand,' he said. 'Why shouldn't I come with Stella?'

The voice seemed to choke at the other end. 'It will upset her father and he is in no condition to be upset. And apart from anything else she is a married woman. You have no right whatsoever to behave with her as you are doing.'

He felt suddenly confident in himself: it was a confidence that Stella had given to him. They had broken down that barrier between them and he was no longer afraid to argue with the wife of Senhor Teape. There was no need to be rude; he was simply firm. 'I'm sorry,' he said, 'but Stella has invited me to go with her and I have accepted. And I know you won't be able to change her mind, either.'

He heard her sob a moment at the other end, and then she said, 'Shall I tell you why, Eduardo? Do you want to know why?'

'If you want to, but it won't make any difference at all.'

'Very well,' Joy said. 'I shall tell you the reason and then you will know. Whether you tell Stella is up to you, Eduardo. The reason is that Stella's father – her father is *your* father. Now do you understand? You and she are the same blood. You are half-brother and sister. It has been a secret between your mother and – and – It has been a secret for many years. Can you hear me? Hullo? Eduardo?'

The front door slammed. Stella was back. He heard Joy's voice again on the telephone, and quickly rang off. Stella came into the room, with her shoes in a paper bag.

'They did it while I waited,' she said. 'Who phoned?'

He was still dazed by what Joy had told him. 'It – was a wrong number,' he said.

She frowned in disbelief. 'Funny sort of wrong number. You look as though you've seen a ghost.'

He avoided her eyes.

'It wasn't a wrong number, was it?'

He shook his head.

'Who was it?'

'Tia Joy.'

'Oh yes. What did she want?'

There was no way out. He looked back at her. 'I'm not going to be able to come north with you.'

She threw the shoes down on the sofa, suddenly aggressive. 'Why not?'

'I – just can't. That's all.'

'What did she say to you?'

'It wouldn't work, Stella. You know it wouldn't.'

'We discussed this. We agreed that we would go up together, whatever anyone said. Have you forgotten that?'

'No, I haven't forgotten.'

'Then what's she said to change things?'

'I can't explain.'

'Why not? Why can't you explain?'

He stared at her, shook his head. She turned away from him because she was suddenly afraid. She found her cigarettes, struggled with a card of matches that wouldn't light. 'Oh fuck,' she whispered, and threw the matches and the cigarette away. He was still staring at her when she turned back to him.

'You're looking at me as if I were something – dirty,' she said.

The silence hung between them.

'Can't you say anything at all, Eduardo?'

He remained silent, unable now to look into the hurt, the accusation in her eyes.

'What did that – bloody woman say? Was it because of my father? Is it because she's frightened we'll upset him?'

'Partly,' he mumbled. 'Yes.'

'Well what else was there? Was there something else?'

He nodded.

'What was it?'

He turned right away from her, tried not to listen to her.

'Didn't you understand why I needed to do this? Don't you understand that we both need to do it? Don't you realise that it's a question of confidence for you, as well?'

He heard her sobbing: it was a terrible noise, not like a human at all, but a low-pitched panting that was almost bestial. There had not been enough time to think it out: he shrank from telling her what Joy had said because he could not entirely believe it himself. He needed time: time to question his mother, time to decide whether to tell Stella at all, and if so –

Suddenly, she was wrenching at his shirt, screaming at him, out of control. 'Tell me! Tell me what's happened! Was that Tia Joy? Or was it someone else? Is that it? Have you had enough of me?'

He shook his head. 'I can't explain. I've – I've just got to think.'

She said things then that he knew she did not mean. She screamed at him and cursed him in English and Portuguese. She ran quickly into the kitchen and returned with two pottery mugs which they had chosen together only a few weeks before. They had spoken to the potter and he had put both their names on each mug, with a heart and an arrow between them. She brought them to him, showed them to him and smashed them deliberately, throwing them down on the tiled floor with all her strength, so that the pieces shot outwards all over the room.

There was nothing he could say. He tried to mumble an apology, but she stopped him, saying she didn't want to hear it; so he left the house and went quickly up the hill, out of Cascais, walking and running along the coast road to the Quinta da Luz, where Natália still worked.

He found her in the basement, ironing.

'*Filho!*' she said, pleased to see him. 'What a surprise.'

It was a bare little room with yellow walls and a single electric light without a shade. There was a smell of freshly ironed linen.

'I've found out about my father,' he said.

VI

Stella went from room to room, looking at herself in mirrors, looking at the furniture, her belongings, standing in the hall, holding on to herself to stop herself shaking. She drank some whisky from the bottle, but not very much, and lit a cigarette. I am really behaving extremely well, she told herself.

It didn't matter what Joy had said to him. What mattered was that he had allowed himself to be influenced by her. If he had resisted, if he had been able to fight back, then she would have known that they had something real and worthwhile and lasting; she would have known that he really was totally and completely hers, as she had believed him to be. But he was not. He had given in to what had no doubt been the wishes of her father, faithfully transmitted by the ever attentive Joy. What she, Stella, had said and wanted and explained stood for less, carried less weight, finally, than what Joy had said.

She laughed to herself. 'I have turned him into a swine,' she said aloud. 'He is the same as all of them. Dear Pig, are you willing to sell for one shilling your *thing*.' She heard her own voice going on, saying other things, but she didn't pay much attention to it because what she was saying and what she was thinking were oddly different. What was in her mind was not in word form yet, but she knew it was there and she was afraid of it.

She went into the bedroom and took off her clothes. She stood in front of the mirror and looked at what she mentally referred to as her colonial mansion. She held herself to stop herself shaking, and then she went to the bathroom and ran the bath.

She opened the wash cabinet, and some tubes of ointment and bottles of pills fell out. The bathroom filled with steam and the gas roared in the water heater. She watched the water level rise and adjusted the mixture of hot and cold to ensure she achieved a really hot bath. There's nothing worse than a tepid bath, she thought, and laughed because the thought amused her.

'There's nothing worse than a tepid bath,' she announced to the empty house.

She turned off the taps and got in. She lay down in the scalding water and relaxed. She remembered the T.S. Eliot quotation of Phillida's. Was that appropriate in this case? It didn't really matter, did it? All that mattered now was that Joy, her father, Sam, the colony – even Phillida and Eduardo – should be made to understand that none of them and no one could ever control her or manipulate her or force her to do anything which she chose not to do, or not to do anything she wanted to do. That was all that mattered, and soon she would make them realise it, once and for all.

Natália sat on the upright chair by the ironing board and wept. Eduardo watched her, horrified by the hurt he had already caused, but at the same time angry that she had never told him the truth about his parentage.

'Why didn't you tell me?' he asked. 'Why didn't you warn me when I first told you about *menina* Stella?'

'There was no need,' Natália sobbed. 'It was not necessary.'

'Of course it was necessary. If I'd known, I'd have ended everything between us straight away. Can't you see that?'

Natália shook her head. 'It doesn't concern *menina* Stella.'

'Mother – don't you understand? Stella and I – we're the same blood!'

She caught her breath, looked up at him. 'What do you mean? You can't possibly be the same blood.'

Was she being deliberately stupid? Or was she trying to conceal something from him? 'It's no good pretending any more,' he said. 'I know. I know about you and her father.'

'You don't think that he's *your* father?'

'I know he is.'

'Who told you this?'

'Stella's Tia Joy.'

'She's wrong, Eduardo. He may think he's your father, but he isn't.'

He stared at her. 'I don't understand.'

She was overtaken by a fresh wave of sobbing. She buried her head in her hands. He looked down at her, his mind full of thoughts, suppositions. Though she had never revealed her exact age to him, he had guessed long ago that she had been very young when he was born. He knew that the Teapes had taken her in when she was nearly starving. He imagined her as a young girl in the household, with Teape, a vigorous man. He imagined some sort of affair, or perhaps even a financial arrangement. The very thought of it made him hot with anger.

'Tell me what happened,' he said. 'I must know exactly what happened, mother.'

She looked up at him. 'He took me in his car,' she said. 'I was tired and hungry.'

'And you – you let him?'

491

'No. It wasn't like that. He forced me. He was strong and I was frightened. But I was already pregnant, Eduardo. I was already carrying you.' She made the sign of the Cross. 'I swear by the Mother of God that he is not your father.'

'Then who is?'

She was silent for a long time, and then she said, quietly: 'It was a fisherman.'

VIII

It was dark when he walked back through Cascais to Stella's house. A wind had got up and leaves were falling from the plane trees by the church at the top of the town.

He felt cautiously optimistic now. He had decided that he would tell Stella exactly what had happened, what both Tia Joy and his mother had told him. Tia Joy would have to be told the truth, and perhaps Teape, as well. But truth would heal a number of wounds: it would make the reconciliation between Stella and her father complete; it would make it possible for himself and Stella to be open about their affair, as Stella had intended.

He let himself into the house with the key that Stella had given to him three weeks before. He called, 'Stella?' and after going into the living room and kitchen he went upstairs.

He saw steam in the bathroom. The door was open. 'Are you in the bath?' he asked, going in to her.

She was in the bath.

Her head was right back and her mouth wide open. Her eyes stared upward, and blood still trickled from the gaping wound across her throat.

He ran out, down the stairs and out into the street, and he heard his own voice screaming.

IX

The grape must was warm and clinging to the legs; it squelched between the toes. The faces of the treaders were flushed from the drinking of *bagaceira*. An electric light hung overhead, and the slowly moving figures threw large shadows upon the whitewashed walls: shadows that seemed to dance in slow motion, as if performing some strange ritual.

When the English arrived after their dinner and Bobby Teape appeared, the treaders turned to stare, and the manager bustled up to wish him and his wife good evening.

The treaders continued moving about in the must, glancing from time to time at the group of people who talked together, and at the children who had also come to watch. It was the same almost every night of the vintage at Saborinho: the English always came down after their dinner, and the manager always talked to the *patrão*.

One of the English ladies was asking a question. Why was there no dancing? Why no accordion? And the manager was explaining that this year it had not been the wish of the people to have such music. What a great shame, the lady was saying, and the treaders grinned to each other at the overheard remark.

The manager drew the attention of the English to a new cassette tape recorder which had been brought along: he switched it on and the building filled with the strident voice of a Portuguese woman folk singer. She sang to an accordion at full volume, and the percussion was provided by the sound of clogs on wooden boards.

The English decided that they would dance. The treaders watched and grinned; one of the English twins who had arrived that day was dancing with Sr Teape: the treaders clapped in time, and some of the other English also started to dance.

The old man danced with the girl and pumped her hand up and down in time with the music. She giggled and watched her feet in order to make the correct steps. The lady was telling the old man to stop, and he was saying no, but eventually she insisted, and he did stop, and all the other English were laughing and clapping.

It was time to finish the treading for the night now, and the people were stepping out of the stone *lagar* to wash the purple juice off their legs. One old man was drunk: his pants did not cover him sufficiently and he grinned about inanely. The English smiled embarrassedly and looked the other way. One of the children was told not to stare. She turned away and put her finger in the must and tasted it.

The water from the tap splashed on the stone floor and the treaders queued to wash their white legs and afterwards put on their trousers. The English moved along to look at the other *lagares* where the must had been left to ferment, and where two men were mixing it gently with wooden implements called *macacos*, or monkeys. The manager kept close to the *patrão* all the time, talking a great deal so that the English might be impressed by his efficiency.

While this was happening, Sr. Remington came into the building and went to speak to the wife of the *patrão*. He drew her to one side, and their faces were serious and without the humour that had been there before. They went quickly out of the *lagar*, past the queue of people at the tap and the old man struggling into tattered trousers.

Outside, the vine terraces rose above them, dark under the stars. Light spilled out of the building, and the voice of the woman on the tape recording stopped abruptly.

James had received the telephone call in the chalet only five minutes before. The police at Cascais had telephoned to say that Stella had taken her life.

That was all he knew, all he could tell Joy as she stood there, dazed by the news. What would this do to Rob? she asked. How was she going to tell him? Why did Stella have to do this? And why now, of all times.

'We shall have to go south tomorrow,' she said.

'Yes. So Bobby will have to be told either this evening or tomorrow morning. We'll cancel the lunch of course.'

'My poor Rob!' Joy whispered. 'My poor, darling Rob!'

James put his arm round his elder sister's shoulders and comforted her. 'I don't know if he will be able to withstand a shock like this,' she said. 'It could kill him. You realise that?'

'We can't keep it from him. Or the twins, for that matter.'

They looked in through the open door of the *lagar*. The music had started again, and Teape was bowing formally to Clare and requesting the pleasure of the next dance with her.

'Would you like me to tell him?' James asked.

She shook her head. 'No. That's my duty.'

'When will you do it? Now? This evening?'

'Does anyone else know up here?'

'Just the two of us.'

'In that case I shall tell him in the morning. When he's had a night's sleep.' The music blared forth into the night. 'Damn her!' Joy whispered. 'Damn her!'

X

Bobby Teape awoke the following morning to the sound of someone tapping on the window, and he was out of bed before Joy could stop him.

'What is it?' she asked. 'What are you doing?'

'It's the must,' he said shortly, and opened the window. A face appeared outside. It was the manager, doffing his cap and producing a copper cup full of the new fermentation for Teape to sample. They wished each other a very good morning, and Teape took a mouthful of the juice, rolling it round his mouth and eventually spitting it out on to the ground outside the window.

He stood in his paisley pyjamas and talked to the farm manager, asking him whether the temperature of the must was still correct, which areas were to be picked that day, what the weather looked like doing, and how the grapes from the outlying farms compared with the Teape grapes at Saborinho. He already knew the answers to most of these questions, but he had never forgotten the advice his mother had once given him: it was necessary to show enthusiasm in order to be successful, and he attributed much of the success of Teape & Co. to the enthusiasm he and his co-directors had always shown.

495

The manager took off his cap and put it on again and wished him a very good day for the second time. Bobby Teape returned the greeting, and closed the window.

'You haven't had the must brought in the morning for years!' Joy said when he was back in bed.

He laughed. 'No. But I thought, well – you know.'

'Did you sleep well?'

He smiled. 'I always do, up here.'

She got out of bed.

'Getting up already?'

'No. I'm coming in with you.'

He frowned and smiled: it was a long time since she had come into his bed in the morning. He moved over to make room for her. Then he saw her expression.

'Is anything the matter?'

She nodded. 'Bobby darling, I have some bad news for you. You will have to be very brave.'

'It's Stella, isn't it?' he said. 'She can't come up, after all.'

'No, she can't.'

'Never mind,' he said. 'I didn't really expect her to, you know.'

'It's worse than that, Bobby.'

'How – worse?'

When she told him, it seemed that he did not really understand what he had heard. She took his hand between hers and held it to her lips. He breathed through his mouth; his eyes searched about as if he were suddenly lost.

'Why?' he whispered. 'Why?' And again: 'Why?'

XI

He walked slowly up the track that led away from the chalet, between the vine terraces. A little way distant the pickers were already at work, and the young men were carrying the baskets of grapes down the hill.

He had declined to eat breakfast and had told Joy that he

496

wished to be alone until it was time to go. She had tried to prevent him going off on his own like this, but he had insisted. She had tried to comfort him, but he had wished for no comfort.

He had often walked along this track. It was the old path, the path that had been in use before the road had been built. He had gone along it by mule many times on his way to visit other farms; he had accompanied his father along it, and this stretch of it in particular evoked a jumble of mixed memories.

He rested on a low stone wall and looked down over the wide stretch of water, the reflected mountains, the railway line winding its way along by the river and into a tunnel. He listened to the sounds of the valley, watched an eagle soar overhead, and when he had been sitting there for a very long time, he was suddenly startled by a child's voice. It was Mia. She had come quietly up to him from a different direction. She said simply, 'Hullo.'

He looked round. She stood on the terrace above and behind him, a stringy girl in faded jeans and shirt. She came down to him and sat beside him on the wall. She looked him full in the face, and she was frighteningly like Stella had been at the same age.

'How did Mum die?' she asked.

'You wouldn't understand,' he said.

'Yes I will. Aunt Joy wouldn't tell me, but I want to know. Will you tell me?'

She slipped her hand into his. She had never shown him affection before, had always held herself away from him.

'Did she drive over a cliff?' she asked.

He stared at her.

'She often said she might.'

'She said that?'

Mia nodded. 'Lots of times. When she was feeling mizzy. Just you wait, she said. One of these days, I'll drive over a cliff.'

He wept.

Mia watched him, surprised and a little puzzled by his breakdown and unsure what to do about it. At the same time, she knew that she was at the centre of something important, something that mattered, and although she was sorry her mother had died, she was also a little glad that she was there on the mountainside with her grandfather.

She knew the best way to comfort people, too: it was the way her mother had always comforted her. You stroked their heads gently, using your fingers like a comb, pressing down a little with the tips. That was the way her mother had always soothed them when they were ill or hurt or very unhappy or frightened by a bad dream. She wondered if her grandfather would like it if she did it to him; she watched him for some time and decided that he would.

She reached out with her hand and started doing it. His hair was thin and white and his scalp was a little nobbly in places. That was what it got like when you were old.

She could not have known that Stella had learnt this way of soothing from Ruth, nor that Ruth had, on a few occasions, used it upon Bobby. So she couldn't understand why, when she started, her grandfather seemed overwhelmed by an even deeper, more racking sorrow. All she knew was that suddenly he had taken her into his arms and was holding her to him very closely and that she was sharing with him a grief that was so deep it seemed to engulf the whole world.

When Joy came to collect him they were still there, grandfather and granddaughter, sitting on the wall, her arm round his shoulders, his head bowed.

'Come along, Bobby,' Joy said. 'Time to go.'

They went down the hill. The cars were ready and the luggage packed. Joy chivvied people along. James and Joanna were going to lead the way, and Penny and Martin were remaining behind to oversee the vintage.

Bobby Teape was helped into the car. Engines started and doors banged. And then they were gone, and two clouds of pale dust were zigzagging up the mountain, up to the skyline, and out of sight.

⚜ 21 ⚜

IF YOU DRIVE NORTH from Cascais on the coast road that leads to the Guincho beach, you will see a few restaurants along the way. Among these, built right out on a cliff, is the Casa Natália. Inside, there are twenty or so tables laid with blue and white tablecloths, and gleaming cutlery and glass. The windows overlook jagged volcanic rocks where, in the winter storms, the Atlantic rollers spend themselves in a last fury of white surf.

When the Casa Natália opened in 1977, it took some while to break even, and there was a time when its joint owners – Rui Cardoso, Eduardo and Natália herself – considered closing it down. But with Eduardo's growing reputation as a singer, the restaurant was suddenly 'discovered' and it is now a popular place to eat both among the tourists in the summer and the locals in the off-season.

Eduardo usually waits until late in the evening before he appears. He stage manages his entrance carefully, and sings the *fado* in a gentler, less strident way than is traditionally accepted as the norm. He stands in the dimmed lighting, a big, friendly man with a broken-toothed smile; and when he sings, it is as if he is speaking personally to each member of his audience.

There is always tumultuous applause. Sitting behind him, out of the light, his mother joins in. She is in her sixties now, and must be comparatively wealthy. People say that she has had some tragedy in her life which she will never discuss. The restaurant is doing very well indeed. Visits for groups of tourists are arranged by the hotels in Estoril and Cascais, and each is warned that absolute silence is required from the

499

audience during performances.

Eduardo sings one song that is particularly popular. It tells of a fisherman lost at sea, and his daughter waiting on the harbour wall for him to return. He sings with an intensity which the critics say will bring *fado* to a new height of popularity in Portugal; and they no longer say of him that his singing is lacking in depth, or passion.